Who wouldn't like to spend the night with a
sexy Italian? Or be married to one?

Latin Lovers
ITALIAN HUSBANDS

Three fabulous stories from some of our
readers' favourite authors: Kate Hewitt,
Rebecca Winters and Alison Roberts

D1464182

LATIN LOVERS COLLECTION

COLLECT ALL SIX!

Latin Lovers
ITALIAN HUSBANDS

Kate
HEWITT

Rebecca
WINTERS

Alison
ROBERTS

Mills & Boon, an imprint of Harlequin (UK) Limited, Eton House, 18-24 Paradise Road, Richmond, Surrey TW9 1SR

LATIN LOVERS: ITALIAN HUSBANDS
© Harlequin Enterprises II B.V./S.à.r.l. 2011

The Italian's Bought Bride © Kate Hewitt 2008
The Italian Playboy's Secret Son © Rebecca Winters 2008
The Italian Doctor's Perfect Family © Alison Roberts 2007

ISBN: 978 0 263 88995 6

027-1211

Harlequin (UK) policy is to use papers that are natural, renewable and recyclable products and made from wood grown in sustainable forests. The logging and manufacturing processes conform to the legal environmental regulations of the country of origin.

Printed and bound in Spain
by Blackprint CPI, Barcelona

THE ITALIAN'S BOUGHT BRIDE

Kate Hewitt

Kate Hewitt discovered her first Mills & Boon®
romance on a trip to England when she was
thirteen, and she's continued to read them ever
since. She wrote her first story at the age of five,
simply because her older brother had written one
and she thought she could do it too. That story was
one sentence long—fortunately they've become a
bit more detailed as she's grown older.

She has written plays, short stories, and magazine
serials for many years, but writing romance
remains her first love. Besides writing, she enjoys
reading, travelling, and learning to knit.

After marrying the man of her dreams—her older
brother's childhood friend—she lived in England
for six years, and now resides in Connecticut with
her husband, her three young children, and the
possibility of one day getting a dog.

Kate loves to hear from readers—you can contact
her through her website: www.kate-hewitt.com

To Abby,
for being a wonderful friend and confidante.
You've seen my tears! Love, K.

CHAPTER ONE

STEFANO CAPOZZI SAT in the well-appointed office of one of Milan's top psychiatrists, his eyes glittering in a face set like stone.

'It has been eight months,' he said flatly, even though Renaldo Speri had the case notes on his desk. 'Eight months of every treatment available, imaginable, and no change.'

Speri smiled in sympathetic understanding. 'You cannot expect a miracle cure, Signor Capozzi. You may not be able to expect a cure at all.' He trailed off as he took in Stefano's unrelenting gaze.

Stefano shook his head. 'I want better.'

He would have better. He wouldn't accept brush-offs or excuses. He'd come to Milan to find the best therapist for the child in his charge, and he would have it.

Speri ran a hand through his thinning hair and sighed. 'Signor Capozzi, you must face the very real possibility that Lucio falls on the spectrum of pervasive development disorder—'

'No.' After eight months of Lucio's silence and stress, he would not accept it. He was used to obstacles in business, and personal ones would prove no different, no more difficult. 'Lucio was normal before his father died. He was like any other child—'

'Autism often manifests itself at three years of age,' Speri explained gently. 'Lucio had only a little speech before his father's death, and lost it completely in the months afterwards.'

Stefano raised one eyebrow in scathing scepticism. 'And you are now trying to tell me that the two aren't related?'

'I am trying to tell you that it is a possibility,' Speri said, his voice becoming strained with patience. 'As difficult as it may be to accept.'

Stefano was silent for a moment. 'There is no cure for autism,' he finally said. He'd done his research. He'd read the books, seen the statistics.

'There are therapies, diets, that alleviate some of the symptoms,' Speri said quietly. 'And it also depends where he falls on the spectrum—'

'He's not on the spectrum.'

'Signor—'

'I want something else.' Stefano levelled his gaze at the psychiatrist and waited.

After a moment Speri raised his hands in a defeated gesture. 'Signor Capozzi, we have tried therapies and grief counselling, and as you've reminded me, there has been no change. If anything, Lucio has descended deeper into his own iron-walled world. If this were a case of normal grief—'

'What,' Stefano asked icily, 'is normal about grief?'

'The grieving process is normal,' Speri said steadily. 'And accepted. But Lucio's behaviour is not normal, and there should have been signs of improvement in communication by now. There have been none.'

On his lap, out of sight, Stefano's hand curled into a fist. 'I know that.'

'Then accept that he might fall on the spectrum, and turn to the therapies and treatments that can help him best!'

Stefano was silent. Carefully, deliberately, he flattened his hand, resting it on the desktop. When Lucio's mother, Bianca, had asked him to help, to come to Milan and tell 'those doctors' that her son was not autistic, Stefano had accepted. He had believed Bianca then, but now he felt the first flicker of doubt.

He would do anything for Bianca, anything for Lucio. Their

family had saved him all those years ago, had pulled him up from the mire of his upbringing, giving him the steps and tools to be the man he was today.

He would never forget it.

'Surely there is something we haven't tried,' he said at last. 'Before we accept this diagnosis.'

'The psychiatrists involved in an autism diagnosis are very thorough,' Speri said. 'And competent. They do not make such a judgement incautiously.'

'Agreed,' Stefano said tersely. 'But still—is there something else?'

Speri was silent for a long moment. 'There is,' he finally said, his voice reluctant, 'a therapist who had success with a child who'd been diagnosed with autism. Misdiagnosed, as the case turned out. He'd suffered a severe trauma the therapists working with him were unaware of, and when it was uncovered he began to regain his speech.'

Hope—treacherous, desperate—unfurled within him. 'Then couldn't Lucio be like that boy?' Stefano demanded.

'I don't want to offer you false hope,' Speri said, and the reluctance in his voice became more pronounced. 'That was one case—an anomaly, a fluke—'

Stefano cut him off; he didn't want to hear about anomalies. He wanted hope, he wanted certainty. 'Who is this therapist?'

'She's an art therapist,' Speri said. 'Often creative therapies help children release suppressed emotions and memories, as was the case with this child. However, Lucio's symptoms are more severe…'

'Creative therapies,' Stefano repeated. He didn't like the sound of it. It sounded abstract, absurd. 'What exactly do you mean?'

'She uses the creative arts to provide an outlet, whether through art, song or performance, for a child's suppressed emotions. Sometimes it is the key that can unlock a child who has been unable to be reached.'

Unlock. It was an apt word, Stefano thought, when he considered Lucio's blank face and staring eyes. And no words. Not one word spoken in nearly a year.

'All right, then,' he said shortly. 'We'll try it. I want her.'

'It was one case—' Speri began, and Stefano silenced him with a raised hand.

'I want her.'

'She lives in London. I read of the case in a journal and we corresponded briefly, but I don't know…'

'She's English?' Disappointment sliced through him. Of what use to him—to Lucio—was an English therapist?

'No, I wouldn't have mentioned her if that was the case,' Speri said with a faint smile. 'She's Italian, but I don't believe she's been back to Italy in many years.'

'She'll come,' Stefano said firmly. He would make sure of it—offer whatever enticements or inducements she needed. 'How long did she work with this other child?'

'A few months—'

'Then I want her in Abruzzo, with Lucio, as soon as possible.' Stefano spoke with a finality that took the psychiatrist aback.

'Signor Capozzi, she'll have other patients, responsibilities—'

'She can get rid of them.'

'It's not that simple.'

'Yes,' Stefano said flatly. 'It is. It will be. Lucio can't be moved; it's too upsetting for him. She'll come to Abruzzo. And stay.'

Speri shifted uncomfortably. 'That will be for you to negotiate with her, of course. Such an intensive course is to be recommended, although there are no guarantees, but it is also costly…'

'Money,' Stefano replied with the barest flicker of a smile, 'is no object.'

'Naturally.' Speri looked down at his notes; Stefano knew the highlights of his own CV were sketched there. Stefano Capozzi, founder of Capozzi Electronica. Liquidator of a dozen of Italy's top electronics firms. Unrivalled.

'I'll give you her details,' Speri said with a little sigh of capitulation. 'I have the article about her and the case I mentioned here. I should tell you she's young, quite newly qualified, relatively inexperienced, but of course that case was remarkable…'

'That boy recovered? He spoke again?' Stefano demanded. He didn't like the flicker of compassion—or was it pity?—in the doctor's eyes.

'Yes,' Speri said quietly, 'he did. But it isn't that simple, Signor Capozzi. And Lucio might be different. He might indeed be—'

'Her details, please.' Stefano held out his hand. He didn't expect things to be simple. He just wanted them *started*.

'Just a moment…' Speri looked through his papers again. 'Ah, here's the article I mentioned.' He smiled and handed Stefano a medical journal, opened to a folded page. 'Here she is…a lovely photograph, don't you think? Allegra Avesti is her name.'

Stefano didn't hear the last part of what Speri had said, but then he didn't need to. He knew her name. He knew her.

Or at least, he once had.

Allegra Avesti. The woman who should have been his wife, the woman he no longer knew.

His concern for Lucio fell away for a moment as he gazed at the caption: 'Allegra Avesti, Art Therapist, with patient'. Memories swam to the surface and he forced them back down again, drowning them as his dispassionate gaze moved to the photo. He saw that she was older, thinner. She was smiling in the photo, hazel eyes glinting as she looked at the child by her side, his little fists pounding a lump of clay.

Her head was tilted to one side, her hair, a thousand shades of sunlight, piled in a careless knot, tendrils escaping to trail her cheek, her shoulder.

Her eyes sparkled and her smile was wide, encouraging, full of hope. He could almost hear the tinkling promise of pure joy. She had dimples, he saw. He'd never known. He'd never seen them. Had she not laughed like that in his presence?

Perhaps not.

He stared at the picture—the ghost of a girl he'd once known, an image of a woman he'd never met.

Allegra.

His Allegra…except she wasn't, he knew that, had known it when he'd waited while she'd walked away. For ever.

He closed the journal, handed it back to Speri. Thought of Lucio. Only Lucio. 'Indeed, a lovely picture,' he said without any intonation or expression. The look of joy and hope on Allegra's face would be an inspiration to many a fearful and weary parent, seeking answers for their child. 'I shall contact her.'

Speri nodded. 'And if for some reason she is occupied, we can discuss…alternatives…'

Stefano acknowledged this statement with a brusque nod. He knew Allegra would not be busy. He would make sure she was not. If she was the best, if she'd helped a child like Lucio, he would have her.

Even if it was Allegra.

Especially if it was Allegra.

The past, he vowed, would not matter when it came to helping Lucio. The past would not matter at all.

Allegra Avesti gazed into the mirror of the ladies' powder room at the Dorchester Hotel and grimaced. Her hair was meant to be in a carelessly elegant chignon, but it looked as if she'd only succeeded with the first part of that plan.

At least her dress hit the right note, she decided with satisfaction. Smoky-grey silk, cut severely across the collarbone and held up by two skinny straps on each shoulder, it was elegant and sexy without being too revealing.

It had cost a fortune, far more than she could afford on her earnings as a therapist. Yet she'd wanted to look good for her cousin Daphne's wedding. She'd wanted to feel good.

As if she fitted in.

Except, she knew, she didn't. Not really. Not since the night she'd fled her own wedding and left everyone else to pick up the scattered pieces.

With a little sigh she took a lipstick and blusher out of her handbag. She didn't think of that night, chose never to think of it—the shattered dream, the broken heart. The betrayal, the fear.

Yet her cousin's wedding this evening had brought her own almost-wedding to the forefront of her mind, and it had taken all her energy and emotion to push it back into the box where she liked to keep those memories. That life.

The wedding had been lovely, a candlelit ceremony at a small London church. Daphne, with her heart-shaped face, soft voice and cloud of dark hair, had looked tremulously beautiful. Her husband, a high-flyer at an advertising firm in the City, seemed a bit too self-assured for Allegra's taste, but she hoped her cousin had found happiness. Love. If such things could truly be found.

Yet, during the ceremony, she'd listened to the vows they'd spoken with undisguised cynicism.

'Will you love her, comfort her, honour and protect her, and, forsaking all others, be faithful to her as long as you both shall live?'

As the words had washed over her, Allegra couldn't help but think of her own wedding day, the day that never happened, the vows she'd never spoken.

Stefano hadn't loved her, wouldn't comfort her or honour her. Protect her? Yes, she thought wryly, he would have done that. Faithful? Doubtful…

Yet she still felt, sitting in that dimly lit church, an unidentifiable stab of longing, of something almost like regret.

Except she didn't regret anything. She certainly didn't regret walking out on Stefano. Although her uncle—and sometimes it seemed the rest of society—blamed her for that fiasco, Allegra knew the real fiasco would have been if she'd stayed.

But she was free, she told herself firmly. She was free and happy.

Allegra turned away from the mirror. She'd survived Daphne's wedding, slipping out before anyone could corner her, but she wasn't looking forward to the reception tonight. She was in a melancholy mood, didn't feel like chatting and laughing and dancing. And although she loved Daphne and her Aunt Barbara, her relationship with her Uncle George had always been strained.

She hadn't spoken to her uncle more than a handful of times in the seven years since he'd first sheltered her when she'd fled Italy, and those conversations had been uncomfortable at best.

Straightening, she left the luxurious powder room. It had been a hell of a day—running from appointment to appointment at the hospital, grappling with one serious and seemingly hopeless case after another. There had been no breakthroughs, no breath of hope.

Not today.

She loved her job, loved it with an intensity that some said should be replaced with the love of—and for—a man, but Allegra knew she was happy as she was. Happy and free, she reminded herself again firmly.

Still, the hopelessness of some of her cases, the children who had seen far too much suffering, too much sorrow, wore her down. She only had a few moments with them, perhaps an hour a week at most, and doctors expected breakthroughs. Parents expected miracles.

Once in a while, God was good. Once in a while they happened.

But not today.

The reception was being held in the Orchid Room, with its walls of delicate blue and ornate painted scrollery. A string quartet had been arranged near a parquet dance floor, and guests circulated amidst waiters bearing trays of hors d'oeuvres and sparkling champagne.

Allegra surveyed the glittering crowd and lifted her chin. She wasn't used to this. She didn't go to parties.

The last party she'd attended—a party like this, with society in full swing—had been for her own engagement. She'd worn a poufy, pink dress and heels that had pinched her feet, and she'd been so happy. So excited.

She shook her head as if to banish the thought, the memory. Why was she thinking—remembering—those days now? Why was she letting the memories sift through her mind like ghosts from another life—a life that had never happened? A life she'd run away from.

It was the wedding tonight, she decided. It was the first one she'd attended since she'd abandoned her own.

Forget it, Allegra told herself as she plucked a flute of champagne from one of the circulating trays and made her way through the crowd. Her cousin's wedding was bound to stir up some unpleasant memories, unpalatable feelings. That was all this mood was, and she could deal with it.

Allegra took a sip of champagne, let the bubbles fizz defiantly through her and surveyed the milling crowd.

'Allegra…I'm so glad you could come.'

She turned to see her Aunt Barbara smiling uncertainly at her. Dowdy but cheerful, Barbara Mason wore a lime coloured evening gown that did nothing for her pasty complexion or grey-streaked hair.

Allegra smiled warmly back. 'I'm glad to be here as well,' she returned a little less than truthfully. 'I'm so thrilled for Daphne.'

'Yes…they'll be very happy, don't you think?' Barbara's anxious gaze flitted to her daughter, who was chatting and smiling, her husband's arm around her shoulders.

'I'm afraid I don't know much about the groom,' Allegra said, taking another sip of champagne. 'His name is Charles?'

'Charles Edmunds. They met at work. You know Daphne's been a PA at Hobbs and Ford?'

Allegra nodded. Although her uncle disapproved of Allegra keeping in touch with his family, she still spoke to Barbara on the telephone every few months, and several times Daphne had defied her father to meet Allegra for lunch.

She'd learned at one of those outings that Daphne had secured a job as PA at an advertising firm, despite her obvious lack of qualifications. Her father's, apparently, had been enough.

'I'm happy for them,' she said. She watched Charles Edmunds as he glanced down at his wife, smiling easily. Then he raised his eyes, surveying the ballroom with a gaze that was steely and grey. Looking for business contacts, associates? Allegra wondered cynically. Someone worth knowing, at any rate, she decided as his eyes passed over her and Barbara without a flicker.

So much for true love, she thought with a little grimace. Charles Edmunds was a man like most others—cold, ambitious, on the prowl.

'Barbara!' Her uncle's sharp voice cut across the murmur of the crowd. Both Allegra and her aunt tensed as George Mason strode towards them, his narrow features sharpened by dislike as he glanced at his niece.

'Barbara, you should see to your guests,' he commanded tersely, and Barbara offered Allegra a quick, defeated smile of apology. Allegra smiled back.

'It was good to see you, Allegra,' Barbara murmured. 'We don't see enough of you,' she added with a shred of defiance. George motioned her away with a shooing gesture, and Barbara went.

There was a moment of tense silence and Allegra swivelled the slick, moisture-beaded stem of her champagne flute between her fingers, wondering what to say to a man who had ordered her from his house seven years ago. The few times she'd seen him since, at increasingly infrequent family gatherings, they'd avoided each other.

Now they were face to face.

He looked the same as ever, she saw as she slid him a glance from beneath her lashes. Thin, grey-haired, well-dressed, precise. Cold eyes and a prim, pursed mouth. Absolutely no humour.

'Thank you for inviting me, Uncle George,' Allegra finally said. 'It was good of you, considering.'

'I had to invite you, Allegra,' George replied. 'You're family, even though you've hardly acted like it in the last seven years.'

Allegra pressed her lips together to keep from uttering a sharp retort. She wasn't the one who had ordered so-called family out of his house, and who had made it increasingly difficult for Allegra to stay in touch.

Running away had been her only crime, and her uncle never failed to remind her of it.

For in running away she'd shamed him. Allegra still remembered her uncle's fury when she'd shown up, terrified and exhausted, on his doorstep.

'You can stay the night,' he'd said grimly, 'and then you need to be gone.'

'He does business with Stefano Capozzi,' her aunt had explained, desperate for Allegra to understand and not to judge. 'If he's seen sheltering you, Capozzi could make life very unpleasant for him, Allegra. For all of us.'

It had been an *unpleasant* insight into her former fiancé's character. She had wondered then if Stefano would come for her, find her. Make life unpleasant for *her.*

He hadn't, and as far as she knew he'd never made life unpleasant for her uncle. She wondered sometimes whether that had been a convenient excuse for George Mason to wash his hands of her, especially when her own defection had been followed so quickly by her mother's.

Her mother…another person, another life, Allegra chose not to remember.

Now she met her uncle's cold gaze. 'I needed help and you gave it to me,' she said levelly. Her fingers tightened on the stem of her glass. 'I'll always be grateful for that.'

'And you'll show it by keeping out of my way,' George finished coolly. 'And Daphne's. Her nerves are strung high enough as it is.'

Allegra felt a flush creeping up her throat, staining her face. She kept her chin high. 'I certainly don't want to cause any dismay to my cousin. I'll pay my respects and leave as soon as possible.'

'Good,' he replied shortly before moving off.

Allegra straightened proudly. She felt as if every eye in the faceless crowd was focused on her, seeing, knowing, condemning, even though she knew no one cared.

Except her uncle and his family.

A waiter passed and Allegra placed her nearly untouched champagne on his tray.

Murmuring her excuses as she moved through the crowd, she found a secluded corner of the ballroom and took her position there, half hidden behind a potted palm.

She took a deep breath and surveyed the circulating crowd. No one was paying any attention to her, she knew, because she wasn't important. Her flight from Italy seven years ago was little cause of concern or even gossip these days.

She'd kept her head down and well out of society's glare these last years, working two jobs to pay for her schooling. She was far, far from this glamorous crowd, the glittering lifestyle. Yet the people who knew her, who were supposed to love her…what had happened seven years ago still mattered to them. And it always would.

It didn't bother her on a day-to-day basis. She didn't need these people. She had a new life now, a good one. When she'd left that night, she'd gained her freedom, but the price for that freedom had been, quite literally, everything.

It had been a price worth paying.

The music died down and Allegra saw everyone heading to the tables. Dinner was about to be served.

Taking another deep breath, she moved through the crowds again and found her place card. She was at a table tucked in the back with a motley handful of guests who looked to be nearly as out of place as she was. Distant, vaguely embarrassing relatives, colleagues and friends who necessitated an invitation yet were not an asset to the sparkling and successful party George Mason intended for his daughter.

An art therapist with a disreputable past certainly fitted into that category, Allegra thought ruefully.

With a murmured hello, she took her place between an overweight aunt and a weedy looking businessman. The meal passed in stilted conversations and awkward silences as eight misfits attempted to get along.

Allegra let the conversation wash over her in a meaningless tide of sound and wondered just how soon she could leave.

She wanted to see Daphne but, with the cold, ambitious Charles Edmunds at her cousin's side, Allegra wasn't expecting a cosy cousinly chat.

The plates were cleared and her uncle stood up to speak. Allegra watched him posture importantly, talking about how he knew Charles Edmunds, cracking business jokes. At one point he pontificated on the importance of family and she smothered the stab of resentment that threatened to pierce her composure.

Soon after, the music started up again and Allegra excused herself from the table before anyone could ask her to dance. The junior from Charles's office had been eyeing her with a determined expression.

She moved through the crowds, her head held high, her eyes meeting no one else's.

Daphne stood apart with her husband, pale and luminous in a designer wedding gown that hugged her slight figure before flaring out in a row of ruffles.

'Hello, Daphne,' Allegra said.

Her cousin—the cousin she'd shared summers in Italy with, swimming and laughing and plaiting each other's hair—now turned to her with a worried expression.

'Hh… Hello, Allegra,' she said after a moment, her apprehensive gaze flicking to her husband. 'Have you met Charles?'

Charles Edmunds smiled coolly. 'Yes, your cousin came to our engagement party. Don't you remember, darling?'

He made it sound as if she'd crashed the party. She supposed that was what her attendance felt like. Still, she'd wanted to come, had wanted to show that no matter what they did or thought, she was still family.

'Daphne, I only wanted to congratulate you,' Allegra said quietly. 'I'm afraid I'm going to have to leave a bit early—'

'Oh, Allegra—' Daphne looked both relieved and regretful '—I'm sorry…'

'No, it's fine.' Allegra smiled and squeezed her cousin's hand. 'It's fine. I'm tired anyway. It's been a long day.'

'Thank you,' Daphne whispered, and Allegra wondered just what her cousin was thanking her for. For coming? Or for leaving? Or for simply not making a scene?

As if she ever would. She'd only made one scene in her life, and she didn't plan on doing so again.

'Goodbye,' she murmured, and quickly kissed her cousin's cold cheek.

In the foyer, she found the cloakroom and handed the attendant her ticket. She watched as the woman riffled through the rack of luxury wraps for her own plain and inexpensive coat.

'Here you are, miss.'

'Thank you.'

She was just about to pull it on when she heard a voice—a voice of cool confidence and warm admiration. A voice that slid across her senses and into her soul, stirring up those emotions and memories she'd tried so hard to lock away.

It all came rushing back with that voice—the memories, the fear, the regrets, the betrayal. It hurtled back, making her relive the worst night of her life once more, simply by hearing two little words that she knew, somehow, would change her world for ever.

'Hello, Allegra,' Stefano said.

CHAPTER TWO

Seven years earlier

TOMORROW WOULD BE her wedding day. A day of lacy dresses and sunlit kisses, of magic, of promise, of joy and wonder.

Allegra pressed one hand to her wildly beating heart. Outside the Tuscan villa, night settled softly, stealing over purple-cloaked hills and winding its way through the dusty olive groves.

Inside the warm glow of a lamp cast the room into pools of light and shadow. Allegra surveyed her childhood bedroom: the pink pillows and teddy bears vying for space on her narrow girl's bed, the shelf of well-thumbed Enid Blyton books borrowed from English cousins, her early sketches lovingly framed by her childhood nurse, and lastly—wonderfully—her wedding dress, as frothy a confection as any young bride could wish for, swathed in plastic and hanging from her cupboard door.

She let out a little laugh, a giggle of girlish joy. She was getting married!

She'd met Stefano Capozzi thirteen months ago, at her eighteenth birthday party. She'd seen him as she'd picked her way down the stairs in her new, awkward heels. He'd been waiting at the bottom like Rhett Butler, amber eyes glinting with promise, one hand stretched out to her.

She'd taken his hand as naturally as if she'd known him, as

if she'd expected him to be there. When he'd asked her to dance, she'd simply walked into his arms.

It had been so easy. So right.

And, Allegra thought happily, there hadn't been a misstep since. Stefano had asked her out a handful of times, to restaurants and the theatre and a few local parties. He'd written her letters from Paris and Rome, when he was on business, and sent her flowers and trinkets.

And then he'd asked her to marry him…to be his wife. And he would be her husband.

Another giggle escaped her and she heard an answering echo of a laugh from outside, low, throaty, seductive. Allegra opened the shutter and peeped out; she saw a couple in the shadow of a tree, arms, bodies entwined. The woman's head was thrown back and the man was kissing her neck.

Allegra shivered. Stefano had never kissed her neck. The few times he'd kissed her, he had been chaste, almost brotherly, yet the brush of his lips against her skin had sent a strange sensation pooling deep inside, flooding through her with an unfamiliar, new warmth.

Now she watched, fascinated, as the unknown couple's bodies moved and writhed in a sensuous dance.

She drew in a little breath, her eyes still fastened on the couple, the balmy night air cooling her flushed face. Suddenly she wanted to see Stefano. She wanted to say…what?

That she loved him? She'd never said those three little words, and neither had he, but it hardly mattered. Surely he saw it shining from her eyes every time she looked at him. And, as for Stefano…how could she doubt? He'd sought her out, he'd courted her like a troubadour. Of course he loved her.

Yet now she wanted to see him, talk to him. Touch him.

A blush rose to her face and she turned away from the window and the couple, who had moved further into the shadows, her hands pressed to her hot cheeks.

She'd only seen Stefano with his shirt off once, when they'd all gone swimming in the lake. She'd had a glimpse of bare, brown muscle before she'd jerked her gaze away.

And yet tomorrow they would be married. They would be lovers. She knew as much; even she, kept away in convent school, knew the basics of life. Of sex.

Her mind darted away from the implications, the impossibilities. What vague images her fevered brain conjured were blurred, strange, embarrassing.

Yet she still wanted to see him. Now.

Stefano was a night owl; he'd told her before. Allegra didn't think he'd be in bed yet. He'd be downstairs, in her father's study or library, reading one of his fusty old books.

She could find him.

Taking a breath, Allegra opened her bedroom door and crept down the passage. The soft September air was cool, although perhaps she was just hot.

Her hand was slick on the wrought iron railing as she went down the stairs. In the hall, she heard voices from the library.

'This time tomorrow you will have your little bride,' her father, Roberto, said. He sounded as sleekly satisfied as a tomcat.

'And you will have what you want,' Stefano replied, and Allegra jerked involuntarily at the sound of his voice—cool, urbane, indifferent.

She'd never heard him speak in such a tone before.

'Yes, indeed I will. This is a good business arrangement for us both, Stefano…my son.'

'Indeed it is,' Stefano agreed in a bland tone that still somehow made Allegra shiver. 'I'm pleased that you approached me.'

'And not too bad a price, eh?' Roberto chuckled, an ugly, indulgent sound. Allegra's flesh crawled at the sound—a sound she realized she'd never heard, a sound she'd been protected from. Her father's own callousness. Towards her.

'Allegra's mother has raised her well,' Roberto continued. 'She'll give you five or six *bambinos* and then you can keep her in the country.' He chuckled again. 'She'll know her place. And *I* know a woman in Milan…she's very good.'

'Is she?'

Allegra choked, one fist pressed to her lips. What was her father saying? What was *Stefano* saying?

Their words beat a remorseless echo in her numb brain. *Business arrangement.* A deal to be brokered. A bargain to be had.

A woman to be sold.

They were talking about a marriage. Hers.

She shook her head in mute, instinctive denial.

'Yes,' Roberto said, 'she is. There are many pleasures for the married man, Stefano.'

Stefano gave a light answering laugh. 'That I believe.'

Allegra closed her eyes, her hand still against her mouth. She felt dizzy and strange, her heart thudding hopelessly in her chest.

She took a calming breath and tried to think. To trust. Surely there was some explanation why Stefano was saying the things he was, sounding the way he was. If she just *asked*…it would be all right. Everything would be just as it had been.

'Allegra! What are you doing here?'

Her eyes flew open. Stefano stood in front of her, an expression of concern—or was it annoyance?—on his face. Suddenly Allegra couldn't tell. She wondered if she'd *ever* been able to tell.

Even now, her gaze roved hungrily over his features—the bronzed planes of his cheekbones, the thick chocolate-coloured hair swept away from his forehead, his amber eyes glinting in the dim light.

'I…' Her mouth was dry and the questions died in her heart. 'I couldn't sleep.'

'Too excited, *fiorina?*' Stefano smiled, but now everything had been cast into doubt and Allegra wondered if she saw arrogant amusement in that gesture rather than the tenderness she'd always supposed. 'In less than twelve hours we will be man and wife. Can you not wait until then to see me?' He cupped her cheek, letting his thumb drift to caress her lips. Her mouth parted involuntarily and his smile deepened. 'Go to bed, Allegra. Dream of me.'

He dropped his hand and turned away, dismissing her. Allegra watched him, watched the clean, broad lines of his back, tapering to narrow hips, watched him move away from her.

'Do you love me?' As soon as she'd asked the question, she wished she could bite back the words. Gobble them up and swallow them whole. They sounded desperate, pleading, pathetic.

And yet it was a reasonable question, wasn't it? They were about to be *married*. Yet as she saw Stefano turn slowly around, his body tense and alert, she felt as if it wasn't.

She felt as if she'd asked something wrong. Something stupid.

'Allegra?' he queried softly, and she heard a stern note of warning in the sound of her name.

'I heard you…and Papa…' she whispered, wanting even now to explain, to understand. Yet the words trailed off as she saw Stefano's expression change, his eyes turning blank and hard, the mobile curve of his mouth flattening into an unforgiving line.

'Business, Allegra, business between men. It is nothing you need concern yourself with.'

'It sounded…' Her mouth was dry and she licked her lips. 'It sounded so…'

'So what?' Stefano challenged.

'Cold,' she whispered.

Stefano raised his eyebrows. 'What are you trying to say to me, Allegra? Are you having second thoughts?'

'No!' She grabbed for his hand and after a second he coolly withdrew it. 'Stefano…I just wondered…the things you said…'

'Do you doubt that I'll care for you? Protect and provide for you?' he demanded.

'No,' Allegra said quickly, 'but Stefano, I want more than that. I want—'

He shook his head with slow, final deliberation. 'What more is there?'

Allegra gazed at him with wide, startled eyes. *What more is there?* So much more, she wanted to say. There was kindness, respect, honesty. Sharing joy and laughter, as well as sorrow and heartache. Bearing one another's burdens in love. Yet she saw the hard lines of Stefano's face, the coldness of his eyes, and knew that he was not thinking of these things.

They didn't matter.

They didn't exist.

Allegra licked her lips. 'But Stefano…' she whispered, although she didn't know what to say. She barely knew what to feel.

Stefano held one hand up to stop her half-spoken plea. Something twisted his features, flickered in his eyes. Allegra didn't know what it was, but she didn't like it. When he finally spoke, his voice was calm, cold and frightening. 'Are you questioning what kind of man I am?'

His voice and face were so harsh, unfamiliar. Allegra shook her head. 'No!' she gasped, and it came out in a half sob for she knew then that she was. And so did he.

Stefano was silent for a long moment, his gaze hard and fastened on hers, until Allegra could bear it no longer and stared at the floor.

She realized he was treating her like a child—a child to be charmed or chastened, placated or punished.

With sudden, stark clarity, she realized he'd *always* treated her this way. She'd never felt like a wife, or even a woman.

She wondered if she ever would.

'Go to bed, Allegra.' He tucked a tendril of hair behind her ear, his thumb skimming her face once more. 'Go to bed, my little bride. Tomorrow is our wedding day. A new beginning, for both of us.'

'Yes…' she whispered. Except it didn't feel like a beginning. It felt like the end. Her throat was raw and aching and she couldn't look at him as she nodded. The implications of what he had said to her father—what he had now said to *her*—were flooding through her, an endless tide of confusion and fear. 'Yes…all right.'

'Do not be afraid.'

She nodded again, jerkily, as she moved backwards up the stairs. Stefano gazed up at her, his eyes burning into her mind, her heart, her soul. Burning and destroying.

She turned around and ran the rest of the way up.

'Allegra!'

Gasping aloud in frightened surprise, she saw her mother, Isabel, striding down the upstairs corridor. Allegra glanced behind her, but she could no longer see Stefano.

'What is the meaning of this?' Isabel demanded, belting her dressing gown, her long, still-blonde hair streaming behind her in a smooth ripple.

'I…I couldn't sleep.' Allegra stumbled into her bedroom and her mother followed. Everything was unchanged, she saw—the teddy bears, the tattered books, her wedding dress. All signs of her innocence, her ignorance.

'What is wrong?' Isabel asked. Her face, with its austere beauty, was harsh. 'You look as if you've seen a ghost!'

'Nothing is wrong,' Allegra lied quickly. 'I couldn't sleep and I went for a drink of water.'

Isabel arched one eyebrow and Allegra shrank back a little. She wasn't frightened of her mother, but she couldn't help but be nervous around her. After a lifetime of nannies and boarding school, she sometimes wondered if she even knew her mother at all.

Isabel's cold eyes swept over Allegra's dishevelled appearance. 'Have you seen Stefano?' she asked, and there was a sly note in her voice that made Allegra's skin crawl even as she shook her head.

'No. No, I—'

'Don't lie to me, Allegra.' Isabel took her daughter's chin in her hand, forcing her to remain still, as pinned as a butterfly uselessly fluttering its fragile wings. 'You never could lie to me,' Isabel said. 'You've seen him. But what's happened?' There was a cruel note in her voice as she added, 'Has the fairy tale been tarnished, my dear daughter?'

Allegra didn't know what her mother meant, but she didn't like her tone. Even so, she felt trapped, helpless. And alone.

And she wanted to confide in someone, anyone, even her mother.

'I saw him,' she whispered, blinking back tears.

There was a tiny pause that spoke far more than anything her mother could have said in words. 'And?'

'I heard him talking to Papa...' Allegra closed her eyes, shook her head.

Her mother exhaled impatiently. 'So?'

'It's all been a business arrangement!' This came out in a wretched whisper that caught on the jagged edge of her throat. Tears stung her eyes. 'Stefano never loved me.'

Her mother watched her with cool impassivity. 'Of course he didn't.'

Allegra's mouth dropped open as another illusion was ripped away. 'You knew? You knew all along...?' Yet even as she spoke the words, Allegra wondered why she was surprised. Her mother had never confided in her, never seemed to enjoy her company. Why shouldn't Isabel know? Why shouldn't she have been in on the sordid deal, the business of brokering a wife, selling a daughter?

'Oh, Allegra, you are such a child.' Isabel sounded weary rather than regretful. 'Of course I knew. Your father approached Stefano before your eighteenth birthday and suggested the match. Our social connections, his money. That was why he was at your party. That was why you *had* a party.'

'Just to meet him?'

'For him to meet you,' Isabel corrected coolly. 'To see if you were suitable. And you were.'

Allegra let out a wild laugh. 'I don't want to be suitable! I want to be loved!'

'Like Cinderella?' It would have been a taunt if her mother didn't sound so tired, so bitter. 'Like Snow White? Life is not a fairy tale, Allegra. It wasn't for me and it won't be for you.'

Allegra spun away, her hands scrubbing her face, bunching in her hair as if she could somehow yank the memory from her mind, forget the words Stefano had spoken to her father and then to her. Both conversations had damned him.

'It's not the Dark Ages, either,' she said, her voice trembling. 'You speak of this...this as if people can just barter brides...'

'For women like us, well-placed, wealthy, it is not so far,' Isabel returned grimly. 'Stefano seems like a good man. Be thankful.'

Seems, Allegra thought, but was he? She thought of the way he'd spoken to her father, the way he'd spoken to her, the coldness in his eyes, how he'd scolded and then dismissed her. *What more is there?*

She realized she didn't know him at all.

She never had.

'Honourable,' Isabel added, and now true bitterness twisted her words, her face. 'He has treated you well so far, hasn't he?' She paused. 'You could do worse.'

Allegra turned to stare at her mother, the cool beauty transformed for a moment by hatred and despair. She thought of her father's words, *I know a woman in Milan,* and inwardly shuddered.

'As you did?' she asked in a low voice.

Isabel shrugged, but her eyes were hard. 'Like you, I had no choice.'

'Papa spoke...Stefano said...things...'

'About other women?' Isabel guessed with a hard laugh. She shrugged. 'You'll be glad for it, in the end.'

Allegra's eyes widened. 'Never!'

'Trust me,' Isabel returned coldly.

Allegra was compelled to ask, her voice turning ragged, 'Have you *ever* been happy?'

Isabel shrugged again, closed her eyes for a moment. 'When the *bambinos* come…'

Yet her mother had never seemed to enjoy motherhood; Allegra was an only child and she'd been tended by nannies and governesses her whole life, until she'd gone to the convent school.

Would children—the hope of children—be enough to sustain *her* through a cold, loveless marriage? A marriage she had, only moments ago, believed to be the culmination of all her young hopes. Now she realized she had no idea what those hopes had truly been. They had been the thinnest vapour, as insubstantial as smoke. Gone now. Gone with the wind.

She thought of how she'd compared Stefano to Rhett Butler and she choked on a terrible, incredulous laugh.

'I can't do it.'

A crack reverberated through the air as her mother slapped her face. Allegra reeled in shock. She'd never been hit before.

'Allegra, you are getting married *tomorrow.*'

Allegra thought of the church, the guests, the food, the flowers. The expense.

She thought of Stefano.

'Mama, please,' she whispered, one hand pressed to her face, using an endearment she'd only spoken as a child. 'Don't make me.'

'You do not know what you're saying,' Isabel snapped. 'What can you do, Allegra? What have you been prepared to do besides marry and have children, plan menus and dress nicely? Hmm? Tell me!' Her mother's voice rose with fury. 'Tell me! What?'

Allegra stared at her mother, pale-faced and wild eyed. 'I don't have to be like you,' she whispered.

'Hah!' Isabel turned away, one shoulder hunched in disdain.

Allegra thought of Stefano's smooth words, the little gifts, and wondered if they'd all been calculated, all condescensions. *Not too bad a price.* He'd bought her. Like a cow, or a car. An object. An object to be used.

He hadn't cared what she thought, hadn't even cared to tell her the truth of their marriage, of his courtship, of *anything*.

Something hardened then, crystallised into cold comprehension inside her.

Now she knew what it was like to be a woman.

'I can't do it,' she said quietly, this time without trembling or fear. 'I won't.'

Her mother was silent for a long moment. Outside, a peal of womanly laughter, husky with promise, echoed through the night.

Allegra waited, held her breath, *hoped...*

Hoped for what? How could her mother, who barely cared for her or even noticed her at all, help her out of this predicament?

Yet still she waited. There was nothing else she could do, *knew* to do.

Finally Isabel turned around. 'It would destroy your father if this marriage fell through,' she said. There was a strange note of speculative satisfaction in her voice. Allegra chose to ignore it. 'Absolutely destroy him,' she added, and now the relish was obvious.

Allegra let her breath out slowly. 'I don't care,' she said in a low voice. 'He destroyed me by manipulating me—by giving me away!'

'And what of Stefano?' Isabel raised her eyebrows. 'He would be humiliated.'

Allegra bit her lip. She'd loved him. At least, she'd thought she did. Or had she simply been caught up in the fairy tale, just as her mother said?

Life wasn't like that. She knew that now.

'I don't want to create a spectacle,' she whispered. 'I want to go quietly.' She nibbled her lip, tried not to imagine the future ahead of her, looming large and unknowable. 'I could write him a letter, explaining. If you tell him tomorrow—tell Papa—'

'Yes,' Isabel agreed after a short, telling pause, her face a blank mask, 'I could do that.' Her eyes narrowed. 'Allegra, can you give this up? Your home, your friends, the life you've been groomed to lead? You won't be allowed back. I won't risk my own position for you.'

Allegra blinked at her mother's obvious and cold-hearted warning. She looked around her room. Suddenly everything seemed so beautiful, so precious. So fleeting. She sat hunched on her bed, hugging her old patched, pink teddy bear to her chest. In her mind she heard Stefano's voice, warm and confident.

Tomorrow is…a new beginning, for both of us.

Maybe she was wrong. Maybe she was overreacting. If she talked to Stefano, asked him…

Asked him what? The answer she'd been hoping for, *desperate* for, but he'd failed to give. He hadn't told her he loved her; he'd reprimanded her for asking the question in the first place.

There could be no future with him.

And yet what future was there for her without Stefano?

'I don't know what to do,' she whispered, her voice cracking. 'Mama, I don't *know.*' She looked up at her mother with wide, tear-filled eyes, expecting even now for Isabel to touch her, comfort her. Yet there was no comfort from her mother, just as there never had been. Her face looked as if it were carved from the coldest, whitest marble. Isabel gave a little impatient shrug. Allegra took a deep breath. 'What would you have done? If you'd had a choice back then? Would you still have married Papa?'

Her mother's eyes were hard, her mouth a grim line. 'No.'

Allegra jerked in surprise. 'Then it wasn't worth it, in the end? Even with children…*me…*'

'Nothing is worth more than your happiness,' Isabel stated, and Allegra shook her head in instinctive denial. She'd never heard her mother speak about happiness before. It had always been about duty. Family. Obedience.

'Do you really care about my happiness?' she asked, hearing the naked hope in her voice.

Her mother gazed at her steadily, coldly. 'Of course I do.'

'And you think…I'll be happier…'

'If you want love—' Isabel cut her off '—then yes. Stefano doesn't love you.'

Allegra recoiled at her mother's blunt words. Yet it was the truth, she knew, and she needed to hear it. 'But what will I do?' she whispered. 'Where will I go?'

'Leave that to me.' Her mother strode to her, took her by the shoulders. 'It will be difficult,' she said sternly, her eyes boring into hers, and Allegra, feeling as limp and lifeless as a doll, merely nodded. 'You would not be welcome in our house any longer. I could send you a little money, that is all.'

Allegra bit her lip, tasted blood, and nodded. Determination to act like a woman—to choose for herself—drove her to reckless agreement.

'I don't care.'

'My driver could take you to Milan,' Isabel continued, thinking fast. 'He would do that for me. From there a train to England. My brother George would help you at first, though not for long. After that...' Isabel spread her hands. Her eyes met Allegra's with mocking challenge. 'Can you do it?'

Allegra thought of her life so far, cosseted, protected, decided. She'd never gone anywhere alone, had no prospects, no plans, no abilities.

Slowly she returned the pink teddy bear to her bed, to her girlhood, and lifted her chin. 'Yes,' she said. 'I can.'

She packed a single bag with trembling hands while her mother watched, stony-faced, urging her on.

She faltered once when she glimpsed on her dressing table the earrings Stefano had given her the day before, to wear with her wedding gown.

They were diamond teardrops, antique and elegant, and he'd told her he couldn't wait to see her wearing them. Yet now she would never wear them.

'Am I doing the right thing?' she whispered, and Isabel leaned over and zipped up her bag.

'Of course you are,' she snapped. 'Allegra, if I thought you could be happy with Stefano, I would say stay. Marry him. See if you can make a good life for yourself. But you've never wanted a good life, have you? You want something great.' Her mother's smile was sardonic as she finished, 'The fairy tale.'

Allegra blinked back tears. 'Is that so wrong?'

Isabel shrugged. 'Not many people get the fairy tale. Now write something to Stefano, to explain.'

'I don't know what to say!'

'Tell him what you told me. You realized he didn't love you, and you weren't prepared to enter a loveless marriage.' Isabel reached for a pen and some lined notebook paper—childish paper—from Allegra's desk. She thrust the items at her daughter.

Dear Stefano, Allegra wrote in her careful, looping cursive. *I'm sorry but...* She paused. What could she say? How could she explain? She closed her eyes and two tears seeped out. 'I don't know what to do.'

'For heaven's sake, Allegra, you need to start acting like an adult!' Isabel plucked the pen from her fingers. 'Here, I'll tell you what to write.'

Isabel dictated every soulless word, while Allegra's tears splashed on to the paper and smeared the ink.

'Make sure he gets it,' she said as she handed the letter to her mother, scrubbing the tears from her eyes with one fist. 'Before the ceremony. So he's not...not...'

'I'll make sure.' Isabel tucked the letter in the pocket of her dressing gown. 'Now you should go. You can buy the ticket at the station. There's money in your handbag. You'll have to stay at a hotel for a night at least, until George returns.'

Allegra's eyes widened; she'd forgotten her uncle was staying in the villa. 'Why can't I just go with him?' she asked, only to have her mother tut impatiently.

'And how would that look? You can manage a hotel. I'll tell him tomorrow what's happened. They'll be back by the next day, no doubt. Now go, before someone sees you.'

Allegra gulped down a sudden howl of panic. She was so

afraid. At least marriage to Stefano had seemed familiar, safe. And yet, she asked herself, would it have been? Or would it have become the strangest, most dangerous thing of all—being married to a man who neither loved nor respected her?

Now she would never find out.

Isabel picked up the small bag that held nothing more than a few clothes, toiletries and keepsakes and thrust it at her daughter.

Allegra, now dressed in a pair of jeans and a jumper, clutched it to her chest.

'My driver is waiting outside. Make sure no one sees you.' Isabel gave her a little push, the closest she'd probably ever come to an embrace. 'Go!'

Allegra stumbled back to the door, then inched her way down the hallway. Her heart thudded so loudly she was sure the whole villa could hear it.

What was she doing? She felt like a naughty child sneaking out of bed, but it was so much more than that. So much worse.

She slipped on the stairs and had to grab on to the banister. Somewhere a floorboard creaked, and she could hear a distant sound of snoring.

She tiptoed down the rest of the stairs, across the slick terracotta tiles of the hall. Her hand was on the knob of the front door and she turned it, only to find it was locked.

Relief poured through her for a strange, split second; she couldn't get out. She couldn't *go*.

So she would go quietly back to bed and forget she'd ever had this mad, mad plan. She'd half-turned back when the door was unlocked from the outside. Alfonso, her mother's driver, stood there, tall, dark, and expressionless.

'This way, *signorina*,' he whispered.

Allegra glanced back longingly at her home, her life. She didn't want to leave it, yet she would have been leaving it all tomorrow anyway, and for a fate surely worse than this.

At least now she was in charge of her own destiny.

'Signorina?'

Allegra nodded, turning back from the warm light of her home. She followed Alfonso into the velvety darkness, her trainers crunching on the gravel drive.

Wordlessly, Alfonso opened the back door and Allegra slipped inside.

As the car pulled away, she gazed at her home one last time, cloaked in darkness. Her eyes roved over the climbing bougain-villea, the painted shutters, everything so wonderfully dear. In the upstairs window Isabel stood, her pale face visible between the gauzy curtains, and Allegra watched as her mother's mouth curved into a cold, cruel smile of triumph that made her own breath catch in her chest in frightened surprise.

Tears stinging her eyes, her heart bumping against her chest in fear, Allegra pressed back against the seat as the car moved slowly down the drive, away from the only home she'd ever known.

CHAPTER THREE

STEFANO WATCHED ALLEGRA stiffen, her fingers stilling on the buttons of her cheap coat. Her head was bent, her face in profile so he could see the smooth, perfect line of her cheek and jaw, a loose tendril of hair curling on to the vulnerable curve where her neck met her shoulder.

When he'd come here tonight—finagled an invitation all too easily from the ever striving Mason—he'd intended to speak to Allegra about business only. All he cared about was obtaining the best care for Lucio.

He didn't—wouldn't—care about the past, wouldn't care about Allegra. She was simply a means to an end.

Yet now he realized their history could not be so smoothly swept away. The past had to be dealt with…and quickly. Easily. Or at least appear as if it was.

He moved forward so his breath stirred that stray tendril of hair—as darkly golden as he remembered—and said, 'You're not leaving so early, are you?'

Slowly, carefully, she turned around. He saw her eyes widen, her pupils flare in shock as if, even now, after he'd spoken, she was surprised—afraid?—to see him there.

Stefano smiled and slipped the coat from her shoulders. 'It's been a long time,' he said. The memories, which pulsed between them with a thousand unnamed emotions, he firmly pushed to one side.

He saw Allegra gaze up at him, her eyes wide and luminous, reminding him so forcefully of the girl he'd known too many years ago. He felt a lightning streak of pain—or was it anger?—flash through him at that memory and he forced himself to smile.

All he could think about, care about, was Lucio. Not Allegra. Never Allegra. He let his smile linger as he asked, 'Won't you come into the party with me?'

It was bound to be a shock. Allegra knew that. Yet she still hadn't expected to be so affected, so aware. Of him.

Even now, she found herself taking in his appearance, her eyes roving almost hungrily over his form, the excellently cut Italian suit in navy silk, the lithe, lean strength of him, the utter ease and arrogance with which he stood, holding her coat between two fingers.

'Stefano,' she finally said, drawing herself up, bringing her scattered senses back into a coherent whole. 'Yes, it has been a long time. But I was actually just leaving.'

She'd envisiaged a scenario such as this many times—how could she not? Yet in each one she'd imagined Stefano furious, indifferent, or perhaps simply unrepentant. She'd never, in all of her imaginings, seen him smiling, looking like an old acquaintance who wanted nothing more than for them to catch up on each other's lives.

Yet perhaps that was precisely what they were. Seven years was a long time. Who knew how either of them had grown, changed? And Stefano had never really loved her in the first place; his heart hadn't been broken.

Not like hers had.

He hadn't given her her coat, she realized. He hadn't said a word, just smiled faintly in that aggravatingly arrogant way.

'My coat, please,' she said, trying not to sound annoyed, even though she was.

'Why are you leaving the party so early?' he asked. 'I've just arrived.'

'That may be, but I'm going,' she said firmly. She couldn't help but add, as curiosity compelled her, 'I didn't realize you knew my uncle's family that well.'

'Your uncle and I do business together.' His smile, still faint, now deepened. 'Did you not realize I'd been invited?'

'No,' she said shortly.

'From what I've gathered, your uncle and you are not on favourable terms.'

Allegra's gaze jerked up to his; he was staring at her with a quiet understanding that quite unnerved her.

'How do you know that?'

'I hear things. So do you, I imagine.'

'Not about you.'

'Then let me take this opportunity to fill you in,' he said, smiling easily. Too easily. Allegra shook her head in instinctive, mute denial.

She wasn't prepared for this. She'd expected to encounter hostility, hatred, or perhaps at worst—or at best—indifference.

Yet here he was, smiling, relaxed, acting like her friend.

And she didn't want to be his friend. She didn't want to be anything to him.

Why? Was she still angry? Did she still hate him? Had she ever hated him? The questions streaked through Allegra's mind like shooting stars and fell without answers.

'I don't think we really have anything to say to each other, Stefano,' Allegra said when she realized the silence had gone on too long, had become pregnant with meaning.

Stefano raised his eyebrows. 'Don't we?'

'I know a lot has passed between us,' Allegra said firmly, 'but it's all in the past now and I—'

'If it's in the past,' Stefano interjected smoothly, 'then it doesn't matter, surely? Can't we share an evening's conversation as friends, Allegra? I'd like to talk to you.'

She hesitated. Part of her howled inside that no, they couldn't, but a greater part realized that treating Stefano as a friend, an acquaintance, was the best way to prove to him, and to herself, that that was really all he was.

'It's been a long time,' he continued quietly. 'I don't know anyone here but George Mason, and I'd rather have more congenial company. Won't you talk with me for a while?' His smile twisted and the glint in his eyes was both knowing and sorrowful. 'Please?'

Again Allegra hesitated. All those years ago she'd left Stefano, left her entire life, because he'd broken her heart.

Yet now was her chance to show him, herself, the world, that he hadn't. Or, even if he had, she'd come out of the experience wiser, stronger, happier.

'All right,' she whispered. She cleared her throat and her voice came out stronger. 'All right, for a few minutes.'

His hand rested on the small of her back as he guided her back into the Orchid Room. Even though he was barely touching her, she burned from the mere knowledge of those fingers skimming the silk of her dress.

His touch. She'd once craved it, although in all of their engagement he'd never given her more than the barest brush of a brotherly kiss.

And now her body, treacherous as it was, still reacted to him, her senses screaming awake from the mere brush of his fingers.

At least she knew, Allegra told herself, and recognized it. At least she was aware of his power over her body. That, in itself, was power.

And after tonight, she would never see him again.

'Let me get you a drink,' he said as they entered the ballroom amidst a flurry of speculative looks and murmurs. 'What do you drink now? Not lemonade any more, is it?'

'No…' She found herself cringing at the memory of just what a child she'd been. 'I'll have a glass of white wine, dry, please.'

'Done.'

Allegra watched him disappear towards the bar and resisted

the urge to plunge back through the crowd, through the double doors, out of the hotel. Away from here…from him.

No, she needed this reckoning. Perhaps she'd been actually waiting for it, waiting for the day when she saw Stefano face to face and showed him that she was no longer the silly, star-struck girl who'd thought herself so lucky, so *blessed,* to have someone like him fall in love with her.

Just the memory of her own *naïveté,* of Stefano's deception, was enough to stiffen both her spine and her soul. Seeing him had been a shock; that was to be expected.

But she was different now, and she would show him just how different. How changed. They would have a drink for old times' sake, and then…

And then what?

Turning her back on the crowd, as well as the unfinished thought, she found another innocuous spot to station herself.

'There you are.' Stefano stood in front of her, two glasses of wine cradled in one hand, his smile wry. 'I thought you'd given me the slip.'

Allegra swallowed. Her throat felt too tight and dry to make any kind of reply. Given him the slip—as she had once before?

She reached for the glass of wine. 'Thank you.'

Stefano glanced at her, shrinking in the shadowy corner of the ballroom, and quirked one eyebrow. 'Why are you hiding, Allegra?'

'I'm not,' she defended herself quickly. 'This isn't exactly my crowd, that's all.'

'No? Tell me what your crowd is, then.' He paused before adding, 'Tell me about yourself.'

She glanced up at him, saw him looking down at her with that faint, cool smile that chilled her far more than it should. She found her own gaze sweeping over his features, roving over them, looking for changes. His hair was shorter and threads of silver glinted at his temples. His face was leaner, the lines of his jaw and chin more angular and pronounced. There was a new hardness in his eyes, deep down, like a mask over his soul. Or perhaps that had always been there and she hadn't known. She hadn't seen it, not until that last night.

'You're being rather friendly,' she said at last. 'I didn't expect it.'

Stefano rotated his wineglass between strong brown fingers. 'It's been a long time,' he said finally. 'Unlike your uncle, I try not to hold grudges.'

'Nor do I,' Allegra flashed, and Stefano smiled.

'So neither of us is angry, then.'

'No.' She wasn't angry; she just didn't know what she felt. What she was supposed to feel. Every word she spoke to Stefano was like probing a sore tooth to see how deep the decay had set in. She didn't feel the lightning streak of pain yet, but she was ready for it when it came.

Unless it never did. Unless she'd really healed her heart, moved on, just like she intended to show him. Just as she'd always told herself she had.

He took a sip of wine. 'So, what have you been up to these last few years?' he asked. Allegra suppressed the impulse to laugh, even though nothing felt remotely funny.

'I've been working here in London,' she finally said. She could feel him gazing at her, even though her own eyes were averted.

'What kind of work?' His voice was neutral, the carefully impersonal questions of an acquaintance, and for some reason that neutrality—that distance—stung her.

'I'm an art therapist.' He raised his eyebrows in question and Allegra continued, genuine enthusiasm entering her voice. 'It's a kind of therapy that uses art to help people, usually children, uncover their emotions. In times of trauma, expressing oneself through an artistic medium often helps unlock feelings and memories that have been suppressed.' She risked a glance upwards, expecting to see some kind of sceptical derision. Instead he looked merely thoughtful, his head cocked to one side.

'And you enjoy this? This art therapy?'

'Yes, it's very rewarding. And challenging. The opportunity to make a difference in a child's life is incredible, and I'm very thankful for it.' Her mouth was dry and she took another sip of cool wine. 'What about you?'

'I still own my company, Capozzi Electronica. I do less research now it has grown bigger. Sometimes I miss that.'

'Research,' Allegra repeated, and felt a surprising pang of shame to realize she'd never known he'd done any research at all. He'd never told her all those years ago, and she'd never asked. 'What kind of research?'

'Mostly mechanical. I develop new technology to improve the efficiency of industrial machinery.'

'You've lost me,' Allegra said with a little laugh and Stefano smiled.

'Most of it wouldn't concern your day-to-day living anyway. My research has been centred on machinery in the mining industry. A selective field.'

'Capozzi Electronica is a big business though,' Allegra said, 'isn't it? I've seen your logo on loads of things—CD players, mobile phones.'

Stefano shrugged. 'I've bought a few companies.'

She opened her mouth to ask another question, but Stefano plucked her wineglass from her fingers and gave her a teasing smile. 'Enough of that. The music is starting again and I'd like to dance. Dance with me?'

He held one hand out, just as he'd done all those years ago on her eighteenth birthday, when she'd walked down the stairs and into what she'd thought was her future.

Now she hesitated. 'Stefano, I don't think…'

'For old times' sake.'

'I don't want to remember old times.'

Stefano smiled faintly. 'No, neither do I, come to think of it. Then how about for new times' sake? New friendships.'

She stared at his hand, outstretched, waiting. The fingers were long and tapered, the skin smooth and tanned. 'Allegra?'

She knew this was a bad idea. She'd wanted to chat with Stefano like an old friend, but she didn't want to dance with him like one. Didn't know if she should get that close.

And yet something in her rebelled. Wanted to see how they were together, how she reacted to him. Wanted, strangely, to feel that lightning streak of pain…to see if it was there at all.

Mutely she nodded.

His hand encased—engulfed—hers and he led her on to the dance floor. She stood there woodenly, her feet shuffling in a parody of steps, while couples danced around them, some entwined, some holding themselves more awkwardly, all of them sliding her and Stefano speculative glances.

'This isn't a waltz, Allegra,' Stefano murmured and pulled her gently to him.

Their hips collided in an easy movement that was far too intimate…more intimate than anything that had passed between them during their engagement.

She felt the hard contours of him against her own softness, unyielding and strong. Allegra stiffened and jerked back even as her limbs went weak.

'I'm sorry,' she murmured, 'I don't dance that often.'

'Nor do I,' Stefano murmured back, his lips close—too close—to her hair. 'But I hear it's like riding a bike. You never forget.'

His arms were around her waist, his fingers splayed on her lower back. 'Do you remember how we danced? On your eighteenth birthday?' A glimmer of a smile lurked in the mobile curve of his mouth, although his eyes were shuttered. 'You clung to me for balance because you'd never worn heels before.'

Allegra shook her head, closed her eyes before snapping them open once more. 'I was a child.'

Stefano frowned, his eyes flickering across her face. 'Perhaps,' he said at last. 'But you aren't one now.'

'No,' Allegra agreed, 'I'm not.'

They danced in silence, swaying to the rhythm, their bodies—

chests, hips, thighs—all too tantalisingly close. Allegra felt herself relaxing, even though there was a taut wire of tension running
through her core, vibrating with awareness.

She'd never expected it to happen like this. And yet, she
realized, she'd expected to see Stefano again. A part of her, she
acknowledged now, had been waiting for their reunion since the
night she'd fled.

Why? she wondered, and her heart knew the answer. To
show him how strong she was, how healed and healthy and
happy she was…without him.

'What are you thinking?' Stefano murmured, and Allegra gazed
at him through half-closed lids, soothed by the music and wine.

'How odd this is,' she admitted in a husky murmur. 'To be
dancing with you…again.'

'It is odd,' Stefano agreed, his voice pitched low to match
hers. 'But not unpleasant, surely.'

'I expected you to hate me.' Her eyes opened, widened. Waited.

He shrugged. 'Why should I, Allegra? It was a long time ago.
You were young, afraid. You had your reasons. And, in the end,
we didn't know each other very well, did we? A handful of
dinners, a few kisses. That was all.'

Allegra nodded, accepting, though her throat was tight. He'd
distilled their relationship down to its rather shallow essence,
and yet it had been the most profound experience of her life.

'Do you hate me?' Stefano asked with surprising, easy
candour. Allegra looked up, startled, and saw a shadow flicker
through his eyes.

'No,' she said, and meant it. 'No. I've moved past it,
Stefano.' She smiled, tried to keep her voice light. Breezy. 'It
was a long time ago, as we've both agreed, and I've realized
that you never lied to me. I just believed what I did because I
wanted to.'

'And what did you believe?' Stefano asked softly. Allegra
forced herself to meet his gaze directly.

'That you loved me…as much as I loved you.'

The words seemed to reverberate between them and for a strange second Allegra felt like the girl she'd been seven years ago, standing before Stefano and asking, *Do you love me?*

He'd never answered then, and he didn't now.

Allegra let out a breath. What had she expected? That he'd tell her he *had* loved her, that it had all been a mistake, a misunderstanding?

No, of course not. It hadn't been a mistake. It had been the right thing to do. For both of them.

Stefano hadn't loved her, hadn't even considered loving her, and she would have been miserable as his wife. She'd never regret her choice, never even look back. Not once. Not ever.

That you loved me…as much as I loved you. The words played a remorseless echo in Stefano's brain, even as he continued to dance, continued to feel Allegra's soft contours so tantalizingly close to him. He fought the urge to pull her closer, and closer still, and make her remember how they could have been all those years ago, if they'd been given the chance.

If she'd given him a chance.

But she hadn't, she'd made her decision that night, and he'd accepted it.

Hell, he'd made peace with it. Or at least he would now, for Lucio's sake.

Lucio… He forced his mind as well as other parts of his body away from Allegra's tempting softness and thought of his housekeeper's son, the grandson of the man who'd given him everything—shelter, food, opportunity—even at his own expense.

He wouldn't repay Matteo by neglecting his duty to his grandson. He wouldn't let Allegra distract him in his purpose… or, if it came to it, have him distract her.

His lips curved as he considered how many ways in which he could distract her…

No. No, the past was over. Finished.

Forgotten.

It had to be.

The music ended and they swayed to a stop before Stefano quite deliberately stepped away. It was time to tell Allegra the real reason why he was here…why he was dancing with her, or talking to her at all.

Allegra felt Stefano's arms fall away and resisted the urge to shiver. Out of the corner of her eye, she saw her uncle glowering and she looked away.

Stefano glanced around at the crowd of striving socialites and smiled. 'This crowd isn't really to my taste. What would you think about getting a drink some place more congenial?'

Allegra felt a leap of both anticipation and alarm in her chest. 'I don't…'

Stefano raised an eyebrow. 'Care to finish that sentence?' he asked dryly and Allegra realized she'd trailed off without knowing what to say. What to think.

What to feel.

'It's late,' she murmured, and wondered what she wanted Stefano to do. Take her reluctance as refusal or refuse to take no for an answer?

It galled her that she didn't know what she wanted him to do; she just wanted him to choose.

'It's not even ten o'clock yet,' Stefano said. There was a lazy lilt to his voice that made Allegra feel as if a purring cat had just leapt on to her lap. She wanted to stroke it, test its softness. 'One drink, Allegra. Then I'll let you go.'

'All right,' she said, her voice cautious, yet with not nearly as much reluctance as she knew she should have.

She wondered why she was reluctant, why she was afraid.

They'd just shown how grown up and civil they could be. The past was truly forgotten.

She wasn't that girl any more.

Stefano threaded her fingers with his own as he led her off the dance floor and away from the party.

This was strange, Allegra told herself as Stefano handed her her coat. Yet it was nice too, she realized as they headed out into the night, the September air cool on her flushed cheeks.

Too nice, perhaps.

'Where to?' Stefano stood on the kerb, an expensive woollen overcoat draped over one arm, his eyebrows raised in faint question.

'I'm afraid I don't know London nightspots very well.'

'Nor do I. But I do know a quiet wine bar near here that can be quite relaxing. How does that sound?'

'Fine. Lovely.'

She didn't see Stefano gesture to the doorman, but he must have for a cab pulled sleekly to a halt at the kerb. Stefano brushed the doorman aside and opened the car door himself, ushering Allegra in before he joined her.

Their thighs touched as he slid next to her, and Stefano did not move away. Allegra wasn't sure whether she liked the feel of his hard thigh pressing against hers or not, but she was certainly aware of it. Her hand curled around the door handle, nerves leaping to life.

They rode in silence, and Allegra was glad. She didn't feel up to making conversation.

After a few minutes, the cab pulled to a halt in front of an elegantly fronted establishment in Mayfair and Stefano paid the driver before he helped Allegra out. His hand was warm and dry and Allegra forced herself to let go.

She could not let herself be attracted to Stefano now. Not when she had a life, admittedly a small, humble one compared to his wealth and status, but one that was hers and hers alone.

Not when she knew what he was like. What he believed. Tonight was about being *friends.* That was all.

That was all it could be.

The wine bar was panelled in dark wood, with low tables and comfortable armchairs scattered around. It was like entering someone's study and Allegra could see immediately why Stefano liked it.

'Shall I order a bottle of red?' he asked, and Allegra bit her lip.

'I think I've had enough wine already.'

'What is an evening with friends without wine?' He smiled. 'Just drink a little if you prefer, but we must have a toast.'

'All right.' It did seem rather prim and stingy to sit sipping iced water.

Stefano ordered and they were soon seated in two squashy armchairs. Allegra even kicked off her heels—her feet had been killing her—and tucked her legs up under her.

'So,' Stefano said, 'I want to hear more about what you've been up to these last seven years.'

Allegra laughed. 'That's a rather tall order.'

He shrugged; she'd forgotten how wide his shoulders were, how much power and grace the simplest of movements revealed. 'You're an art therapist, you said. How did that come about?'

'I took classes.'

'When you arrived in London?'

'Soon after.'

The waiter came with the wine and they were both silent while he uncorked the bottle and poured. Stefano tasted it, smiled and indicated for the waiter to pour for Allegra.

'*Cin cin,*' he said, raising his glass in the old informal toast that reminded her of her childhood, and she smiled, raising her own.

She drank, grateful for the rich liquid that coated her throat and burned in her belly. Despite Stefano's easy manner, Allegra realized she was still feeling unsettled.

Seeing him brought back more memories than she'd ever wanted to face. Memories and questions.

She had chosen not to face them when she'd left. She'd quite deliberately put the memories in a box and unlike Pandora, she'd had no curiosity to open it. No desire for the accompanying emotions and fears to come tumbling out.

When you didn't face something, she knew, it became easier

never to face it. It became quite wonderfully easy to simply ignore it. For ever.

Yet now that something was staring her straight in the face, smiling blandly.

Whatever Stefano had felt seven years ago, he'd clearly got over it. He'd put his ghosts, his demons to rest and had moved on.

And so had she.

Hadn't she?

Yes, she told herself, she had. She *had*.

Stefano crossed one long leg over the other, smiling easily. 'Tell me about these classes you took,' he said.

'What is there to tell?' Her voice came out too high, too strained. Allegra took a breath and let it out slowly. She even managed a laugh. 'I came to London and I lived at my uncle's house for…a little while. Then I got my own digs, my own job, and when I'd saved enough money I started taking night classes. Eventually I realized I enjoyed art and I specialised in art therapy. I received my preliminary qualification two years ago.'

Stefano nodded thoughtfully. 'You've done well for yourself,' he finally said. 'It must have been very difficult, starting out on your own.'

'No more difficult than the alternative,' Allegra retorted, and then felt a hectic flush sweep across her face and crawl up her throat as she realized the implication of what she'd said.

'The alternative,' Stefano replied musingly. He smiled wryly, but Allegra saw something flicker in his eyes. She didn't know what it was—hidden, shadowy—but it made her uneasy.

It made her wonder.

'By the alternative,' he continued, rotating his wineglass between lean brown fingers, 'you mean marrying me.'

Allegra took a deep breath. 'Yes. Stefano, marrying you would have destroyed me back then. My mother saved me that night she helped me run away.'

'And saved herself as well.'

Allegra bit her lip. 'Yes, I realize now she did it for her own ends, to shame my father. She used me as much as my father intended to use me.'

A month after her arrival in England, she'd heard of her mother's flagrant affair with Alfonso, the driver who had spirited Allegra away. Allegra had lost enough of her *naïveté* then to realize how her mother had manipulated her daughter's confused and frightened state for her own ends—the ultimate shaming of the man she despised, the man who had arranged Allegra's marriage.

Her husband.

And what had it gained her?

By the time Isabel had left, Roberto Avesti was bankrupt and his business, Avesti International, ruined. Isabel hadn't realized the depth of her husband's disgrace, or the fact that it would mean she would be, if not broken-hearted, then at least broke.

Allegra bit her lip, her mind and heart sliding away from that line of conversation, those memories, the cost her own freedom had demanded from everyone involved.

'Even so,' she said firmly, 'it's the truth. I was nineteen, a child, I didn't know who I was or what I wanted.'

Stefano's face was expressionless, his eyes blank, steady on hers. 'I could have helped you with that.'

'No, you couldn't. Wouldn't.' Allegra shook her head. 'What you wanted in a wife wasn't—isn't—the person I was meant to become. I had to discover that for myself. Back then I didn't even know I was missing anything. I thought I was the luckiest girl in the world.' Her voice rang out bitterly.

'And something made you realize you weren't,' Stefano finished lightly. 'I know it shocked you to realize our marriage was arranged, Allegra, as a matter of business between your father and me.'

'Yes,' she agreed, 'it did. But it wasn't just that, you know.'

Stefano cocked his head, his eyes alert. 'No? What was it, then?' His voice was bland and mildly curious yet Allegra still felt a strange *frisson* of fear. Unease.

Suspicion.

'You didn't love me,' Allegra said, striving to keep her voice steady. 'Not the way I wanted to be loved, anyway.' She shrugged. 'It doesn't matter now, does it?' she said, trying to keep her voice light. 'It's all past, as you said.'

'Indeed.' Stefano's voice was chilly, the expression in his eyes remote at best. 'Still,' he continued, his voice thawing, turning mild, 'it must have been difficult for you to set up a new life here, leave your family, your home.' He paused. 'You've never been back really, have you?'

'I've been to Milan, for professional reasons,' Allegra replied, hearing the defensive edge to her voice.

Stefano shrugged in dismissal. 'But you have not been home.'

'And where's home, exactly?' Allegra asked. 'My family's villa was auctioned off when my father declared bankruptcy. My mother lives mostly in Milan. I don't *have* a home, Stefano.' Her voice rang out clear and sharp, and she looked down, wanting to recover her composure, wishing it hadn't been lost.

She didn't want to talk about her family, her home, all the things she'd lost in that desperate flight. She didn't want to remember.

'Is London your home?' Stefano asked curiously, when the tense silence between them had gone on too long. Too long for Allegra's comfort, at any rate.

She shrugged. 'It's a place, as good as any, and I enjoy my job.'

'This art therapy.'

'Yes.'

'And what of friends?' He paused, his fingers tightening imperceptibly on his wineglass. 'Lovers?'

Allegra felt a *frisson* of pure feeling shiver up her spine. 'That's not your business,' she said stiffly and he smiled.

'I only meant to ask, do you have a social life?'

She thought of her handful of work acquaintances and shrugged again. 'Enough.' Then, since she wasn't enjoying this endless scrutiny, she asked, 'And what of you?'

Stefano raised his eyebrows. 'What of me?'

Suddenly she wished she hadn't asked. Wasn't sure she wanted to know. 'Friends?' she forced out. 'Lovers?'

'Enough,' Stefano replied, a faint feral smile stealing over his features. 'Although no lovers.'

This admission both startled and pleased her. Stefano was so virile, so potent, so utterly and unalterably male that she would have assumed he had lovers. *Loads.*

Probably he only meant he had no lovers currently, Allegra thought cynically. No arm candy for the moment, none for this evening.

Except her.

He was with *her* tonight.

'Does that please you?' Stefano asked, breaking into her thoughts and making her gaze jerk upwards in surprise.

'It doesn't matter,' she countered swiftly.

'No, of course not, and why should it?' Stefano's smile turned twisted, cynical. 'Just as it doesn't matter to me.'

Allegra nodded, uncertain. Of course, the words were right, yet the tone wasn't. The feeling wasn't.

She saw something spark in Stefano's eyes, something alive and angry, and she set her wineglass on the table. 'Perhaps this was a bad idea. I was hoping we could be friends, even if just for an evening, but maybe, even after all this time, we can't. I know memories can hurt. And hurts run deep.'

Stefano leaned forward, his fingers curling around her wrist, staying her.

'I'm not hurt,' he said, his voice quiet and firm, and Allegra met his eyes.

'No,' she said, suddenly, strangely stung, 'you wouldn't be, would you? The only thing that was hurt that day was your pride.'

His eyes glinted gold, burned into hers. 'What are you saying?'

'That you never loved me.' She took a breath and forced herself to continue. 'You just *bought* me.'

He shook his head slowly. 'So you claimed in that letter of yours, I remember.'

Allegra thought of that letter, with its girlish looping hand-writing and splotchy tear-stains and felt the sting of humiliation.

He wasn't even denying it, but it hardly mattered now.

'I think I should go,' she said in a low voice and Stefano released her, leaning back in his chair. 'I never meant to bring all this up, talk about it again.' She tried to smile, even to laugh, and wasn't quite able to. 'Perhaps it would have been better if I'd left before you came into the party. If we hadn't seen each other at all. We almost missed each other, as it was.'

Stefano watched her, smiled faintly. 'That,' he said, 'wasn't going to happen.'

Allegra felt a lurch of trepidation, as if everything had shifted subtly, suddenly. 'What do you mean?'

'We weren't going to miss each other this evening, Allegra,' Stefano said with cool, calm certainty. 'I came to the party— to London—to see you.'

CHAPTER FOUR

'ME?'

Stefano watched the emotions chase across Allegra's features: shock, fear, pleasure. He smiled. Even now, she wanted his attention. His touch.

And he couldn't stop touching her, whether it was her back as he'd steered her through a crowded ballroom, or her thigh in the darkened confines of a city cab. He was drawn to her, despite both his desire and intent to the contrary. He wanted to touch and to know the woman he'd once believed he could love.

Love. *You never loved me.* How many times had she told him now, he wondered cynically. How many times had she thrown it in his face? No, he hadn't loved her, not the way she'd wanted. Not like Galahad, Rhett Butler, or whatever ridiculous caricature of a man she'd imprinted in her childish mind.

It hardly mattered now anyway. Love was not the issue; Lucio was.

He smiled, broke the silence. 'Yes, you,' he said.

Allegra blinked. Stared. She heard a buzzing in her ears. Felt it in her soul. 'What do you mean?' she finally said, though she'd heard what he'd said. She just couldn't believe it.

'I knew you would be at this wedding, and I wangled an invitation from your uncle. It wasn't difficult. He was thrilled to be getting such a notable guest.' His lips curved in a mocking smile that had Allegra gritting her teeth at his unshakeable arrogance.

'Why?' she whispered. 'Why did you want to see me, Stefano?'

Stefano cradled his wineglass between his hands, staring into its ruby contents before he raised his head. His expression was stony, bleak. 'Because I've been told you're the best art therapist for children in this country.'

Allegra jerked back, startled. She hadn't expected *that*. What, a mocking little voice asked, did you expect? For him to declare that he'd missed you? *Loved* you?

'I think that's overstating the case rather a lot,' she said after a moment. 'I've only been qualified for two years.'

'The doctor I spoke to in Milan recommended you unreservedly.'

'Renaldo Speri,' Allegra guessed. 'We corresponded regarding a case I had, a boy who had been misdiagnosed with autism.'

'And he wasn't autistic?'

'No, he was severely traumatised from witnessing his mother's suicide.' She grimaced in memory. 'It was a remarkable breakthrough, but I can't really take the credit for it. Anyone could have—'

'Speri thinks highly of you,' Stefano said with a shrug. 'He seems to think you're the best. And I want the best.'

Allegra watched him for a moment. The best. So she was a commodity, a possession. Just as she'd been all those years before. Would Stefano ever think of her otherwise? Did he even know how?

At least the difference now, she thought cynically, was that the arrangement was mutual.

'Why didn't you tell me this when we first met, Stefano? Why come to the reception at all?' Why ask her to dance, take her for a drink, talk about *lovers?*

She shook her head, felt a tide of humiliation wash over her at the realization of how Stefano had been manipulating her…as he had before. Softening her up for the request. The kill.

She felt another wave of humiliation crash over her as she

remembered her own thoughts, the pleasure she'd felt at believing Stefano wanted to be with her. Treacherous, half-acknowledged desires that Stefano had undoubtedly surmised. She closed her eyes briefly, sickened by his deception, and by herself for falling for it…again.

She opened her eyes and met Stefano's blank gaze with a stern one of her own. 'If you were interested in me professionally, you should have come to my office, made an appointment—'

Stefano shrugged, unrepentant. His face was expressionless, yet his eyes blazed into hers. 'You know it's not as simple as that, Allegra. The past still lies between us. I needed to see how things would be between us. If we would be able to work together.'

'And can we?' she asked, eyebrows raised, her voice sharpened with both sarcasm and curiosity.

'Yes.' He spoke flatly, with cold certainty. 'We can.' He leaned forward, his eyes intent on hers, trapping her with his unrelenting gaze. 'The past is forgotten, Allegra.'

Yet it hadn't felt forgotten a moment ago, Allegra thought, suppressing a shiver of unease. That flash of something dark and primal in Stefano's eyes had made her feel as if it wasn't forgotten at all.

'And for this you needed to ask me to dance? Invite me out for a drink?' She shook her head. 'If you want me to help you, Stefano, help whatever child you are thinking of, then you need to be honest with me. From the beginning. I won't abide liars.'

Stefano's eyes narrowed. 'I am not a liar,' he said coldly. 'How was I not honest, Allegra? We had a past. I wanted to make sure it wouldn't interfere with what I am proposing before I set it before you. That's all.'

She pressed her lips together against a useless retort…a *revealing* retort. There was nothing Stefano had done, she acknowledged silently, that she could point her finger at. Accuse him of. Yet she was still cross, still *hurt,* and she still felt uneasy, uncertain. Uncomfortable.

'All right, fine,' she said at last. 'Why don't you tell me what exactly you're proposing?'

Stefano paused. 'The hour's late,' he said. 'And it's been a long evening. Why don't we talk about it another time? Tomorrow, perhaps? Over dinner?'

Allegra frowned. 'Why not Monday, in my office?' she countered.

'Because I'll be back in Rome on Monday,' Stefano replied with firm finality. 'Allegra, I am interested in you only as a professional—'

'I know that!' she said, a flush rising to her cheeks.

'Then why not converse over dinner? We've just shown how we can be reasonable this evening. We can even, perhaps, be friends.' He smiled, his amber eyes glinting with a promise Allegra remembered all too well. A promise of tenderness and compassion, of understanding and caring. Of love.

False. All false.

Allegra took a breath. Stefano was right; she *was* letting the past cloud the present issue, which was presumably a hurting child.

She had to forget it, had to move on as she knew she'd done all those years ago. Yet seeing Stefano had brought it rushing back.

She lifted her chin. 'All right. Tomorrow.'

'Tell me your address and I'll fetch you.'

'There's no need—'

'I'll fetch you,' Stefano repeated. He didn't raise his voice, didn't need to. He simply smiled. Smiled and waited.

Allegra chose to capitulate gracefully. Some battles, she knew, were not worth fighting. Not yet.

She gave it to him, then rose from her chair. He stood also. 'Goodnight, Stefano,' she said, and she held out her hand.

He glanced down at it, smiling wryly, before he took it in his. Her hand felt so small in his, small and fragile.

'Good night, Allegra,' Stefano said, his voice a husky murmur. 'Until tomorrow.'

* * *

All the next day Allegra's mind hurtled from alarm to anticipation, marking quite a few assumptions along that perilous mental route.

Stefano wanted to contract her services as an art therapist for a child. A *child*.

His child?

His wife?

She probed these possibilities with careful, clinical precision. Did it hurt? How much pain?

She wasn't jealous, she knew that. She wasn't even that surprised. So what did she feel?

She didn't know. Couldn't answer. More thoughts, more emotions to tuck away in that box.

As day darkened into twilight, Allegra surveyed the slim pickings of her wardrobe.

She'd splurged on the dress for Daphne's party, and there was nothing else remotely as sophisticated or expensive in her wardrobe. Her work clothes were generally plain and comfortable, and the few dresses she had were stodgy and serviceable.

Allegra sighed. Why hadn't she considered this before? She'd have had the time, if not the money, to buy something at the shops.

Why, that objectionable little voice whispered inside her, do you care? Are you trying to impress him? *Attract* him?

'No,' Allegra said aloud but, even alone in her bedroom, her voice sounded flat and false.

With a growl of impatience, she turned to the rack of clothes and picked a dress out at random. It was an olive green coat dress that she'd bought on sale for an interview, and while it presented a reliable if rather depressing image for work, it was hardly something one wore to dinner…especially if that dinner was at one of London's classiest restaurants, which Allegra had no doubt it would be, knowing Stefano.

Knowing Stefano… Did she really know him?

Seven years was a long time for both of them. She'd never have expected him to act as he had last night, putting the past behind them. Wanting to be her friend. Caring about what she thought.

And the only reason he'd done those things, she reminded herself, was because he wanted something from her.

She slipped on the coat dress, only to grimace in rueful dismay at her reflection. She looked awful, drab and dreary, and she was vain enough to want to look at least half-decent for Stefano.

Not beautiful, not sexy, not alluring. But attractive, at least. Attractive and professional, confident and calm.

She chose a pair of slim-fitting black trousers and a white silk blouse that was plain but well-tailored.

Catching her hair up in a chignon—nothing careless about it this time—she nodded at the rather austere image she presented. Professional, puritanical.

'For the best,' she reminded herself. After all, she was having dinner with Stefano in her professional capacity, not personal. Nothing personal. Nothing *ever* personal.

The intercom for the front door sounded, and Allegra hurried to buzz him through.

The walls were so thin, she could hear the creak of the stairs and his tread down the hall and her heart started to hammer.

She grabbed her coat and handbag and met him in the hallway.

'Thanks for coming,' she said quickly. 'I'm ready.'

Stefano raised an eyebrow. He looked devastating in a charcoal-coloured suit, a crisp white shirt and mulberry-coloured silk tie. 'We could have a drink first.'

'Let's go out,' Allegra suggested. 'My flat's tiny.' She realized with a little pang of shame that she didn't want him to see her poky flat with its second-hand furnishings. Art therapists, even ones who'd had significant successes, didn't make much money.

She was proud of her flat, but she knew it would seem pathetic to him—the little life she'd built for herself—compared with what he had. What he'd been prepared to offer her.

Stefano made no comment, merely shrugged one shoulder

before gesturing for her to lead the way down the cramped hallway.

Out in the street, traffic blared along with the stereo systems propped in windows, and there was an overwhelming smell of greasy kebab on the air.

Allegra smiled brightly. 'Where to? We could walk…'

Stupid, she told herself. Stefano would have made reservations at a place far from here.

'I have a car.' He gestured to a black luxury car idling at the kerb. A few passers-by were giving it curious—and envious—looks as the driver hopped out and opened the back door for them.

'I hope you don't mind…?' Stefano asked politely. 'If you wanted to eat more locally—'

'No,' Allegra hastened to assure him, 'this is fine.'

It was more than fine. It was amazing. She'd spent the last seven years in severely squeezed circumstances and she'd forgotten that this was the kind of life she'd once been accustomed to. The kind of life Stefano had always known.

'Thank you for giving me a lift,' she said stiffly as the car pulled away from the kerb. 'I could have taken a cab, met you at the restaurant.'

'Yes,' Stefano agreed, his voice pleasant and mild, 'you could have.'

Allegra was conscious of the enclosed space, the forced intimacy of their shared seat, thighs and shoulders brushing, touching. She sneaked a glance at Stefano, saw the clean, strong lines of his cheek, his jaw, and curled her fingers into a fist in her lap.

'So why don't you tell me about the child in need of therapy?' she said after a moment when the only sounds had been the muted traffic from outside and their own breathing.

'Let's wait until we get to the restaurant,' Stefano replied. 'Then we won't be interrupted.'

Allegra nodded. It made sense, but the silence that stretched between them was unnerving, and she didn't even know why.

This wasn't personal, she reminded herself. It was professional. Stefano was nothing more than another parent in desperate need of help for his child. As long as she remembered that…

'Allegra,' Stefano said softly. He smiled as he put one large hand on her leg. Her thigh. Allegra stared down at his fingers, tense, transfixed. 'Relax.'

She realized how tense she was, coiled tightly, ready to strike or to flee. She smiled, tried to laugh, tried to relax, and failed at both. 'I'm sorry, Stefano. This is just a bit strange for me.'

He smiled, his gaze flickering over her features. 'Me too.'

'Is it?' she asked frankly, and his smile deepened.

'Of course. But what's important now, what has to be important, is Lucio.'

'Lucio,' Allegra repeated. His son. 'Tell me about him.'

'I will, soon.' He gazed down at his own hand, her leg, as if suddenly aware of what he had done. How he'd touched her.

He didn't move his hand, and the confines of the car suddenly seemed airless, tiny. Allegra couldn't remember how to breathe. He has a son, she told herself, which means he has a wife.

Finally, with a little smile, he removed his hand and Allegra drew in a lungful of air. Had he always affected her that way, she wondered hazily, or was it new?

Whatever it was, it didn't matter. It wouldn't.

They rode in silence for a quarter of an hour before the car pulled up to a luxury hotel on Piccadilly.

Stefano ushered her up the steps and through the doors and then, surprisingly, to a lift. They rode up in silence and when the lift doors opened Allegra gave a little gasp of pleasure, for they were at the top of the hotel and beyond the elegantly set tables and tall glass vases of creamy lilies, the whole of London's skyline stretched enticingly to the dark horizon, spangled with lights, glittering with promise.

A waiter ushered them to the most private table, tucked in an alcove with long windows on either side of them. Allegra sat down, felt the weight of the heavy linen napkin as the waiter placed it in her lap.

'Is this all right?' Stefano asked and she smiled mischievously.

'I suppose it will have to do.'

Stefano smiled back, his eyes glinting in the dim light, and for a moment they seemed complicit in their own little joke, their own world. It caused Allegra's heart to skip two beats and a bubble of laughter to well up in her throat.

She felt the cares and worries that had been tightening like an iron band around her heart ease. They very nearly slipped away altogether and she let them go, even gave them a little push.

This could work, she told herself. It was working. They were interacting in a professional way, friendly and relaxed. Just as it should be.

Allegra took a sip of water. 'Tell me, do you come to London often?'

'Occasionally on business,' Stefano replied, 'although mainly I've been doing business in Belgium.'

'Belgium? What's there?'

He gave a little shrug. 'That industrial machinery I told you about. Mining industry.' He smiled faintly. 'Very boring.'

'Not to you, I suppose.'

'No,' he agreed, his expression darkening as if a shadow had passed briefly over him, 'not to me.'

'I don't even know what made you interested in that,' Allegra acknowledged ruefully. 'I feel like I actually know very little about you.' When they'd met all those years ago, he'd asked her questions about herself. She'd been happy to chatter on about all of her silly, girlish interests. He'd been happy to listen. She winced now at the memory.

And what had she known of him? He was from Rome; he owned his own company; he was rich and handsome and he had wanted her.

Or so she'd thought...until she'd realized that all he'd wanted was her social status, her family's standing.

Not her, never her.

'I suppose I thought you knew what was important,' Stefano replied.

'Like what?'

'That I'd protect and provide for you,' Stefano replied. He spoke calmly, easily even, and yet Allegra felt chilled.

He was the same, she realized with a sickening stab of disappointed longing. Protection. Provision. Those were what had mattered, what still mattered. Not love, respect, honesty, or even common interests, shared joys. Just the careful handling of an object. A possession...something bought and paid for. That wasn't love, she thought, wondering why it mattered. Why she cared. That kind of love wasn't real. It was worthless.

Why should she have thought—*hoped*—he'd changed? That kind of belief was the bedrock of a man's soul. It didn't change. It didn't even crumble.

'Yes,' she murmured, taking another sip of water to ease the sudden dryness of her throat, 'I knew that.'

'Why don't we look at the menu?' Stefano suggested and there was a knowing gleam in his eye. Allegra had no doubt that he'd realized how dangerously deep the waters swirling between them had become, and he was steering them to safer, shallower eddies.

She glanced down at the menu, the elegant gold script, half of it in French, and swallowed a laugh.

Stefano glanced at her over the top of his menu. 'You learned French in school, didn't you?'

Allegra thought of the convent, the lessons she'd learned there. Silence. Submission. Subservience. 'Schoolgirl stuff,' she dismissed with a little smile, and stared back down at her menu. 'What are langoustines?'

'Lobster.'

'Oh.' She gave a little grimace; she'd never liked seafood. Stefano chuckled softly. 'Perhaps we should have gone somewhere a bit less international.' He perused the wine menu, adding carelessly, 'You seem to have become rather English.'

Allegra didn't know why she felt stung, except that it sounded like an insult. 'I am half English,' she reminded him and he glanced up at her, his eyes dark, fathomless.

'Yes, but the girl I knew was Italian to her core...or so I thought.'

Allegra put down her menu. 'I thought we agreed that we didn't know each other very well back then. And anyway, we're different people now.'

'Absolutely.' Stefano put down his own menu. 'Have you decided?'

'Yes. I'll have the steak.'

'And to start?'

'The herb salad.' She pressed her lips together, because she knew he was going to order for her and it irritated her. Another way of providing, she thought sardonically, gazing out of the window.

The waiter, aware of the precise second they'd put down their menus, came to the table.

As Allegra had thought, Stefano ordered for both of them.

'How would madam like the steak done?'

Stefano began to speak and Allegra interjected frostily, '*Mademoiselle* would like it medium rare.'

There was a moment of surprised silence and Allegra realized she'd just spoken like a child.

Acted like one.

Felt like one.

Why did Stefano do that to her? she wondered wearily. Why did she allow him to? Even now, when she was here as a professional, when he wanted her for her expert services?

'If you wanted to order for yourself,' Stefano said mildly once the waiter had gone, 'you could have told me.'

'It doesn't matter,' Allegra dismissed firmly, although Stefano still looked unconvinced. 'Why don't we talk about Lucio now?' she suggested. No more raking up the past, the memories swirling about like fallen leaves around them. 'He's your son?'

Stefano looked genuinely startled. 'No, he's not. I don't have a son, Allegra.' He paused, and she thought she saw something flicker in his eyes—that darkness again, a glimpse of his soul. Then he continued, 'I'm not married.'

'I see.' She took a sip of water and tried to frame her thoughts. Her feelings. Relief was the overwhelming emotion, and on its heels came annoyance for she'd no business being relieved about Stefano's single status. 'I just assumed,' she explained. 'Most adults who come to me are the parents of the child in question.'

'Understandable,' Stefano replied, 'and in truth Lucio is like a son to me. A nephew, at the very least. His mother, Bianca, is my housekeeper.'

And mistress? Allegra wondered. She pressed her lips together to stop herself from voicing her suspicion aloud, knowing just how petty and petulant she would sound. 'I see.'

Stefano smiled although there was a hardness in his eyes. 'You probably see quite a lot that isn't there,' he replied, and Allegra blushed. 'But, in fact, Lucio and Bianca are like family to me. Bianca's father, Matteo…' He stopped, shrugged. 'The relevant details are that Lucio's father, Enzo, died nine months ago in a tractor accident. He was the groundskeeper for my villa in Abruzzo. After his death, Lucio began to lose his speech. Within a month of the accident he stopped speaking completely. He hasn't…' He paused, his expression darkening, eyes shadowed with painful memory.

'He's retreated into his own world,' Allegra surmised softly. 'I've seen it before, when children experience a sudden and severe trauma. Sometimes the easiest way of coping is by not coping at all. Just existing without feeling.'

'Yes,' Stefano said, and Allegra heard ragged relief in his voice. 'That's just what he's done. No one can reach him, not even his own mother. He doesn't cry, doesn't throw tantrums…' He shrugged helplessly, hands spread wide. 'He doesn't do anything, or even seem to feel anything.'

Allegra nodded. 'And you've tried therapies before this, I presume? If this has been going on for nine months?'

'He's been evaluated,' Stefano explained heavily. 'Although not as quickly as he should have been.' Regret turned his voice harsh. 'At the time of his father's accident, Lucio wasn't even four years old. He was a quiet boy as it was, and so his condition went undetected. Bianca had taken him to a grief counsellor, who said that some withdrawal was a normal sign of grieving.' Stefano's head was bowed and Allegra felt a tightening pang of sympathy for him and his situation. It was so familiar from her work, but it always hurt. Always.

'Then,' Stefano continued, 'as he began to lose speech, develop certain behaviours, the counsellor recommended he be evaluated. When he was, he was diagnosed with pervasive developmental disorder.'

'Autism,' Allegra finished quietly and Stefano nodded. 'What types of behaviours was he exhibiting?'

'You can look at his case notes, of course, but the most obvious one was lack of speech or eye contact. Methodical, or repetitive, play. Abnormal level of sustained concentration, resistance to cuddling or physical contact.' Stefano recited the litany of symptoms in a flat voice and Allegra could imagine how he—and Lucio's mother—had felt when they'd heard the doctor. No one wanted to hear the news that their child was flawed in some way, especially when the problems associated with autism were not easily treated.

The waiter came with their first courses and they spent a few moments eating, both grateful for the slight respite. When their plates had been cleared, Stefano continued.

'He was first diagnosed with autism a few months ago but Bianca resisted. She felt certain that Lucio's behaviour stemmed from grief rather than a disorder, and I feel the same way.'

Allegra took a sip of water. 'I presume it has been explained to you,' she said gently, 'that the symptoms associated with autism often manifest themselves at Lucio's age.'

'Yes, of course, but right around the time his father died? It's too much of a coincidence.'

'It also doesn't make sense for Lucio to lose speech and develop other worrisome behaviours months after a trauma,' Allegra countered, her voice steady and quiet. 'Especially at such a young age.'

'Are you trying to tell me you think he's autistic?' Stefano demanded.

'It's a possibility,' Allegra replied. 'A misdiagnosis among professionals is rare, Stefano. Psychiatrists aren't just slapping a label on a child without care or reason. They draw on extensive evaluation and data—'

'I thought you'd had experience with a child who was misdiagnosed,' Stefano replied coolly.

'Yes, one. One child in hundreds, thousands. And it simply happened that he responded to art therapy, and I happened to be his art therapist.' She shook her head. 'I'm not a miracle worker, Stefano. If you want to hire me to prove Lucio isn't autistic, then I can give you no guarantees.'

'I don't expect guarantees,' Stefano replied. 'If, after extensive work, you come to the same conclusion as the other medical professionals, then Bianca and I will have no choice but to accept it. However, before that time, I want to give Lucio another chance to heal. For the last several months, the doctors involved have been treating him for autism. What if his real problem is grief?' He lifted his bleak gaze to meet hers and Allegra felt a wave of something unfamiliar, something tender, sweep over her.

'It is possible,' she allowed, 'and I couldn't really say any more until I saw his case notes. Why do you think art therapy in particular might help Lucio?'

'He always loved to draw,' Stefano said with a little smile. 'I have a dozen thirty-second masterpieces by my desk. And while I'll admit I was sceptical with the idea of creative therapy—' he shrugged, his mouth quirking cynically '—at this point, I'm willing to try anything. Especially when I heard about your success with a similar case.'

'I see.' She appreciated his honesty, and it was no more than what most parents initially expressed. 'So Lucio lives in Abruzzo?'

'Yes, and I won't move him. Bianca had to take him out of nursery because he couldn't abide strange places any more. Regular trips to Milan or further afield would not be possible.'

'So,' Allegra surmised slowly, 'you need an art therapist— me—to come to Abruzzo.'

'Yes, to live there,' Stefano completed without a flicker. 'For at least a few months initially, but ideally…' he paused '…as long as it takes.'

He poured them both wine from the bottle the waiter had uncorked and left on the side of the table. Allegra took a sip, letting the velvety-smooth liquid coat her throat and burn in her belly.

Several months in Abruzzo. With Stefano.

Professional.

'That's quite a commitment,' she said at last.

'Yes. I imagine you have some cases you'd need to deal with, business that would have to be wrapped up. I'm returning to London in a fortnight. You could be ready by then?' There was a slight lilt to his voice, but Allegra knew it wasn't really a question.

Stefano wasn't even *asking* her to come to Abruzzo. He was expecting her. Telling her.

As high-handed as ever, she thought. As arrogant and pre-sumptuous as he'd been when he'd patted her on the head and told her to go to bed.

Dream of me.

What more is there?

She shook her head, a tiny movement, but one Stefano still noticed. 'Allegra?' he queried softly. 'Two weeks surely is enough to do what you need to do here?'

Questions clamoured in her throat. 'What if I can't come to Abruzzo, Stefano?' she asked, and heard the needling challenge in her voice. 'What if I say no?'

Stefano was silent, his eyes blazing into hers for a long, heated moment. 'I didn't think,' he said finally, quietly, enunciating every syllable with chilling precision, 'that you would allow the past, our past, to threaten the future of an innocent child.'

Allegra's face flushed with anger. 'This isn't about the past, Stefano! It's about the present, and my professional life. I'm not your star-struck little fiancée to order about at will. I'm a qualified therapist, a *professional* you are seeking to contract.' She broke off, letting her breath out sharply.

An all too knowing smile flickered across Stefano's face and died. 'Are you sure it's not about the past, Allegra?' he asked softly, and at that moment Allegra wasn't.

Their second courses arrived, and she looked down at her succulent steak with absolutely no appetite.

'Let's eat,' Stefano suggested. 'You can take the time to consider any more questions you might have regarding this situation. I'm happy to answer them.'

'Will you be in Abruzzo for the entire time?' Allegra asked abruptly. Stefano stilled, and she felt exposed, as if she'd revealed something too intimate by that simple question.

Perhaps she had.

'No,' he answered after a moment. 'I'll divide my time between Abruzzo and Rome. You'll deal mostly with Lucio's mother, Bianca, although, of course, I will continue to take an interest.'

'I see.' Relief and disappointment coursed through her, each emotion irritating in its complexity.

They ate then and Allegra found, a bit to her annoyance, that her appetite had returned and the steak was delicious.

By the time their meal was finished, she felt her calm, cool, impersonal demeanour return. She was grateful for it; it gave her armour. 'I'll need to see Lucio's case notes, of course,' she said as the waiter took their plates. 'And speak to Dr Speri, and anyone else who has interacted with him.'

'Of course.'

Allegra glanced at Stefano and saw, despite his carefully neutral expression, the hope in the brightness of his eyes, the determined, drawn line of his mouth. 'I'm not a miracle worker, Stefano,' she reminded him gently. 'I may be no help at all. As I said before, you have to contend with the possibility that Lucio is indeed autistic.'

A muscle bunched in Stefano's jaw and he gave a little shrug. 'Just do your job, Allegra,' he said, 'and I'll do mine.'

Allegra nodded, slightly stung by his tone, although she knew she shouldn't be. 'I'll need a few days to look over all the material on Lucio's case,' she said after a moment. 'I'll let you know my decision by the end of this week.'

'Wednesday.'

She wanted to protest, felt a cry clamour up her throat, straight from her gut, her heart. She wanted to tell him he couldn't order her around her any more, that she knew—she *knew* what kind of man he was.

Yet she pressed her lips against such useless retorts. The past was forgotten. She just seemed to keep having to forget it.

Besides, Stefano's behaviour was only that of a concerned adult. He wanted answers, and he wanted them quickly.

'Wednesday,' she repeated with a small, brisk nod. 'I'll do my best, Stefano, but there is no point rushing me. You're asking a lot of me, you realize, to give up my entire life in London for an extended period—'

'I thought you'd appreciate a professional challenge,' Stefano countered. 'And a few months is hardly a long time, Allegra. It's not seven years.'

She glanced at him sharply, wondering what he meant by such a comment. She didn't feel like asking. She didn't want to fight.

'Even so, this is a decision which should be considered carefully on both sides. As you reminded me yourself, it's Lucio we have to consider foremost.'

'Of course.' He spoke as if it were assumed, automatic. As if he hadn't considered anything else, hadn't for one second been caught up in the emotions that Allegra felt swirling around and through her, making her think, wonder.

Remember.

'Will you be having dessert?' The waiter had come to their table, and they ordered dessert, a chocolate gateau for Stefano and a sticky toffee pudding for her. When the waiter had gone and the menus were cleared Stefano faced her again, brisk and businesslike.

'I'll ring you on Wednesday, then.'

'Yes, fine.' Allegra licked her lips, felt the deepening pang of doubt. 'Stefano, perhaps you should consider another art therapist. There are plenty available, and even though the past is forgotten, it still exists.' She toyed with her fork, unable to quite meet his eyes as she confessed quietly, 'It could be difficult at times for both of us.'

Stefano was silent long enough for Allegra to look up and meet his knowing gaze.

'There isn't another art therapist who has the experience you do,' he replied, his tone flat and final. 'One who is also Italian, who has the ability and willingness to spend several months in a rather remote place.'

'You're assuming rather a lot—' Allegra interjected and Stefano smiled, although it was a gesture tinged with sorrow.

'Am I? The girl I knew would have done anything—gone anywhere—to help someone in need. But perhaps you've changed.'

'It's not that simple, Stefano,' Allegra replied. She wouldn't be manipulated or emotionally blackmailed. She wouldn't let Stefano use those tactics on her. Not now. Not again.

'It never is,' he agreed, and Allegra was silent.

Their desserts came and Stefano turned the conversation to easier topics—films, the weather, London's sights. Allegra was relieved to talk without considering how every word she said might be interpreted, and what every rejoinder of Stefano's might mean.

It was quite late in the evening when they finally left the restaurant. Stefano's car was waiting as they left the hotel, and Allegra wondered how he did that.

Had Stefano rung the driver? Had the driver waited there the whole evening? How did everything come so easily to people in power?

Except, perhaps, where it mattered. She thought of Lucio, and how much he obviously meant to Stefano, with a compassionate pang.

They drove back to Allegra's flat in virtual silence. Allegra didn't know if she was imagining the heavy expectancy of that silence, as if something had already been decided.

As if something was going to happen.

A light, misting rain was falling, softening the street into a grey haze, as Stefano pulled up to Allegra's building.

'You don't have to come in,' Allegra protested vainly, for Stefano was already through the front door.

'I'll see you safely to your door,' he said, but there was nothing safe about his presence, filling up the tiny hallway. He was too big for the space, she thought, too *much*. He towered over her, near her.

'It's perfectly safe,' she protested and Stefano just smiled. He was gazing at her, that familiar glint in his amber eyes, a spark Allegra knew could become a fully-fledged blaze. She swallowed, pressing against the wall as if she could put some distance between them.

'Stefano…' she began, and then stopped because she didn't know what else to say.

'I wondered what it would be like, when I saw you again,' Stefano said. His voice was pitched low, a husky murmur that still managed to make Allegra tremble.

'I have too, of course,' she said, and tried to keep her voice light, friendly. She failed.

'I wondered if you would be the same,' Stefano continued. He lifted his hand as if to touch her and Allegra held her breath.

'I wondered,' he continued, his voice turning huskier, 'if you would look at me the same way.'

'We're different, Stefano,' Allegra said. She wished she could tear her eyes away from his burning gaze, wished she could keep her body—and perhaps even her heart—from reacting. Wanting. 'I'm different,' she added, but it was no deterrent. He smiled, his fingers touching her cheek, tucking a tendril of hair behind her ear.

'Yes,' he murmured, 'you are.'

The light touch of his fingers was enough to send sensation spiralling through her. Enough to make her dizzy, to close her eyes. She snapped them open.

'Don't do this, Stefano,' she whispered. She didn't have the will power to pull away and it shamed her. 'You're hiring me in a professional capacity. You shouldn't do this.'

'I know I shouldn't,' Stefano agreed, but there was no regret in his voice, only decision.

He was moving closer, his body inches from hers—chest, torso, stomach, thighs. She felt his heat come off him in intoxicating waves and she took a deep, gulping breath.

'We should say goodnight,' she managed, her voice turning breathless because suddenly it seemed as if there was no air in the hallway, no air in her lungs. Her body was transfixed, her eyes on his, watching his lids lower, his lashes sweep his cheeks and still he moved closer. 'We should shake hands,' she added desperately, for she knew it wasn't going to happen.

Something else was.

'We should,' Stefano agreed. His fingers drifted down her cheek, traced the full outline of her lips. His fingers left a trail of tiny shocks along her skin and Allegra forced herself to remain still, not to lean into his hand, into *him,* because at that moment she wanted nothing more.

'Of course,' Stefano continued, 'we could seal a business deal with a kiss.'

'That's not how I do business,' she countered, choking on air.

'Don't you want to know, Allegra?' he whispered, his lips a

scant inch from hers. 'Don't you want to know how it is between us…how it could have been, for all these years?'

She tried to shake her head, tried to frame a word, a thought. Why was it so hard to think? Her mind was as misty as the evening outside, her thoughts evaporating into haze.

Then his lips came down on hers, a mere brush turning into something hard, demanding, a possessive brand.

Mine.

His.

Allegra realized dimly in the last cogent part of her brain that Stefano had never, not even remotely, kissed her like this before. The kisses they'd shared all those years ago had been chaste pecks, brotherly brushes, and she'd thought those had sent a spark spiralling through her body!

This kiss turned her to fire.

His mouth moved on hers, his tongue tasting, testing and finding.

Her arms came up around his shoulders and she revelled in the sheer size and power of him, her hands bunching on his arms, her nails digging into his skin.

Stefano's arms came around her, holding and supporting her for Allegra realized she'd sagged bonelessly against him, needing his strength.

When he finally lifted his mouth from hers, his arms still around her, she had not a single thing to say. To think.

The feelings blazing through her were simply too much.

'Sealed with a kiss,' he whispered in satisfaction and stepped back. 'I'll ring you on Wednesday,' he promised. 'But now I'll leave you to your dreams.'

Dream of me.

'Goodnight, Allegra.'

Wordlessly she nodded, watched him open the door and disappear into the drizzle. In the shattered silence of the hallway she let out a choked gasp, a half-laugh, her mind and heart seething with both confusion and unfulfilled desire.

She touched her fingers to her lips as if she could still feel him there, his sure possession, and thought numbly that the past was *not* forgotten.

As his car pulled away from the kerb, Stefano could still see Allegra in the hallway. She sagged against the wall, one hand touching her lips, and he smiled—smiled with a hard satisfaction that settled in him, through him, with savage pleasure.

She wanted him. Just as before. Perhaps, he thought musingly, more.

She wanted him, even though she didn't want to, even though she denied it. Denied it to him as well as to herself.

And yet that kiss, wonderful as it was, had been a mistake. He couldn't afford to tangle with Allegra, for Lucio's sake as well as his own.

Wouldn't.

He'd been down that road once before, knew where it ended, and it was nowhere he wanted to be.

He leaned his head against the back of the seat and closed his eyes. He'd kissed Allegra because he'd wanted to; he'd wanted to feel her lips under his, her body against his. He'd wanted to discover if the reality lived up to his dreams.

And did it? he wondered with a cynical smile.

Perhaps, but it didn't matter. He wasn't going to kiss Allegra again.

She was Lucio's therapist, nothing more.

Never, he told himself savagely, anything more again.

CHAPTER FIVE

WEDNESDAY AFTERNOON FOUND Allegra in her office, Lucio's case notes scattered on her desk. She gazed unseeingly out of the window at a dank, grey London sky and waited for Stefano's call.

She'd been quite determined, after that shocking, *shattering* kiss, not to take Lucio's case. The personal conflict was obvious and overwhelming.

There were plenty of other art therapists, she told herself. Ones who were more experienced as well as not personally involved.

Yet was she personally involved? Her mind staunchly said no, but the rest of her, her body still remembering that tide of desire, spoke differently.

Yet she wanted to take the case, she realized. She was professional enough to separate any feelings for Stefano from her work with Lucio, and she wanted to help this boy whose case notes spoke of a tragic, silent eight months. She wanted to help him for his own sake as well as for her own.

The idea of working intensively with one child for a prolonged period of time was inspiring, exciting. No more forty-five minute slots while parents waited, desperate for her to have made a difference.

No endless slog of case after case without hope or happiness.

She wanted this change, this chance.

Even if Stefano was involved.

Especially if Stefano was involved.

For while this could be an opportunity with Lucio, it was also an opportunity to put the past to rest. Redeem it, even.

And show Stefano, once and for all, that she was not that girl any more, the girl he thought he knew, the girl who'd loved him.

The phone trilled, startling Allegra out of her thoughts. She picked it up.

'Hello?'

'Allegra.' It sounded like a caress somehow, even though his voice was brisk. 'You've seen Lucio's case notes?'

'Yes.'

There was a moment of pulsing silence and Allegra realized how hard her heart was beating.

'And?'

'Yes, I'll take the case, Stefano. Although…'

'You have some reservations.'

'Yes.'

'Because of our kiss the other night.' He spoke steadily, without apology or concern, yet Allegra found her hand gripping the telephone receiver far too tightly.

'Yes,' she said after a moment of tense silence. 'Stefano, as we've said, I'm coming to Abruzzo in a professional capacity. There can't be—'

'There won't.'

She blinked, swallowed, strangely, stupidly stung that he sounded so certain. 'Even so,' she forced herself to continue, 'I don't want there to be any…tension…because of what has happened between us. It would be best for Lucio, as well as for ourselves, if we could be friends.'

'Then we will be.'

Allegra gave a shaky laugh, for she knew it wasn't that simple, and surely Stefano knew it as well. You couldn't will yourself into being friends; you couldn't will feelings or memories to disappear.

You could just put them in a box.

'You never kissed me like that when we were engaged,' she

blurted, and then wished she hadn't. Stefano was silent although she could hear him breathing.

'You were nineteen,' he finally said, his voice flat. 'A child, as you pointed out to me. I was taking my time with you, Allegra.' He paused, she waited. 'You weren't, however, a child last night. But have no fear. It's an incident that will not be repeated.'

He spoke so firmly and finally that Allegra was left with nothing left to do but accept.

'All right, then,' she finally said. She knew there was no point trawling old ground over the telephone.

'I'm flying to London next Friday,' Stefano said. 'That should give you time to hand off any cases, and you can return to Rome with me. From there we'll go to Abruzzo.'

'All right.'

'Email me with anything you'll need for your work,' Stefano said, 'and I'll arrange for it to be there when you arrive.'

'Fine…'

He gave her his email address and then, when the only thing left to say was goodbye, he surprised her.

'Allegra,' he said. 'Thank you.'

'You're welcome,' Allegra said. 'I'm looking forward to it, Stefano. I want to help Lucio.'

'So do I.'

More silence, and Allegra longed to say something, but she didn't know what it was. What did you say to someone you'd been planning on spending the rest of your life with? Having his children?

Loving him?

What did you say to someone who had never loved you back, who had planned to marry you for your name and your status and nothing else?

What did you say to someone who had broken your heart?

'Goodbye,' she finally said quietly, and put down the telephone.

In the end, it was remarkably easy to hand off her few cases. Since she freelanced, her work wasn't permanent anyway, and within a week she'd cleared her desk, sublet her flat and packed two suitcases with the things she thought she'd need.

It was strange and a bit disturbing to realize how easily she'd dismantled her life, a life she'd built with her own sweat and tears over the last seven years. None of it had been easy, and yet now, for the present, it was gone.

It was a cloudy day in mid-September, the leaves drifting down in lazy circles under a wispy blue sky, when Stefano arranged to pick her up.

Allegra waited outside since it was warm, felt nerves leap to life as she gazed down Camberwell Road for the first sign of Stefano's luxurious black car.

When it finally pulled sleekly into view, she was calm, focussed on the firm purpose of her journey and its destination.

Stefano exited the car. He was dressed in a dark suit, a mobile phone pressed to his ear, and his manner was so abrupt and impersonal that any anxiety Allegra had felt about seeing him again since their kiss trickled shamefacedly away.

At the moment, he looked as if he didn't even remember her, much less their kiss. She wondered if he'd spared it a moment's thought, while she'd given it several hours' confused contemplation.

Stefano was still on his phone as the driver put her bags in the boot and Allegra climbed into the car.

They pulled away from her street, her home, her life, and Stefano hadn't even said hello.

Twenty minutes into their journey, Stefano finally finished his conversation.

'I apologise,' he said. 'It was a business call.'

'So it would seem.'

He smiled, his eyes glinting with a rare humour. 'I told Bianca about your arrival, and she's looking forward to meeting you. You're providing a new hope for all of us, Allegra.'

Allegra nodded. 'Just remember there are no guarantees, no promises.'

'No, but there aren't with anything in life, are there?' He spoke lightly, yet Allegra heard an undercurrent of bitterness, saw it flash across his face. Was he referring to something else? Their own disappointed dreams?

She gave herself a little shake and gazed out of the window as they came on to the motorway. She had to stop reading innuendo and remembrance into every word Stefano said.

The past was *forgotten*.

It felt like a prayer.

They took a private jet to Rome. Allegra realized she should have expected no less, yet the blatant, if understated, display of Stefano's wealth and power awed her.

'Are you richer now than seven years ago?' she asked curiously when they were seated on the plane, the leather seats huge and luxurious.

Stefano glanced at her over the edge of his newspaper. 'A bit.'

'I know my father was wealthy,' Allegra said, 'but, to tell you the truth, I don't feel I saw much of it.'

'You were comfortable?' Stefano asked, his eyebrows raised, and Allegra laughed.

'Yes, of course. Trust me, I'm not giving you some poor little rich girl story.' She shrugged. 'I just saw very little of life, and I think that's why I was so swept away when I met you.'

'I see.' His voice was neutral, betraying no indication of agreement.

Allegra gazed out of the window. The plane was rising above the grey fog that covered London and a bright, hard blue sky stretched endlessly around them.

She had a strange urge to talk about the past, even though she knew there was no point, no purpose. She wanted to exorcise it, to show Stefano how little it mattered, how utterly *over* it she was.

It was a childish impulse, she knew, and worse, she wasn't even sure if she could pull it off.

Yet what was there to talk about? What was there to say, that hadn't been said that night?

Do you love me?

What more is there?

Even if their marriage hadn't been a business arrangement, Allegra knew, it wouldn't have been a good match. It wouldn't have made her happy. Stefano hadn't loved her, not in a real or worthwhile way. He'd only thought of her as a possession, something to be protected and provided for, tucked on a shelf. Taken care of.

Nothing else, nothing equal or giving or real about it.

And he'd shown her in a thousand tiny ways since then that he was the same. Thought the same, loved the same, which really wasn't love at all.

Worthless.

Allegra turned back to Stefano. He was reading the paper, his head bent, his legs crossed.

'You have a flat in Rome,' she said. 'Which part?'

He glanced up, smiling at her faintly, the glint in his eyes making Allegra feel as if he were simply humouring her. 'Parioli, near the Villa Borghese.'

'I've never actually been to Rome,' she admitted, a bit embarrassed by her own inexperience. Her life in Italy had consisted of home and convent school, summers at their villa by the lake, and nothing more.

'I'd show you the sights, if we had the time,' Stefano said.

'We'll leave for Abruzzo right away?'

'Tomorrow. I have a business dinner tonight. A social occasion.' He paused, his gaze sliding away from hers. 'Perhaps you would care to come with me.'

Allegra stiffened, felt the confusion of conflicting emotions. Alarm, surprise, pleasure. 'Why?' she asked. Her question was blunt but necessary.

Stefano raised his eyebrows. 'Why not? Most people bring dates and I don't have one.'

'I'm not a date.'

'No, you're not,' he agreed, unruffled, unconcerned. 'But you're with me, and there's no point in you staying alone in the villa, is there?' He smiled again, humour flashing briefly in his eyes. 'I thought we were supposed to be friends.'

'We are,' she said quickly. 'It's just—'

Eyebrows still raised, Stefano waited. Allegra realized he'd tangled her up in her own words. Yes, she wanted them to be friends, and therefore these innocent, innocuous occasions should provoke no alarm or anxiety. And yet…

And yet they did. They did, because they weren't just friends. No matter how much she wanted to dismiss their kiss, their entire past, she couldn't. Not as much as she wanted to.

And yet she couldn't avoid it. Perhaps the only way across this swamp of memory and feeling, Allegra thought, was straight through. It might mean getting muddy, wet, dirty, and even hurt, but she couldn't avoid Stefano, or what was and had been between them. She didn't even want to.

The past, forgotten as it might be, had to be dealt with. Directly.

'All right,' she said, and gave a little nod. 'Thank you. That should be…' she sought for a safe word and finally settled on '…pleasant.'

'Pleasant,' Stefano repeated musingly. He turned back to his paper. 'Yes. Indeed.'

She turned back to the window.

They didn't talk again until the jet landed at Rome's Fuimicino airport, and Stefano helped her from the plane.

The air wrapped around her like a blanket—dry, hot, familiar. Comforting.

Home.

She took a breath, let it flood through her body, her senses. The air was different here, the light brighter.

Everything felt different.

'It's been a long time,' Stefano said, watching her, and Allegra shrugged.

'Six years.'

'You came back for your father's funeral.'

'Yes.' They were walking across the tarmac to the entrance to customs, and Allegra kept her head averted. Her father's funeral. Her father's suicide. More things she chose not to think about. To remember.

'I'm sorry about his death,' Stefano said after a moment, his voice quiet and far too understanding.

Allegra shrugged. When she spoke, her voice sounded as hard and bright as the sky shimmering above them. 'Thank you. It was a long time ago.'

'The death of a parent still hurts,' Stefano replied, his gaze searching hers, and Allegra shrugged again and looked away.

'I don't really think of it,' she said, and felt as if she'd revealed something—had exposed it to Stefano's unrelenting gaze, unrelenting *knowledge*—simply by making that throw-away comment.

Mercifully Stefano dropped the subject and they spent the next short while dealing with customs and immigration.

Stefano had all of their papers in order and it didn't take long. All too soon they were pulling away in yet another hired car, the ocean a stretch of blue behind them, the flat, dusty plains in front and the scattered brown hills of Rome against the horizon.

Allegra felt exhaustion crash over her in a numbing wave. She'd been physically busy these last few weeks but, more to the point, emotionally she'd been in complete overdrive. She leaned her head against the leather seat and closed her eyes.

She didn't realize she'd actually dozed until Stefano nudged her awake. The sedan had pulled to a stop in front of a narrow street of elegant town houses, all with painted shutters and wrought iron railings.

'We're here,' Stefano murmured, and helped her from the car. Allegra followed him into the town house. It was elegantly decorated with antiques, sumptuous carpets and priceless paintings, yet it did not have the stamp of individuality on it, of Stefano.

It was impossible, Allegra thought even as she admired what looked like a Picasso original, to know anything about the person who lived here except for the fact that he was fabulously wealthy.

She wondered if Stefano wanted it that way. She was realising, more and more, that she'd never really known him when they'd been engaged. She'd thought that before, of course, when she'd overheard that terrible conversation with her father. Yet now she thought of it in a different, more intimate way, a way that wasn't fraught with anger and hurt, only a certain sorrowful regret.

She wanted to ask him what books he liked, what made him laugh. The things she should have known and delighted in when she'd been his almost-bride.

And she wouldn't ask those questions, she told herself sternly, wouldn't even *think* of asking them, because there was no point. *Professional.*

'I know you're tired,' Stefano said, 'and you can rest upstairs if you like. I'll have the cook prepare something light for lunch.'

'Thank you.' Allegra hesitated. 'The dinner tonight…I assume it's a formal occasion?'

'Yes.'

'I don't have anything appropriate to wear, I'm afraid,' Allegra said. She kept her voice light, even though she felt embarrassed. 'Evening gowns aren't usually required in my line of work.'

Stefano gazed at her, his face expressionless, yet Allegra saw—sensed—a flicker of something in his eyes. She wished she knew what he was thinking, wished she could ask.

He gave a brief nod. 'I'll send someone to the shops to select something for you. Unless you'd prefer to go yourself?'

Allegra shook her head. She wouldn't know what to choose, and just the thought of wandering around Rome by herself exhausted her.

'Very well. I need to attend to business, but Anna, my house-keeper, will show you your room.'

As if on cue, a kindly, slight, grey-haired woman emerged from the back corridor.

'This way, *signorina,*' she said quietly in Italian.

'*Grazie,*' Allegra murmured, and the language—her native tongue—felt strange to her ears. She'd spoken English, only English, for years.

Had it been a deliberate choice? A way to forget the past, harden her heart against who she was?

A way to become the person she was now—the English Allegra, Allegra the art therapist. Not Allegra who had stood at the bottom of the stairs, her heart in her eyes for all to see.

She followed Anna up thickly carpeted stairs to a beautifully appointed bedroom. Allegra took in the wide double bed with its rose silk cover, the matching curtains, the antique walnut chairs flanking a marble fireplace. It was far finer than anything she'd ever known, even in her father's villa.

She smiled at Anna. '*Grazie,*' she said again and Anna nodded and left.

Allegra sank onto the bed, overwhelmed and overawed. Even though it was only early afternoon, she stripped off her clothes and slipped beneath the cool, smooth sheets.

She could hardly credit that she was here, in Stefano's house, in Stefano's bed...one of them, anyway. She laughed aloud, but the sound held no humour. Alone in the huge bedroom, it sounded lonely. Little.

Allegra closed her eyes. Emotions had been flickering through her since she'd first seen Stefano again, flickering to life after seven years of numbness, and she was tired of them, tired of feeling. She didn't want to analyse how she felt, what she thought, what Stefano felt or thought.

She just wanted to *be.* To do her job, as Stefano had told her to. She hoped, when she finally met Lucio, she could forget about Stefano completely...

On that hazy thought, sleep overtook her.

She woke to a light knock on the door as late afternoon sunlight slanted across the floor.

'Allegra?' Stefano called softly. 'You've been asleep for four hours. We need to get ready for the dinner.'

'I'm sorry,' she mumbled, pushing a tangle of hair from her eyes. Stefano opened the door and Allegra was conscious of her dishevelled appearance, the fact that, even with the coverlet held up to her chest, it was quite obvious she was wearing only a bra and panties.

Stefano's gaze swept over her for one blazing second, and Allegra felt an answering awareness fire her nerve endings, turn her breathless.

Then his face blanked and he gave her a polite, impersonal smile. 'There is a selection of evening gowns for you to choose from downstairs. I'll bring them up.'

'A selection?' Allegra repeated in surprise, but Stefano had already gone.

Allegra took the opportunity to slip out of bed and throw on the clothes she'd left discarded on the floor. She was just tying her hair back when he reappeared a few moments later with several elegantly embossed carrier bags.

'Everything you need should be in there,' he said. 'We need to leave in a little under an hour. Anna is going to bring you up some antipasti. You missed lunch.' He smiled briefly, a teasing, affectionate look in his eyes that did something strange—something pleasant—to Allegra's insides.

'Thank you,' she managed, 'for being so thoughtful.'

He inclined his head. 'You're welcome.'

It was a simple exchange, almost meaningless, and yet, as Stefano left, closing the door behind him, Allegra realized she'd enjoyed it. She liked things simple. She liked not wondering what the hidden meaning or feeling was.

She wanted to enjoy. Enjoy an evening playing dress up like a little girl let loose in her mother's wardrobe.

Smiling at the thought, Allegra reached for the carrier bags.

Stefano had provided everything—three different designer gowns, all with matching shoes and wraps, as well as undergarments and tights.

She let the silky, luxurious fabrics slide through her fingers. She hadn't had such beautiful clothes in seven years. Hadn't needed them and certainly hadn't been able to afford them.

She was touched by Stefano's thoughtfulness, even though she knew it was simply his way of operating. She was in his care, so he would provide for her. Everything, always, whether she liked it or not.

She chose a slim-fitting knee-length gown in taupe silk. It was simple yet elegant and clearly well made. She liked the way the silk rippled over her, smoothing to a silhouette as she tugged up the zip.

In the bottom of one of the bags, Stefano had left a small velvet box and when Allegra opened it she let out a small shocked gasp.

They were the earrings he'd given to her the day before the wedding. The earrings he'd told her he couldn't wait to see her wearing. The earrings she'd never worn, just as there had been so many things she'd never done.

She slipped them from their velvet bed, saw the way the lamplight glinted off their myriad facets, and blinked back tears.

She didn't know why she felt like crying; she couldn't untangle the way she felt. Yet, at that moment, she didn't feel like a possession—she felt like a treasure.

This was dangerous, she knew. Dangerous to let herself feel this way, to flirt on the blurred edge of friendship. It would be far safer to keep her distance from Stefano, to maintain that professional facade.

Yet at this moment, beautifully dressed and about to embark on an evening of entertainment, she didn't want to.

At this moment, she wanted to be treasured.

She slipped the earrings on and left her hair down, tumbling over her shoulders.

Then she went downstairs.

Stefano was already in the marble hallway, dressed in a tuxedo. He quite literally took her breath away as he turned to face her, his eyes glittering with honest admiration when he saw her.

'You look stunning,' he said, and there was nothing but simple sincerity in his voice. His eyes rested on her ears, the diamond teardrops sparkling against her skin, and he smiled, an intimate gesture that spoke more than any word.

Allegra realized she was smiling back, glowing as if she'd swallowed the sun. As if Stefano had handed it to her.

'Thank you.'

He held out his hand and Allegra took it with only a second's hesitation. She wasn't going to let herself think too much. This was one evening, one evening only, and she planned to enjoy it.

They took a car to the St Regis Grand Hotel. As they pulled up to the hotel's front, Allegra couldn't help but be impressed by its ornate facade. They were in the heart of Rome, minutes from the Spanish Steps and the Trevi Fountain, worldly, witty people moving, talking and laughing all around them along with the trill of mobile phones and the hum of mopeds.

And Allegra was a part of it. She *felt* a part of it.

The mid-September air was a balmy caress as they climbed the steps to the hotel. As they entered, Allegra was struck by the huge chandelier suspended glittering above them, the tinkling music from a grand piano, the marble columns and sumptuous carpets that almost caught her heels, all conspiring to create an overwhelming sense of luxury and privilege.

Stefano guided her into the Sala Ritz, yet another sumptuous room decorated with marble pillars soaring to a ceiling with hand-painted frescoes and possessing the same aura of accustomed wealth. Businessmen and their well appointed wives mingled among black-frocked waiters bearing trays of champagne.

Allegra saw the heads turn as Stefano moved through the room, one hand on the small of her back. She saw the eyes slide speculatively towards her, heard the silent questions.

She shook her hair back and smiled proudly. Possessively.

Stefano joined a small group of men and introduced Allegra to his associates.

'Gentlemen, my friend, Allegra Avesti.'

My friend. Something she'd never been to him before. And she wondered now, distantly, if that was what she really was. If she *could* be that to Stefano. If she wanted to be.

Yet what other choice was there?

She watched surprise flicker across their faces as they heard the words *my friend*. A few jaws dropped, and Allegra wondered why they were so surprised.

Surely Stefano had come to business occasions with a woman before—a woman who was not a steady girlfriend or perhaps even a date.

Or was it something else? Unease prickled uncomfortably through her, up her spine and along her insides. Was it that he did come to these functions with a woman, a particular woman, and she was not that woman?

There was no time to consider such a question, or how it had made her feel, as she was soon swept up in the pre-dinner conversation, and took comfort in the innocuous chatter.

'All right?' Stefano murmured, his hand holding her elbow, and Allegra felt his breath graze her cheek, felt her whole body shiver at the touch and sound of him.

'Yes,' she murmured back, 'I'm all right. Enjoying myself, actually.'

'Good.' There was a note of possessive satisfaction in his voice that should have alarmed her, should have reminded her that Stefano simply thought of her as an acquisition, and a recent one at that. Services purchased and rendered.

But she didn't want to think, didn't even want to feel, at least not too much. She just wanted to enjoy. So she smiled lightly and let Stefano guide her to the table.

Dinner was served and Allegra was seated next to Antonia

Di Bona, a bony, sharp-faced woman in black crêpe. 'Stefano's kept you quiet,' she remarked, her voice light yet no less catty.

Allegra swallowed and glanced at Stefano across three feet of white damask. He was intent on a conversation with a colleague and she turned to smile coolly at Antonia. 'I'm just a friend.'

'Are you?' Antonia raised thin penciled-in eyebrows. 'Stefano doesn't have too many female friends.'

'No?' She felt a wave of relief flood through her although, coupled with it, was the needling awareness that Antonia knew something she didn't and was savouring the moment when she would tell her.

They ate their first course without much more conversation, but then Antonia turned to her again and there was malicious intent in her mocking smile.

'Have you known Stefano long, then?'

'Long enough,' Allegra replied carefully. Although there were probably few people who remembered or cared about her flight seven years ago, she knew they existed. How could they not, when their wedding had been fêted as the social event of the decade?

An event that had never happened. Allegra sought comfort in knowing that she'd called it all off early enough. No one would have gone to the church, no one would have known. She'd never asked her mother for details, how Stefano had responded when he'd been given her note, what he'd done or said.

She hadn't wanted to know, and she still didn't. The past, she reminded herself firmly, was forgotten.

'Long enough,' Antonia repeated. 'I wonder how long that is.' She leaned forward. 'You don't seem his type, you know. He prefers…' she paused, her hard, dark eyes sweeping Allegra's form with clear criticism '…more glamorous women. Do you go out with him very often?' She raised her eyebrows, smiling sweetly.

'No,' Allegra said coolly. Her face burned from Antonia's casual, cruel assessment, even though she told herself there was no reason to care. Antonia was simply one of those women who

enjoyed taunting and tormenting other women. She wouldn't
be happy until she was the last one standing and everyone else
bore the scratches from her three-inch fake talons. 'I'm actually
rather busy,' Allegra said, 'as is Stefano.' She knew she should
explain that she was associated with Stefano only in a professional capacity, but she somehow couldn't form the words.
Antonia probably wouldn't believe her, anyway.

Antonia gave a humourless little chuckle. 'Stefano is always
busy. It's how he's become so rich.' She raked Allegra once with
her cold eyes, then, bored, clearly dismissing her, added almost
as an afterthought, 'It's also why his marriage failed.'

CHAPTER SIX

ALLEGRA FELT AS if she'd frozen, as if the very air around her had turned to ice and snow. She closed her eyes, then opened them. Across the table, she saw Stefano's gaze sweep over her, concern flickering across his features.

His marriage. He'd been married. Married, to someone else. Not to her, never to her. He'd loved someone else, had been with someone else, had said his vows to someone else.

Who?

She swallowed a sudden impulse to laugh, to laugh wildly and loudly until there was nothing left inside.

Why had he not told her? Where was his former wife?

Why was she so *hurt?*

A restive, rational part of her brain told her there was no reason to react this way, to *feel* this way. So Stefano had been married. True, he hadn't mentioned it, but why should he?

Professional.

Friends.

And yet nothing felt professional or friendly about their relationship right now. All Allegra could feel right now was the burning brand of Stefano's lips on hers, the hurt inside that she'd held back all these years, the girl inside who was still—still—crying out,

Do you love me?

She closed her eyes, willing the flood of feelings to recede.

She hadn't broken down for seven years and she wasn't about to break down now.

She wasn't about to break down ever.

She stiffened her shoulders, lifted her chin. Next to her, Antonia let out a raucous bird-like laugh as she chatted and flirted with the man on her other side.

Allegra heard the murmur of conversation around her, knew no one was paying attention to her, and tried to relax. She stared down at her uneaten dessert, a custard flan in a golden pool of syrup, and felt her stomach roil and rebel.

Relax.

So Stefano had been married. It didn't mean anything; it *wouldn't* mean anything to her.

And yet still…still. Still it mattered, still it meant something. She didn't want to think what, couldn't bear to analyse the feeling. Yet she already knew.

Hurt. It was hurt.

Allegra picked up her fork and took a bite of her dessert. It might as well have been cardboard for all she could taste; she was too preoccupied with this new awareness, this new hurt. Understanding and accepting it…and then dismissing it.

Why was she hurt? Why did she let him get under her skin, into her heart now? Still?

Always.

Allegra shook her head in instinctive, desperate denial. No. She wasn't that girl.

Do you love me?

She wasn't; she knew what he was like, had known for years. He'd bought her, had bought her like an object, a thing. And, worse, he'd treated her like one.

Not a treasure.

Never a treasure.

No matter what she'd wanted to convince herself of for a single evening's enjoyment.

She pushed her dessert away, took a sip of wine and felt

Stefano's eyes on her. He was chatting with a business colleague across the table, but his considering glance swept over her, and out of the corner of her eye Allegra saw his mouth tighten and knew he was aware that she was upset. He just didn't know why.

Dessert was cleared, coffee served, and Allegra forced herself to make small talk with the dowdy housewife on her left. Antonia had abandoned her completely, and Allegra could only be relieved. She didn't need any more well-placed catty remarks right now.

After the meal the guests circulated, chatting and laughing, while music from a string quartet played softly. Allegra moved through the elegant crowd, saw Stefano sweep the room with a hawk-eyed gaze. She wound her way through the throng and leaned against a cool marble pillar. She didn't know what she'd say to Stefano now, didn't even know what to think.

'Why are you hiding again?' Stefano had come behind her without her realizing it, and now she stiffened.

'I'm not hiding,' she retorted and he raised one eyebrow.

'You were avoiding me.'

She lifted her chin. 'Don't be so arrogant.'

'You're denying it?'

'I didn't feel like talking, Stefano, to you or anyone. I'm tired, and this isn't exactly my crowd.'

In answer he touched her chin with his fingertips, levelled her gaze to meet his own. 'What's wrong?' he asked quietly.

Something ached in Allegra. If only it were so simple, if only he really wanted to know. To understand.

If only he could make it better.

'Nothing,' she said through numb lips.

'You're upset.'

'Stop telling me what I am!' Allegra snapped, her voice rising enough so there was a lull in the conversation.

'You could mingle,' Stefano said mildly. 'Get to know people.'

Allegra kept her gaze averted. 'I don't feel like it.'

'I was hoping,' he continued in that aggravatingly calm voice, 'that we could enjoy ourselves this evening.'

She hunched one shoulder, her face averted. 'I'm tired, and I'm not really here to be your escort, am I, Stefano? Remember? I'm here to help Lucio. That's all.'

'You think I don't know that?' There was a savage edge to his voice that made Allegra's gaze slide nervously yet curiously to his. She was shocked to see his face, the hard lines and harsh angles of a man set in bitterness. In anger. 'You think I don't remind myself of that every day?' he demanded in a low voice.

Allegra shook her head, not daring to consider what he might mean. What he might want. 'Stefano...'

'Allegra, all I'm asking is that you act normally. Socialise. Chat. You used to be able to talk the hind leg off a donkey. I never got a word in edgewise. Have you changed so much?' He smiled then, and Allegra felt the revealing prickle of tears behind her lids.

She remembered those conversations, how she'd chattered and laughed about anything and everything—stupid, girlish, *childish* dreams—and Stefano had listened. He'd always listened.

'Stefano, don't,' she whispered.

He touched his thumb to her eyelid and it came away damp. 'Don't what?'

'Don't,' Allegra repeated helplessly. *Don't make me remember. Don't make me fall in love with you. You broke my heart once; I couldn't stand it again.*

The realization that it was in fact a possibility should have terrified her, but right now all Allegra felt was sad. She felt, perhaps for the first time, the sweet, piercing stab of regret.

She blinked, and Stefano's thumb came away wet again. 'Why are you crying?' he whispered and there was surprise and sorrow in his voice.

Allegra shook her head. 'I don't want to think about the past. I don't want to remember.'

'What about the good bits?' Stefano asked. 'There were some, weren't there?'

'Yes, but not enough.' She took a deep, steadying breath and then stepped away from Stefano's touch. 'Never enough.'

'No,' Stefano agreed, his voice odd, flat. 'Never enough.'

'Besides,' Allegra agreed, emboldened now that he wasn't touching her, 'you talk as if we had something real and deep and we didn't.' Another breath, more courage. 'Not, presumably, like you did with someone else.'

Stefano stilled, his expression deepening, darkening into a frown. 'What are you talking about?'

'I heard, Stefano,' Allegra said. She took another breath; her lungs hurt. Or maybe it was somewhere else, somewhere deeper that had absolutely no business being hurt. 'Antonia told me you were married.'

Even now Allegra expected him to deny it, to laugh even, or make some remark about how the closest he'd come to marriage was with her. Instead, a muscle flickered in his jaw and he gave a tiny shrug.

'It wasn't relevant.'

Allegra laughed; the sound carried on the air and people looked their way. 'It would have been nice to know.'

'Why, Allegra? Why would you need to know?' There was a fierce, blazing look in his eyes and on his face that had Allegra stepping back again.

'Just…just because,' she said, and her reasons and self-righteousness deserted her, leaving her with nothing but a few stammered excuses. 'It's the kind of thing I should—'

'Know?' Stefano finished. His voice was soft and dangerous. 'Do you ask all the adults you come in contact with about their marital history? The parents of the children you work with?' He smiled mockingly, his eyes hard and cold.

'You know it's not that simple,' Allegra snapped. 'Stop turning the tables on me, Stefano. You conveniently forget and remember the past—*our* past—however the mood strikes you! Well, allow me the same courtesy!' She realized, belatedly, that her voice had risen yet again. People were staring.

'This is not the place,' Stefano said between his teeth, 'for this discussion.'

She ignored him, shaking her head, the implications exploding through her mind. 'I don't even know if you're divorced. If you have children.'

'I'm widowed,' he bit out. 'I told you before, I have no children.' His hand clamped down on her elbow. 'Now we're going home.'

'Maybe I don't want to go home with *you!*' she said, jerking away from him, her voice rising to a shriek—a shriek people heard.

There was a moment of embarrassed silence, and then the conversation resumed at double speed and sound.

Allegra swallowed, felt colour stain her face and throat. She was making a scene. A big one.

And Stefano was angry about it—perhaps angrier than she'd ever seen him before.

'Are you quite finished?' he asked in a voice of arctic politeness.

Allegra couldn't look at him as she nodded. 'Yes. We can go,' she whispered.

'Perhaps we should stay,' Stefano told her in a deadly murmur, 'and brazen it out. But I'll have mercy…on both of us.' He took her elbow once more and guided her none too gently out of the ballroom.

She managed to hold her head high even though her face was aflame as Stefano escorted her from the room amid a hiss of speculative murmurs. They were both silent all the way to the car.

Vespas and taxis sped around them in a glitter of lights as they drove from the hotel to the quieter Parioli district.

Allegra sagged against the seat. Her behaviour, she knew, had been inexcusable. She should have waited to talk to Stefano back at his town house rather than force a full confrontation in the middle of an important business engagement.

She closed her eyes against the prickling of tears. He should have told her he'd been married.

No matter what he said now, what arguments he so reasonably gave her, he should have told her.

She should have known.

Why didn't she know? Allegra wondered. Why had she never heard? Surely, somewhere, somehow she should have known.

Perhaps she should have felt it.

And yet, a mocking voice asked her silently, why should you have known? Didn't you sever all ties when you left that night? She'd never seen her parents again; her father had died less than a year after, and her mother…

Her mother had got what she wanted. She lived her own life now in Milan, bankrolled by a steady stream of lovers.

As for anyone else who might have known of Stefano's marriage…who? Who were those people? The girls she'd known at convent school? The relatives who'd shunned her?

She'd made choices in life, instinctive choices that had kept her well away from Stefano and his circle. And, really, she hadn't wanted to know, had never asked anyone about Stefano, had avoided talking or even thinking about him. It was precisely this kind of information that she'd never wanted to hear.

Yet, in the end, none of it had worked, for here they were together, in this very car, the silence freezing and hostile, their knees still touching. And her heart was hurt, crying out once more.

The car pulled up to the town house and Allegra followed Stefano inside. She watched as he stalked into the drawing room and poured two fingers of Scotch into a glass and tossed it back.

He stood in front of the fireplace, one hand braced against the marble mantle. Outside, a car drove past and washed the room in sickly yellow light. Allegra closed the double doors, drew the curtains and turned on a lamp. All tasks to keep her from the reckoning she knew would come. What she knew she had to say.

'I'm sorry.'

'For what?' Stefano asked, a trace of sarcasm sharpening his tone. 'For seeing me again? For agreeing to help Lucio? Or perhaps for walking out on me in the first place?'

There was such savagery in his voice that Allegra could only push it away, refuse to consider the implications of his words, the turn in his tone.

'No,' she said quickly, 'for my behaviour tonight. I was shocked that you were married and I...I overreacted at the party.'

'Yes, you did.'

Her fingers nervously pleated the silk of her gown. 'Why didn't you tell me?'

'Why should I have?'

'Because...' She tried to think of a reason, a safe one. 'Because I deserve to know,' she finally said. 'We've acknowledged the past and forgotten about it, but...'

'But it's still there.'

'Yes.' Allegra bit her lip. 'I never heard that you'd married.'

'Did you ever ask?'

'No, of course not. Why would I...?' She trailed off, not wanting to follow that line of thought and its inevitable conclusions.

'You wouldn't have heard,' Stefano said after a moment, his voice resigned, 'because it was kept quiet. By me.'

'Why?' she whispered.

He turned around and Allegra was surprised and alarmed by the weariness etched into his features. 'Because I regretted it almost as soon as the ceremony was over.'

He ran a hand through his hair before sinking into a cream silk armchair. 'If you want the facts, Allegra, I'll give them to you. I suppose I should have considered that someone might mention my marriage to you tonight, but I didn't want to deal with it. Not yet, anyway. So I just pushed it away and didn't think about it.' A smile flickered and died, and his eyes were shrewd. 'A habit I believe we share.'

Allegra looked down. The man in front of her was one she

wasn't used to. Here was Stefano being candid, open. Vulnerable. He sat sprawled in a chair, his tie loosened and the top two buttons of his shirt undone, his whisky tumbler still held loosely in one hand.

'So what are the facts?' she asked in a low voice.

'I was married to Gabriella Capoleti for six years.'

'Six years!' It came out in a shattered, shocked gasp. Six *years*. 'When did you marry her?'

'Three months after you left me,' Stefano said flatly.

Left me. Not Italy, not the wedding, no innocent, innocuous phrases. *Left me.* Because that was what she'd really done.

Allegra felt dizzy, and she steadied herself by placing one hand on the back of a chair. 'Why?' she whispered. 'Why so soon?'

Stefano shrugged, gave the ghost of a smile. 'My first marriage didn't happen, so I planned another.'

'That simple,' Allegra whispered.

Stefano smiled, although his eyes were hard. 'Yes.'

She swallowed. Why did this hurt? This was old ground they were covering. She'd raked it over in her own mind years ago, had laid it to rest. Yet now it felt fresh, raw, achingly painful.

It hurt.

'I meant to marry you for your name, Allegra, remember? The Avesti name.' He laughed dryly, without humour. 'Not that the Avesti name has any standing these days.'

'Don't—'

'No, you don't like to face that, do you?' Stefano said, his voice as sharp and cutting as a blade. 'You don't like to face the facts. Well, neither do I. I try not to think of my marriage. Ever.'

'Why not?' Her throat felt like sandpaper; her eyes were dry and gritty. 'Did you love her?'

'Does it matter?' Stefano asked in a soft hiss. 'To you?'

Yes. 'No.' Allegra drew herself up. 'No, of course not. I just wondered.'

Stefano was silent; so was she. Waiting. Wondering. Outside she heard the muted blare of a car horn, the trill of a woman's laughter.

'I married Gabriella for the Capoleti name, just as I was going to marry you for yours,' Stefano finally said. His voice was as flat as if he were reciting a list of dry, dusty facts. 'I needed someone from an old, established family.'

'Why did you need a name so much?' Allegra asked, wondering even now why she hadn't asked this, thought this before. She'd just shut it all out.

His lips curved in a smile and his eyes glittered like topaz. 'Because I don't have one myself, of course. I have money. That's all.' She heard a bleak note in his voice that she didn't completely understand.

'And so Gabriella accepted this arrangement?' Her voice sharpened as she added, 'Or did you deceive her as well?'

Stefano gazed at her for a moment, his expression assessing. Knowing. 'As I deceived you?' he finished softly. 'How you cling to that, Allegra. How you need to believe it.'

'Of course I believe it,' Allegra snapped. 'I heard it from my father's mouth, from your own! Our marriage was nothing more than a business deal, brokered between the two of you.' Rage and self-righteousness made her stand tall, straight. Proud. 'How much was I worth in the end, Stefano? How much did you pay for me?'

Stefano laughed softly. 'Didn't you realize? Nothing, Allegra. I paid nothing for you.' She blinked; he smiled. 'But I *would* have paid a million euros for you, if you'd shown up that day. A million euros your father had already gambled away. That was why he killed himself, you know. He was in debt— far more than a million euros in debt. And, when you didn't marry me, he got nothing.'

Allegra closed her eyes, wished she could close her mind against what Stefano was saying.

'More facts,' Stefano said softly, 'that you've never wanted to face.'

He was right, she knew. She'd never wanted to face the fallout of her flight, had never wanted to examine too closely why her father had killed himself, why her mother had run.

'It's not my fault,' she whispered, and her voice cracked.

'Does it really matter?' Stefano returned.

She shook her head, shut herself off from those memories, those emotions. 'What of Gabriella, then? Tell me about your marriage.'

'Gabriella was thirty years old then—two years older than me at the time. Desperate, to be blunt. She agreed to the marriage, to the *arrangement,* and it all happened rather quickly.'

'So it would seem.' Allegra sank into a chair. She felt sick. She'd always known that Stefano had his reasons for marrying her... Hadn't her mother said, *Our social connections, his money?* Yet here was the proof, right in front of her that he'd never loved her, had never cared in the least. He was giving it to her.

He was telling her, and he didn't even sound sorry. Just resigned.

'Why did you keep it quiet,' she finally asked, 'if you wanted her name? Shouldn't you have...let people know?' Her voice wobbled with uncertainty and Stefano raised his eyebrows.

'Cash in on my investment? In theory, yes. But I realized after I married Gabriella that I didn't want her damned name. I didn't want her, and she didn't want me.' He laughed dryly, but Allegra heard something else in that sound, something sad and broken. 'And, in the end, I realized I didn't want to build my business on someone else's shoulders. I'd got as far as I had by myself, or nearly, and I'd continue the same way.' He gave the ghost of a smile.

Allegra gave a little jerk of assent, her eyes sliding from Stefano and the bitterness and cynicism radiating from him in icy, intangible waves.

'So what happened?' she finally whispered. 'She...she died?'

'Yes.' Stefano raised his eyes to meet her startled gaze. 'But six weeks after the wedding Gabriella left me. I don't blame her. I was miserable company and a poor husband.' He leaned his head back against the chair. 'She went to live in Florence, in a flat I provided for her. We agreed to live completely separate lives. When she died in a car accident six months ago, I hadn't seen her for nearly five years.'

'But...but that's horrible,' Allegra whispered.

'Yes,' Stefano agreed bleakly, 'it is.'

'What...what did you do that made her so miserable? To leave you?'

He raised one eyebrow, his smile darkly sardonic. 'My fault, is it?'

'You admitted it was!'

Stefano was silent for a long time, his head back, his eyes closed. Allegra wondered if he'd actually fallen asleep.

Then he spoke, his eyes still closed. 'I realized I wanted something else from marriage. Something more. And so did Gabriella. Unfortunately, we couldn't give it to each other.'

'What was it?' Allegra asked in a whisper.

Slowly Stefano raised his head, opened his eyes. Allegra felt transfixed by his sleepy gaze, gold glinting in his irises. 'What do you think it was, Allegra?'

'I...' She licked her lips. She didn't know. What more did Stefano want from a marriage? He'd got the social connections, he had the money. What more was there to be gained? 'I...I don't know.'

'I wonder,' Stefano mused, turning his tumbler around and around between his palms, 'why you were so startled by the fact of my marriage. It almost seemed as if you were *hurt*.'

Allegra jerked back. 'Of course I was startled! It's rather a large fact to keep secret—'

'But you've kept secrets, Allegra,' Stefano interjected softly, 'haven't you? I haven't been celibate for the last seven years. Neither, I believe, have you.'

Allegra felt as if she'd been nailed to the chair. The last thing she'd expected now was for him to turn the spotlight on *her*.

'What does that matter?' she finally asked, trying to keep her voice cool. Logical.

'Exactly. What does that matter? If I choose to ignore your past, then you should ignore mine, don't you think? Because it doesn't matter, since you're merely here in a professional capacity.' His eyes glittered and he leaned forward. 'Does it?'

'No,' Allegra said, her voice sounding hollow to her own ears, 'it doesn't.'

She felt the truth of what he was saying, what he was implying, like a series of electric shocks to her heart. Because it did matter. It did hurt.

And the only reason it could was because Stefano still mattered. To her.

'How many lovers have you had, Allegra?' Stefano asked softly.

Allegra felt as if an icy finger had trailed along her spine, drifted across her cheek. She didn't like the look in Stefano's eyes, the intent, the anger. 'Stefano,' she said, her face pale, her voice thready, 'it doesn't matter. I never married you, I was free. I'm not yours to command, to possess. It doesn't matter how many lovers I've had.' Her voice shook. 'You shouldn't even ask.'

'But it does matter,' Stefano replied, his voice still so soft, so dangerous. 'It matters to me.'

'Why?' She was trembling—actually trembling—under the onslaught of his blazing gaze.

He didn't answer, just smiled. 'Who was the man who touched you first?' he asked softly. 'Who touched you where I should have touched you?'

Allegra closed her eyes. Images danced in the darkness of her closed lids; imaginary images that had never taken place, memories of Stefano and her that had never been made.

'Don't, Stefano,' she whispered. 'You don't want to do this.'

'No, I don't,' Stefano agreed, his voice pleasant, a parody. 'I know I don't, and I shouldn't. But I'm going to do it anyway. Who was he? When did you have your first lover?'

Her eyes were still closed, but she heard—felt—him move. He closed the small space between them and she knew he was standing before her. She heard him drop down to kneel in front of her, felt his hands on her knees. She tensed, he waited.

The moment was endless. They were so close, yet a yawning chasm had opened between them, a chasm caused by memories they'd both claimed didn't matter. Memories they'd said they'd forgotten.

Allegra felt them tumble through her mind; she saw Stefano smile, she remembered the light touch of his carefully chaste kiss, she even felt the exploding joy within her at being loved.

She'd thought she'd been loved.

But, of course, she hadn't. Not then, and certainly not now.

She gave a little gasp as she felt his fingers skim her knees, testing, teasing. Touching.

And his touch, as it had all those years ago, caused sensation to explode in her stomach, to spiral upwards from her heart. Her *heart*.

'Stefano…' she whispered, and stopped, because she didn't know what she was saying. She didn't even know what she was wanting.

She knew that if they continued down this path it would be dangerous. Deadly. How could they recover, continue the polite parody of their relationship, when *this* had happened?

This. Desire. Regret. Wonder.

Slowly, Stefano slid his hand along the tender, untouched skin of her thigh. Allegra shuddered lightly, but kept her eyes closed. She didn't want to open them, didn't want to see the expression on Stefano's face. She was afraid of what it would be, what he was feeling.

What *she* was feeling.

'Did he touch you here?' he whispered. His hand slipped along her thigh, his fingers drifting higher, closer. Allegra felt her legs part, leaving her passive to his calculated caress.

She shook her head, not even sure what she was denying, admitting. Wanting him to stop, yet also wanting him to continue. Treacherously, terribly, wanting him to continue, even now.

'What about here?' Stefano whispered. His fingers played with the elastic of her underwear, his thumb skimming over her most sensitive flesh. 'Did you enjoy it? Did you…?' His finger slipped beneath her underwear. 'Did you think of me?'

She gasped aloud, whether in pleasure or shame even she didn't know. Her eyes were still closed, clenched shut. She gave a little shake of her head.

She opened her eyes, saw his blaze into hers with feeling. Anger. *Hatred.*

Shock reverberated through her at the savage expression on his face, his soul reflected so openly, so terribly, if only for a moment.

'What is this?' she choked out. 'Some kind of *revenge?*'

Stefano's eyes burned into hers for one fiery second before he cursed under his breath and jerked back. Allegra watched him stalk across the room, his back to her, heard the clink of glass as he poured himself another whisky.

She sagged against the chair, limp, lifeless. He was treating her like a possession, she thought. Just as she'd feared he would all those years ago, just as she'd always known. A possession. *His.* His to punish.

He was *punishing* her, she knew with a cold fury quite apart from the desire he'd sent spiralling through her.

Punishing her, for having had a lover when he'd been married. The realization of such a disgusting double standard cleared her head, gave her strength.

'It was a doctor at the hospital where I was training,' she said, and her voice was clipped and cold. Stefano stilled but did not turn around. 'David Stirling. We were lovers for two months, until I realized he was just about as controlling and possessive as you are. And,' she added, her voice shaking, 'we didn't sleep together until last year. So I waited six years to give myself to someone else, Stefano. You waited three months.'

He still didn't turn around, and she wanted to hurt him, wound him, as he'd wounded her. Yet she knew she couldn't, because he didn't care.

And she did. Damn it, she did.

'And you're right, it doesn't matter. It doesn't matter because you don't care about me, Stefano. You never did. You never loved me. The only thing that was hurt when I left was your wretched pride. You showed it tonight—someone else got to play with your toy! That's all I am, have ever been, to you. And,' she continued, trembling with emotion, with the river of suppressed feeling coursing through her in a terrible, unrelenting stream, 'even if you had loved me, I didn't want the kind of love you were prepared to give—a kind that didn't involve honesty or joy or anything that really matters.'

Protection. Provision. *What more is there?*

He still didn't turn around, didn't acknowledge her in any way but the stiffness of his shoulders.

Allegra felt a blinding anger driving through to a needlepoint of pain, anger and pain that fuelled her words. 'The kind of love you offer, Stefano, isn't love. It's nothing! It's *worthless.'*

Stefano jerked, though he didn't turn around. For a triumphant second Allegra actually thought she'd got to him. Hurt him. Yet even as she felt a blaze of victory, she realized it didn't feel the way she wanted it to—deep and satisfying, a direct hit.

She felt low, cheapened somehow by her own actions as well as Stefano's.

She took a breath, trying to calm herself. 'Coming here was obviously a mistake but it's also a business arrangement.' She laughed, a sharp, brittle sound. 'Just like our marriage was meant to be! Funny, how it all comes round. I'll stay, Stefano, for Lucio's sake. I want to help him. But when I have, and the next few months, or however long it takes, are over, I'll thank God that I never have to see you again. A welcome thought for you as well, I'm sure.'

Trembling, still aching to hit him, hurt him, make him at least turn around and acknowledge her, Allegra left the room. She slammed the door on the way out.

Stefano knew he shouldn't have a third whisky but he felt like it. He wasn't a man who normally drank, but now he needed the fiery relief burning all the way to his gut.

Rage and remorse coursed through him in an unrelenting river of emotion. Emotion he didn't want to acknowledge, much less feel.

Damn it. Why had he talked to her, treated her like that?

Allegra. The woman who was going to help Lucio. The woman meant to be his wife. He hadn't forgotten. He could never forget the moment when he'd realized, when he'd known that she'd left. And she hadn't bothered to say goodbye, to explain.

Nothing but a note.

That moment was burned into his memory, into his very soul. It felt as much a part of him as his family, his job, his every ambition or fear. He'd carried it around with him for seven years; he wasn't about to let it go.

Yet, for Lucio's sake, he had to. He had to try.

When he'd decided to seek Allegra out, to hire her, he'd convinced himself that the past didn't matter. *She* didn't matter.

There was no reason to care what she'd done, who she'd been with, who she'd loved. He'd been married, of all things; he could hardly accuse her for taking a lover. She was twenty-six years old and she had every right to find romance, love, *sex,* with someone else.

Someone other than him.

Yet the reality of it had been much harder to bear than the mere possibility.

It wasn't the idea of another man touching her that wounded, Stefano realized with profound bitterness, although that certainly stung. It was the fact that Allegra had chosen—had preferred—

someone else. She'd walked away from him to seek solace in another's arms, and nothing—*nothing*—could change that.

Even worse, perhaps, was the cold, hard knowledge that he'd done the same thing. And failed.

The only solace he'd found was in knowing he'd made a mistake, and doing his best to rectify it. Giving Gabriella her life, her freedom back had been a relief for both of them.

Stefano dragged in a long, laborious breath and set his tumbler down. He walked slowly from the room, up the stairs to Allegra's bedroom.

He didn't try the knob; he had a feeling it would be locked and he didn't want to find out. He placed his palm flat on the door, leaned his forehead against the smooth wood. All was silent, but he spoke anyway.

'Allegra.'

He thought he heard a tiny sniff, a little gasp. He continued. 'I'm sorry. I shouldn't have said or done what I did downstairs. It was wrong of me. I…' He paused, his throat closing against the clamour of things he felt but didn't know how to say. 'Goodnight,' he finally managed, and walked slowly down the corridor to his own empty bedroom.

CHAPTER SEVEN

THE NEXT MORNING the town house was silent as Allegra made her way downstairs, but after a few seconds she heard the quiet clink of china from the dining room and saw Stefano in the mahogany-panelled room, drinking a cappuccino, his head bent over the newspaper.

She watched him silently for a moment, the hard plane of his cheek and jaw, the soft sweep of his hair, the way he absently ran his long-fingered hand through it before turning a page.

Looking longer she saw lines of strain on either side of his mouth, shadows of fatigue under his eyes.

What had kept him up last night? she wondered. His own behaviour, or hers? The past or the future?

It was wrong of me.

She'd heard him through her door, as she huddled on her bed. She'd heard the regret in his voice, but it barely made a dent in her hardened heart.

He'd treated her like an object. A possession. He'd revealed himself in that one cold, calculated caress—what he thought of her, what he couldn't forget.

And even though the light touch of his fingers had made her tremble, had made her want, she wouldn't let it weaken her will.

She was not Stefano's possession. She would not let him treat her as one. *Ever.*

And, Allegra resolved as she stood in the doorway of the

dining room, she would tell Stefano so. Now, not with whispered words of regret through a closed door, but face to face, eye to eye.

'Stefano.'

His head jerked up, his eyes wary, hooded before he smiled. '*Buon giorno.*'

'*Buon giorno.*' She sat at the table and picked up a *cornetti,* taking a knife and buttering it with fingers that only trembled a tiny bit. 'We need to talk.'

He folded his paper and placed it on the table, a look of polite expectancy on his face. 'Of course. What is it?'

She shook her head slowly. Was he going to pretend that last night hadn't happened? That the truth, painful and broken as it was, hadn't been revealed?

'When we both agreed to this business arrangement,' she began, keeping her voice firm and purposeful, 'you told me that we were different people. That the past didn't matter.'

'Yes,' Stefano confirmed, a touch of coolness in his voice. He took a sip of his coffee and Anna bustled in from the kitchen with a cappuccino for Allegra.

'*Grazie,*' she murmured, her gaze still fastened on Stefano's. 'But that wasn't true, was it, Stefano?' she asked softly when Anna had left. 'The past does matter, and perhaps we haven't changed as much as we think we have. As much as we want to have changed. And I won't allow the past to affect the present or the future. Not my future, not yours, and certainly not Lucio's.'

'I wouldn't expect it to,' Stefano drawled. He sounded bored.

'You may have hired me,' Allegra continued, her voice still thankfully firm, 'but I'm not your possession. I won't be treated like one—'

'Allegra, I apologised for my behaviour last night,' Stefano cut her off coldly. 'I was angry with what had happened, not seven years before, but a few hours ago. You behaved in a childish way at the dinner, and I responded by behaving in a childish manner here. Again, I'm sorry.' He gave her a tight, perfunctory smile that sent fury coursing through her in a cleansing stream.

'I'd accept that,' she said, 'if you'd called me names or thrown a tantrum. *Childish* behaviour. But that wasn't it, was it, Stefano? It was something more.' She paused, took a breath. Stefano waited, one eyebrow raised in scathing scepticism. 'The truth is,' Allegra continued, 'you can't forget the past, you can't pretend it doesn't affect the present and any future. I believed we could because I wanted to believe it, because it was easier. But in the end ignoring it will only make it more difficult, for you, for me, and for Lucio—'

'That's quite an interesting load of psychobabble,' Stefano cut her off. 'Did you learn it on your art therapy course?'

'No, I learned it through dealing with you,' Allegra snapped. 'The way you treated me—' She stopped, pressed her lips together and refused to think about how his fingers had sought her, punished her, thrilled her. And then, worst and most hurtful of all: the blazing look of contempt, *cruelty* in his eyes. 'But last night proved to me that you're the same man you were seven years ago, treating me the same way.' The words rang with contempt and condemnation, but Stefano didn't react. He merely stilled, his face blank, his eyes hard. Silence. Yet again the only response to her words, her plea for understanding, was silence.

She heard the ticking of the clock, the clink of china as Stefano carefully, slowly stirred his coffee. 'Think what you like,' he finally said. He looked up, smiled in a way that was utterly chilling to Allegra. It was the smile, she thought numbly, of a person who didn't care at all. And, she realized, even now she wanted him to care.

'It doesn't really matter. I apologised for my behaviour, and it won't happen again. As you said,' Stefano continued in a voice of determined pleasantness, 'you're here to help Lucio. We don't need to deal with each other at all.'

'It's not that simple—'

'It will be,' Stefano said, and there was hard finality to his words, his face. 'It will be.'

Allegra tried once more. 'Unless we deal with it, with our feelings—'

Stefano laughed. Allegra didn't like the sound. 'But I don't have *feelings* for you, Allegra, remember? I bought you. I treated you like a possession. I *thought* of you as a possession…you told me so yourself. Why should I have feelings for an object?'

Allegra opened her mouth, closed it, and then opened it again. 'But…'

'So if I didn't have feelings for you then,' he continued, cutting across her useless, incoherent denial, his voice horribly soft, 'why should I now?'

But he wasn't finished. His eyes glittered as he leaned forward, his voice thrumming with power and knowledge. 'You want to talk about *feelings,* Allegra?' he challenged. 'What about yours?'

Allegra drew back. 'What about mine?'

'You think I'm the only one who doesn't like to talk about the past? What about you? What about the fact that you haven't seen your mother or your father since that night you ran away?'

'My father's dead,' Allegra said. 'Stefano, this has nothing—'

'To do with it? Perhaps it does. You don't want to face what you've done. Well, neither do I.' His voice was quiet and controlled, yet Allegra felt as if he were shouting. She felt as if he were shouting at her. 'Why did you cut off all contact with your family? You stayed at your father's funeral for less than an hour. I know. I was there.'

Her mouth opened, yet no words came out. He gave her a faint feral smile, yet she saw a bleakness in his eyes, a bleakness Allegra felt herself.

'I watched you from afar. You never saw me.'

'Why did you come?'

'I knew your father too, Allegra. I shared in the guilt for his death. He was a foolish man, even an immoral one, but no one deserves to suffer such despair.'

Allegra held up one hand as if to ward off his words, as if they were blows. 'Don't—'

'It hurts, doesn't it?' Stefano said softly. 'To remember.'

'*Stefano*—'

'You cut yourself off from everything and everyone you'd ever known, Allegra,' Stefano said, every word a condemnation. 'Even yourself.'

'You don't know—'

'Because you couldn't face it. You don't want to face it. So don't ask me to face anything, when you've been running from the past for seven years, and you *still* haven't stopped.'

'This is not about me!' Allegra shrieked. Her voice felt as if it had been ripped from her lungs and her chest, heaving with emotion, hurt. 'This is not about me,' she said again, and this time her voice cracked.

'No? None of it's about you?' Stefano rose from the table, his face harsh, his voice utterly merciless. 'What about your father, Allegra? Did he have nothing to do with you? I know he was crushed by your betrayal. I know it was one of the reasons he killed himself.'

'No.' She wouldn't think of it. She wouldn't allow him to make her think of it. Like a steel trap, the lid of the box Stefano had ripped open snapped shut. Allegra felt herself go numb—numb and cold, blessedly blank. She rose from the table too, curling her hands around the back of her chair to steady herself. 'You don't know what you're talking about,' she said in a flat, cold voice quite unlike her own.

Stefano laughed shortly. 'I think I know all too well. But it's better this way, isn't it? For both of us.' He turned away. 'We leave for Abruzzo within the hour.'

'Fine.' Allegra nodded, still numb. It was so much easier not to feel. Not to feel anything.

Yet, as he left, she found her legs going weak and it all came rushing back, a tide of emotion she couldn't deal with. Wouldn't deal with. Allegra sank into her chair, dropped her head in her hands.

Whatever either of them tried to believe, the past was not forgotten. It was alive and well and vibrating between them with a thousand torturous memories.

The sun was high and bright in the sky when they pulled away from the narrow street and into the clogged city traffic. Stefano was dressed casually in jeans and a crisp white shirt, the sleeves rolled back against his forearms.

'I think you'll like Abruzzo,' he said when they'd cleared the traffic and the road stretched endlessly ahead of them, winding through dusty brown hills and fields of sunflowers ready for harvest. He spoke in a pleasant, impersonal tone that Allegra knew she should be thankful for but instead it grated on her nerves, made her hands clench in her lap. 'It's very relaxing there, very quiet. A good place for you to work with Lucio.'

'I look forward to it,' she said tersely, her face averted.

'Good.'

They'd silently agreed on a tense truce, and Allegra wondered how long it would last. For Lucio's sake, she couldn't be distracted by Stefano when she worked with him. She knew that, saw it as her first consideration, and she knew Stefano did as well.

At least on that point—the only point, it seemed—they were in agreement.

They both lapsed into silence and drove that way for an hour as the plains and fields around Rome turned hilly, and then mountainous. In the distance Allegra glimpsed rolling fields of saffron, the small purple flowers with their distinctive red-gold stigma stretching to the craggy, snow-topped peak of Gran Sasso.

Stefano turned off the motorway and they drove on a small winding road through several hill towns, huddled against the unforgiving landscape as if they had but a desperate, precarious hold on this earth.

Allegra glimpsed an old woman, dressed from head to toe in black, leading a bony cow along the road. She grinned toothlessly at them, her eyes lost in wrinkles, and Stefano raised one hand in greeting as the car passed by.

There could be no mistaking that this region of Abruzzo was impoverished. Although she'd seen signs on the motorway for ski resorts, spas and luxury hotels, here the hill towns showed no signs of such wealth. The streets were narrow and near empty, the few houses and shops sporting peeling paint and crooked shutters. It was as if time had simply passed by these places, Allegra thought, and no one living there had even noticed.

They drove through another town and out into the countryside again, the rolling, rocky hills leading to mountains, a few falling down farmhouses huddled against the hillside, half a dozen sheep grazing on the desolate landscape.

'What made you buy a farmhouse out here?' Allegra asked, breaking an hour long silence.

Stefano's fingers flexed on the wheel. 'I told you, it's my home.'

'You mean you grew up here? I always thought you were from Rome.'

'Near Rome,' Stefano corrected, his eyes on the twisting road. 'We're less than a hundred kilometres from Rome, believe it or not.'

Allegra couldn't believe it. The harsh beauty of this landscape was so different from the ostentatious wealth and glamour of the Eternal City.

She also couldn't imagine that Stefano came from this place. She'd always assumed he was urban, urbane, born to wealth and luxury if not aristocratic pedigree and privilege.

'Your family had a villa here?' she asked cautiously and he gave a short laugh.

'You could say that.'

He swung sharply on to an even narrower road, little more than dirt and pebbles, and they drove in silence for a few minutes more before coming to a sleepy village with only a handful of shops and houses. A few old men sat outside a café, playing chess and drinking coffee, and they looked up as Stefano drove through. They squinted at the car before cheers erupted from the café crowd and Stefano slowed the car to a stop.

'Just a moment,' he said, and Allegra watched in bemusement as he climbed out of the car and approached the men. They were impoverished old farmers, their remaining teeth tobacco-stained, greasy caps crammed on their heads.

Allegra watched as the men embraced Stefano in turn, kissed his cheeks and clapped him on the back. She looked on with growing surprise and wonder as Stefano kissed them back, held them by the shoulders and greeted them with the respect and love of a beloved son.

They talked for a few moments, loudly and with much excitement and agitation, and then Stefano turned to her, his expression tense and still, and beckoned for her to come out of the car.

Slowly Allegra did so. She was not a snob, and she'd certainly been among the lowest of society's offerings in her seven years in London.

Yet, she realized, she'd thought Stefano was a snob. After all, he'd wanted to marry her for her social connections. He'd married someone else for them.

He put paid to that assumption by the way he laughed and smiled with these men, old and incredibly poor. He looked upon them as if they were his family, Allegra thought. As if he loved them.

'*Por* Lucio,' Stefano said. 'She is going to help him.'

Allegra heard a chorus of grateful and delighted cries. *Fantastico! Fantastico! Grazie, grazie, magnifico!* And then she was embraced as he'd been, her face cradled by weathered hands as kisses were bestowed on each cheek, and she heard the men murmuring *'Grazie, grazie'* in a heartfelt chorus of thankfulness.

Tears stung her eyes at their easy affection, their unsullied joy. She smiled back, found herself laughing, returning the warm embraces even though she knew not one person's name.

She felt rather than saw Stefano watching her, felt both his tension and approval. The men wouldn't let them go back in the car until they'd drunk a toast, the conversation continuing with a round of questions.

Would she stay long? Did she know Lucio—such a wonderful child? And Enzo—a man with such wisdom, such kindness! It was a tragedy, such a tragedy...

Allegra listened, nodding with deepening sympathy for this close community and the sorrow that had ripped it apart.

And yet Enzo's death *hadn't* ripped it beyond repair, she realized. If anything, it had made these men, this community, stronger. Closer. They clearly all cared deeply about Lucio, about Bianca...about Stefano.

She thought of her own family, the sorrow and betrayal which had left it in shreds. She thought of Stefano's words only this morning, *You haven't seen your mother or your father since that night you ran away,* and then her mind slid gratefully away.

She turned her thoughts back to Stefano, saw him smiling and laughing good-naturedly, his arm around the shoulders of one of the men who looked at him with the love of a father shining in his eyes.

Finally Stefano made his excuses and they returned to the car. People crowded around the windows, women in black and ragged children who laughed and slapped the windows in excitement.

Stefano honked the horn a few times to many more delighted cries, and then they drove off.

They drove in silence for a few minutes. Allegra's mind whirled with questions. She hadn't expected Stefano to act like that, to have such a genuine camaraderie with a bunch of poor farmers.

She glanced at him, saw his eyes on the road, and ventured cautiously, 'Those men loved you.'

'They are fathers to me,' Stefano said. He spoke in a voice that brooked no questions, no comments. Allegra nodded even though her mind seethed with both.

She was ashamed to realize she knew nothing about Stefano's family. Where was his own father, mother? Did he have brothers or sisters? What kind of childhood, what kind of *life,* had he had?

She didn't know.

And, she realized with a rush of surprise, she wished she did. She wished she'd asked when she'd had the chance.

It was too late for that, she thought. Too late for both of them. The only relationship that could exist between them was one of distant professionalism. It was what she'd wanted all along, what she'd insisted on, yet now it made her sad.

Stupid. How could she be wanting something from Stefano now—*now*—when it was so clear that he wanted to give her nothing? Nothing she needed, anyway.

Finally Stefano turned into a long dirt drive, twisted oak trees shading the lane. Allegra glimpsed a farmhouse on one side of the road, a crude place with its roof caving in. She wondered why Stefano left such an eyesore on his property before her sights and senses were taken with the villa in front of them.

It was not ostentatious, Allegra saw at once, but it possessed every comfort. Begonias and geraniums spilled from hanging baskets and terracotta urns that lined the flagstone path up to the front door.

A young woman with luxuriant dark hair caught up in a bun opened the door and called a welcome. A little boy with the same dark, glossy hair stood next to her, keeping himself close to his mother yet also strangely, inexorably apart.

'My housekeeper, Bianca,' Stefano said quietly, 'and that is Lucio.'

Allegra nodded, saw the boy stare into an unknown—and safe—middle distance. They climbed out of the car and she noticed that the air was sharp and cool, scented with pine and cedar.

'Bianca.' Stefano greeted her warmly and Allegra was ashamed to feel a piercing little stab of jealousy. 'Hello, Lucio.' He ruffled the boy's dark hair, but Lucio didn't look at him, didn't say a word.

Stefano introduced her to Bianca, who shook her hand and smiled with hopeful gratitude. Allegra crouched down so she was eye-level with Lucio. His eyes didn't meet hers, but still she smiled as if he were looking at her.

'Hello, Lucio,' she said quietly. 'I'm happy to meet you.'

Lucio didn't look at her, didn't acknowledge her at all. It was as if she hadn't spoken, or even as if she wasn't even there.

Allegra hadn't expected him to speak or even look at her, yet his utter indifference betrayed by not even one flicker of understanding was discouraging. Still she remained there, crouched down, for several long moments. She knew Lucio had to be aware of her on some level, and that would have to be enough. For now.

She stood up and Bianca ushered them into the house.

Allegra glanced around, surprised again. Stefano's town house in Rome had been the epitome of tasteful, if impersonal, luxury. This house had no obvious antiques or original paintings, no clear signs of wealth or status.

Yet it was a home—comfortable and well cared for. Well loved. Bianca led them into the kitchen rather than the lounge, and Allegra could see that this was the heart of the house. A wide oak table occupied one side of the room, the gleaming kitchen appliances the other. In the middle an alcove had been made, three sides were windows to the world.

Allegra stepped into the alcove and gasped, for it had been built directly on to a rocky outcrop and she felt as if she were standing on a mountain top. She felt as if she could fly.

'Careful, don't fall,' Stefano murmured from behind her. His hand lightly touched her waist.

'I feel like I could topple right off,' Allegra admitted with a little laugh. 'But it's wonderful.'

'I'm glad you like it.'

She glanced at him. 'Did you build this house yourself?'

'I helped design it.'

Bianca bustled over to them. 'You must be hungry from your journey. Lunch, *signor?* And *signorina?* You can eat here or in the dining room.'

'Here,' Allegra said with decision. She gazed out at the hills stretching emptily, endlessly to the magnificent peaks of the Apennines and felt a small, surprising *frisson* of happiness.

She liked it here, she realized. She liked the solitude, the possibility of serenity. She liked the idea that this house was a glimpse into Stefano's life, the man he was now...and perhaps had been all along. A man different from the one she thought she'd known.

Good things could happen here, she told herself. Good things for Lucio, and perhaps even good things for herself. She just didn't know what those things might be. She couldn't—wouldn't—even begin to guess.

Bianca served lunch and Allegra tucked in to spaghetti alla chitarra—square strands of pasta with a spicy tomato sauce and the local pecorino cheese.

Despite both her and Stefano's urging, Bianca refused to eat with them, and Lucio still didn't say a word or even look at them. Allegra told Bianca it would take a few days for Lucio to accept her presence, and until then the real work—the art therapy—could not begin. Bianca nodded, although disappointment flashed briefly in her dark eyes.

No matter what anyone said or didn't say, Allegra knew, everyone secretly wanted a miracle.

Did she?

The thought surprised her with its unexpectedness as well as its force. Bianca and her son had left for their own rooms in the back of the house, and she and Stefano were alone.

She glanced at him now, preoccupied and yet more relaxed than he'd been in either London or Rome.

Was she expecting a miracle with Stefano? Why, when she shouldn't expect anything?

He didn't love her; he never had. And while she'd once loved him with all the passion and feeling in her childish heart, she didn't love him now. He'd treated her terribly last night; she should hate him.

As he, perhaps, hated her.

And yet she still found herself wondering about the man he really was…the man who had designed this amazing villa, who had embraced those poor farmers like fathers and friends. The man who cared deeply about his housekeeper's son, a boy other wealthy, prominent businessmen wouldn't even be aware existed.

Who was that man? she wondered. And why had she never bothered to find out? Seven years ago, it had been enough that Stefano loved her, or at least seemed to. His attention, his little gifts, even his smile had been enough.

Now, Allegra realized, she wanted more. She wanted intimacy, understanding. She wanted to see him turn to her with laughter and warmth instead of distance and wary regard. She wanted him to touch her with desire that was not tarnished by anger, by memory.

She wanted *more*.

More, and yet there could be nothing between them, for Lucio's sake, and certainly for their own. The past was forgotten and there was no future.

Allegra toyed with her pasta. Stefano's gaze had settled on the distant hills and he seemed lost in his thoughts.

'This is your home,' she stated after a moment, and Stefano smiled faintly.

'Yes, I said it was.'

'What I mean is…' She took a sip of the local red wine Bianca had poured and tried to frame her thoughts. 'You're at home here,' she finally said.

Stefano was quiet for a long moment, his shuttered gaze still on the mountains. 'Yes,' he finally said, and it sounded like a reluctant confession.

Allegra knew better than to press. Not now, not yet.

After lunch Bianca showed Allegra to her room while Stefano went to his home office to deal with business. Allegra took in the wide oak bed and dresser, simple yet adequate furnishings. There was no decoration in the room save a pair of gauzy white curtains framing the only artistry the villa needed, the view outside.

She stood at the window and took several deep, clean lungfuls of air. The scent of pine was sharp, and she heard the lonely bleat of a sheep on a distant hillside.

Stefano's words from this morning reverberated yet again through her mind and her heart. *You want to talk about feelings? What about yours?*

Yes, she had feelings, as much as she longed to deny them even to herself. She didn't like to consider those feelings fermenting inside her—memories, regrets, fears and disappointments. They bubbled up, demanding to be recognised, to be *felt,* and she pushed them down, again and again. It was so much easier not to think.

Not to feel.

She wondered if Stefano was the same. She knew he had things he refused to consider.

Like the fact that he was angry with her. Still. Now. Allegra wasn't sure if he even knew it. Or if knew it, like her, it was simply one more emotion to suppress.

He'd denied it this morning and yet Allegra knew—*knew*— he'd been angry with her last night. Deeply angry, angry in a way he had no right to be.

Her lips twisted in a cynical smile. Of course, Stefano would think he had a right. He'd thought of her as a possession all those years ago, prized perhaps, but an object nonetheless. Something to be owned.

And he was the same now. He'd shown her last night; he thought of her in those terms still.

And it hurt, she knew, because just as he was still the man

he'd been all those years ago, the man who'd coldly asked her, *'What more is there?'* so she was still that same girl, wanting to believe, begging for love.

Allegra closed her eyes. Neither of them had changed as much as they thought they had.

As much as they'd wanted to.

'I want to show you something,' Stefano said. He stood in the doorway, one shoulder propped against the door-frame.

Allegra kept her back to him and spread her arms wide as she gazed out at the vista. 'What more could you show me?'

Stefano laughed softly. 'You like the view?'

'Yes,' Allegra said simply.

'Come with me.'

He had moved behind her, and Allegra could feel his presence, his breath. She resisted the urge to lean back against him. It was a ridiculous urge, she told herself, as ridiculous and inappropriate as her thoughts had been earlier, expecting a miracle.

She felt Stefano's tension vibrating between them, a tension born of an awareness of each other—bodies, minds, memories.

'All right,' she said, and turned around.

Stefano led her down the upstairs corridor and to another bedroom on the southern side of the villa.

'Here.' He opened the door and ushered Allegra in before him. She looked around in surprise.

It wasn't a bedroom; it was a studio. The room had windows on two sides and was flooded with clear, perfect light. It contained everything she could possibly need for her work with Lucio: an easel, sketchbooks, paints and pastels, charcoals and chalks, brushes and pencils and pens. There was a stool by the easel and a comfortable chair in the corner, wrapped in sunlight.

Allegra moved slowly through the room. It was incredibly thoughtful of Stefano to provide it for her and Lucio, yet even now she felt a finger of unease creeping up her spine.

All the art supplies in the world weren't going to make Lucio talk. That, she knew, was one thing Stefano couldn't buy.

He looked around the room in satisfaction. 'I had only the best brought here, flown by helicopter from Rome.' There was a hidden vulnerability in his eyes as he turned to her. 'You like it? It will be enough?'

Looking at him, at the room he'd provided for Lucio with such complete, considering care, Allegra felt her heart contract.

'Stefano, it's amazing.' She crossed over to him and, standing on tiptoe, she kissed his cheek. 'Thank you.'

His eyes flared in surprise, in awareness. 'You're welcome.'

They stood that way for a moment, a hand span apart, and Allegra felt desire and something deeper uncoil in her belly, spiral upwards. She wanted him to take her in his arms. She wanted to go there.

It would have been so easy, so devastatingly easy, to take that one last step towards him, to let him pull her into his arms, brush his lips against hers. She could feel it; she could almost taste it.

She wanted it.

But he didn't take that step, didn't touch her. Of course he didn't. She shouldn't have wanted it; she certainly shouldn't expect it. Not now, not ever.

Stefano gazed down at her, a smile quirking the corner of his mouth without reaching his eyes.

Allegra smiled back and stepped away.

'I'll leave you alone,' Stefano said, moving towards the door. 'I'm sure there are things you need to do, in preparation for your work with Lucio. We usually eat around seven.'

Allegra spent the rest of the afternoon reviewing Lucio's case notes. According to Bianca, he had been napping in the villa when Enzo had died. She'd told him about the accident that night, had always talked about Enzo in warm and loving terms to keep his memory alive. At first, Lucio had responded, grieved, seemed normal. Then slowly he'd begun to withdraw verbally, physically, emotionally.

Over the ensuing months he had retreated further and further into his own safe, silent world. When he was forced out of it, it was as if a switch had been flipped and he became agitated, screaming incoherently, banging his head against the floor or wall.

Bianca had been forced to withdraw him from the nursery in the local village and soon it had become difficult to take him to shops or church. He greeted the world with blank, staring eyes, didn't interact with anyone or anything.

Lost in thought, Allegra gazed out of the window, the sun sinking behind the rugged mountain peaks. While all of Lucio's behaviours fell into the normal spectrum of childhood grief, the length and depth of them did not.

A grieving child should begin to respond to therapy, to improve, even if it was a two steps forward, one step backward type of improvement. Yet Lucio was not improving. He was slowly, steadily growing worse.

Allegra uncurled herself from the chair and wandered around the studio as a settling twilight lengthened the shadows on the floor. She let her fingers drift over the stiff new bristles on the paintbrushes, the untouched paints, unopened packets of crayons and felt-tip pens.

Worry gnawed and nibbled at her insides. She'd come here to help Lucio; that, of course, always, had been her primary goal. Yet now she doubted. What if she couldn't help him? What if he really was autistic?

What if, a little voice whispered inside her heart, she'd really come here for a selfish reason? And what was that reason?

To see Stefano again.

She gave a little, instinctive shake of her head. *No.* Surely not. *Please.*

Yet she couldn't deny that seeing him again had stirred something to life inside her she'd long thought dead. Something she wanted to be dead.

She didn't want to care about Stefano, didn't want to hand him her heart so he could carelessly grind it with his heel.

Do you love me?

No, she wouldn't go there, wouldn't let herself. She'd shut herself off from the past for the last seven years, and she could continue to do so. Love, if that was what this was, was just another emotion to suppress.

Outside, a wolf howled, a distant, lonely sound. It was now nearly completely dark and Allegra realized the hour had to be quite late.

'Allegra?'

She stiffened, turned. Silhouetted against a spill of light from the hallway was Stefano.

'What is it?' she asked, and her voice came out sharper than she meant it to be. She felt rather than saw Stefano stiffen in response, and then saw that reaction resolutely change into a more predictable one: he shrugged.

'Dinner is ready. I thought you'd want to know.' Without waiting for her, he turned and left.

After a few moments, Allegra followed.

Downstairs, the kitchen was warm and cosy, with light and steam from several pots, their savoury contents bubbling merrily. Bianca stood at the sink, scrubbing a pan, while Stefano stood next to her, chopping a tomato for a salad.

They were chatting and laughing like friends, while Lucio stood by the window, methodically tapping the windowsill with a wooden spoon.

Stefano turned his head, caught sight of Allegra, and his eyes blazed into hers for a second before he beckoned her in and then turned back to his chopping.

Yet that moment of intensity struck Allegra to her core, and she wondered if that blaze of feeling had been anger or affection, or something else altogether.

They all ate together in the kitchen. Lucio sat next to Bianca, everything about him sombre and silent, his face and eyes blank. Allegra sat on his other side and, even though he didn't respond to her, she included him in the conversation, smiling and making eye contact as much and as naturally as she could.

Bianca and Stefano chatted easily with her over the meal of pasta with sausage and beans, a simple, hearty speciality of the region.

After dinner, Allegra insisted on helping Bianca with the washing-up. In typical Italian style, Bianca shooed Stefano out of the kitchen.

'We don't want him here anyway,' Bianca said with a mischievous smile. 'Women's work and women's talk, eh?'

Allegra gave a little laugh, choosing not to take offence at the inherent sexism in her remark.

'I'm glad you agreed to help Lucio,' Bianca said as they scraped the plates. 'It can't have been easy, considering.'

'Considering...?' Allegra asked, her eyebrows raised. Bianca's head was bent, her eyes on the dirty dishes in the sink.

'Considering that you and Stefano nearly married,' she said quietly, and Allegra experienced a cold ripple of shock.

'I didn't realize you knew our history,' she said after a moment. Her voice came out calm, normal, and she was glad.

Bianca looked up, surprised. 'Of course I knew. I've known Stefano since I was a baby and he was a boy. When his father died, my own took him in. He's like a brother to me.'

Allegra nodded. At least now she understood Lucio's importance to Stefano, as well as Bianca's.

'I know you had your reasons for leaving,' Bianca continued quietly, 'and I expect they are good ones—'

'Yes,' Allegra couldn't help but interject, 'they are. Were.' She turned to the table to collect more dishes. 'Stefano and I have agreed to put the past behind us. It's best for Lucio and, frankly, I think it's best for us.'

'Easier said than done,' Bianca said quietly.

Allegra turned around. 'What do you mean?'

'I see the way he looks at you,' Bianca replied with a shrug. 'He loved you then, and I wonder if he perhaps loves you still.'

The remark, made with such stark simplicity, caused Allegra to give a short laugh of disbelief. 'Bianca, Stefano never loved me! He told me as much. And I am quite certain he doesn't love me now. We…we don't really know each other any more. I don't think we ever did.'

Bianca shrugged again. 'If that is easier to believe…'

'It's easier to believe,' Allegra replied, 'because it's the truth. Trust me. Stefano never loved me, never even considered loving me, and he's made that clear many, many times.'

'But,' Bianca surmised softly, 'you love him.'

Allegra's breath came out in a short, surprised rush. 'No,' she said, and heard the doubt in her own voice. Her horrified gaze lifted to meet Bianca's knowing one. 'No!' She shook her head. 'No, I did love him—terribly—seven years ago. But now? No.' Another shake of her head, and her voice came out firm, strident. 'No, I don't,' she continued, talking as much to herself as to Bianca. 'Of course, seeing him again is bound to make me remember—feel—certain things, but no.' Now she met Bianca's sombre smile, her own smile dazzling, determined in its certainty. 'No, I don't love him,' she stated with a strange triumph, and her heart sank as Bianca merely smiled, shrugging in a way that managed to convey her scepticism and sympathy without saying a word.

After the dishes were done, Bianca went to put Lucio to bed and Allegra wandered through the darkened, empty rooms of the villa until she came to the lounge. The double doors were only partly ajar and warm light spilled from within.

She peeped inside, saw Stefano in an overstuffed armchair, intent on reading an old leather-bound book. She realized with a little jolt that he wore reading glasses. This tiny weakness made him somehow more approachable, and she stepped inside.

Stefano looked up and smiled briefly, coolly. 'All right?'

'Yes. I'm all right. Bianca's putting Lucio to bed.'

'Good.'

She came further into the room, perched on the edge of a sofa. The room was cosy and warm, decorated in warm red fabrics and mahogany, a haven against the unrelenting darkness outside.

'Do you think Bianca will marry again?' she asked.

Stefano glanced up. 'Perhaps, in time. There are not many men out here, though.' He smiled faintly. 'You saw the pickings in town, at the café.'

'Yes.' She paused, looked at him. 'Bianca mentioned that you lived with her family when your father died.'

Stefano stilled, the expression in his eyes shadowed, hidden. Allegra saw his long tapered fingers tense on the cover of his book.

'Yes, I did.'

'What happened to your family?' Allegra asked. 'Your mother, your brothers and sisters?'

'They went elsewhere.'

She shook her head, confused. 'Why?'

'Why are you asking these questions, Allegra?' There was a wary sharpness to his tone and Allegra faced it.

'Because I realize I should have asked them before. I should have thought to ask them, wanted to ask them.'

'Before?'

'When we were engaged. When I was nineteen.'

Stefano took off his reading glasses. He was silent for a moment, his head bent, his expression hidden. Then he looked up and smiled mockingly. 'Having regrets, Allegra?' he asked softly.

'No,' she retorted, still buoyed by her conviction earlier. 'No, of course not. I'll never regret what I did, Stefano, because it was the right thing to do. We would have made a terrible couple.'

His mouth twisted. 'Then why do you care?'

'It's called making conversation.' She lifted her chin, held her breath and waited.

Stefano was silent for a long moment. His fingers tapped a staccato rhythm on the cover of his book and then he let out a short bark of laughter.

'All right, *fiorina*,' he said, and it sounded like a taunt. 'You want to know? My father died when I was twelve. My family had no money, nothing, and so we were all farmed out while my mother went to work in Naples at a firework factory. Bianca's father took me in, and I was fortunate.'

'What about your sisters?' Allegra whispered.

'Elizabetta went with my mother, to Naples, and died in a factory accident. Rosalia stayed with an aunt in Abruzzo, met a mechanic and married. She's happy the way she is, hasn't wanted anything from me.' A quick, short shrug. 'And little Bella, who was younger than me, she did okay until I started giving her money, sent her to boarding school, gave her the means to better herself, and all it did was finance a drug habit that eventually killed her.' His smile was cold, a coldness that seeped straight into Allegra's soul. 'So that's my family history. Satisfied?' And, without another thought, he flipped open his book, readjusted his glasses and began to read.

Allegra stared at him, her heart aching. No, she was not satisfied. Not in the least.

Slowly she walked towards him and laid a hand on the page of his book. Stefano stilled again. 'Why did you never tell me this before?'

'When was I to mention it?' Stefano asked in a disbelieving drawl. 'It's not the kind of pedigree that would have impressed your parents, or you for that matter.'

'Still…'

He looked up, his mouth twisting in mockery. 'Did you really want to know, Allegra? Or did you want to keep believing that I was the dashing prince you thought me to be?'

She shook her head. 'No, Stefano, I wanted to know the real you. I loved you—'

'You loved the man you thought I was.' Stefano cut her off with cruel, cutting precision. 'And when you learned I wasn't, that my feet were made of clay, you hightailed it to England. So spare me all the misunderstood melodrama now, please.' With two fingers he removed her hand as if it were something slimy and distasteful and it fell helplessly to Allegra's side.

She stood there, feeling the shock waves pulse painfully

through her. Stefano's assessment had been so cold, so cruel, so *clear*. There could be no doubt now what he thought of her…what he'd always thought of her.

Stefano closed his book. 'I'm leaving tomorrow,' he announced in a neutral voice. Allegra's startled gaze flew to his. He met her gaze with a stare as blank as Lucio's.

'Tomorrow? Why so soon?'

'It's for the best, don't you think? I don't want to distract you from your work with Lucio.'

Allegra nodded, accepting that Stefano would be a hopeless distraction, as much as she didn't want him to be.

'When will you return?' she asked and he shrugged.

'I don't know,' he replied. He sounded so casual, so indifferent, that Allegra was stung.

'Very well,' she said, trying to match his tone, his shrug. Stefano smiled faintly. He laid his book on the table and rose, closing the small space between them in just a few steps.

He stood before her, reached out to tuck a tendril of hair behind her ear before drifting his hand along her cheek. It was a gesture born of tenderness, like a phoenix rising from the ashes of his earlier anger.

Allegra looked up at him, saw not anger in his eyes but sorrow. Grief.

'It's better this way, *fiorina*,' he whispered. 'For both of us.' Lightly—so lightly—he rested his forehead against hers. Allegra felt his breath stir her hair, felt the sorrow and regret that wrapped them both in a fog of feeling.

She wanted to speak, opened her mouth, but all that came out was a tiny choked cry, as feeble and useless as a baby bird's. Silently, she reached up and touched Stefano's fingers, pressing them against her cheek before he tugged his hand gently from hers and stepped away.

'Goodnight,' he murmured, and walked out of the room, leaving her there with the darkness and the memories.

CHAPTER EIGHT

THE SUN WAS streaming through the wide windows when Allegra awoke. She lay in bed, waiting for memories and feelings to catch up and play havoc with her heart.

She thought of Stefano's assessment of her love, herself, and still felt stung, stunned. Then she remembered his sad smile, a smile that had cut through her defences in a single stroke and left her wondering.

She threw off the covers and jumped out of bed, showering and dressing quickly. She couldn't think of Stefano; she needed to concentrate on Lucio. He was the reason—the only reason—she was here.

The villa was surprisingly quiet as she came downstairs. She saw Bianca in the kitchen, washing dishes. Lucio was at the table, running a toy car methodically along its wooden surface.

'Bianca?' Allegra stepped into the welcoming warmth, instinctively looking for Stefano.

'Stefano went back to Rome,' Bianca said. 'Early this morning.'

Allegra nodded. She'd known he was leaving, of course, and yet she'd wanted to say goodbye. Perhaps they had said goodbye last night. It had, in a way, felt like a farewell.

'He said he had business there,' Bianca continued, a knowing compassion in her dark eyes. 'He'll be back in a few weeks.'

A few weeks. Allegra nodded, tried to smile. It was for the best, she knew. 'Can I help with breakfast?' she asked.

'No, no, it's all made,' Bianca said, and served Allegra with cappuccino and pastries.

After breakfast, Bianca left for another part of the house and Allegra began her work with Lucio. She intended to spend the first few days simply observing him, allowing Lucio to become accustomed to her presence. He didn't even look at her as he played, running his car over and over again along the table's surface, his expression blank and fixated on the seemingly mindless activity.

After a few minutes of this, Allegra began to talk, making friendly, interested comments about his car, the house, the view of mountains outside. She didn't expect answers, only waited a few seconds for them before she continued cheerfully. Lucio didn't even look her way, but at least he tolerated her presence.

The next few days continued in much the same way. Lucio allowed Allegra to be in the same room with him, played his mindless, methodical games while she sat next to him and chatted. But he never looked at her, never responded in any way, and Allegra had to admit to herself that she was discouraged.

One evening after Lucio had gone to bed, Bianca approached her. 'Is it not working?' she asked, her fingers knotted together, her eyes filled with disappointed sorrow.

Allegra, curled up on the sofa in the lounge, looked up from the notes she'd been studying. 'It's not a question of whether it's working or not, Bianca,' she explained quietly. 'Lucio needs time. I don't want to begin proper therapy with him until he's comfortable with me.'

Bianca nodded. 'It's hard to wait.'

'Of course it is,' Allegra agreed. She touched Bianca's hand. 'You know, though, that Lucio may indeed be autistic? Even though that is a diagnosis that is difficult for any parent to accept, especially if their child did once have speech and other behaviours that would contradict such a diagnosis. Still, it's a possibility.'

Bianca swallowed. 'I know.'

'I'll do my best,' Allegra promised, 'but if his silence and other behaviours are trauma induced, then it's likely we're missing something. His level of emotional suppression is severe and extraordinary.' She paused, letting Bianca take a moment to digest this. Then she asked, 'Have you tried speaking with Lucio about his father? I know sometimes it seems easier—and kinder—not to talk about it, but Lucio needs an outlet for his feelings.'

'I talked with him at first,' Bianca said. 'But he would grow agitated and I didn't want to upset him. Then he started just to fall silent instead and, as you know, it worsened until he wasn't speaking or even responding at all.' She bit her lip. 'It was hard for me too—talking about Enzo.'

'Of course it was,' Allegra murmured.

'Lucio always loved to draw, though,' Bianca said and, although her voice wobbled, there was hope in her eyes. 'When Stefano mentioned the idea of art therapy, even without the experience you've had with a child like Lucio, I felt encouraged. He hasn't drawn anything since he stopped speaking, but if you help him…guide him…' She trailed off, looking to Allegra for reassurance, comfort.

Allegra smiled. She was used to the conflicting mixture of scepticism and hope, the intense desire for change coupled with the disbelief that it could ever happen.

She felt that way about Stefano. The thought shocked her. She and Stefano didn't even have a relationship. They'd agreed to keep their distance.

And yet. And yet.

She couldn't deny her own feelings resurfacing after all these years, still wanting something he couldn't give her.

Love.

The kind of love she needed, wanted.

'I'm sorry,' Allegra said after a moment, realizing her thoughts had scattered, her mind spinning. 'Yes, I think art could help Lucio. But whether or not it's the key that unlocks his silence…' she shrugged, smiling sadly, '…only time will tell.' Allegra reached over to cover Bianca's hand with her own. 'I'll do my best to reach him, Bianca,' she said softly, and the other woman's eyes shone with unshed tears.

'It hurts,' she said simply, 'to love.'

Yes, it did, Allegra knew. It hurt when your dreams were disappointed, your hopes crushed.

It hurt so much.

And was Stefano hurt? The question whispered through her mind, her heart, as it had in the days since he'd left.

Was he angry because his pride was hurt, or was it something more? Something deeper?

And why, Allegra wondered hopelessly, did she want it to be?

The next day Allegra took Lucio to the art studio upstairs. He was surprisingly docile, allowing her to lead him down the corridor and into the room, the pale floorboards washed in the morning sunlight. He stood in the middle of the room, his eyes flickering around the art materials before coming to a rest, gazing out at a mindless middle distance.

'Stefano told me you like art,' Allegra said. 'He has some of your drawings by his desk. Do you like to draw with crayons?' She sat on the floor in the middle of the room and took a handful of crayons from a plastic tub.

She named the colours one by one, let them fall through her fingers. Lucio watched, silent, his eyes flickering over the crayons.

'Would you like to draw?' Allegra asked gently. She took a wide white sheet of paper and laid it in front of him and waited.

Lucio stared at the blank paper for a long moment and then looked away.

Still Allegra persevered, chatting easily. She drew a few streaks of colour to show him, not wanting to guide or influence him too much, but still Lucio did nothing, said nothing.

They stopped at lunch time and Lucio followed her silently down to the kitchen. Allegra felt the heavy burden of disappointment and helplessness. She wasn't reaching Lucio, just as no one had been able to reach him.

Most children she worked with weren't nearly as traumatised as Lucio was, if it was indeed trauma that was causing his silence. The children she usually encountered were more than willing to scribble with felt-tips, pound clay, splatter paint. Allegra facilitated their creativity, helped them work through their emotions by helping them expand and complete their pictures.

She wasn't used to this—stone walls of silence, blank stares, *nothing*. Lucio was giving her nothing to work with, and she realized she felt completely out of her depth.

He needed an experienced psychiatrist or grief counsellor, not an art therapist who had only been qualified for two years. Yet she couldn't abandon Lucio now, even if she wanted to, which she didn't.

Still, Allegra resolved, when Stefano returned she would impress upon him the importance of entrusting Lucio's care to additional professionals.

It was not a job she could manage on her own, and she felt the burden of both Bianca and Stefano's expectation and hope weigh heavily on her.

That evening, after Lucio was in bed, Bianca came into the lounge where Allegra was reading. 'The telephone,' she said, holding out the receiver. 'It is Stefano, for you.'

Allegra's heart tumbled over. She smiled, murmured her thanks and took the phone. Bianca withdrew.

'Hello?'

'Allegra.'

She was surprised to hear the emotion in his voice—what was it? Relief, perhaps, and regret. Something unfathomable and deep.

'Hello, Stefano,' she said quietly.

'How are things progressing with Lucio?' he asked, reverting to a more impersonal tone.

'Slowly. You can't expect much yet. It's early days.'

'No words?'

'No. But I wouldn't judge success by his ability to speak,

Stefano. If suppressed trauma is indeed the cause of his symptoms, he needs to remember first. And feel. He hasn't grieved properly and he needs to.'

'How,' Stefano murmured, 'do you allow someone to grieve?'

'Give him a safe place to express himself,' Allegra replied quietly. 'Lucio is an extreme case, I'll confess.' She paused before continuing carefully. 'I don't think we can rule out an autism diagnosis.'

Stefano let out a short, sharp breath before saying evenly, 'You've been with him less than a week.'

'I know that,' Allegra said, 'but I also want to make sure you and Bianca understand what to expect…or not to expect.'

'Barring autism, what do you think could be the source of his trauma?'

Allegra nibbled her lower lip, thinking. She'd given this very question a great deal of thought over the last few days, wondering what secret or surprise Lucio was withholding, perhaps without even knowing it. 'I almost wonder,' she said slowly, 'if there isn't something more that he's suppressing, something none of us knows about.'

'Like what?' Allegra heard the bite of impatience in Stefano's voice and knew that, like Bianca, he was disappointed and frustrated.

No matter what she'd said, he wanted answers. Miracles.

'Something about Enzo's death?' Allegra guessed. 'It could be anything. If he saw Enzo—'

'Impossible. Bianca said he was asleep.'

'Perhaps he overheard something, then,' Allegra suggested. 'A small child can easily take adult remarks out of context and apportion blame to himself—'

'You think he blames himself for his father's death?' Stefano asked, and she heard the incredulity in his voice.

'I don't know,' she replied, struggling to keep her own voice quiet and even.

'Well, find out,' Stefano snapped and then, before Allegra

could frame a reply, he sighed and said, 'I'm sorry. I know you are doing all you can.'

'I'm trying,' she whispered and they were both silent, listening to each other's breathing. There were other things Allegra wanted to say, things that had nothing to do with Lucio and all to do with her and Stefano.

Yet she didn't even know where to begin. She didn't even know what to *feel*. And neither, it seemed, did Stefano, for he too remained silent; both of them quiet and listening without speaking a word.

They should have said goodbye, should have said *something*, but neither of them did.

The phone wire provided a strange, intimate connection between them. A temporary connection, for after that endless, aching moment, Stefano said quietly, 'Goodnight, Allegra,' and severed it.

The next morning Allegra took Lucio to the art studio again. She tried clay, finger-paints and crayons, but he showed no interest.

Deciding to take a different approach, Allegra drew a picture for him.

'This is the view from my window,' she said, smiling, as she drew a simple scene of mountains, sun and sky. 'I love looking at it every morning.' She held it out to him. 'Is there anything you'd add to that picture, Lucio? What do you see when you look out of the window?'

Lucio stared at the picture for a long moment—long enough for Allegra's arms to ache and she almost put it down. Then he looked down at the crayons and she held her breath.

Lucio picked a black crayon and took the picture. Then, systematically, as methodically as he'd done everything else, he drew with the black crayon, not stopping until the entire drawing was covered in blackness.

She watched him draw, watched the fierce concentration on his face, made more pitiable by his complete silence.

She looked down at the picture. In places the paper had ripped from the force of his crayon.

He'd made an astonishing statement; he'd communicated. And the message was clear—clear and terrible.

Lucio was trapped, she thought, trapped and tormented by suppressed memories and emotions—emotions that held him in their snare and refused to let him go, just as he couldn't let go of them.

Just as she and Stefano couldn't.

Allegra put the blackened drawing aside and gently laid her hand on Lucio's shoulder. He didn't flinch, didn't move.

'When my father died,' Allegra said quietly, 'I sometimes felt empty inside, as if there was nothing inside of me. And, other times, I felt so *full,* as if I was going to explode if I didn't do something. But I never knew what to do.'

She waited, letting Lucio hear what she was saying, allowing it to filter through his consciousness. Then she retrieved a lump of clay and put it on the floor between them.

'Would you like to make something with the clay?' she asked gently. 'Squish it between your fingers, if you like. It's soft.'

After a long silent moment Lucio reached out and touched the clay, stroked it with one finger. Then he dropped his hand. Allegra knew they'd done enough for one day.

'We can work with the clay tomorrow, if you like,' she said and, standing up, led Lucio from the room.

Late that afternoon, when the peak of Gran Sasso was touched with gold, Allegra took a walk down the front drive. Bianca had taken Lucio with her to collect eggs from the hen house, encouraged by the small step, awful as it had been, that Lucio had taken. Allegra was grateful for a few moments' relaxation.

The wind whispered through the oak trees, their leaves already touched with a deep, mellow gold. In the distance a cow lowed mournfully and she heard the tinkling of its bell.

It was peaceful here, she realized, even though concern for

Lucio overshadowed that sense of serenity. She was glad there was a crack of communication in the walls he'd built around himself, relieved that it indicated he might not be autistic. Yet she was also intimidated by the depth of Lucio's trauma, and the amount of work that would have to be done to help him recover—work she could not do on her own.

Yet today the realization of his hidden hurt and anger, a terrible grief he'd suppressed so completely, made her conscious of her own veiled emotions in a way she'd never been before.

She'd always known that she didn't think about her former life, ended so abruptly the night she'd run away. She'd quite consciously put those memories in a box, had done it on purpose as a way to build her own future. Yet she hadn't realized that those memories held so much pain—pain and hurt, fear and guilt.

She hadn't realized until Stefano had come back into her life, forcing her to confront not just the past, but her own self. The girl she'd been, the woman she was.

Am I so different? Have I changed?

She'd spent the last seven years rushing, straining, trying to prove herself in a thousand different ways and here she found herself resting at last.

It was hard to let go of that sense of urgent striving, hard to let the cares and worries tumble from her. Her heart and mind resisted, her body tensed. She wanted to keep it all at bay and yet she couldn't.

She couldn't…she was afraid of what might happen when she finally let it all go.

Something black flashed between the trees and after a moment Allegra saw what it was: Stefano's car. She stood uncertainly by the side of the road and watched as the vehicle, and Stefano, drew closer to her, finally slowing to a stop right in front of her.

Stefano climbed out, stood with one hand resting on the bonnet of the car, his eyes fathomless, his face blank.

'What are you doing?' he asked.

She shrugged. 'Going for a walk.'

'What about Lucio?'

She flushed at the implication that she was neglecting her responsibility. 'He's with Bianca. We had a productive session this morning.'

'Did you?'

'Yes.'

'Is he speaking?'

'I told you, it's not that simple, Stefano. He isn't just going to magically start talking and be better.'

Stefano ran a hand over his face and Allegra realized how tired he looked.

'You're back,' she stated unnecessarily. 'Why?'

'I wanted to see how Lucio was doing.'

Allegra nodded, swallowed. Of course, that was to be expected. She was disappointed, delusional, to think he'd wanted to see her.

Stefano's gaze slid away from hers, resting among a copse of trees by the twisting road. 'I haven't been down here in a while,' he said.

Allegra didn't know what he meant—they were standing on the main drive, after all—when she saw Stefano start to walk towards the trees.

She looked over her shoulder and saw the dilapidated structure huddled in a copse of elms—the building she'd seen when they'd first arrived.

Stefano walked towards it, mindless of the long grass catching on his finely tailored suit.

Wary and intrigued, Allegra followed him.

He stopped in front of the hovel. The timbers were rotting, the windows gaping, shutters askew. Most of the roof had fallen in and terracotta tiles lay scattered around. A stunted sapling grew determinedly through the hole in the roof.

'I haven't been over here in years,' Stefano said, half to himself. 'I'm not sure it's safe to go inside.'

Allegra was inclined to agree, but Stefano still moved forward, picking his way through the fallen stone, the rotting timber, and ducked his head under the low lintel.

'Stefano…?' she asked uncertainly. She had no idea why he was here, what he was thinking.

Dusk was falling; the peak of Gran Sasso, touched with gold only moments before, was now cloaked in darkness. A chill had crept into the air, wound its way through the mountains, into Allegra's bones.

Stefano appeared in the doorway. 'This is my home,' he said simply. It took Allegra a moment to understand.

This was his home. This falling-down two-room hovel. This.

Allegra surveyed the tumbled stone and rotting wood. 'You grew up here?' she asked, trying not to sound incredulous.

'I told you the other night my family had nothing.'

Allegra swallowed. 'I know. I just didn't think—'

He laughed. 'That I was *this* poor? Well, I was. Believe it.' There was a savage note to his voice as he added, 'I worked hard to lose my country accent, my country manners.'

'You succeeded,' she said with a small smile, but there was pain in her heart, a pain she saw reflected in Stefano's eyes. 'Tell me,' she said.

Stefano gave a little shrug. 'My father was a farmer. We had a few sheep, a couple of cows. Then the agricultural industry collapsed in this region and my father left our farm to seek work in the mines in Wallonia, in Belgium.'

'You work in the mining industry now,' Allegra said after a moment. She felt as if she'd been given a handful of scattered puzzle pieces and she had to work out where they fitted.

'Yes.' Stefano paused. 'My father died in a mining accident. When I started my business, one of my goals was to make machinery that would keep miners safe, keep men like my father from dying needlessly.' He smiled, although his voice was hard and held no humour. 'It also happened to make me rich.'

They were both silent, listening to the creak of the trees, the slap of a loose shutter in the wind.

Allegra thought of her mother's words, *Your social connections, his money,* and it made sense, a horrible sense when she realized just how important, how necessary those social connections must have been.

'I suppose,' she said slowly, 'for business, it would help to be socially connected.'

Stefano's gaze flicked to her face and he nodded, understanding where her trail of tangled thoughts had led her.

'Yes. There were plenty of men in Milan and other cities who wouldn't do business with me because I didn't have their manners, didn't go to their schools and clubs. I was a rough country boy and they knew it. No matter how much I tried to hide it from them…from you.'

The last came out as a confession and his gaze slid away from hers once more, resting on the distant darkened hills.

'Why?' Allegra met his gaze, searched it. 'Why hide how far you've come? Who you are? You should be *proud.*'

Stefano smiled faintly. 'I'm glad you think so.' He lapsed into silence, lost in thought, one hand resting on the cracked lintel of his family home. 'When my father went to work in the mines,' he began after a moment, his gaze still averted from hers, 'my mother didn't want him to go. She'd heard about the kind of work there. It's a hard life.' He paused, ran his hand down the rough-hewn stone. 'But he went because he knew it was the only way of providing for his family. The only way,' he said, 'of loving them.' He spoke flatly, matter-of-factly. There would be no arguing with that sentiment, Allegra knew. No dispute.

She gazed at him, lost in shadow, in darkness, and understood how much Stefano had revealed with that statement, had revealed it without even realizing.

'And he died there,' she said quietly. He nodded.

'Yes, three years after he went. In all that time, he never came home. He didn't want to waste the money on the train fare.'

There was no regret in Stefano's voice, no anger or hurt or sorrow. There was only fierce, unrelenting pride.

'Didn't your mother miss him?' Allegra asked in a whisper. 'Didn't she want to see him? Didn't he want to see her?'

'Yes,' Stefano said, the conviction in his voice still unshakeable, 'but it didn't matter. He was providing for her, Allegra. He was doing what needed to be done…because he loved her.'

Allegra stared unseeingly at the darkness that cloaked the mountains outside, a darkness that was not pierced by a single light or hope.

What more is there?

Now she understood what he'd meant that awful, never-ending night. She'd known how he loved, but she hadn't realized why. She hadn't understood what it meant, that it could mean *anything*.

She'd said his love was worthless, yet now she realized that perhaps it wasn't.

It wasn't worthless. It just wasn't enough.

How could two people who had loved each other not have been able to find happiness together?

And now? she wondered. Could they still? The question was pointless; Stefano didn't love her any more. And she wasn't willing to ask herself if she loved him. She couldn't think that much—feel that much—yet. Not when her heart was already overflowing, her barriers breaking. Not when it was getting so desperately difficult to hold everything back, at bay.

They walked back to the villa in the dark, in silence. Warm light spilled from the windows. While Stefano went to check his messages, Allegra decided to see if she could help Bianca in the kitchen.

Dinner was a surprisingly cheerful, chatty affair, and it felt right to have Stefano among them again. Yet still Allegra felt the undercurrents of tension, of remembrance, pulling at her own heart.

She saw Stefano glance at her, an understanding and knowledge in his eyes that made her own gaze slide away.

Everything was conspiring to make her think, make her feel. Perhaps it was being in the mountains, perhaps it was seeing Stefano again, perhaps it was the intensive work she was doing with Lucio, so different from her weekly sessions with a dozen different patients.

Now she found those barriers cracking completely, the memories and feelings threatening to rush over and engulf her. And, strangest of all, she found herself wanting it. Craving it, needing it.

She wanted to open the box she'd closed all those years ago and scatter the feelings and fears to this clean, healing wind.

She just didn't know how to begin. How to prise open the lid, how to deal with the questions. The memories.

The feelings.

Later, when Bianca was putting Lucio to bed, Allegra went upstairs to the art studio. It was shrouded in darkness, the only light coming from a spill of moonlight through the wide windows.

Allegra sat on a stool, ran her fingers over the drawing Lucio had blackened. Its desecration had been the first key to his healing.

Yet it was not his healing she was reflecting on now, but her own. She felt an ache, deep within, of sorrow and regret, loss and grief. It was an ache she'd become accustomed to; it had become a part of her own self, dull, and steady, so easy to ignore.

Yet now she felt it rise up in her chest, threaten to erupt in a never-ending howl of misery that she couldn't deal with on her own. Couldn't accept.

She bowed her head, willing the tears, the pain back.

She'd almost succeeded, felt her eyes become dry and gritty, her throat sore and aching with effort, when she heard a sound at the door.

'Allegra.'

She gave a tiny shake of her head, her hair tumbling over her shoulders, shrouding her face in a tangle. She couldn't bear it if Stefano was kind now; she couldn't bear to feel anything more.

He walked into the room, laid a strong hand on her shoulder.

'Don't,' Allegra pleaded in a tiny whisper. 'I can't...'

'Yes,' Stefano said, 'you can.'

She closed her eyes, clenched her fists. *No.* She wouldn't cry. She wouldn't cry in front of Stefano; she couldn't let him see all the pain and the hurt, the *mess* that was inside her. She couldn't show him how little she'd changed from the girl he'd known, the girl who had loved him so utterly, so uncontrollably...

No.

Stefano crouched down, his face level with hers although Allegra still didn't—couldn't—look at him, her hair tangling against her flushed cheeks and thankfully obscuring her vision.

Stefano's hand was still on her shoulder and with his other hand he cupped her cheek. Allegra let out a little choked cry, tried to resist as he slowly, inexorably, drew her to him.

His chest was hard and solid against her cheek, and she found herself nestling against his shoulder, her lips pressed to the hollow of his throat.

And then it came, the tide of sorrow she'd willed back for so many years, the tears she'd refused to shed or even acknowledge.

Her shoulders shook with the force of her sobs, shook her with silent, healing tremors.

She felt as if she should stop, and once she tried to pull back, to get herself under control, but Stefano wouldn't let her. He held her to him, his arms gentle yet strong, but instead of a prison it had become a sanctuary.

She felt safe. Safe and loved, protected and provided for in a way she'd never dreamed of, had never imagined possible.

Protection. Provision.

And still she cried, tears streaming down her cheeks, running into her nose and mouth, dampening her hair. She was a mess, inside and out, an open, unlovely, desperate mess, and she didn't care.

Stefano didn't care.

She'd held herself together for so long and now all the pieces were coming unstuck, the lid of that box blown clear off.

She didn't know how long she cried—a few minutes, an hour?—but eventually the tears subsided, and her body relaxed, sagged against Stefano.

He was seated on the floor, cradling her like a child, washed in moonlight.

They didn't speak for a long time. Allegra listened to the silence, heard the quiet rasp of their breathing, the beating of their hearts. Outside, darkness had settled like a cloak of velvet and she heard a wolf give a long, lonely howl.

She didn't know what to say. She wanted to apologise, but she resisted the urge to explain away what had happened or, worse, to pretend that it hadn't happened at all.

'Thank you,' she finally whispered, and Stefano smoothed her hair back from her face, tilting her chin so that their eyes met. She couldn't quite see his expression in the darkness, but she felt it.

Felt the compassion and tenderness emanating from him in warm, engulfing waves.

'How is it,' he murmured softly, 'that a woman who has dedicated her life to helping children uncover their emotions has hid hers away for so long?'

Allegra gave a trembling laugh. 'I don't know. I suppose I knew I was doing it, but I didn't...I didn't realize quite how much.'

Stefano continued to smooth her hair with careful, gentle hands. 'Tell me,' he said quietly, 'what you were crying for.'

'Everything,' Allegra whispered. Yet she knew she couldn't leave it there, knew she had to explain. Explain everything. 'For my father,' she began slowly, feeling the words, feeling her heart wrap around them. 'For how he used me, and how I know I hurt him. If I'd known he'd made so many investments, needed the money...I...'

'You would have married me?' Stefano queried gently. '*Fiorina,* it wasn't your fault. You cannot blame yourself for your father's death.'

'I know that,' Allegra said. 'At least, in my head. But my heart…'

'We can't always control our hearts,' Stefano murmured wryly.

'No. It's been easier not to think of it. To simply not think of it at all.'

'And his funeral?'

'It was too hard,' Allegra said simply. 'So I left. But it still hurt. It always hurts.'

Stefano nodded, stroking her hair. 'Yes,' he murmured, 'of course it does.'

'And my mother,' Allegra continued, quieter, calmer now. 'I know she used me. I realized it as soon as she left my father and took up with Alfonso. He was the one who drove me to the train! She wanted only to humiliate my father, and I was a means to that end, nothing more. Never anything more.' She shook her head, still cradled in Stefano's arms. 'Yet it still hurts,' she whispered. 'It hurts that I was nothing but a bargaining chip to them…' She trailed off, unsure if she should— could—continue. Stefano waited, stroking her hair, her cheek. 'And it hurts,' Allegra finally said, her voice little more than a thread of sound, 'to think that that's all I was to you. You, whom I loved most of all.'

Stefano's hands stilled, tightened, then continued their stroking.

Allegra pressed her face against his shoulder, seeking comfort from the one who had hurt her, the one who now could offer her the healing she needed. 'I loved you so much,' she whispered, her voice choking on the words, the memories. 'And that last night, when we spoke, you…you treated me like a naughty child. Like a possession, a prop. You looked at me as if I were an annoyance to you, and it felt…it felt…*horrible.*' She closed her eyes, squeezed them shut, and still Stefano said nothing. 'Worst of all,' she continued after a moment, 'is the thought, the possibility, that I made a mistake all those years ago. That perhaps I shouldn't have walked—run—away. It torments me now, the thought of what might have happened if I'd stayed.'

Stefano's arms tightened around her. 'Allegra,' he said, his voice roughened with emotion, 'you cannot think about the what-ifs. We were different people then…'

'Were we?' she whispered. '*Were we?*'

'I wouldn't have made you happy,' Stefano said after a long moment, and she heard the regret as well as the certainty in his voice and knew he spoke the truth.

He couldn't have made her happy then, couldn't have been the man she needed.

But now…? Was he the man she needed now?

Slowly Allegra tilted her head until their eyes met. Stefano held her gaze for an endless moment, his eyes searching hers.

Then his lips came down and brushed hers in the barest question of a kiss.

Allegra answered. She answered with her lips, her heart, her whole body. Her arms came around his shoulders, bringing him to her, needing his closeness, his warmth, his strength. Stefano kissed her with a sweet tenderness that shook her to her soul, her very marrow. His tongue gently explored the contours of her lips, her teeth, her mouth, and she clung to him, wanting him, needing him, needing *this*.

His touch was a balm, a blessing, and she felt herself opening up in response, blossoming like the most beautiful and precious of flowers.

Stefano broke the kiss for the barest moment, took a breath, and, lit by a sliver of moonlight, their eyes met, clashed, and something changed.

It was the space of a heartbeat or a breath, yet it felt endless. Stefano kissed her again and this time it was urgent, demanding, angry.

What had been sweet turned savage, a gentle yearning metastasizing into reckless craving.

Stefano's mouth turned hard against hers and her own hands curled into claws, bunching on his arms as fabric pulled and buttons broke and scattered.

Somehow the jar of paintbrushes was knocked to the floor and Allegra distantly heard the shattering of glass, felt a hard brush poking into her back.

How had this happened? she wondered dizzily, even as she answered Stefano kiss for kiss, each touch a brand, as if they were in a desperate race to possess one another, to punish as well as to pleasure.

Desire coursed through her, desire and anger and hurt, all flowing together into one rushing river of emotion. She felt her hands smooth Stefano's bare chest, felt her fingers curl inward, sharp, digging. She heard Stefano's surprised gasp of both pleasure and pain, and laughed aloud with a strange sense of victory.

He pushed her back, his face savage with desire as he pulled her shirt up, lowered his head. She gasped now too, her hands fisted in his hair.

His hands found her, fingers seeking, blazing along her bare skin, touching her in a way she'd never been touched and she gasped as she felt his hand on her breast, her navel, and lower still—so knowing, so intimate, so...

Wrong. This was wrong. She didn't want it like this—on the floor, hard and angry and urgent. They were both angry and they *wanted* to hurt each other.

The thought was horrible, humiliating.

How could you love someone and feel this way? How could you love someone and act this way?

You couldn't. Surely you couldn't.

Her hands stilled, her heart heavy. She didn't want Stefano to look at her, didn't want to see the pain in his eyes, didn't want to feel it in her own heart.

Yet she wanted him—*him*—the man who had hurt her, the man who could heal her.

'Stefano...' she whispered, and choked on the sound. He paused, poised above her, his own expression ravaged, his breathing ragged. They stared at each other for a long moment and then Allegra reached up and cupped his face, felt the rough stubble against her fingers.

Stefano let out a choked cry and rolled away from her, mindless of the broken glass crunching beneath him, one arm thrown over his face.

Broken. Everything felt broken.

Lying there, her clothing in disarray, her dignity in shreds, Allegra wondered if she'd imagined the tenderness, the understanding that had existed between them only moments ago. Now all she felt, all she knew, was anger and pain, hurt and fear.

And then, in the stillness of the shattered night, she heard another sound—a sound that chilled her, made her bolt upright.

Lucio was screaming.

CHAPTER NINE

ALLEGRA STRUGGLED UPWARDS, pulling her clothing to order even as Stefano did the same.

'Lucio—' she said, an explanation, and he nodded.

Stefano hurried down the corridor to Bianca and Lucio's rooms, the little boy's shrill cries still renting the air.

It was a constant, appalling, almost inhuman sound, the sound of an animal in desperate anguish.

Stefano stopped at the threshold of Lucio's room. Bianca sat on his bed, trying to cradle and comfort her thrashing child.

'Lucio,' she begged, tears streaming down her face, 'Lucio, please, it's Mama. *Mama.* Let me hold you—'

It was as if he couldn't hear her. His face was a blank mask of terror, tears streaming from his eyes, his mouth opened in a wide 'O' of endless fear and memory.

Bianca reached to hold him, but he pushed her away, his arms flailing so violently that she would have fallen off the bed if Stefano had not moved forward to steady her.

'Lucio—' Bianca tried again, sobbing.

It was a scene from hell, a scene of personal devastation and torment. There was no healing for Lucio here, Allegra thought, nothing but the overwhelming sense of his own grief and fear.

'Do something,' Stefano said in a jagged voice, and Allegra moved forward.

She sat next to Lucio on the bed, laid a hand on his trembling, jerking shoulder. With her other hand she caught his flailing fist and firmly but gently returned it to his lap, where it continued to shake.

'It's all right, Lucio,' she said in a quiet voice. 'It's all right to feel like this. It's all right to be scared. To be sad. It's *all right.*' Lucio tensed, his body still quivering, and Allegra motioned to Bianca to put her arms around him. 'It's all right,' she continued steadily. 'You don't need to stop. Your body is shaking; just let that happen. It's all right to cry. It's all right to feel.'

She felt Stefano's eyes on her, knew she was talking as much to herself as to Lucio. *It's all right to feel. It was all right to hurt.*

She continued murmuring, affirming the emotions that ripped through his body and mind with exhausting force, until at last he sagged against his mother's shoulder, half-asleep. In that last moment before he lost consciousness, his eyes flickered open and he stared straight at Allegra.

'I saw,' he whispered, his voice scratchy and small. 'I saw and I ran away.'

Allegra stiffened in shock, even as Lucio relaxed into sleep. Bianca held him, stroking his hair, tears streaking silently down her face.

'You can keep holding him,' she told Bianca. 'For a while anyway, until he's fully asleep.'

'He spoke,' Bianca whispered, her eyes round and wide. 'He spoke. What did he say? Will he…will he be…?' She trailed off, unable to voice the hope they all cherished.

'It's a step in the right direction,' Allegra told her. 'That's good.'

She turned to the doorway, expecting to see Stefano, anticipating his smile of relief, but he was gone.

Allegra moved slowly down the hallway, aching in every part of her body, her mind. Her heart.

Lucio had, she hoped, just begun his journey of healing, and maybe—*maybe*—she had as well. She wanted—needed—to find Stefano and talk about what had happened.

He wasn't downstairs; the rooms were dark and empty. She looked in the art studio, saw only scattered brushes and broken glass.

After a moment's hesitation she turned and walked to the other end of the hallway and stood in front of his closed bedroom door. She knocked.

The soft sound seemed to reverberate through the emptiness in time with her own pounding heart. She knocked again.

After a long, laborious moment Stefano opened the door. Allegra's heart sank at the expression on his face. It was one she knew well; she knew it and hated it.

He smiled faintly, his eyes blank, everything about him distant and remote.

Don't touch me. Don't love me.

But she did, she realized, she did.

'Stefano?'

'Is Lucio all right?' he asked and she nodded.

'I know it's difficult to see, but releasing his suppressed emotion is definitely a step in the right direction.'

'It was a cathartic evening for everyone,' he agreed with that awful faint smile that spoke so clearly. *Don't come in. Don't get close.*

'Stefano...' He waited, eyebrows raised, one arm braced against the door-jamb, blocking her entry. 'May I come in?'

'I don't think that's a good idea.'

'Why are you shutting me out?' she asked, and heard the pain in her own voice. 'After I let you in. *I let you in.* Why?'

He smiled, and she saw a piercing gentleness in his eyes. He touched her cheek, let his fingers drift down her face and then fall away.

Away.

'You needed to tell someone everything that you'd been holding back,' he finally said. 'Like Lucio. But what happened afterwards—between us—was a mistake. Surely you see that. It didn't...' He paused, and she filled in the blanks.

'We were angry,' she said quietly. 'It wasn't right. I know that, but—'

Stefano shrugged his agreement. 'It's a good thing we stopped. That Lucio stopped us.'

'Why?' It hurt to ask, to be so vulnerable, so needy, but she wanted to know. She needed to know. 'Why?' she asked again. 'Stefano, I don't want us to be angry, but maybe we both need to finally address what is happening between us, what we *feel*—' She wanted to cry out, *I love you,* but she couldn't. Not yet, not when he was being so distant. She couldn't bear another silence, damning and endless.

She saw something like regret flicker across Stefano's features before he shook his head. 'Allegra, we agreed to put the past behind us, to be friends. So let's leave it at that.'

'Is that what you really want?'

Stefano was silent for a long moment, long enough for Allegra's fingers to curl into desperate claws, bunching against her legs, long enough for tears—yet more tears—to sting her eyes, to pool obviously, pathetically.

Long enough for him to realize how she felt, how she loved him, and still he didn't say anything.

And when he did finally speak, she wished he hadn't.

'Yes.' And, with that single devastating word, he gently— ever so gently—closed the door in her face.

On the other side of the door Stefano leaned against the wall and listened to Allegra's ragged breathing.

He'd hurt her. He knew that, and he was sorry.

So sorry, so damn *sorry,* but it was necessary.

He couldn't let her love him, not with all that hope and faith shining in her eyes, not when she was so willing to believe— again—that he could give her what she needed.

He couldn't. He knew he couldn't, and he was glad he knew, because now he wouldn't hurt her any more.

And he wouldn't hurt.

Nothing could be gained by their relationship, he knew, because he'd learned, finally, that he couldn't make her happy. He couldn't give her what she needed; his love was worthless and he'd only disappoint—devastate—her in the end.

And himself.

It was better this way, he told himself, even as he heard her choke back a sob of misery, even as he felt the answering howl in his own chest.

He closed his eyes, willed her to go before he opened the door and took her in his arms, kissed her and told her he didn't care if he couldn't make her happy, he wanted her anyway.

And he would have her.

Go.

Stefano's hand reached for the knob, curled slickly around it. He bit down hard on his lip, his eyes still clenched shut.

And then finally, slowly, he heard her retreat, the soft, disappointed patter of her footsteps down the hall.

Away.

Stefano pushed himself off the wall, sank on to his bed, one hand raking through his hair, hard enough to hurt.

Hurt.

It was better this way, he told himself, and tried desperately to believe it.

The next morning the sky was hard and bright, the sunshine pouring in the windows, bathing the room in light.

Allegra woke up from a disjointed, restless sleep, her hair tangled and sweaty against her face, her body aching as much as her heart was.

She hadn't realized until Stefano had closed the door in her face how much she'd counted on him to love her. Love her, she realized, as he always had. At nineteen, it hadn't been enough. She'd wanted more. She hadn't wanted the reality of love, its mess and complications. She'd wanted, as her mother had told her so cynically, the fairy tale.

But love wasn't a fairy tale. Love was hard, it was messy, it was painful and miserable and it made life worth living. For wrapped up in that pain, was unspeakable joy, unshakeable happiness, and she could have that with Stefano.

If he wanted it…

She felt her own hurt heart harden. He hadn't answered her seven years ago—*Do you love me?*—and he wouldn't answer now.

Why? *Why?*

Allegra sat up in bed and drew her knees up to her chest. She'd believed for so long that Stefano hadn't loved her. It had become the bedrock of her soul, of her outlook. She'd clung to it because it justified her own actions, her own feelings.

She'd seen him tender, terrible, and everything in between, all the emotions in a tangle, just like hers were.

She loved him, and she'd fought it with every ounce of her being. What if Stefano was the same way?

What if he loved her and didn't want to? Was afraid to, even?

What if he felt just like she did?

The thought was quite literally incredible, yet it was also wondrous and frightening.

If Stefano loved her…then all she needed to do was make him admit it. Confess.

An impossible task.

Allegra shook her head. She couldn't think about Stefano, couldn't let her thoughts get in such a hopeless tangle. She needed to concentrate on Lucio and his recovery. And, to do that, she needed help.

She showered and dressed quickly before heading downstairs for breakfast. Bianca was in the kitchen and Lucio was at the table eating breakfast.

'Hello, Bianca,' Allegra greeted the housekeeper. Bianca had shadows of fatigue under her eyes but she looked happy. Relieved. 'Hello, Lucio,' she said, crouching down to meet Lucio's reluctant gaze, one hand steady and firm on his shoulder.

He was silent for a long moment, his gaze sliding away from hers, but Allegra waited. Finally he jerked his head in a greeting and whispered, 'Hello.'

Bianca beamed; Allegra smiled. 'Would you like to do art with me today?'

Another jerking nod. Allegra accepted it; it was enough. She sat down to breakfast.

Stefano didn't appear as she ate, and she didn't need Bianca to tell her that he'd returned to Rome.

He was the one running away now, she thought with a sad smile. When would he return? And what would she say? Do?

After breakfast she took Lucio up to the art studio. Thankfully, someone had cleaned up the broken glass and brushes, and Allegra wondered who it was. Bianca, being polite? Or Stefano, trying to forget what had happened between them…deny that it ever had?

'Why don't you take a look around, Lucio?' she suggested. 'Would you like to draw something? Paint? We could take the clay out.'

Lucio went tentatively to the crayons. He selected a green one and began, ever so carefully, to draw grass. A field.

Allegra watched silently as his picture, and his memory, slowly took shape. A field, a red box with black circles on one side—a tractor, Allegra realized, overturned.

And, behind a rock, a stick figure. A boy, with oversized tears, big black drops, falling from his circle of a face.

After a long moment Lucio thrust the picture at her. His face was hard, determined.

'Is this what you saw, Lucio?' Allegra asked gently. 'You saw your father in the tractor?'

His lip trembled and his eyes filled as he nodded. 'I should have been in bed…I wanted to see Papa… He looked over at me and waved…' He stopped talking, started to shake.

Allegra put a hand on his shoulder. She could guess the rest. Enzo, while waving to his son, had taken his eyes from the field, hit a rock or tree stump, and the tractor had overturned. Lucio had seen the whole thing and, terrified, had run away.

I ran away.

'Lucio, thank you for telling me. I know that was a hard thing to do. It's hard to tell the truth. But it's not your fault that your papa died, even if you feel it is. It's not your fault.'

Lucio gulped back a sob, shook his head. 'I ran away.'

'You were scared. You didn't know what to do. It's not your fault.' Allegra spoke gently, firmly, but Lucio just shook his head, unable to believe, to accept the absolution Allegra offered him.

'I want Mama,' he whispered and after a moment Allegra nodded.

'Let's go find your mama,' she said, slipping his hand into hers and leading him from the room, from the pain of his memories.

Later, when Lucio was sleeping, she spoke to Bianca and explained what had happened.

'And he saw…?' Bianca's face was pale, horrified. 'My poor Lucio! And all this time he's held it in?'

'He feels guilty,' Allegra explained. 'Guilty for being there in the first place, and then for running away. He'll need to talk to a psychiatrist, Bianca. He'll need therapy, more than I can provide, to process and accept what has happened.'

Bianca nodded. 'But do you think…in time…?' she whispered.

'The more support he's given, the better chance there is of Lucio accepting what has happened and moving on,' Allegra said, trying to keep her voice encouraging even as she felt mired by doubts.

Did anyone have a chance of accepting the mistakes and tragedies of the past and moving on? Living, loving again?

'I hope so,' she said with a watery smile. 'I pray so.'

Bianca nodded fervently. 'So do I.'

They sat in silence for a moment, the shadows lengthening, the mountains wrapped in the soft violet light of dusk.

'I'd like to go to Milan,' Allegra said after a moment, 'and talk to Dr Speri. He's a gifted psychiatrist, and he'll have some recommendations for Lucio, what course of action to take next.'

Bianca nodded. 'Whatever you must do.'

Allegra tried to keep her voice diffident as she asked, 'Do you know when Stefano will be back?'

'He didn't say.' Bianca smiled sadly. 'He looked terrible this morning, as if he hadn't slept at all.'

Allegra nodded. 'I didn't sleep much, either,' she admitted.

'What is happening? You're in love, *si?*'

Allegra was silent for a long moment. Yes, they were in love. She believed—she had to believe—that Stefano loved her. Finally she shrugged, her smile one of sorrow and regret. 'Sometimes,' she said, 'love isn't enough.'

'Love is always enough,' Bianca protested, and Allegra wished it could be true. Yet it hadn't been true seven years ago. Love hadn't been enough then, not nearly enough.

She knew, in her heart, she'd been right to run. Even though she loved him now, she could never have made Stefano happy then, and he would have made her miserable.

Funny, she thought without any humour, when she felt that he could make her very happy now, if he'd let himself. And she could make him happy—she hoped—if he let her in.

She left the next morning for Milan. Bianca drove her to the train station in L'Aquila, Lucio sitting in the back seat. It was the first time he'd been away from the environs of the villa in months, and Allegra was glad that he seemed to accept it.

The train journey took a few hours—hours which she spent leaning her head against the window, watching the barren mountains and empty fields turn to hill towns and prosperous suburbs, and then finally the busy, glittering metropolis of Milan.

She'd rung Dr Speri the previous afternoon and he'd agreed to spare her an hour to talk about Lucio.

Sitting in his office, she explained the situation, the progress Lucio had made.

'The poor boy,' Dr Speri said after she'd spoken. 'To suffer so much, and so silently.'

'I feel out of my depth,' Allegra confessed frankly. 'He needs more intensive therapy than I can provide.'

'You've done wonders, Allegra, as you did before,' Dr Speri said with a smile. 'I'm impressed.'

Allegra gave a short laugh. 'It isn't me, Dr Speri. It's the children. They reach a point where they're willing to confront their emotions and memories, and I happen to be there.'

'I think it's a bit more than that.'

Allegra smiled, but secretly she wondered if it really was. How had she been able to help children like Lucio when she'd hidden from her own self for so long?

Yet now that was going to change. She wasn't going to run away, she wasn't going to hide. She would face the truth and she would make a future.

There had been another reason to come to Milan.

After leaving Dr Speri with several recommendations for local child psychiatrists, she took a taxi to a quiet neighbourhood of tall, elegant town houses. Minutes from the fashionable Via Montenapoleone, the neighbourhood reeked sophistication and snobbery.

It was where her mother lived.

Allegra pressed the doorbell with a shaking but determined finger. She didn't know if her mother would be home; she didn't know if she wanted her to be.

After a moment she heard footsteps and wondered who would actually open the door: a harassed maid, a scantily clad lover, or her mother herself?

It was the last, looking older and harder than she had seven years ago. She was more polished, more brittle, her hair expertly highlighted to a platinum blonde, her face Botoxed, her nails long, false, and painted a glossy hot pink.

Her thin red lips curved in a knowing, mocking smile. 'Well, well,' she said. 'The prodigal daughter returns.'

'Hello, Mama,' Allegra said. 'May I come in?'

'By all means.' Her mother threw an arm out in a wide, expansive arc, ushering Allegra into her home.

Allegra moved into a drawing room that was elegant, impersonal and cold. She stood in the middle of the room while her mother sprawled on to a white leather divan.

'Go on, make yourself comfortable,' she said with a little laugh. Allegra perched on the edge of a spindly antique chair.

'I came,' she said after a moment, watching as her mother lit a cigarette and blew a long thin stream of smoke in the air, 'because I wanted to make peace with you.'

Her mother took another drag on her cigarette. 'How very touching.'

'I've been angry at you, you and Papa both, for a long time. I didn't even realize how angry or hurt I really was until recently, and I want to make it right.'

Her mother's thin, perfectly plucked eyebrows rose in disbelieving arcs. 'It must be very convenient,' she said dryly, 'to blame other people for your own mistakes.'

Allegra stared at her. 'What do you mean?'

'You aren't seriously telling me,' her mother continued, 'that you've blamed me for walking out on your poor fiancé all those years ago? You aren't, surely, going to lay all that at my door?' Her smile was so vicious that Allegra felt as if she'd been assaulted.

'No, of course not,' she said after a moment. 'I take responsibility for what I did. I chose to leave, even if you gave me a push in that direction. I almost turned back—'

'But you didn't, and you shouldn't have,' Isabel cut in. 'Allegra, you thought Stefano was your knight in shining armour. When you realized he wasn't, you deserted him. It's really that simple.'

Allegra's mouth dropped open. It was so close to what Stefano had intimated before, and yet it was wrong. *Wrong.* 'It wasn't that simple,' she said, fighting to keep her voice steady. 'The marriage was arranged and no one told me!'

'Oh, really? And you just thought Stefano appeared at your party by magic? And wanted to dance with you, be with you— you, a pathetic little frump of a child?'

Allegra forced herself to meet her mother's scathing gaze. Kept her chin held high, even though it hurt.

It hurt.

'Yes, I did,' she said. 'I realize now just how innocent— ignorant—I truly was, but I believed, and no one told me otherwise.'

'And why should we?' Isabel demanded. 'Stefano was attentive to you, kind and considerate. He might not have loved you—how could he have?—but that could have come in time.'

'Then why didn't you tell me that at the time?' Allegra demanded, her voice shaking, her composure starting to crack.

'I did,' Isabel replied succinctly, 'but it wasn't enough for you.'

'You urged me to leave,' Allegra said in a low voice. 'You told me you would have left yourself—'

'And I would have,' Isabel replied. 'I did, in the end. But your father was a very different man from Stefano. Cruel, callous and utterly unfaithful.'

'You said Stefano would be the same! That I'd be glad, in the end, if he turned to other women—'

'I was speaking from experience,' Isabel said in a bored voice. 'And what does it matter? You chose for yourself, Allegra. You chose to listen to me. Accept it.'

'Stefano treated me like a possession, a child—'

'You were a child,' Isabel said with a laugh. 'How else was he supposed to treat you?'

Allegra shook her head. 'No. It wouldn't have worked. We wouldn't have worked.' She couldn't believe that it had all been a mistake. She wouldn't. 'You might have used the situation to your own advantage to shame Papa, but I know I was right.'

'I'm so thrilled for you,' Isabel stated dryly.

Allegra lifted her eyes to meet her mother's hard, unflinching gaze. 'Why?' she asked. 'Why did you want to shame him so much?'

'Because he shamed me every day of our marriage,' Isabel snapped, and there was a savage edge of pain to her voice that Allegra had never heard before, a sound that made her sad. 'And shame him I did,' she added, gloating now. 'In front of five hundred people, sweating in his suit, humiliated beyond endurance! It was a beautiful moment.'

Allegra watched her mother smile in twisted, triumphant memory, felt the words—the realization—penetrate.

'What are you talking about?' she whispered. 'I told you— you said—you'd give my note to Stefano before the ceremony! So he wouldn't be shamed—'

Isabel shrugged. 'I changed my mind.'

'What! Are you telling me that Stefano went to the church thinking I would be there? That he *waited?*'

Isabel smiled, cruel enjoyment dancing in her eyes. 'As your father did. I didn't care about Stefano, although you obviously did. But yes, he stood there. He waited.' She laughed. 'And all of his peasant relatives waited too! I knew Stefano had money, but his family obviously grew up on a pig farm. His mother had about three teeth, dressed all in black. She looked like the worst kind of drudge.'

'Don't talk about them like that!' Allegra's voice rose in a sharp cry. She thought of the men in the village, kissing her, bestowing their blessings.

They'd been there, she realized with a sickening wave of understanding. They'd all stood by Stefano—Bianca too—and had watched him wait.

Had watched him be shamed.

She imagined the prissy shock and gloating malice of her family's snobbish friends, pictured Stefano standing still and straight as the minutes ticked by and no bride came. She wondered when he'd realized she wasn't coming, when he'd finally walked out of the church and five hundred staring guests.

The only thing that was hurt that day was your pride.

And how hurt it was! She'd never known, never realized...

'Don't tell me you didn't know that,' Isabel said in disbelief. 'How could you not have heard? George would have told you, or Daphne—'

'No.' Allegra shook her head. She hadn't let anyone speak of the wedding; she hadn't wanted to hear. 'No.'

'Then you really did stick your head in the sand,' Isabel said with an almost admiring laugh. 'Well, let me pull it out for you. Yes, he waited. He waited for hours. Even after the guests had gone, after his family told him to leave. Your father had already started drinking, demanding money, calling in his debts.' Isabel shook her head. 'If I'd realized how thinly he'd spread himself—I didn't get one euro out of it!'

'Papa *shot* himself,' Allegra said, her voice trembling, tears starting to fall.

'Yes, I know. I was there, remember? You weren't.' Isabel shrugged, unmoved. 'In the end, he was a pathetic waste of man.'

'As you are a waste of a mother! How could you do that to Stefano? To me?'

'Why do you care now?' Isabel asked coolly. 'You were perfectly content to shame him in leaving him, Allegra. Leaving him with nothing but a note—a note you couldn't even write yourself! Not one word of explanation or understanding. And yet you blame me.'

'I never wanted to hurt him,' Allegra whispered.

'Yes, you did.' Isabel's voice was forceful, violent. 'You might not want to admit it, even to yourself, not then and not now, but you did. You wanted to hurt him as he'd hurt you—treating you like a child, telling you he didn't love you. So you did it the only way you knew how—the coward's way. And I, being the gracious mother I am, helped.' Isabel's teeth were bared in a horrible smile.

Allegra shrank back. 'No.' And yet, no matter how coldly or cruelly her mother phrased it, she heard the truth. She knew it, recognised it even after seven years of self-righteous blame and denial.

She'd wanted to hurt Stefano, even to shame him. Hadn't cared about the consequences, hadn't wanted to know.

And now they were staring her down, crowding her out. Memories. Feelings. Regrets.

No wonder Stefano was angry, she thought hollowly. No wonder he pushed her away, told her he didn't want her any more. No wonder he didn't want to love her.

Why would he? Why would he, when she'd treated him so terribly? Who would sign up for that kind of love, that kind of life, again?

But he hurt me.

Yes, he'd hurt her and she needed to forgive him. And he, Allegra realized, needed to forgive her.

Only then could they go forward. Only then could love— wonderful, painful, messy love—be enough.

'Thank you,' she told her mother stiffly, 'for enlightening me so thoroughly.' She'd come here for closure and instead had the past ripped open all the more. Yet she'd needed to know. She'd hidden from the truth of her own heart for so long; she wouldn't hide from the truth of her actions. 'I won't be seeing you again.'

Isabel waved a hand with languid indifference. 'Fine.'

Allegra walked on legs that felt wooden to the door of the drawing room, then turned around. 'I feel sorry for you,' she stated in a calm, cool voice.

Isabel stared at her, nonplussed, and Allegra shook her head. 'You can't be happy.'

For a moment Isabel's face was naked in its desolate emotion, the unassailable loneliness of her life and the choices she had made. Then her cold composure returned, and she shrugged with defiant indifference.

'Goodbye, Mama,' Allegra said quietly, and left the town house.

All the way back to L'Aquila, her thoughts sifted and seethed.

Truth, memory, hurt, forgiveness.

They'd both tried to forget the past and pretend it didn't matter. But they couldn't; no one could.

The past wasn't forgotten until it was forgiven.

Forgiveness—forgiveness and being forgiven—was hard. It was messy and painful, just like love.

She closed her eyes, dreading and desiring the confrontation ahead, the reckoning that had needed to come since she'd met Stefano in the hotel foyer—no, since she'd left him one moonlit night.

It would come now. She would make it so.

Allegra took a taxi from L'Aquila back to the villa. As the old car wound its way up the twisted roads, past the half-deserted hill towns, she realized that it felt like coming home.

Home. Home was where Stefano was, and who knew when he would be back?

Yet she would wait and, if necessary, she would find him. She would do whatever it took to confront the past. To heal it.

Bianca greeted her with a warm embrace when the taxi pulled up at the villa and even Lucio came and touched her hand, smiling shyly.

Over coffee in the kitchen, Allegra explained what Dr Speri had told her.

'There is support available locally,' she said. 'He gave me the names of therapists and psychiatrists in L'Aquila, as well as grief counselling for both of you.' She smiled and squeezed Bianca's hand. 'It won't be easy, but it will be better. It will help.'

Bianca nodded. 'I never expected it to be easy,' she said. 'I am just glad that finally we can do something. Thank you.'

Allegra smiled and nodded her acceptance. She watched Lucio playing on the floor, his face still fixed in concentration, and knew it wouldn't be easy or simple.

Nothing was. Love wasn't.

'Have you heard from Stefano?' she asked, and Bianca heard the intensity in her voice and smiled sadly.

'No, but he will come back. He will have to.'

Allegra nodded, knowing that Bianca spoke with the unshakeable conviction that Stefano loved her. Yet still she wasn't so sure.

She wanted to be sure, wanted to believe, to hope, but how could she, when he'd left her without a word?

Not even a note.

Yet what she was sure of—finally, futilely, perhaps—was that she loved Stefano.

And she would tell him so.

Yet, as the days passed, the wind sharpening, the leaves beginning to flutter disconsolately from the trees, Allegra wondered if she would be given the opportunity.

Stefano had not rung, hadn't written. Hadn't come home.

She had no idea where he was, what he was doing, what he thought.

She'd spent the days with Lucio, continuing his therapy as well as travelling to L'Aquila to work with the new grief counsellor he and Bianca would be meeting together.

Lucio spoke now—few, halting words, his face still sometimes lost in shadow, transfixed by tragedy—and Allegra knew it would take a lot of time and a lot of healing before he could move on.

But she was optimistic, determined, and so was Bianca.

A week after her trip to Milan, Allegra decided to leave again. Lucio needed her less, as he was regularly meeting a psychiatrist and grief counsellor, as well as starting up again with his nursery school.

Although she didn't like to leave the villa and Lucio, she knew he could tolerate her absence for a few days…enough time to find Stefano.

She'd start with his flat in Rome, she decided. It was one of two links she had, as he'd also given her his email address.

Laying her suitcase on her bed, she began to pack for a trip that would end where? And with what?

She had no idea, only hope and the sure knowledge of her own feelings at last.

Her suitcase was half-packed and she was sorting through a few clothes when she heard her door swing open, heard the sudden, hostile hiss of indrawn breath, and before she could even turn, words of bitter condemnation, utter judgement.

'So,' Stefano said, 'you're running away again.'

CHAPTER TEN

ALLEGRA WHIRLED AROUND, shock turning her rigid. 'Stefano!'

His face was twisted with rage, with bitterness, with pain. Hurt.

'Running away,' he spat, 'without even telling me where you're going or why. I should have expected it. I've been waiting for it.'

It took Allegra's mind a moment to catch up, to realize what Stefano had assumed simply from a half-packed bag. When she realized his mistake, relief poured through, sweet and exhilarating. She almost laughed. 'Stefano, no, no, this isn't—'

'Why, Allegra?' His voice was ragged. 'Why, after all this time, can you not spare the decency of an explanation? A conversation, face to face? What are you scared of?' His voice rose on both a plea and an accusation. 'Or do you just not care?'

'I do care,' Allegra whispered. 'I do.'

'You have a bizarre way of showing it,' Stefano said. He turned away, jerking his shoulder in a shrug. 'Go, then. Go and don't come back.' And with that he strode from her room, slamming the door, leaving her alone and stunned.

She took a few calming breaths. This went deeper, required more than a simple sentence of explanation. A lot more.

It took Allegra a few seconds to gather her courage, her conviction, but when she did she was unshakeable. She stormed from the room, stalked down the hall and met him in his bedroom.

He stood by the window, head bowed in defeat, fingers fisted in his hair, and Allegra's heart ached. Broke.

Her self-righteous indignation trickled away as she knew it should have done long ago.

'Stefano, I'm not going anywhere,' she said quietly. He didn't answer, didn't even turn. 'I was…' she continued, 'I was planning on going to Rome—to find you. To tell you—'

'It doesn't matter,' he said. When he looked up, his face was blank, his voice cold. 'To tell you the truth, Allegra, I really don't care.' He turned from the window and moved past her with supreme indifference. He stood by the door and Allegra realized he was waiting for her to leave. Her mouth opened in shock.

'You do care!' she cried. 'You just showed me you cared!'

'I was disappointed,' Stefano corrected with cold disdain, 'for Lucio's sake. I thought you cared more about him and your own work—'

'No, Stefano. This is not about Lucio. It's about us. *Us.*' Allegra's voice shook. 'You don't care just for Lucio. You care about yourself. You care about me. And I'm beginning to realize that you always did.'

Stefano was silent for a long, terrible moment. Allegra stood her ground, waiting for him to look at her. When he did, her heart lurched at the sardonic gleam in his amber eyes.

'Oh?' Stefano queried softly. He raised one eyebrow. 'But I treated you like a possession, Allegra, remember? Like an *object*. You told me so yourself, you found me out.' He moved towards her with lithe, lethal grace and, although she trembled, Allegra didn't move. She would stand her ground this time, no matter what.

She wouldn't run away.

'What's made you think I care about you, Allegra?' he asked when he was just a whisper away. He reached out and touched her cheek, let his hand drift with mocking knowledge to her breast.

Allegra trembled, but she didn't move. His eyes blazed into

hers and he pulled his hand away with a sound of disgust. 'Or are you simply so desperate, so pathetic, that you've managed to convince yourself despite the evidence otherwise?'

Allegra's face flamed, then paled. She felt her fingers curl into slick fists. 'You're saying these things,' she said steadily, 'because you're angry.'

'Angry?' Stefano sounded incredulous. 'Why should I be angry? From what I hear, you've made wonderful progress with Lucio. You've done everything I asked.'

'Stefano, this isn't about Lucio!' Allegra's voice rose in a frustrated shout. She strove to calm herself, to reach him when he was trying so hard to be remote, removed. 'I told you, it's about us. And yes, you're angry. I saw it that first evening, at Daphne's reception. It was in your eyes.'

Stefano folded his arms. 'This all sounds very melodramatic,' he commented in a bored drawl.

'I felt it,' Allegra continued, 'the night after the party in Rome. The way you touched me—'

'Like a possession,' Stefano cut her off swiftly. 'As you accused me. Well, it's true, isn't it? Everything you've said is true.' His voice rang with condemnation—condemnation of himself as well as her—and it shamed Allegra. She'd believed the worst of him…always.

Except now.

'Stefano, please. Listen to me. I spoke to my mother today—'

'Cosy times,' Stefano drawled and she closed her eyes, praying for patience. She had so much to say, to ask, and it was impossible when he was like this, cutting her off before she could even begin to get close.

Because he didn't want her to get close. He didn't want to get hurt…again.

It was such a strange and humbling thought, to consider that Stefano had been hurt—truly, deeply wounded—by her actions all those years ago. And for that she had to ask his forgiveness…if he would even let her. If he would admit to being hurt, which she was beginning to doubt he would. *Could.*

'My mother told me,' Allegra tried again, forcing her voice not to waver, 'that you waited at the church for me, all those years ago.'

He gave a short laugh of disbelief. 'Of course I did, Allegra. We were getting married, remember? We'd actually agreed to meet there, funnily enough.' His eyes were hard, his mouth flattening into a thin line of anger and disgust.

'Would you believe,' Allegra asked, 'that I didn't know? That I asked her to give you my letter the evening before? I didn't want you to be humiliated in front of everyone.'

He stared at her for a long, hard moment, his eyes raking over her in judgement. 'I don't know why we're talking about this now. It doesn't matter.'

'You're right,' Allegra agreed. 'It doesn't matter that I wanted to give you the note the night before, because I still ran away. I left everyone else to deal with my mess because I was young and afraid. And selfish,' she added. 'I was selfish. When I heard you talking with my father, and then with me, it was as if you were a different man—one I was almost afraid of. And when you didn't answer me when I asked you if you loved me, I assumed you didn't.' She paused, her throat aching with the effort of this confession, spoken to a stone wall of indifference. Stefano gazed at her, arms still folded, a bored look on his face.

Why did this have to be so hard? Why couldn't he *say* something?

Yet she knew somehow that this was right, this was fitting. She'd faced his silence before and she'd run away. She'd been too afraid, too young, too silly to voice all the fears and needs in her heart, and now she would.

Now she would say everything.

'I should have told you what I was feeling,' Allegra continued. 'But I was a child, Stefano, as you knew I was. And I loved you like a child. You were right: when I saw you weren't my

perfect prince, I ran away. I couldn't face it and I ran away.'
He gave a little shrug, unmoved, and she took a breath. 'But
now I'm a woman, and I love you like a woman, and I'm not
running away.'

Something flickered across his face. His mouth twisted and
his shoulder jerked and then he spun away, stalked to the
window. Allegra watched as he braced one arm against the
window frame, his body taut with suppressed tension.

'Stefano…'

'Once upon a time,' he said in a harsh voice, 'I would have
given much—anything—to hear you say that. But not now.
Not now.'

'I know,' Allegra said after a moment, her voice trembling,
'that I need to ask you to forgive me. I know why you've been
angry, and you have a right to be, Stefano. When I think of you
standing there, waiting for me, and all your family, your mother,
the men from the village there—' She broke off, tears starting
and then streaming down her face. 'I'm sorry,' she whispered.
'I'm so sorry. Will you forgive me?'

Stefano's back was still to her. He straightened, raking one
hand through his hair before dropping it lifelessly to his side.
Slowly, sorrowfully, he shook his head. 'You're right, I have been
angry. Like you, I fought my emotions. My memories. I'd convinced myself I didn't feel anything for you, never did. I almost
believed that all I'd ever really wanted from you was your name.'

Allegra held her breath, waited.

'I almost succeeded,' Stefano continued, his back to her as
he gazed out of the window at the deepening twilight. 'I married
Gabriella and I thought I could manage it. But she made me miserable, as I told you, and I did the same to her. It was bitter then
to realize what a mistake I'd made, what a fool I'd been. I'd exchanged something I'd believed to be deep and real for something shallow and false. I didn't want a marriage simply for a
name. I didn't want a *possession.* I wanted you. I wanted love.'

Allegra opened her mouth, made a tiny breath of sound, but

realized she didn't know what to say. Stefano must have heard her too, for he continued.

'But it wasn't deep or real, was it? Because it fell apart at the first gate.'

Allegra wanted to deny it, yet she knew she couldn't. Every word Stefano spoke was true, terribly true. Their love hadn't survived the first test, and she knew it never would have survived a marriage. She'd been too young, too idealistic and impressionable. And Stefano? Stefano had had his own weaknesses, his own faults—ones that he was acknowledging now.

If only, Allegra thought, he could believe they were different now. Stronger.

'I know you believed I didn't love you,' Stefano said into the silence. 'And that I thought of you as an object. And I know now that my love was flawed. Perhaps, in some ways, I did think of you the way you believed I did. It's hard to remember now. Yet, when I saw you again, I wasn't prepared to feel anything. I still managed to keep convincing myself that I never felt anything for you, and then to see you…and want you…and know that, even though you desired me, you also reviled me.'

'I didn't—'

Stefano shrugged. 'It's unimportant now.' He straightened, and she wished she could see his face. She wanted to look into his eyes and see *something* there.

'So yes, I forgive you, Allegra,' Stefano said, 'since you seem to need to hear that. I forgave you a long time ago. I know you were young and frightened, influenced by your mother. *Da tutti i san,* I'm not a monster. I wasn't then, though I know you thought me one.'

'I didn't—' Allegra tried again, but stopped as Stefano half-turned to her.

In the lengthening shadows she saw him smile sadly. 'The way you looked at me? I knew, Allegra. I knew every thought in your head. I knew you realized I wasn't your dashing prince, and I knew you questioned what kind of man I was. Why ask me if I loved you, if you were sure?'

'*Did* you love me?' Allegra whispered and he laughed, a broken, empty sound.

'Even now you don't know? Even now you have to ask?' He turned around, spread his hands wide, his head thrown back. 'But of course you do. Because the kind of man I am, the kind of love I offer is *worthless* to you! Well, I know it. You've told me time and time again. You don't want what I have to give, Allegra. It's never enough for you. I saw that seven years ago. I realized it when you asked me those questions, when you looked at me as if somehow I could make it all right again. And I knew I couldn't. I never could.' His voice was ragged, his eyes bleak with a despairing knowledge. 'And I can't give it to you now. You've shown me, you've told me. Even moments ago...' He broke off and rubbed a hand over his face. 'I came back from Rome to tell you I loved you, and you seemed to have already guessed it, but it doesn't matter. It doesn't matter. So why are we putting ourselves through this? We won't work, Allegra. Love isn't enough.'

It was what she had said to Bianca, what she'd believed, yet now she knew it wasn't true. Knew it with her heart, soul, body and mind.

Love was enough.

'Love is enough, Stefano,' she said, 'when it comes with honesty, like we're being now, and with forgiveness. And all the other things you can give me, that you've already given me. You showed me how you love when you took me in your arms and wiped away my tears. And before then—when you look at Lucio. When you embraced those men. When you spoke about your family. Stefano!' Her voice rang out clear and strong. 'Your love is enough.'

He began to shake his head, but she stopped him. She crossed to him, certain now, her doubts and fears falling away in the light of the one simple truth that made all the difference:

they loved each other. She knew it now, saw it in Stefano's eyes, felt it in her own soul.

They loved each other, and it was enough.

It would be.

She stood in front of him, stood on tiptoe to cup his face in her hands. She felt the stubble on his cheeks, glinting gold in the settling dusk, and felt with her thumbs a dampness near his eyes.

'The only question I have to ask now is this,' she said softly. 'Is my love enough for you?'

Stefano gave a small, choked cry of assent, then reached up to press her hand against his cheek. Allegra blinked back tears as he dropped his hand to pull her into a closer, deeper embrace.

'Yes,' he whispered. '*Yes.*'

She'd never felt so comforted, so safe—so protected, so provided for—than she did in the shelter of Stefano's arms.

They stood that way for a long time, silent, still, and utterly content, as twilight settled softly over the villa, cloaking the distant peaks in a soft purple light that brought peace to the world.

Everything was different this time. Allegra stood in the vestibule of the tiny church and smiled at her reflection. Instead of ruffles and lace, she wore a simple silk sheath in palest ivory. Her hair was down, tumbling over her shoulders in a cascade of sunlight, and diamond teardrop earrings sparkled at her ears.

She felt a small hand tug on her dress and she looked down and smiled at Lucio. He smiled back shyly and ducked his head.

Lucio had been in therapy for three months and he was doing much better. The strides were slow but they were there, and Allegra was thankful.

She was thankful for so much.

There were only a handful of people in the church for the ceremony. No glittering names or faces, just a few friends from the village, Bianca and Lucio, and another couple of people from London. Neither of them wanted a spectacle.

They wanted a ceremony—simple, sacred.

It was enough.

'Are you ready?' Bianca's father, Matteo, stooped and in a wrinkled suit that smelled faintly of mothballs, stood by Allegra's elbow.

'Yes,' she said, and took his arm.

The organ played music, but Allegra barely heard it as she walked down the narrow aisle of cracked stone. Stefano stood at the end of it, dressed immaculately in a charcoal grey suit, his hands folded at his front, love blazing from his eyes.

Allegra's heart swelled and she almost stumbled, still, after all this time, not used to heels.

Matteo steadied her and she walked firmly the rest of the way to stand proudly by Stefano's side.

Both of their voices rang out with clear purpose as they said their vows.

'Noi promettiamo di amarci fedelmente, nella gioia e nel dolore, nella salute e nella malattia, e di sostenerci l'un l'altro tutti i giorni della nostra vita...'

We promise to love each other faithfully, in the joy and the pain, the health and the disease, and to every day support each other in our life.

Allegra knew they both meant it, every word.

They had a wedding supper at the villa, and then Bianca left with Lucio to spend the night at her father's. Stefano had wanted to take her to a hotel, somewhere luxurious and opulent, but Allegra simply wanted this—to be home, *home,* with him.

She stood by the window where they'd found each other at last just over three months ago and watched as darkness crept over the mountains. She'd never tire of the view, she thought, watching as the first stars twinkled on the jagged horizon.

Stefano came to stand beside her, his hands on her shoulders. He bent to kiss the nape of her neck, and Allegra shivered with pleasure.

She turned to face him and he kissed her, deeply, with a passion that was tender and yet powerful in its force.

She looked up at him, into his eyes, saw the light of his love shining there. There were no shadows, no flickers, no doubts, no fears. No anger.

'Come,' Stefano said, lacing his fingers with hers, and with gentle purpose he led her to their marriage bed.

* * * * *

THE ITALIAN PLAYBOY'S SECRET SON

Rebecca Winters

Rebecca Winters, whose family of four children has now swelled to include three beautiful grandchildren, lives in Salt Lake City, Utah, in the land of the Rocky Mountains. With canyons and high alpine meadows full of wild flowers, she never runs out of places to explore. They, plus her favourite vacation spots in Europe, often end up as backgrounds for her Mills & Boon® novels because writing is her passion, along with her family and church.

Rebecca loves to hear from her readers. If you wish to e-mail her, please visit her website at: www.cleanromances.com.

CHAPTER ONE

"Two more laps and it's yours, Cesar."

Nothing was ever "yours" until you crossed the finish line with the best time, but he didn't say that to his crew chief talking to him through the mic in his helmet.

"You're coming up on turn four. Watch out for Prinz. He's starting to make his run."

"I see him."

"Rykert has hit the cement wall. There's debris. Go inside."

Cesar made the correction. Coming out of the turn he saw what was left of Rykert's car. Smoke poured from it like a genie escaping a bottle. Then his heart failed him as part of Prinz's chassis flew at Cesar out of nowhere. Zero hope of escape. This was it.

"I'm a dead man."

No sooner did the words leave his mouth than the impact of gut-crunching debris tossed him in an arc across the track. He experienced blinding flashes of light before being sucked into an acrid-smelling black vortex.

"Cesar?"

He felt hands on his shoulders, shaking him gently.

"Cesar?"

Cesar de Falcon, known as Cesar Villon in the Formula 1

racing world, awakened gasping for breath. His torso was vibrating like a jackhammer. He saw his doctor leaning over him with a concerned look in his eyes.

"You're all right, Cesar. Your nightmares about the crash have begun. Do you remember any of them?"

"No." Everything from after a tire change at his last pit stop until he awoke in a hospital in Sao Paulo was a complete blank to him. He lifted an arm to wipe the perspiration off his forehead. His body was lying in a pool of sweat.

"I'll see you're bathed and changed immediately."

While Cesar waited for his heart rate to slow down, two of the nursing staff came in to clean him up and change his bed. Then his doctor was back.

"They left your breakfast, but I see you haven't touched it yet."

Still shuddering from the nightmare of a crash he couldn't remember, the last thing he wanted was food. "Feed it to some poor devil who gives a damn."

What he needed was a pill to keep him awake so he wouldn't have to experience another night of nameless terror like last night. But being awake proved to be equally horrendous.

He lay on his back, unable to move his legs.

Dead from the waist down.

Six years before his heart had also died. His demise was now complete.

"Your physical therapy *must* begin today."

One bronzed arm covered his eyes. "Why?"

"Surely I shouldn't have to point out that you need to keep up your strength in order to get through it." The doctor spoke as if Cesar hadn't said anything. "Putting it off any longer won't help you walk again," he said as he took Cesar's vital signs.

Cesar grabbed the doctor's hand to prevent him from doing anything more. "It isn't going to happen. Save your speech for someone who's gullible enough to believe it. Don't you understand? Look at me!" The cords stood out in his neck. "I've lost my body and my mind."

"You're only feeling that way because your nightmare is still upon you. But believe me—you're alive and well in every other way. I've told you repeatedly it's too soon to tell if there's permanent damage to your spine. After that crash on the track, it's a miracle you're in such good sha—"

"Get out, *dottore!*"

The rage in his voice sent a shudder through Sarah Priestley's body. She'd been standing outside the hospital room door. The doctor had left it open, making it possible for her to see and hear Cesar for herself so she'd know what she was up against.

Though she didn't speak or understand Italian, his violent response revealed the depth of his despair. Sarah cringed, unable to imagine what life must be like for him now.

As the doctor came out of the room, he took her aside. "Cesar had a very bad night. I'm positive he was dreaming about the crash, but he couldn't recall it when he woke up. It's his mind I'm worried about. He needs to remember in order to help the healing process. Everything else is good. His body is strong and healthy, which is vitally important in his case.

"Unfortunately he won't stay that way long if he refuses to eat or get started on crucial therapy. He's like a wounded animal that won't let anyone come near."

"Then he's got to be lured out of that dark place where he's living," she whispered, sick at heart for him. Until now he'd walked away from his other track accidents without severe injury.

Sarah had always feared there would come a time when the law of averages caught up to him. Now that day was here…

The doctor nodded for her to go in, but his expression said that she entered at her own risk.

Risk was right!

But Sarah had to do this. Yesterday she'd flown from San Francisco to Rome with her son, Johnny. A taxi had taken them to their hotel. From there they'd come straight to the hospital.

After being denied information or access to Cesar since he'd declared himself strictly off-limits, she'd made an appointment to talk to the doctor. But until he'd seen Johnny with his own eyes, he'd refused to discuss the case with her. At that point he was forced to concede that Sarah and Cesar had a history together and agreed to tell her what he knew.

To her dismay she learned Cesar had refused all visitors, including his parents and brother who were starting to panic. If there was an important woman in his life at the moment, the doctor had no knowledge of her. Cesar had demanded to be left alone.

With the exception of his private personal hospital staff brought in to take care of the absolute basics, he'd been given his wish. Since being flown to Italy after the ghastly crash on the racetrack in Brazil a week ago, Cesar had gone downhill steadily. No one could get through to him.

"Is it true then he's suicidal?" she'd asked the doctor yesterday, dreading the answer. "I heard it on television, but I didn't believe it. That doesn't sound like Cesar. He's a fighter."

The doctor frowned. "He's in a severe depression. Frankly I'm worried he's reaching that stage."

She shuddered. "Tell me about his injury."

"The chain of nerve cells that runs from the brain through the spinal cord out to the muscle is called the motor pathway. Normal muscle function requires intact connections all along that pathway. Cesar's has been damaged in one area, enough to have reduced the brain's ability to control the muscle movements in his legs.

"After studying all the X-rays, I have reason to believe it's only badly bruised. In time there could be nerve regrowth. Therefore he needs to be undergoing physical therapy to retrain his limbs. It will maintain and build any strength and control that remain in the affected muscles."

"Then it's not impossible that he'll get feeling back!"

"No."

That was all she needed to hear. "Does he know he has everything to live for?"

The doctor nodded. "But his mind—despairing and traumatized by the nightmares—is keeping him from believing it."

"How soon can I see him, Doctor?"

He eyed her speculatively. "Your visit could be the kind of shock therapy Cesar needs to provoke a reaction from him. I'll arrange it for tomorrow morning."

"Thank you." It was worth anything if she could pull him out of the black sinkhole burying him alive.

"I'm counting on you, Signorina Priestley," he murmured in a grave tone.

Little did the doctor know she was counting on *Johnny*...

If Sarah hadn't witnessed for herself Cesar's precarious mental state in front of the doctor just now, she might not have found the courage to follow through with her plan. But the situation called for drastic measures.

One of the nurses named Anna was keeping her son company at the nursing station down the hall. She spoke enough English to communicate with him. When it was time, Sarah would get him and bring him to the hospital room. Of course that depended on Cesar...

After taking a fortifying breath, she stepped over the threshold into his territory.

A thin sheet covered the lower half of his body where he lay flat in the bed. Sarah could hardly tell he'd been in a crash, one that neither he nor the two other drivers could have prevented. It had sent all of them to the hospital. Cesar had been the most seriously injured.

Her heart quaked. *Cesar—my love—*

His millions of adoring fans located throughout the world would be horrified to see the great Cesar Villon, five time world champion of the Formula 1 Grand Prix, lying helpless in a hospital bed, unable to move his legs. The cruel media had already predicted he was crippled for life.

He was part Italian through his mother's titled Varano family, and part Monegasque through his titled father, the Duc de Falcon of Monaco. Between a week's growth of black beard and his black curly hair more unruly than usual, the thirty-three-year-old race car driver was the epitome of the ultimate, dashing, aristocrat bachelor.

With his eyes closed, the black lashes against his gorgeous olive skin accentuated the bruised hollows beneath, the only surface evidence of the crash's impact. It was a miracle he'd survived something that had demolished the fabulous race car his engineering brother Luc de Falcon had designed several years ago.

Called the Faucon, the French name for falcon, toy manufacturers had made a facsimile of it. Her son had a collection of miniature Formula 1 race cars, but he prized his daddy's Faucon. In fact he was the keeper of the scrapbook they'd kept about his famous father. He pored over it every night before saying his prayers.

When she was a few feet from the left side of Cesar's bed, she finally found the courage to speak. "H-hello, Cesar." Her voice faltered.

His eyes flew open.

The last time she'd seen him in person, they'd been a beautiful, translucent gray burning with desire for her. These eyes were the color of a dark funnel cloud that had touched ground, destroying everything in its path.

Her mouth went dry. She couldn't swallow. "I-it's good to see you again after so long," she stammered.

At thirty-three, he was more attractive than ever. But the

low, menacing curse that escaped his bloodless lips was evidence that Sarah was the last person Cesar had expected to see walk into his room.

She supposed it was at least something that he still recognized her.

The last time they'd been together she'd been twenty, and proud of the fact that she'd never cut the hair that had hung down her back to her waist.

Six years later it was now styled in a jaw-length feather cut, bringing out the oval of her face, and dark fringed eyes.

Time had added curves to her slim, five-foot-seven body. His narrowed gaze took in all of her. Heat filled her cheeks to realize he knew every centimeter of what lay beneath the soft crepe dress in periwinkle covering her figure. If anything, he looked repulsed by her.

This was so much worse than she'd imagined, and Sarah had thought she'd imagined the worst—

"You once asked me to join you in Italy." She took a fortifying breath. "Until now there was a good reason why I didn't."

"Your timing's off," sounded the frigid voice before he closed his eyes against her.

Clearly this conversation was over as far as he was concerned.

Though she was terrified of the change in him, she held her ground. "I disagree. The next racing season doesn't start until March. That gives you seven months to recover from this temporary setback. There couldn't be a better time for my visit."

"Go away, Sarah." She could feel his white-hot rage boiling beneath the surface.

"I'm glad you still remember my name."

Another Italian curse pierced the air. Anyone else would have flown from the room by now, but she was on a desperate mission.

"Surely you're not taking back the invitation you once extended me."

"Get the hell out of here—"

All pretense of civility had fled.

While his brutal demand bounced off the walls of the room, his dark head had turned away from the entrance. He'd closed his eyes, undoubtedly believing he'd scared her off for good.

"I don't pity you, you know," she persevered. "The doctor told me you're going to walk again. In truth, I came for an entirely different reason."

Any sensible person would have stayed away, but she wasn't just any person, sensible or not. She'd given birth to Cesar's son. Now was the moment for them to meet.

Heaven help me, her heart cried as she stood there shaking from the inside out.

"Maybe you don't remember what you said to me the morning after we made love, but I do. You said, Sarah? With two more races coming up and the extra practice time I need to put in testing out a new tire, you and I won't be able to be together again like this for a couple of months.

"'When I'm free, I'll send for you to join me for two weeks in Positano like we talked about. After that I'll have to get ready for a race coming up in France, and after that Spain.'"

She shifted her weight nervously. "I would have come for those two weeks, but by the time you phoned me to make final plans, I had just learned some news that would alter both our lives forever."

Another unintelligible epithet escaped his lips.

This was it.

"I—I discovered I was…pregnant."

This brought his head around. His eyes opened to slits. "Pregnant with whose child?" he lashed out, his words dripping acid.

It was hard to breathe. "Yours."

He swore savagely. "Tell me another story. I took precautions."

"I know, but my obstetrician told me no protection is a hundred percent. In case you wanted proof, I brought the results of his DNA with me."

"His?"

"You and I have a little boy, Cesar. He looks so much like you, the nursing staff can't get over it."

In that instant she heard his breath catch in shock.

"I have a *son?"*

Despite his fragile state and his anger toward her, she'd heard unmistakable joy in his voice just now. He couldn't disguise it. That was all she needed to know to carry out the rest of her plan.

"Yes. Since his birth, it's been just the two of us. He's at the nursing station waiting impatiently to meet his famous father."

His face paled. "If this is some kind of joke—"

"It isn't! I swear before God. Give me a moment and I'll be right back with him."

When Cesar didn't tell her no, she hurried out of the room. Johnny saw her and came running toward her. "Hi, honey." She swept him into her arms, wanting to cry out in pain for Cesar who'd been through too much. But she couldn't break down in front of Johnny.

"Did you talk to daddy?" he wanted to know immediately.

"Yes."

"Does he want to see me?"

She hugged him tighter. Cesar's cry of amazement still rang in her ears. He wanted to see Johnny all right. "Of course he does!"

"Is he very sick?"

"No. With a lot of exercise he's going to be fine." *He had to be.*

Johnny seemed satisfied with her answer.

The first time he was old enough to ask about his daddy, she'd explained that his father didn't know about Johnny because he'd gone away long before he was born.

As time wore on and he grew more curious, she told him about Cesar and showed him pictures. She assured him that when the time was right, she would take him to meet his busy father. Finally her son was going to get his wish.

She looked down at Johnny, hoping against hope this first meeting wouldn't end in disaster. Two precious lives were at stake here. Both were so vulnerable. If anything went wrong now…

With her heart racing like the engine of Cesar's Formula 1 car, she took hold of Johnny's hand and they started down the hall toward his hospital room.

Maybe Cesar was in the middle of a dream…

He *had* to be dreaming. His hands balled into fists.

Long ago he'd dispatched memories of Sarah Priestley to the ends of the universe. In the intervening years he hadn't known where she'd gone, or what had happened to her. She'd killed all his feelings for her.

What he'd experienced just now had to be her shadow left over from his nightmare.

You and I have a little boy.

No…

Impossible…

Once upon a time when he'd been wildly in love with her, he'd wondered what it would be like to see her pregnant and watch her beautiful body undergo the changes. But before his imaginings had had the barest hope of becoming a reality, she'd dealt him the death blow.

Right now he needed something strong to blot her out permanently from his subconscious. Panicked, he reached for the button to call the nurse. In the process of doing so he heard a slightly husky feminine voice say, "Honey? This is your daddy."

With those words Cesar's head snapped around. He opened his eyes. There she was again, this time accompanied by a child.

A boy.

A Falcon, as he lived and breathed.

Solemn gray-blue eyes stared at Cesar for the longest time. "I didn't know you had a beard, Daddy. You look different."

Oh, Johnny—

"My papa Priestley says hair makes your skin itch."

Sarah saw the stunned expression on Cesar's face. It prompted her to say, "The doctors have kept your daddy so busy trying to help him get better, he hasn't had time to shave yet. Maybe that's why he's a little grumpy. Kind of reminds me of you when you haven't had enough sleep."

The tension in the room was so thick, she almost lost courage to finish the long overdue introduction. Never would she have imagined it happening under these emotionally perilous circumstances.

"Cesar? I'd like you to meet your son. His birth certificate lists his name as Jean-Cesar Priestley de Falcon, named after you and your father Jean-Louis. Around our house he's known as Johnny Priestley. Your Italian mother will probably call him Giovanni.

"We flew all this way to tell you we're sorry you were hurt in that accident, but we know that pretty soon you're going to be all better."

"Yup," Johnny said. His troubled eyes remained fastened on his father. "We saw you crash on TV. Somebody said you died—" his voice trembled "—but Mommy said you didn't. She promised I could come to see you."

Cesar sat up in the bed abruptly. His action drew her attention to his hard-muscled body covered by the flimsy hospital gown. She noted with satisfaction there was nothing wrong with his reflexes above the waist. He had the most stringent workout ethic known in the racing world. A hundred sit-ups a session was nothing for him.

Though she'd tried to prepare him, Sarah could tell he was so astonished, he still couldn't speak.

"Do your legs hurt?" The fearful question asked in total innocence couldn't have helped but move Cesar who was examining his son in utter disbelief.

Like a man with shell shock he gave a barely perceptible negative shake of his head.

"That's good. Can't you talk?" Johnny asked in alarm.

Sarah saw incredulity in Cesar's eyes before they softened and he said, "Come closer," in a husky voice.

She held her breath as Johnny slowly let go of her hand and walked to the edge of the bed. In a deft masculine movement, Cesar reached for him with those strong, bronzed arms and lifted him onto his lap.

While they studied each other, no conversation passed between them. Both were too fascinated to be aware of her.

Sarah had lavender-gray eyes. They produced the flecks of blue in the gray eyes she and Cesar had bequeathed to Johnny. Her sable hair mixed with Cesar's black hair combined to give their curly headed boy his unique dark hair color.

The rest of him was Cesar's contribution. Besides his olive skin, Johnny possessed enough of the de Falcon and Varano genes in his aquiline features to scream paternity simply by looking at him. He was on the taller side for his age. Talk about Cesar's little lookalike—

"Was that crash scary?" Johnny sounded like he was going to cry, but he was manfully holding back the tears.

She heard Cesar clear his throat. "It happened too fast for me to be scared," he explained in the heavily accented voice that still haunted Sarah's dreams.

"Last week I was riding my bike and crashed into a fire hydrant."

"Did it hurt?" Cesar asked.

"Yes. See my scab?" He raised his pant leg to his knee for his father to inspect. "Mommy put a bandage on it, but it came off."

"That was a pretty big fall."

Johnny nodded. "I cried. Carson told me I was a crybaby."

"Is Carson your friend?"

"Yes."

"Sometimes you can't help it."

"I bet *you* didn't cry."

There were other ways of crying, but Johnny was too young to realize his father was hurting inside. Anxious to change the subject Sarah said, "Do you know what, honey? The doctor told us we could only stay a few minutes. We need to let daddy rest now. He's not used to visitors."

"But, Mom—"

"Johnny's my son, not a visitor," Cesar interjected in that authoritative tone instinctive to him. His acknowledgment of ownership had the undeniable ring of possession. The reaction was so much more than Sarah could have hoped for.

A suntanned hand lifted to tousle the smaller head of dark curls in a fatherly gesture. Johnny was the kind of boy any father would kill to claim for his own. "I'm not in the least tired."

"See, Mommy? Daddy wants us to stay."

Her plan to shock Cesar out of his damaging psychological torpor had succeeded. But this was only the first step. Once she was alone with Cesar, he would take out his fury on her. He had every right.

She didn't expect him to forgive her for keeping their son a secret all these years. Never that. However she was confidant he wouldn't exact his revenge in front of Johnny who'd already seduced his father by simply being the adorable, handsome son of his loins.

Her gaze flicked to Cesar. "If you're really not too tired, do you mind if I eat some of your breakfast? We left the hotel early, and I'm afraid I'm hungry." In actuality she felt faint and reached for an orange, needing the sugar. While she started to peel it, her fingers trembled.

"I'm hungry, too!" Johnny chimed in. "We both had tummy aches this morning, Daddy."

"Is that so," he muttered, but Sarah heard him.

"Yes. I guess your tummy hurts, too," Johnny said, eyeing the full tray.

Cesar had just found out that little boys have big eyes as well as ears.

Sarah extended the roll plate. Johnny took two of them and bit into one. "Mmm. This is good. Here, Daddy."

She was secretly delighted to see that Cesar had little choice but to accept the other roll and take a bite.

"I don't like hospitals," Johnny declared. "Do you?"

"No." The one syllable answer told its own story.

"Do you have to stay in here a long time?"

While she held her breath waiting for the answer she heard Cesar say, "As a matter of fact I'm planning to go home before the day is out."

After Cesar's outburst with the doctor, she could believe it. Knowing how much he loved his freedom, he would feel like a caged animal in here. If she'd arrived a day later it would have been much more difficult to track him down...

"Do you want to come to our house?" came the timid question.

She could hear Cesar's mind working. "In Carmel?"

"Nana and Papa live there. Mommy and I live in Watsonville. In a *town house*."

Close enough to be near the grandparents, far enough away from the racing world for no one to ever make the connection between Johnny and his legendary father.

Avoiding Cesar's probing gaze she said, "Here's some grape juice for you, honey."

"Thanks." He drank several swallows. "Do you want some, Daddy?" His purple moustache was so cute.

"I think I do."

The sight of Johnny seated on Cesar's lap with the two of them drinking from the same glass melted Sarah's heart.

Would knowing he had a son force him to realize he had someone else to live for now? Someone who loved him without qualification? The doctor had said Cesar was fast losing the will to live.

Please, God, let Johnny be the inspiration Cesar needed to dig deep inside himself and fight his way back to a quality life, whatever that might be.

While Sarah finished eating the orange slices, Johnny started asking Cesar questions about the buttons on the remote. Soon he'd pressed all of them. He loved the one that raised the head of the bed so his father could rest against it. Cesar didn't seem to mind.

Suddenly an older nurse appeared in the room. Her eyes widened to see how totally things had changed since Johnny's arrival. Cesar said something unintelligible to her. She nodded as if she were in a daze, then left in a hurry.

"How come you talk different?"

"Because people here speak Italian," she answered. "Your father also speaks French and Spanish, Johnny."

He looked over at her. "We speak American."

"No, honey. We speak English."

Johnny pondered everything and then turned to his father. "What did you say to that lady?" Sarah wanted the answer to that question, too.

"I told her to bring me a razor."

Johnny's eyes lit up. "Can I watch you shave?"

"You'd like that?" Cesar sounded amused.

"Yes!"

Sarah made a snap decision. "Since shaving is a guy thing,

I'll slip out to the rest room down the hall to wash my hands, then I'll be right back. Is that okay with you, honey?"

"Yes."

If she'd left him with anyone else, Johnny would have run after her. Instead she'd gotten an unworried response because he was with his remarkable father at last. For the moment all was right with his world.

As she was leaving the room, she heard him tell Cesar, "Mommy was going to take me to see you race, but you crashed in that other race first."

Johnny had held her to the promise she'd made him to get all three of them together at the U.S. Monterey Grand Prix taking place next month. He'd been living for it. But the accident in Brazil had changed the timing.

Her heart thumping painfully in her breast, she hurried down the hall to the ladies' room. Thankfully no one else was inside the lounge part. She only made it as far as the upholstered banquette before sinking down on it.

It was one thing to suffer guilt over having kept the knowledge of their son from Cesar all these years. The burden had been unbearable, but to see the two of them together at last—to see and feel how much he wanted Johnny and how much Johnny wanted him, deepened her anguish to the point where she felt she could die of remorse.

Sarah hugged her arms to her body, rocking back and forth. What had she done?

"If I were in your place, I would never be able to forgive me, either, Cesar. I don't deserve to live, but that's my punishment." In torment she buried her face in her hands and sobbed.

When the tears finally stopped flowing she lifted her head. On trembling legs she got up to rinse her face and try to repair the damage from her breakdown.

Once she'd refreshed her lipstick, she felt more in possession of herself and left the lounge. The doctor was waiting for her at the nursing station with a pleased expression on his face.

"Your boy is responsible for a minor miracle happening this morning, Signorina Priestley."

"I know." She wiped her eyes, still shaken by the encounter with Cesar after all this time. If the doctor only knew the worst was yet to come.

"You didn't arrive here any too soon. Cesar plans to leave the hospital today."

"I heard him say as much to Johnny."

"You must convince him he *has* to get started on a regimen of physical therapy. At this juncture every minute he works on his recovery is vital."

"I realize that. Unfortunately I have no influence over him, but it's possible Johnny's existence will provide the needed incentive."

"It has already. Wanting to shave is an indication he's coming back to life."

"You're right. Thank you for everything you've done for him."

"He's an icon in my country. What a tragedy if he lets this experience defeat him."

"Not if Johnny and I can help it." She shook his hand before heading for Cesar's room. Almost at the door she met the nurse coming out with the empty food tray. Johnny didn't like eggs, so Cesar must have eaten them. Even if he'd only done that to humor his son, it was better than nothing.

When Sarah walked inside, the first thing she saw was a clean shaven Cesar talking on the phone in rapid-fire Italian from his bed. His transformation back to the physically arresting man she remembered made her breath catch.

She felt his searing glance on her features. Anyone could tell she'd been crying, but it would mean less than nothing to him. Why should it?

He was sitting in an upright position against the mattress. Even without the use of his legs, he had a virile presence that turned her limbs to water.

Johnny stood on a chair pulled up next to him. When he saw her he cried, "Look, Mommy—" He was playing with the electric razor lying among the loose hair that had fallen on the table and settled across Cesar's lap.

A boy toy, one he'd never seen around their town house.

Without saying anything, she took it from him and rolled the table away to clean everything up. In the process she noticed a few gray hairs among the black, evidence that Cesar was six years older than the last time they'd been together. She was six years older, too, and had the stretch marks to prove it.

But the years had only added a few character lines to his face, enhancing the dark, handsome looks every female fan went crazy over. Sometimes she couldn't believe he'd desired her enough to make love to her all night long. Not until she looked at Johnny, who would be a heartbreaker like his father when he was all grown up.

"Johnny?" his father asked the second he'd ended his cell phone call. The name sounded so different when he said it in his heavy Italian accent. "I need to talk to your mother in private. You met Anna a little while ago. She's going to come and take you down to the hospital restaurant for a treat. You can have anything you want. How does that sound?"

"Will it take a long time for you to talk to Mommy?"

Cesar's eyes swerved to Sarah's with piercing intensity. They seemed to say that the answer depended entirely on her. "Not too long."

"Promise?"

"Promise."

"Okay."

With perfect timing, the attractive young nurse poked her

head in the door. "*Ciao,* Johnny. Come with me. We will get a soda. Is that good?"

He nodded and jumped down from the chair.

Sarah gave him a little hug and walked him to the door. "See you in a few minutes, honey."

The nurse smiled at Sarah, sending her a private message that she'd keep him occupied as long as possible. "I will take good care of him."

Johnny looked up at the other woman. "You don't have to take good care of me. I can do it myself."

Anna laughed. "You sound like your papa. You look like him, too!"

When they left, Sarah shut the door. A shiver swept through her body. For the moment she was enclosed in the room with a man whose enmity reached out to her like a living thing.

CHAPTER TWO

"I MUST confess that if I'd put in an order for the perfect son, I couldn't have imagined any child as marvelous in every way as Johnny," he began in a deceptively silken voice. "But for the crash, it begs the question whether I would ever have known him otherwise…"

"Cesar—" She turned to him. Sarah had thought she could handle this, but now she wasn't so sure. "I—I planned for you to meet him when you came to Calif—"

"Basta—" He cut her off abruptly. "The only thing I care to discuss with you is our son's future. You've had everything your own way all this time. He's bonded to you. I could take him away from you legally. In case it has slipped your mind, I have more financial resources than your father ever dreamed of having. But it would destroy Johnny and he would hate me for eternity. And I want equal rights over my child.

"For his sake the only solution is for us to marry."

Marry?

"No, Cesar—"

"No?" he inquired in a lethal tone.

She shuddered. "I mean, let's not talk about that right now. I—I know you despise me and you have every right. As for your family, they would never approve. The important thing here is—"

"For me to get well?" He snarled the question. "No doubt that's the fairy tale you've been reading to him since the accident last week, but it's never going to happen. By bringing an innocent child to my bedside and telling him I'm his father, you've put something into motion no one can undo now."

"I know that. Please listen to me—" she cried, trembling uncontrollably. His words had filled her with new fear, but Cesar was beyond noticing her reaction, or if he did, he didn't care.

"He's seen me in the flesh. He knows beyond any doubt I exist. To *not* make him an official Falcon, my legitimate heir, would be a mortal sin I have no wish to carry to the grave. I leave the heinous sin of omission to weigh on your seductive shoulders, *bellissima*."

"It *does* weigh, Cesar. More heavily than you can imagine. But you never wa—"

"Never wanted marriage before?" he lashed out. "Is that what you were going to say?" A red flush had broken out beneath the skin on his cheeks. "The man you thought you once knew doesn't exist. That man could plant his seed in you and grow a *son!* That man could walk!"

His dark, frosty eyes glittered with rage. "The person you see before you would have to slither off this bed using his arms in order to drag his useless appendages close enough to reach you. Even then he would have to swipe at your legs to bring you down to his level so he could wrap his hands around the slender column of your beautiful white neck and strangle you for what you've done."

Her horrified gasp brought a cruel smile to his lips. "But I can think of a much better way to wring down retribution on your head. Johnny tells me there's a *nice guy* named Mick who comes to the town house *all* the time."

Knowing the erroneous construction Cesar had already put on that information, Sarah's hands curled around the nearest chair back for support.

"Mick sells 'surance," Cesar imitated their son to perfection. "He comes to dinner a lot and he brings me toys. After I go to bed he stays and watches movies with her."

"Mick's a friend, Cesar. Nothing more," she said quietly. "You know I had never been intimate with a man before you, and there's been no one else since." Sarah couldn't. There was no man to equal him.

A frightening curse escaped his throat. "And this is supposed to absolve you of any wrongdoing?"

"No— I'm only trying to explain about Mick because Johnny isn't old enough to understand yet."

"In that case neither you nor Mick should be bothered by any headlines the tabloids will print about our soon-to-be union. 'Nun marries eunuch after nonimmaculate conception six years earlier.'"

"Cesar—" His spirit was so black, she didn't know how to reach him.

"That's how the fairy tale reads, *cara mia.* Lest you've forgotten, let me refresh your memory.

"Once upon a time an enticing red-hot commoner with amethysts for eyes and dark flowing tresses, made incredible, passionate love with her words and her body all night long to a fool of a race car driver who happened to be the second born son of a duc.

"Alas, a curse was put upon them for indulging in such rapture. After she awoke from giving birth, she was no longer possessed by the cravings of the flesh and hid their son away. This was all accomplished unbeknownst to the second born son of the duc who awoke from his fiery crash to discover he was no longer a man."

"Stop it, Cesar!"

His menacing grin crucified her.

"Stop what? The truth? Something you never had the

remotest possibility of telling until the pileup?" he ground out in a murderous tone. "You haven't heard the rest of this tale.

"The son grew up wondering if he had a father. 'Of course you have one,' his mother said. 'He's the one you can see on TV. They're pulling him out of that heap of rubble, which used to be three race cars, and they're taking him away in an ambulance. How would you like to go to the hospital and get a good look at what's left of him?'

"'In case his injuries are life-threatening, we wouldn't want him to die before you have a chance to call him Daddy at least one time, would we? I couldn't possibly live with that on my conscience.'

"'What's a conscience, Mommy?'"

Cesar leaned forward on his fist, ready to lunge at her. "I'd like the answer to that same question," he snarled. The tendons stood out in his bronzed neck. "Where was it when you first had an inkling you were pregnant? Did you ever once give it the slightest thought that I had the right to be *told?*"

Feeling faint she cried, "Do you think I haven't suffered every minute of every day and night for holding this back from you? But you are the Duc de Falcon's son, the world's greatest Formula 1 race car champion who'd had his career planned out for years before we met. A career that allowed no impediments to interfere. No wife, no children. *Niente*—you said. That meant nothing and no one!

"I was seventeen when I first heard that come from your very lips. It was the same litany you repeated every time we saw each other including the night you took me to bed." She swallowed hard. "Those same words came out of your mouth as you slid out of our bed before leaving for your next race in France."

He looked as if despite his injuries he might well leap off the bed to shake her or worse. "Knowing I used protection with you, do you honestly think I would have blamed you if you'd told me we were expecting? One little phone call,

Sarah. Just one. All I needed to hear were two words. 'I'm pregnant.'"

She shook her head while hot tears trickled down her cheeks. "At twenty years of age I was convinced those two little words would have brought embarrassment to your family and changed everything for you.

"I didn't want you to think I was one of those women who was out for anything I could get from you. And you'd convinced me that without total focus, your world standing as a champion would have been jeopardized."

A terrible sound emerged from his throat, frightening her. "Compared to our child being born, my career wins over the past five years mean *nothing* to me. How could you have professed to know me so well, yet not understand the most basic, elemental needs of my makeup?"

She groaned in pain. "I thought I did, but you're right, Cesar. At twenty years of age I had a fatal flaw that prevented me from taking my parents' advice and coming to you. I should have. I'll regret it for the rest of my life, but at the time I didn't even tell them the truth until I started to show.

"Mom and Dad gave me more than one lecture, so please don't blame them. To quote Daddy he said, 'Cesar shares equal responsibility in this. Anytime you sleep with someone, you take the risk of getting pregnant. Cesar knows that. He may be the greatest Formula 1 racer in recent history, but that doesn't absolve him of anything!'"

"Your father was right!" Cesar ground out.

"I know that now, but six years ago you had a race coming up in another month. I was terrified what the news might do to you, so I promised Daddy I would tell you when the time was right.

"He said, 'Cesar will always be preparing for another race. *Now* would be the time to tell him a new career has opened up, one fashioned expressly *by* him, *for* him! Your child will need him.'"

A terrible sound came from his throat. "And still you didn't come forward."

"I wish I could make you understand," she cried. "You'd been enjoying unprecedented success on the circuit. I—I didn't see how you could straddle fatherhood and racing without it affecting your career in precarious ways. I didn't want to be the reason your dreams were dashed, not after the way you'd talked so passionately about your plans.

"I—I couldn't do that to you or our baby who would be the real victim. Our child would suffer from only seeing you once in a while—that is if you wanted to be a father to it."

"*If* I wanted?" he raged, shaking his dark head.

Tears streamed down her face. "I was wrong, Cesar. Totally and completely wrong. My parents told me I'd live to regret it, but in the beginning I held back because I believed it was the right thing for both you and Johnny.

"In order not to cause you any embarrassment, I stayed away from anything to do with the racing world. No one knew about my past association with you.

"I thought maybe you'd come to my parents' home the next time you were in the States, but you never did. I took that as proof you never had the depth of feeling for me that I had for you."

"The way we left it, you were supposed to phone *me,* remember?" His voice sounded like thunder. "After waiting and waiting only to hear nothing from you after six months, why in the hell would I come around looking for you?"

"You wouldn't." Sarah couldn't prevent the sob that escaped. "There were so many times I started to phone you, but I lost my courage. By the time Johnny turned three and started asking questions about you, I determined to take him to Monaco so he could meet you. I had the tickets and was ready to fly over when I read in the tabloids about your involvement with a pregnant woman. It was another ugly scandal I refused to believe, but this time the woman turned out to be your brother Luc's fiancée, Cesar!"

His eyes were filled with pain and rage.

"I honestly didn't know what to do then. In case the baby turned out to be yours, I—I was afraid to fly there with Johnny and complicate matters. So I waited to hear. The time stretched. But there came a time when I realized I couldn't put Johnny off any longer and promised him we'd see you at your next race in Monterey.

"To my horror, you crashed on the track in Brazil before you could fly to California." Tears gushed from her eyes once more. "You'll never know the depth of my pain, Cesar." Without conscious thought she put a hand on his arm. "I'm devastated over what I've done to you."

His eyes bore holes into hers. "Devastated doesn't cover it." In a withering gesture he removed her hand. "I've missed out on Johnny's first five years of life." A bluish white ring had formed around his lips. "I want them back, but since that isn't possible, I'm demanding the rest of them. We're going to get married here at the hospital in a little while."

She wiped her cheeks with her palms. "No one can get married that fast."

He sucked in his breath. "*I* can. It's all been arranged."

As the man he was he could cut through his country's horrendous red tape, even produce a license on the spot.

"But you don't want to marry me," her voice trembled. "You never did or—"

"Or what?"

"N-nothing. It doesn't matter," she whispered.

He stared at her through shuttered lids. "I want my son. I'll do anything to have him, even if it means marrying his mother. After what you've denied me all this time, being condemned to bondage with a man who doesn't desire you—who couldn't do anything about it if he wanted to—might just be a suitable penance for you. Maybe there's some justice in this world after all."

She shook her head. "Take it out on me all you want, but don't let Johnny see how you feel when he's with us. The nurse will be bringing him back in a minute. He's so sweet and loving." Her voice broke.

"You mean the way you used to be?" he sneered. "It's strange. Once upon a time I thought I knew you."

"I guess we've both changed," she said in a raw tone. "You used to have a competitive spirit that nothing and no one could conquer."

"That was before I was put out of commission permanently."

"There's no definitive proof yet," she argued. "The doctor explained that yo—"

"I haven't finished," he said in a voice of ice. "There's only one reality. I'm paralyzed, so we'll start at that point with our son and go from there. I realize my being like this is repugnant to you, but *he* seems to be handling it well. With no expectation comes no future disappointment."

"You don't mean that!" Her heart couldn't take much more. "The doctor believes you'll walk again with hard work and therapy. So do I!"

He swore violently. "You'd better not have fed that lie to Johnny. Have I made myself clear?"

So crystal clear, he'd sent her into shock.

What she'd done to him was unconscionable. But for Cesar to have given up on himself gave proof of a dark side that terrified her. This couldn't be the same man she'd once known and would have given anything to marry.

She'd come to Rome nursing the faintest hope that when he saw Johnny, his anger toward her would soften. At least to the point where they could reason things out together for their son's welfare.

Instead she'd been met with an ultimatum that would bring her nothing but grief no matter what she did. The last thing in the world Cesar wanted was a wife, but he had to take her if he wanted his son. Ironically he was forced to offer marriage to the only person on earth he truly despised.

Sarah had no choice but to meet Cesar's demand. This situation wasn't about her. She knew that. It was about a father and son who needed each other in the most elemental of ways and deserved to know each other's love.

Johnny's happiness was on the line. There'd been too much hurt being deprived of his daddy all this time. To keep them apart now would create an untenable situation that would destroy three lives. She couldn't bear any more guilt on that score.

Sarah was desperate to make recompense, and vowed to dedicate the rest of her life to him and their son.

"Mommy? Daddy?"

Johnny came running into the room before Anna could stop him. Sarah thanked the other woman before shutting the door. Once the three of them were alone, Johnny ran over to the bed. "How come you talked so long?"

Cesar held back deliberately. He was waiting to hear her say the words that would make her son's dreams come true. Johnny looked at her for the answer.

She moistened her lips nervously. "Your father and I had a lot to discuss, honey. H-he wants us to be a family."

"Like Carson's?"

"Yes." Carson had a mother and father who lived together. "Would you like that?"

He blinked before turning to his daddy once more. "You mean you're going to *live* with us?" The wonder in his voice brought tears to Sarah's eyes. She could only imagine what Cesar must be feeling right now.

"You and your mommy are going to live with *me*. In fact I insist on it."

"Hooray!"

Without conscious thought her gaze flew to Cesar whose eyes remained veiled in front of their son. Like black ice they hid his full fury. She'd caught some of it while they'd been alone. Whenever he got her on his own again, he would unleash a little more and a little more.

Her legs shook. The thought of living with him under these circumstances petrified her.

Not so Johnny who was gazing at his father with pure joy. "Where's your house?"

"You mean *our* house." Johnny nodded with happiness. "We have two houses."

"Two?" he cried in astonishment.

"That's right. One is in Monaco where my parents and brother live."

"Is that far away?"

"Pretty far. We'll go there soon and visit your de Falcon relatives."

"Mommy said I have a grandma and a grandpa, and an uncle Luc."

Cesar's eyes flashed in surprise. "That's right. He and your aunt Olivia have a little daughter named Marie-Claire. She's your cousin."

"Can I play with her sometime?"

"Of course. But for right now we're going to our other house. It's here in Italy in a town called Positano. It sits way up on a hillside overlooking the ocean."

"I *love* the ocean."

"Then it's settled."

Six years ago Cesar had asked Sarah to join him in Positano for a two-week vacation. That seemed a century ago.

Cesar leaned toward Johnny. "Have you ever flown in a helicopter?"

"No. Have you?"

"All the time."

"Is it scary?"

"Were you scared on the plane?" Cesar countered with another question.

"Nope."

"Then you don't need to worry about flying to the villa with me."

"What's a villa?"

"That's another name for a house."

Johnny was ecstatic. "When can we leave?"

"Right after your mother and I get married."

His eyes rounded. "But we're in the hospital."

"This hospital has a chapel downstairs on the second floor. Our family priest is coming to officiate. Tell you what. While your mother goes back to the hotel for your bags, you can help me get ready."

"I *want* to help!"

Judging by the sudden telltale sheen filming Cesar's eyes, their darling boy had already worked his way into his father's heart.

"In that case, push this button and the nurse will come and organize us."

Johnny reached for it. "Okay. I did it!"

This was Sarah's cue to leave. She gave her son a kiss on the cheek. "I'll be back in a little while."

He nodded, but it was clear Johnny had much more exciting things on his mind. Getting a father had to be at the top of the list.

"Don't be long."

Cesar's warning almost made her stumble. As she was going out the door, two male nurses came into the room. With Cesar's fiery gaze on her retreating back, she was glad to be able to escape, if only to remove the tension for Johnny's sake.

By sending her to the hotel alone, it was clear he wasn't

taking the chance that she would change her mind and disappear with their son. Surely he knew she would never do that, otherwise she wouldn't have dreamed of bringing Johnny to Italy in the first place.

She left the hospital and took a taxi to the Bernini Palace Hotel about a mile away. Her packing didn't take long. Not knowing how long they'd be in Italy, she hadn't brought many clothes for either of them. Certainly nothing appropriate to wear at her own wedding. Yet she didn't dare hold up Cesar's schedule by shopping for an outfit. To add more crimes to the unforgivable one didn't bear thinking about.

However she'd forgotten that August was the heavy month for tourists pouring into Rome. While she stood in line waiting to check out at the reception desk, she was tormented by her inability to help Cesar understand her frame of mind six years ago. The wall between them was too impenetrable.

Edward Priestley, Sarah's father, was the owner and CEO of the Quenchers soft drink company who'd built the Quenchers racetrack years earlier. It was near Carmel-By-The-Sea.

After the Formula 1 races, he always feted the top racers at their home in Carmel, a Spanish style hacienda overlooking the ocean. It was there that race aficionados gathered with the winners for celebrity photo shots and publicity.

Sarah had been going to the track with her parents and elder sister, Elaine, since she was a little girl. Having grown up with a father who lived and breathed racing, she knew his opinion about romantic entanglements with racers.

"Enjoy their talents, but keep your distance from them," he'd warned his girls. Her mother had said the same thing.

Elaine had listened, but the warning had gone right over the head of a young and foolish Sarah who hadn't taken their advice to heart until it was too late. At the age of seventeen she met Cesar Villon for the first time and developed a painful crush on the dashing twenty-four-year-old race car driver.

From that time on she followed his brilliant career and kept a scrapbook on him. Anything she could find in print about his life whether professional or personal. Whenever he was in the States for a race, he came to the Priestley home where she monopolized his time.

With each visit he sought her out and seemed to enjoy being with her more and more, often staying over at a hotel for several days. During those thrilling interludes they would take long walks along the surf together. Other times they went swimming and boating.

Whatever the activity, they never seemed to run out of things to talk about. She found herself pouring out her heart to him. He shared his dreams with her. Over time her feelings grew into a full-blown love that would never go away.

Cesar had dreams to win seven world championships. Seven was the magic number for him, a higher figure than anyone else in racing history. Then he would quit the circuit and run his business interests. At that point he would take on a wife and family who deserved his full attention.

Though she listened, she didn't really take it in. By the time she turned twenty, she didn't *want* to believe he would stay single that long. Her dream was to become his wife and bear his children as soon as possible.

So she continued to ignore what he kept telling her and played with fire until one night they made love. The experience changed her life forever.

But all he said was that she was the most wonderful girl he'd ever known, and he would make time for her in between racing schedules. Yet again he had reiterated that he had his career mapped out, and couldn't allow anything or anyone to interfere. Otherwise he might as well quit racing because family and Formula 1 didn't mix.

After their night of passion, she'd thought he would miss her so much that he would eventually change his mind and come after her. In her naivete she assumed he couldn't live without her, as she felt she couldn't live without him. She waited in vain for a declaration of love from him, let alone a proposal of marriage.

Two more races in two and a half months went by before he phoned to invite her to come to Italy for a two-week vacation. He'd prepaid her round-trip airfare.

Round-trip...

By then fate had thrown her a curve she hadn't anticipated. She was pregnant with his child, a child she adored from inception. It seemed part of her dream was now realized, but not the way she'd envisioned it. Cesar wasn't her husband nor likely to be in the near future.

If she told him the truth, she had no idea what he'd do. Some men would offer marriage because they were honorable and would want to give their child a name. As far as she was concerned, Cesar was honorable. But he came from a titled family in Monaco. Their prominence guaranteed they wouldn't be thrilled to learn a no account American girl was carrying one of the future heirs to the Falcon dynasty.

In all probability, Cesar would do what he could for their baby financially, but it would fall short of a full commitment. Any contact between them would be behind the scenes, when he was between races. Sarah didn't want her child's heart broken by a phantom father who showed up one day and went out of it the next.

What did she really know about Cesar? One thing was certain. Any feelings he had for her would die or turn to resentment because the pregnancy would have created complications that prevented him from achieving his goals. Too late she'd finally accepted that he'd really meant what he'd been saying all these years. He intended to stay single until he walked away from his career.

For the baby's sake, she knew what she had to do and

turned down his invitation. She used the excuse that she couldn't leave college right then. In truth she had been close to graduating. Her biology classes went in a series and she couldn't afford to miss a course or she would have to repeat it the following year.

At first the line had gone quiet on his end. When he finally did speak, his disappointment sounded deep, if not profound, probably because he wasn't used to any woman turning him down. If he'd begged her, she would probably have lost her resolve to stay away, and would have flown there to tell him the news.

But unhappy as her words made him, he didn't try to persuade her otherwise. Instead he told her college was important and he understood. Therefore he would wait for a phone call from her when she could arrange to go on vacation with him.

He ended the conversation with, "I miss you, *bellissima*. You have no idea how much I long to have you here with me. Call me at the end of this semester and we'll work things out to be together."

Sick at heart, she realized a reunion with him would only last until the return date of the next round-trip ticket. Sarah had to face the bitter truth that he wasn't in love with her to the point that he couldn't live without her.

Now that he'd tossed the proverbial ball in her court, she could phone him back and tell him that he was going to be a father. But the news would change his world.

How could he possibly focus on his career with a new baby needing his attention? Cesar required total freedom to get ready for each race. Such a distraction could severely affect his concentration. His career wasn't like other men's. Until she felt the right time presented itself, she would wait to tell him the truth.

But as it turned out, she never talked to him again.

After graduation she moved out of her parents' home in

Carmel, and rented a small town house in nearby Watsonville where she found a job in an insurance firm. When she couldn't hide her pregnancy any longer, she told her parents who showed no surprise. They knew how much she loved Cesar.

Her mother's sad smile devastated Sarah because she'd urged her to stay away from Cesar when she could see what was happening to her daughter. "Besides having a powerful mistress you can't fight, he's an aristocrat whose family has already chosen someone suitable for him to marry. He'll only be trifling with you. If you're not careful, you're going to get hurt, sweetheart."

Sarah *had* gotten hurt. It was self-inflicted because she hadn't been able to stay away from Cesar. If she felt like she was a widow who'd never been a wife, she had no one to blame but herself.

But the hurt she'd inflicted on Cesar and her son by her silence went so much deeper there was no comparison. She couldn't give them back those years.

Sarah had done irreparable damage. How had she dared to play God with their lives?

With hindsight she could see and understand things she hadn't been capable of six years ago. Back then she'd been too young and immature. Too self-absorbed. She'd never given Cesar the chance to make a decision one way or the other.

She could thank providence it hadn't been too late for her to toss him an unexpected lifeline this morning in the form of his child. Perhaps the only one he would ever father. As for Johnny, he was safe at last in the arms of the daddy he'd always wanted.

But if Sarah had thought this reunion could wipe out those years of guilt and regret, she could think again.

No man could love the woman who'd done this to him. As for Johnny, one day when her son was older he would perceive what she'd done to be selfish and cruel. He would come to resent her, even dislike her for keeping him apart from his father all that time. The gulf between her and the two men she loved beyond all else would never be bridged.

Just deserts for the hell she could look forward to.

CHAPTER THREE

CESAR had asked one of the staff to run out and buy some things for him and Johnny. After being helped to get dressed in a new suit and tie, he picked up his phone again. He'd already made the necessary calls to get everything underway for the ceremony. Now he needed to alert his housekeeper to his plans.

While Johnny occupied himself with some paper and colored pens Anna had brought him, Cesar rang the villa.

"Pronto?"

"Bianca?"

"Cesario—" The sixty-five-year-old woman broke down and wept. "I've been to mass every day praying for you."

Touched by her motherly concern he said, "Someone upstairs heard you."

"You mean you can walk?" she blurted. "Your parents haven't told me the news yet. Not even your brother, Luca."

"No, no, Bianca. That isn't going to happen. No one knows what I'm about to tell you except my doctor."

And Sarah of course.

His free hand crushed part of the bed sheet into a wad. When he'd invited her to come to Italy all those years ago, he'd believed she loved him with the kind of love a man would be lucky to know in one lifetime. She was his darling

Sarah, a woman different from all the others. When she came, he would tell her… He had plans for them…

A curse flew from his lips. So much for that fiction. Now that he'd learned she'd kept his son from him all these years, he realized he hadn't known her at all. How could she of all people be capable of this kind of cruelty?

"It's a blessing you're alive," Bianca insisted.

His blindly loyal housekeeper had always been a rock he could count on. Now it seemed he was going to have to rely on her and her husband Angelo more than ever. "Can I trust you to keep the most important secret of your life?"

"You insult me with that question!"

"*Mi dispiace,* but it's vitally important none of this gets out, not even to the family. Something could leak to the paparazzi. No one must get wind of this until I'm ready for the world to know."

"No one will learn anything from us."

"*Grazie,* Bianca."

"What is it?"

"My plan is to fly to Positano in a few hours, but I won't be alone. I need you and Angelo to organize the staff and get rooms ready for two people who will be living with us."

"I'll see to everything immediately. It's good you're coming home where you can be waited on. This house has been empty too long."

"Get prepared to hear the patter of little feet from now on."

"Little feet?"

"*Si,* Bianca. A five-year-old boy named Jean-Cesar Priestley de Falcon." But for a slight difference in hue, he had Sarah's eyes.

After a pause, comprehension dawned on Bianca. She let out the gasp Cesar had been forced to hold back when Sarah had presented their son to him.

Exactly.

"His mother will be with us."

"Ah—"

Ah… Six years ago his housekeeper had been witness to the shape he had been in after the phone conversation with Sarah that had thrown him into a black void. No one but Bianca and Angelo could have put up with him back then.

"*A presto,* Bianca."

He hung up, his mind still on Sarah whose omission constituted an unforgivable sin in Cesar's mind, but he couldn't fault her for the name she'd given Johnny. Saying it out loud to the housekeeper had filled him with an inexplicable sense of pride. Cesar's parents wouldn't be able to contain their joy.

His brother, Luc, would be blown away to know Cesar had a son older than Luc's.

As for Cesar's best friend and cousin, Massimo was the only person who knew anything about Sarah. In a few days he would phone him in Guatemala and tell him the monumental news.

Until Cesar had seen the son of his flesh and Sarah's, he hadn't wanted to go on living…

Incredible to realize she had become pregnant without either of them realizing it. Of course she and Johnny were indispensable to each other. You didn't break up a mother and child.

If he wanted his son with him day and night, he had no choice but to marry her. For Johnny's sake Cesar was determined to make this wedding special enough that his son would always remember their first memories together with happiness.

The thought of being legally wed to a woman as deceitful as Sarah was anathema to him, but he had to admit she was an amazing mother.

Johnny might be his own spirit—he might have an innate charm all his own—he might possess the kind of good looks and intelligence any man would want in a son, but Johnny's excellent behavior and manners, his breeding, his politeness, his sweet sensitivity and kindness—all those things could be laid at the feet of the woman who'd raised him.

If Cesar were honest with himself, he could see in his son the things he'd loved about Sarah at seventeen.

When she'd first appeared in his hospital room, Cesar figured he was having an irreversible mental collapse, the kind you didn't survive. But after she'd come back in again, everything changed.

Within seconds of seeing that precious five-year-old face and looking into those mirrors of the soul staring at him in such rapt curiosity, Cesar had felt an energizing force surge through his nervous system bringing it back to breathtaking life.

"Mommy!" Johnny cried as Sarah entered the room once more, causing Cesar's gaze to swerve toward the door. He'd been waiting for her return so they could get the ceremony over with and fly away from this claustrophobic prison. She carried two medium-size suitcases.

He was still stunned at the change in her. In six years the enchanting girl he'd lost his head over had turned into a mature woman he hardly recognized without her silky dark hair hanging down her back.

With her standing there on those long shapely legs, he was forced to concede she'd grown into a voluptuous beauty. The birth of a baby did that for some women. It galled him to have to admit he couldn't take his eyes off her, particularly when he was appalled by what she'd done to him… To them…

Sarah felt Cesar's daunting scrutiny and trembled. "I'm sorry it took me so long."

"An hour and a half to be exact," he muttered.

"I know, but the line at the front desk took forever." She put the bags down against the wall.

"We're ready to go get married, Mommy."

When she lifted her head, her breath caught. Cesar had

been helped to a wheelchair. But in the midnight-blue silk suit and impeccable white dress shirt he was wearing, all she saw was the gorgeous, dashing figure of the race car driver she'd fallen in love with years before.

No one seeing him like this could imagine him having an injury that prevented him from walking. In the left lapel he wore a white rose. The contrast of color against his fabulous olive skin and black hair set her pulse racing.

"Here, Mommy. This is for you." Johnny ran across the room to hand her a small paper box. Only then did she notice him dressed in a new dark blue suit and white shirt Cesar had arranged for him to wear. In the left lapel he, too, was wearing a white rosebud.

The sight caused her heart to swell. "Thank you, honey. Don't you look handsome!"

"Daddy and I look alike."

"You surely do." You're the two most beautiful men in the world.

She glanced down to see a corsage of white roses beneath the clear cellophane top. "How lovely!" she exclaimed as she drew off the cover.

"Daddy wants you to wear them."

Cesar wheeled himself over to her. "Lean over and I'll put it on you."

While he drew the corsage from the box, she did his bidding. Her heart was thudding so hard, she knew he could see it by the movement of the material covering her chest. Because the blood was thundering in her ears, he could probably hear it.

As he fastened the flowers to her shoulder, his deft, suntanned fingers brushed against her body. She closed her eyes tightly, afraid to breathe. Through the thin fabric, the heat of contact against her skin had set off an explosion. It sent out shock waves to every atom and corpuscle.

"Are you okay, Mommy?"

His child eyes didn't miss a trick.

"I'm fine."

"Then how now come your eyes are closed?"

"I—I didn't realize they were." She opened them only to discover Cesar's mere inches from hers. The mocking glint told her he knew exactly how his touch affected her. He knew how his hands and mouth and body had always driven her mad with desire.

"Let's go," he said seconds later in a deep, thick toned voice and put his hands on the wheels.

"I'm ready." Johnny stood behind him and helped push the wheelchair toward the door. Anyone else would think they were playing a game, that Cesar was pretending to take a ride to amuse his son. Sarah walked behind them. For her the moment was bittersweet to see Johnny helping his father.

On their way to the elevator they had to pass in front of a flank of hospital staff waiting to offer their congratulations to a man whose name and fame was renowned throughout Europe, particularly in Monaco and Italy. Everyone was in tears. Even the doctor. He sought Sarah's eyes and lifted two thumbs up to her in private salute.

Sarah noted the large number of security guards everywhere. It reminded her that the hospital was sitting on a story that would earn millions of dollars for the media once the public was informed.

Racing and royalty were a dynamite combination, but add the element of the paralyzed playboy bachelor who'd kept his wife and child hidden for six years, and the story would grow legs that marched around the world.

Soon they reached the second floor. The ornate interior of the small chapel surprised Sarah. Everything about Italy, from the style of the buildings and statues to the seductive quality of the language, thrilled her.

An old priest in formal robes urged the three of them forward. "Come closer," he said in English. Except for the hospital staff who stood in as witnesses, they had the chapel to themselves for the ceremony.

When they reached him, he leaned down with a smiling face to shake Johnny's hand. "I baptized your father after he was born. To think he has such a fine son to present on his wedding day. What's your name?"

"Je-Jean-Cesar Priestley de Falcon."

Fighting tears, Sarah cast a covert glance at Cesar. She thought his eyes looked suspiciously bright just then. Their son had said it pretty faultlessly for a five-year-old American boy who'd only had a few coaching lessons from his father in the last hour or so.

"Well Jean-Cesar, it's a pleasure to meet such a wonderful young man. I know you will always be a great comfort to him, especially now while he is recovering from his ordeal."

"Will you bless him so he can walk, Father?"

"I've already done that and will continue to pray to God for him. But it's also up to you, and your father, and your mother, to make the miracle happen."

His raisin dark eyes lifted to Sarah's. He studied her for a long moment and then they traveled to Cesar's. "A strong family is the greatest medicine on earth. Courage, my children, and you'll come out the conquerors. Let us pray."

Before she lowered her head, Sarah saw Johnny and his father bow their dark heads in obedience. Once the priest had offered up beautiful words of hope, he told Cesar to take her hand.

He reached across the arm of the wheelchair to grasp hers. The moment had an air of unreality as they exchanged vows to honor, love and cherish each other in sickness and health all the days of their lives. How many times had she dreamed of this very moment?

But under vastly different circumstances.

"I now pronounce you, Sarah Priestley and you, Cesar Villon de Falcon, husband and wife from this day forward. What God has joined together, let no man put asunder. In the name of the Father, and the Son and the Holy Spirit, Amen." He made the sign of the cross.

"Amen," Sarah whispered.

Johnny let out a big sigh. "Are you married now?"

"We are," Cesar muttered in his deep voice.

"Where's Mommy's ring?"

"At the villa."

"Oh." After pondering that answer he said, "Aren't you going to kiss each other?"

"Yes," Sarah spoke before Cesar could. To save him any embarrassment she leaned down and pressed her lips to his. The gesture made everything seem real enough to the onlookers. But Sarah's heart shattered into pieces because it felt like she was kissing a cold, stone wall.

The second she lifted her head, Cesar grabbed Johnny and pulled him onto his lap. He turned and threw his arms around Cesar's neck. They clung to each other. Two dark curly heads pressed together. Sarah could hardly breathe for the emotions attacking her from all directions.

"You're officially my son now. We'll never be apart again." He kissed the top of his head. "Are you ready for that helicopter ride?"

"Yes."

The priest asked them to step to the back of the chapel where they needed to put their signatures to the marriage documents. When that was done, she shook hands with him. "Thank you, Father."

He turned her to the side away from Johnny and Cesar. "I've known your husband all his life. He guards his heart well." It appeared the priest had seen the truth of the situation with that kiss. "Be patient through the dark times ahead. One day the sun will come out."

Sarah wanted to have his faith, but the words "one day" plunged her to a new threshold of despair.

A group of hospital workers escorted them to another elevator that took everyone to the roof. At five-thirty in the evening, the heat from the sun was almost too much. She walked toward the medical helicopter where she watched an attendant help Johnny inside. Two other workers lifted Cesar.

One of the ground crew stowed her bags onboard while another man helped her inside and handed her the throwaway camera. He'd been the one to take pictures during the wedding ceremony. She thanked him before strapping herself in.

Cesar had put on a pair of sunglasses, reminding her of the many newspaper photos showing the dashing race car driver after another win, or walking along the street in company with an international beauty.

He looked fabulous in his wedding clothes. Before he caught her staring, she quickly flicked her gaze to Johnny. Even without their matching colors, anyone seeing them together would immediately notice the unmistakable resemblance.

"Are you excited, honey?"

"Yup."

His smile didn't fool her. He was scared, but he'd never admit it in front of his father.

Sarah had ridden in a helicopter with her parents when they'd gone to Hawaii, but it was much smaller and built for sightseeing.

The pilot and copilot nodded to her, then the blades began to rotate. At this point she knew Johnny was ready to jump out of his skin. So was she, but for an entirely different reason. Cesar must have sensed his fear. The minute there was liftoff, she saw him put a hand over Johnny's on the armrest.

"This is how it felt the first time I drove around a track in a race car, *mio piccolo*. After a minute I got used to the sensation. Keep your eye on me and everything's going to be fine."

Johnny took his father's advice and looked up at him. His sweet little expression so full of trust in spite of his apprehension, spoke to Sarah's heart.

In a few minutes they'd left Rome and were traveling in a southerly direction. At his father's urging, Johnny finally dared to glance out the window. The sight was so spectacular he forgot to be afraid.

For the next half hour everyone in the helicopter was treated to his bursts of excitement shouted between comments only a child would think to say. The look of fatherly pride in Cesar's eyes, the sound of his low laughter as he responded to his son's unique observations was something Sarah would cherish forever.

The helicopter followed the Amalfi Coast, renowned as one of the most glorious regions in all Italy. Years ago Cesar had borrowed her laptop to show her a map of the whole area including the picturesque town of Positano. He'd pointed to the spot where his villa was located, giving her a graphic description of what to expect when she vacationed with him there.

But nothing prepared her for the breathtaking view assaulting her eyes as they drew closer. The town spilled over the flowering hillside like it had tumbled from the top to the blue bay below, leaving the pink and white, square-shaped Moorish houses almost on top of each other.

"Mommy— See all those cars? They look like tiny bugs marching to war."

She was so captivated by the town's beauty, it took her a minute to realize Johnny was talking about the bumper to bumper traffic lined up along the coastal road as far as the eye could see. Nothing seemed to be moving.

"Good heavens! It looks exactly like that, honey."

"The locals try not to drive here during the summer

months," the pilot commented. "This is the only way to see everything."

"You're right," she whispered, uncomfortably aware of Cesar's silence. No doubt he was thinking of the thousands of moments he'd missed out on by not being with his son.

With those dark lenses, she couldn't tell if he was looking at her or not. But she didn't need to see his eyes to know he felt something deeper than hatred for what she'd done.

"Where's our villa, Daddy?" Johnny was a fast learner.

Cesar leaned closer to him and pointed. "See that pink one on top of the hill?"

Johnny pressed his nose to the window. "It looks like a palace!"

It did. Even down to the number of security men to guard Cesar's privacy.

A low chuckle escaped Cesar's throat. "It's too small for a real palace. Do you like it?"

"I love it!"

Images started to flood her mind in contemplation of what it would have been like if she'd joined him in this paradise six years ago. She wouldn't have been able to hold back telling him she was expecting his baby. And then what?

She hadn't had an answer to that question back then, but she did now. Cesar was overjoyed. His instant transformation from bachelor to father was total. It had happened in a twinkling of Johnny's worshipful gray-blue eyes focused on his daddy.

"We're ready to land," the pilot informed them.

Cesar sat back, but she noticed he'd grasped Johnny's hand and held on to it until after the helicopter had touched ground and the whirring of the rotors slowed down. Who needed whom the most?

The helipad formed part of a small clinic on the east side of the slope. Outside staff took over to help transfer Cesar from the helicopter to a waiting ambucar. Sarah thanked the pilot before she and Johnny climbed inside after him.

She gave Cesar a furtive glance, noting the way his jaw had hardened. After being touted the king of speed for years, to now require assistance from trained health care workers would drain every ounce of that indomitable will just to accept help.

On his own level Johnny showed an uncanny understanding of what was going on inside his father. He patted his smooth shaven cheek. "Are you okay, Daddy?"

Cesar rubbed the back of Johnny's neck. "With you here, how could I be anything else?"

Sarah forced herself to look out of the window. *Keep saying that, Cesar. Keep believing it and you'll get through this stronger than ever.*

Before she and Johnny had made their appearance, Cesar had planned to leave the hospital. But he hadn't anticipated returning home with his own child in tow. This had to be a surreal experience for him.

The driver started up the car. Within seconds they were winding their way along an impossibly narrow lane that climbed past several luxury villas.

After negotiating a hairpin turn, the car slowed down and pulled into a private driveway half hidden by massive overhangs of flowers in shades from shocking pinks to blues and purples. The gate opened to allow them entrance. Soon they drew to a stop at the rear of the pink villa they'd seen from the air.

"We're home," Cesar declared.

"Hooray!" Johnny scrambled from the car, too excited to sit still any longer. Sarah climbed out after him. Perfume from the flowers assailed her senses.

The next few minutes became a blur as the hospital attendant produced a wheelchair and pushed him through a flower-filled arbor to a breathtaking inner courtyard surrounding a rectangular pool.

Johnny had been right. The villa was like a palace.

Once the attendant left to go back to the car, an older woman and man, both with dark blond hair, came running from the portico and converged on Cesar to welcome him back. From their hugs and cries, Sarah could tell his staff adored him.

He removed his sunglasses and reached for Johnny, pulling him onto his lap. "Bianca? Angelo?" he spoke in English. "This is my son, Johnny. Johnny, meet the Carlonis."

"Hi!"

His bright young voice was like a ray of sunshine.

"Such a beautiful boy!" Bianca cried. Sounds of pure delight poured out of the wiry older woman as she leaned over to kiss him on both cheeks.

Angelo, built like a bull, beamed at him. "You look like a young Cesar."

"That's what the pilot said." Obviously Johnny was thrilled over the comparison.

"The Carlonis have lived here for years and take care of me and the house."

"Mommy and I will take care of you."

Cesar kissed the top of his head. "How about we all take care of each other. Sarah?" he called to her unexpectedly without looking at her, almost as if she were excess baggage.

On trembling legs she approached to shake hands with his staff.

Still addressing the others he said, "Meet my wife, Sarah Priestley, now de Falcon."

Her name seemed to mean something to the housekeeper whose black eyes darted to Sarah with an unsmiling expression.

"We were just married in the hospital chapel. No one is to know I'm home yet. Until tomorrow I want everything kept quiet. *Capisce?*"

"*Si*, Cesar," Bianca murmured. Her husband simply nodded.

"Johnny? If you want to come with me and Angelo, Bianca will take care of your mother. Then we'll eat on the terrace."

"The cook has dinner ready," the housekeeper informed them.

Johnny cocked his head. "You have a cook?"

His father smiled at him. "Now you do, too. Her name is Juliana. She'll fix you anything you like."

At those words Johnny jumped up and down with excitement. He seemed perfectly happy to go with his father. If he felt any separation anxiety, he was hiding it well.

"I'll see you in a minute, honey."

"Okay."

Bianca turned to her. "Come with me, Signora Falcon."

She reached for Sarah's bag and led her beneath another portico to the end of the pool. They passed through a set of French doors into a guest bedroom done in shades of aqua and oyster with a modern, en suite bathroom. Every amenity had been provided.

A striped silk spread on the queen-size bed, plus matching stripes on the chairs and love seat made it a beautiful room that reflected the turquoise of the pool.

"This is lovely." She looked around. "Where does that door lead?"

"To the hallway."

"I see. Where have you put Johnny?"

"In his father's suite at the other end of the villa."

Was this Cesar's or Bianca's idea of how things should work?

The housekeeper was civil enough, yet Sarah detected hostility coming from her. Like a possessive mother who turned on anyone hurting her child, she clearly blamed Sarah for this situation and intended to make it up to Cesar.

But Bianca didn't know Johnny. He was still too young and vulnerable to handle this arrangement. Since Sarah didn't want to do anything to alienate the housekeeper further, she would discuss this with Cesar when they were alone.

"Dinner will be served on the west terrace. After you're settled, walk down the hall to the foyer and go straight out the French doors."

"Thank you, Bianca."

With a closed expression, the housekeeper disappeared from the room.

Sarah was having to function one minute at a time. No one at the villa welcomed her here, least of all Cesar. She was only tolerated because she was Johnny's mother. It was something she would have to get used to in order to survive.

She freshened up in the bathroom, changing into white Capri pants and a filmy yellow and white print blouson top. Once she'd slipped into Italian leather sandals, she started for the foyer.

The promise to make a quick call to her parents would have to keep until she went to bed.

Yesterday Sarah had phoned to let them know she and Johnny had arrived safely in Rome. Naturally they had asked her to let them know the outcome of today's hospital visit. They'd be shocked to discover she was already married. Her sister, Elaine, would be elated.

Since they'd never approved of her keeping Johnny a secret from Cesar, she knew they'd be relieved the truth was finally out. For their grandson's sake they'd be happy a marriage had taken place.

But they had no comprehension of Cesar's true state of mind. Under the circumstances Sarah was glad to put off talking to them. For the moment she had no desire to go into detail over the precarious nature of the situation with Cesar. That could wait until she'd gotten her bearings.

After applying some lotion, she took a fortifying breath and went in search of Johnny. She needed the warmth of her darling boy to ward off the chill Bianca had brought into the room.

As Sarah came to find out, the villa was an architectural wonder of latticed passageways forming a structure like an ornate tiara. She moved past more bedrooms to the other part of the house. Fabulous oriental rugs covered the marble floors. Throughout the dining and living room she feasted her eyes on huge brass urns filled with flowering plants. Venetian glass mirrors and wall sconces with tapered candles graced the walls. Against a backdrop that whispered of a sultan's palace, the blend of European furnishings in shades of pale to deep rose silk and damask enchanted her.

She found it difficult to reconcile that a man of the twenty-first century who loved speed and pushed the limits of the latest race car technology to the extreme came from a home steeped in this kind of timeless splendor. His environment and interests proved to be as complex as Cesar himself. A man whose dark hair and sun-kissed skin had captured her attention the first time she'd laid eyes on him.

Tall and buff with eyes that flashed a shimmery silver, she'd never met anyone remotely like him. Without his exceptional skill behind the wheel at an early age, catapulting him to stardom, their worlds would never have collided in Monterey.

He possessed sophistication and intelligence that put him on a level above the other males of her acquaintance, and she had fallen so deeply in love with him. Six years of separation hadn't changed her feelings. If anything, Johnny's birth had only intensified her need for Cesar. He'd spoiled her for anyone else.

Almost to the terrace now, she caught sight of him in the wheelchair. He was pointing out something to their animated son who stood next to him at the wrought-iron railing.

Cesar's exceptional looks and personality made him attractive to men and women alike. She drew closer, noting that Johnny was no exception. Love for his father shone from his eyes. He saw beyond the wheelchair to the man, making no comparisons or judgments. His pure devotion was exactly what Cesar needed.

Even though Sarah felt like she'd walked into a fiery

furnace coming to Italy, she knew it had been the right thing to do. Only time would tell if she could withstand the heat long enough to get past Cesar's bitter rancor.

Johnny saw her first and flew across the terrace to hug her. She'd never been so happy to feel those arms around her. Both he and Cesar had changed into casual shirts and trousers.

"Come and look, Mommy!" As Johnny grasped her hand and pulled her toward the railing overhung with masses of lavender bougainvillea, she felt Cesar's eyes on her. But his punitive gaze couldn't prevent the gasp that escaped her lips.

Surely no spot on earth equaled the sight before her eyes. The villa sat perched on the pinnacle of a steep mount. Once long ago Cesar had told her Positano was gifted with a dramatic beauty that drew the adulation of the world. Now she knew what he meant.

The fragrance of the sultry air, the breathtaking view of a brilliant blue sea and sky separated by the charming town built into the cliffs presented a paradise beyond any words she could conjure.

Johnny pointed toward the ocean. "See those islands?"

She nodded.

"They're called the Galli islands. Daddy said Sirens used to live there and were dangerous. What's a Siren?"

"Didn't he tell you?"

"He said to ask you because you know all about them."

Heat stained her cheeks.

Refusing to look at Cesar she said, "They were imaginary women with birdlike bodies who sang when ships went by."

"How come they were dangerous?"

"Because their songs were so beautiful, they made men want to jump ship and swim over to them," Cesar supplied. "But the men died in the water trying to reach them."

A look of concentration had broken out on Johnny's face. "They shouldn't have sailed near them."

"You're right, *figlio mio*. Unfortunately they learned their lesson too late."

Anger swamped her.

Cesar had made certain he'd escaped her clutches without being swallowed in the depths of the sea. As far as she was concerned he'd gotten his legends mixed up.

If anything she could liken him to the mythical Apollo who raced around mating with many women, never settling down to one. She would love to say something about that to him, but not in front of Johnny.

"It's a pretend story, honey. Come on—let's sit down and eat."

They joined Cesar at the round glass table where a maid named Concetta had just served their food.

"Mommy? Bianca said Juliana made mac and cheese just for me."

"Well aren't you a lucky boy. That's one of your favorite meals."

He nodded. "What's yours, Daddy?"

"I like it, too."

From the way Johnny sat on the chair swinging his legs back and forth beneath the seat, she could tell he was happy.

"Hey, Daddy?" he said after he'd made inroads on his dinner. "What are we going to do after we eat?"

"Your father just got out of the hospital, honey. Since it's been a long day, we're all going to bed early."

Cesar shot her a warning glance before his gaze switched to Johnny. "How would you like to see my gym?"

"Where is it?"

"Down the hall encircling the far side of the pool."

"You mean in *our* house?" Clearly he was surprised.

"*Si, piccolo mio*. It's in a big room where I work out to stay in shape between races."

"What have you got in it?"

"Well, there's a barbell bench, an incline bench, a decline

bench, free weights, dumbbells, a cable machine, a treadmill and a bicycle."

"Whoa— Can I work out with you?"

"We'll do some curls tonight."

"What are those?"

"An exercise. We'll work with the dumbbells to strengthen our biceps."

"What are biceps?"

"These." He patted Johnny's upper arm muscle. "Pretty soon yours will be bigger than Carson's."

"His are kind of little."

"I thought so."

"But you haven't seen Carson before. You're funny, Daddy. I love you."

"I love you, too." He took another bite of macaroni. "Tomorrow we'll go shopping for some toys, and afterward we'll take a swim. It'll feel good after the heat."

"I can't swim very well, but I can dive off the side if Mommy catches me."

"I'm here to catch you now."

CHAPTER FOUR

SARAH had picked up Cesar's warning signal loud and clear. *It's my turn,* it said. She knew. She wouldn't dream of taking this time away from him for anything.

After the black mental state he'd been in at the hospital, she was overjoyed to see that Johnny's presence had sparked fresh life into his psyche. But she was afraid he was going to overdo it and burn out too fast.

Twelve hours ago she and Johnny had just stepped into a taxi to go to the hospital. So much had happened since then, she could hardly process the fact that she was a married woman. From now on she would be referred to as Signora de Falcon, wife of the great Cesar Villon who was a household name to those following the Formula 1 circuit.

When she thought of how his parents and family would react to the news, she trembled with apprehension. His mother would secretly despise her for keeping her grandson from his father all this time.

She tried to imagine how she would feel if someday Johnny had a baby with a woman who didn't tell him about it for years and years. The pain and the hurt for him would be devastating—incalculable.

Yet she was expecting Cesar to be understanding of her reasons for keeping all knowledge of Johnny from him until now.

Her hands clutched the sides of her chair seat. How could she have done this to him? To her little boy? Look how the two of them had already bonded!

While she sat there riddled with pain for her crime, she made a vow to do everything in her power to make up for those lost years. From here on out Cesar's wishes and needs would come first.

No doubt he was hoping she'd leave the table so he could be alone to enjoy his first dinner with his own son, an experience she'd shared with Johnny thousands of times. That much she could do for him.

She quickly finished the rest of her meal, then got up from her chair. Avoiding Cesar's eyes she said, "If you will excuse me, I have a few phone calls to make. Have fun you two."

"Who would you be phoning at four o'clock in the morning California time?"

Cesar's question stopped her cold.

"That's right," she laughed nervously, not only from surprise because she'd forgotten about the time difference, but because Cesar might think she was going to phone Mick. After what she'd told him about them just being friends, he had every reason to be suspicious.

She felt his half shuttered gaze examine her inch by inch before he said, "When I asked Bianca to get the rooms ready earlier, she assumed that in my condition I would need my bedroom to myself. But as Johnny pointed out, Carson's mommy and daddy sleep in the same room. So feel free to move your things to my bedroom now."

The command was implicit. "When you reach the foyer, turn left. It's the room at the end of the hall."

No matter how Cesar couched the words, he wanted them sleeping together. Even if it was for Johnny's sake, a thrill of excitement coursed through her body.

"My room is right next to yours and Daddy's, Mommy."

She could tell their son's fears had been taken away by one word from his father who could fix anything and make everything better.

Her first instinct was to ask Johnny if he wanted to help her move her suitcase to the other part of the house, but she caught herself in time. Unfortunately old habits didn't die right off the bat. She and Johnny had been a twosome for so long, it felt strange to relinquish any responsibility to someone else. Except that Cesar wasn't just someone.

He was Johnny's other parent who'd embraced fatherhood without missing a heartbeat. It had been instant adoration on both their parts. Johnny wanted to be with his father, which meant more free time for Sarah, who didn't really want it.

He'd been her whole world from the moment she'd conceived. Now she would be sharing him the way two parents did in a normal household.

"I'll see you two a little later then."

Without giving Johnny a chance to ask questions she might not be able to answer, she left the terrace and hurried through the villa to her room.

She'd only been in there long enough to change clothes and wash her face, so there wasn't much to gather or tidy. Within a few minutes she had retraced her steps to the foyer with her suitcase and turned left. The tall, ornately carved wood doors at the end had to be the entry to the master suite.

When she opened them she stepped into a dreamy world no doubt created to help Cesar relax after a race. Like the guest bedroom she'd just left, it bordered the pool. However, this breathtaking room with its king-size bed was much larger. Two framed Michelanglo drawings hung above it. A huge hand-painted French armoire in antique white stood against one wall. There was an ornate couch and love seat. They faced an exquisitely carved fireplace.

Two Louis XV striped chairs were placed at either side of

a white marble table. The furniture was upholstered in cream silk with strong accents of café-au-lait woven into the decor, some in stripes, others in an all-over print. Pots of creamy roses completed the enchanting picture.

Opposite the bed, floor to ceiling glass doors opened onto another terrace, offering a spectacular view of the ocean.

Putting her suitcase down, she stepped outside and wandered over to the railing. The beauty from this angle was so indescribable, it hurt. She stood there for a long time drinking it in before tearing herself from the view to explore the rest of the suite.

One door led to Johnny's smaller bedroom with its queen-size bed and en suite bathroom. The lemon-yellow and white decor throughout was a delight.

Behind another door she discovered the luxuriously appointed master bathroom with an oversize jetta tub. A third set of double doors opened into Cesar's study containing state-of-the-art computer equipment.

This room belonged to the race car driver. All his trophies and awards, pictures—everything was here, modestly tucked away from the world's prying eyes.

Where many great sports stars might make their whole house into a shrine, he'd chosen this quiet spot to keep all the mementos precious to him. Cesar had always represented the epitome of class to her. Now she knew why.

Take away his aristocratic background and you would still have the same marvelous man. Deep down he was a very private person who, though he thrived on competition, was amazingly humble about his colossal successes.

It was the race that challenged him. He had an inner drive that provoked him to pit himself against the odds. That's what was important, not the accolades that followed. She blamed the media for the hype about him. Most of it, if not all, was untrue.

In his hospital room this morning, the violence of his

emotions revealed a side of his nature few people would ever glimpse. But she'd seen into his soul and discovered a man who wanted his son more than any prize his sport could bestow on him. She was also convinced that if he hadn't been involved in that accident, he still would have had exactly the same reaction when she introduced him to his son in California.

She saw a hunger in him. The longing to be a father must have always been there. He'd never denied that he wanted to have a family one day, just that he was putting it off until he could commit property. But destiny had decreed that day to come sooner than he'd expected, changing the lives of three people forever.

A sob rose in her throat. She sank down on the bed, running her hand over the luminous cream bedspread.

"Darling Cesar—if there had to be an accident, why didn't it happen to me? Not you, my love. Not you."

A searing ache passed through her body. Suddenly she felt a hand shaking her arm. "Mommy? What's wrong?"

Johnny had slipped into the room so quietly, she hadn't heard him.

"Daddy? Mommy's crying."

"Maybe she's upset because she thought I forgot to give her the wedding ring I promised."

Before turning her head toward them, Sarah hurriedly tried to repair the damage from her crying spell, but nothing escaped Cesar's notice. He'd maneuvered his wheelchair next to the dresser to pull something from the drawer. When he returned to the side of the bed, his penetrating eyes examined her wet cheeks, showing her no mercy.

"See this ruby, Johnny?" He opened his palm to display a ring. "General Napoleon Bonaparte brought it back from his Egyptian campaign. It's called Alexandria's heart."

Johnny picked it up to look at it. "It's really pretty."

"This stone has been in the Varano family for generations. After my mother inherited it, she had it set in gold. On my twenty-first birthday, she gave it to me. She told me I should present this to the woman I wanted to marry."

So his parents hadn't decided his choice of bride after all…

"Give me your left hand, Sarah."

One of the famous Varano jewels—

Little did Cesar's mother realize it would end up on the finger of a little nobody from the States who'd been so careless with her son's heart as to keep his child from him.

But no matter how ludicrous this was she'd made a promise to put his interests first. Every gesture on this red-letter day had a symbolic purpose and would make an indelible impression on Johnny's mind. Already his father was teaching him how things worked when you were born a Varano and a Falcon.

She shifted her position around on the bed to make it easier before extending her hand. Using his left hand to steady her wrist, he slid it onto her ring finger with his right. His sure touch shot fire up her arm. Even after he'd relinquished his hold on her, she still felt his imprint stealing through the rest of her sensitized body.

When she looked down, the facets of the large, fiery red stone had caught the soft light from the lamps placed at either side of the bed. She found it apropos that it looked very much to her like her own bleeding heart.

Johnny stared up at her. "Do you feel better now?"

"Much." She reached out to hug him, aware her new husband was waiting for some kind of response. Over Johnny's shoulder she said, "Thank you, Cesar. It's priceless. I just hope and pray nothing ever happens to it." She was terrified of losing an irreplaceable family heirloom.

"If you do, so be it. When Johnny finds the woman he wants to marry, there are other jewels at the ducal palace in Parma for him to choose from." Beneath his mocking tone she

knew Cesar expected her to carry on his family's tradition, but
he didn't place any faith in her ability to deliver.

"Jewels—can I look at them, Daddy?"

"Of course. We'll take a trip to visit my cousin
Maximilliano and his wife Greer. They have a little boy who
looks a lot like you named Carlo. Of course he's younger.
You're the *oldest* of all your cousins."

A smile broke out on Johnny's face. Evidently the idea
pleased him. "Do I have a lot of cousins?"

Cesar nodded. "My other cousin Nicolas and his wife Piper
just had triplets."

"Triplets—"

"That means three babies at once," Sarah explained. She
couldn't imagine it.

"Whoa."

"Two girls and a boy. Lety, Carolina and Fernando." This
from Cesar. "And I have another cousin Massimo who's a new
daddy. He'll be coming to visit us soon."

Massimo… Sarah knew that name well. There'd been
moments in the last six years when she'd been tempted to call
him and ask his advice. But every time she'd reached for the
phone she'd lost her nerve and couldn't do it. If Cesar ever
found out she'd told Massimo the news first, that would have
made things so much worse.

"What's his baby's name?"

"Nicky di Rocche. His mommy Julie is from Sonoma,
California."

"Hey, we've been there, haven't we, Mommy."

Her eyes met Cesar's for a breathless moment before she
said, "Yes. What a remarkable coincidence."

"Indeed," he murmured, as if to say there was a lot Johnny
had missed out on by being deprived of his father.

Sarah tore her eyes away. So many names and children
Johnny couldn't remember. But she had a suspicion that Cesar

had deliberately gone into detail to make her feel worse about what she'd done to him by depriving him of *his* son.

"My auntie Elaine is going to have another baby."

Cesar cocked his dark head. "I remember her. Does she still have red hair?"

"Yes. And she's afraid her baby will, too."

"Why is she afraid?"

"Cos kids will tease it."

"Sometimes children aren't nice, are they?"

"Nope. Carson wasn't nice when he called me a crybaby."

"I agree."

"Did anybody ever hurt your feelings?"

He sent Sarah a crushing regard. "Yes," came a sound from his throat resembling a hiss.

She had trouble swallowing. "Johnny? It's getting late. You need to have a bath and go to bed."

"Okay."

"I'll turn on the water."

She jumped off the bed, anxious to get away from Cesar. But when she headed for Johnny's room, he told her to wait. "Let him take a bath in our tub. He can swim in it."

"Swim—" He squealed in delight and ran into the master bath to investigate. In two seconds he'd stripped and climbed over the edge of the tub to get in. Soon he was demonstrating his splashing prowess.

Sarah felt Cesar's presence behind her as she knelt down to wash Johnny's hair.

"Look, Daddy— I can hold my breath." He leaned over and kept his head under the water while she rinsed his curls. When he raised it up again with a triumphant smile, he resembled one of the those appealing, mischievous Italian cherubs she'd seen in the chapel. He looked like Cesar.

She quaked inside.

"I'll get your jammies."

"Let me," Cesar forestalled her. "Which ones do you want me to bring, *piccolo mio?* The dinosaurs or the superheroes?"

"A… T-rex!"

"Tyrannosaurus Rex it is."

He wheeled around with a dexterity that proclaimed him an athlete's athlete and left the bathroom. By the time he returned with their son's pajamas and toothbrush, Johnny had climbed out of the tub. He insisted on drying himself with one of the big fluffy tan and white striped towels. Cesar smiled and handed him his jammies. When he'd pulled everything on, he helped himself to Cesar's toothpaste and brushed his teeth.

"I'm ready to go to bed now." His eyes sought his father's. "Will you come in while I say my prayers?"

"Try and stop me." Cesar made a pretend fist below Johnny's chin.

"Let me do that."

Johnny imitated everything his father did. Like a sponge soaking up water, he was constantly absorbing every action and nuance.

Sarah preceded them into the bedroom where their son would be sleeping from now on. She turned down the covers and put the miniature model of his daddy's faucon by the pillow along with a couple of small dinosaurs he'd brought with him.

In a minute the two of them entered the room. Sarah perched on the edge of the bed. Johnny ran over and got down on his knees. Cesar glided over to them. Giving his dad one more glance to make sure he was there he began.

"Dear Heavenly Father— I love my daddy. Thanks for letting us get married. Thanks for not letting me be too scared in the helicopter. Bless Nana and Papa and my grandma and grandpa and all my cousins. Bless Daddy's legs to get better. Bless Mommy so she'll stop crying. Amen."

"Amen." Sarah got up from the bed. "Excuse me for a minute."

* * *

While Cesar's gaze followed her from the room, he reached for Johnny. Emotion gripped him so hard he had trouble speaking. He glimpsed the black racecar that was no more. Sarah had placed it next to a triceratops and a T-Rex. Those little toys that made up his child's world. .

"I love you, Johnny. You've made me happier than I've been in my whole life."

"Me, too."

"Tell me something. Does your mother cry a lot?"

"Yes, cos she loves you so much."

Cesar's eyes closed tightly.

"But she doesn't think I can hear her. I wish she wouldn't," he said wistfully.

"It isn't fun when our mommies cry, is it."

"Nope. Does your mommy cry a lot?"

Probably too much. "I know she cries sometimes."

"Because she's afraid you'll crash, huh."

He patted the boy's sturdy back. "Well she doesn't have to worry about that anymore."

"Cos you had a big crash."

"Bigger than I expected."

Johnny picked up the car and looked at it. "When you get better, are you going to race again?"

His child's naiveté was a bittersweet revelation. "No. I'll be home from now on to enjoy my son."

"I'm glad." After a pause, "Daddy? If I get scared tonight, can I come in your room?"

A smile broke out on his lips. "Where else would you go?" He stroked the damp curls back off his forehead. "But if we leave one of the lamps on, maybe you won't get nervous."

"Thanks." He pressed his soft lips to Cesar's cheek, then crawled into bed pulling the covers over him. "Daddy? Do you want to see my scrapbook before you go to bed?"

"I didn't know you had one."

"I've had it a long time. Mommy helped me make it. I'll get it." After letting go of the car, he got back out of bed and hurried over to the chair where Sarah had put his suitcase. Once he'd undone the locks, he pulled it out and ran back to his side. "Here."

At the sight of it, a tight band constricted Cesar's breathing. With hands not quite steady he opened the cover and came face-to-face with a photograph of himself that Sarah had taken when he was just twenty-four. Nine years of history... It went back a long way.

She'd been seventeen at the time, already a ravishing American beauty. Until they'd started talking at the Priestley home, he'd thought she was older. Then her father walked over to introduce them and put Cesar in the know. He couldn't have made his point any clearer if he'd said, "Hands off."

Her young age and the name Priestley made her untouchable, which was a good thing because he'd been tempted and Edward Priestley had known it.

In the picture Cesar wore a T-shirt with his sponsor's logo and a pair of tight jeans. His hair was longer back than. It was shocking to see how cocky he had been, swaggering around in front of the camera with his trophy in the background, showing off for this girl-woman whose sweetness and beauty called to him like the Siren to Ulysses.

While he looked closer at the picture, Johnny poured over it with him. The idiotic grin on Cesar's face, put there by his first world championship win, made him look drunk with life. Those stars in his eyes were the same stars he saw in Johnny's right now.

"Can I see that trophy?"

"I'll show you everything tomorrow."

"You have a whole bunch, right?"

"Quite a few." But he'd give his soul to have had these years with Johnny instead. Years when a son and father needed each other. Tears stung his eyes. Damn you to hell, Sarah Priestley…de Falcon.

The picture staring back from the page mocked him.

Back then Cesar had felt immortal, ready to smash every previously set racing record. Standing there, he hadn't been capable of imagining the day coming when he wouldn't be able to pose for photo ops on his own two strong legs.

With a trembling hand he turned the page. There was a picture taken of him and Sarah with her family that same night.

"That's Nana and Papa, and Auntie Elaine and Mommy!"

He cleared his throat. "I can see that." Memories flooded his mind. "Did you know the Priestley name has a very important history?"

"It does?"

"Yes. Somewhere way back in your family another Priestley invented a machine to make carbonated water."

Johnny frowned in puzzlement. "What's that?"

"What's your favorite drink?"

"Milk."

Cesar laughed. "Besides milk?"

"Orange soda."

"You're part Italian all right. We Italians love our orange soda. It's made with carbonated water. All sparkling sodas are. That's why your grandfather runs the Quenchers Company now."

"I didn't know that. Who told you?"

"Your mommy."

She'd told Cesar a lot of things that first night. He had to admit there'd been an instant rapport between them, surprising in a woman so much younger than himself. A teenager with enough beauty and charm to lure him back to the Priestley home whenever he flew to the States for a race.

"Papa Priestley says you're the best driver in the world."

And the biggest bastard who ever lived for impregnating his daughter.

"I'm afraid not anymore, *mon fils*."

He helped Johnny get back in to bed and put the covers over him, then he moved on to another page. Thus began a journey into the past. His life unfurled before him in chronological order. There were many shots of him and Sarah on the surf, or sailing on her father's boat.

One picture leaped out at him. It was the Inn along the Big Sur where they'd spent that glorious night. The two of them looked so damn happy it hit him in the gut, making it difficult to breathe.

She'd chronicled his career, leaving nothing out. Every race, every win. All of it documented. Some photo shots from magazines and tabloids had caught him celebrating with various dazzling females and celebrities at favorite jet-set night clubs around the world.

Others featured him standing by a newly won trophy with his parents and brother after the Monaco Grand Prix, or at Monza in Italy with his second cousin and best friend, Massimo.

Sarah had included everything. She'd even found pictures taken of him with his cousins, all of them older. Yet that one unforgettable night with her had produced a son who was the oldest of all his little cousins. Johnny was the most satisfying child he could ever have imagined.

His gaze left the pictures to look at his son who'd finally fallen asleep with his cheek lying on the car. He carefully removed it and put it on the bedside table with the dinosaurs. After such a long, eventful day in his young life, it was no wonder he'd passed out.

Earlier in the morning Cesar had suffered two shocks from which he didn't think he would ever recover. He'd honestly thought he was hallucinating when he'd heard Sarah's voice and saw her standing there like a beautiful frightened doe in the headlights.

After waiting years to hear from her without one damn

word, for her to have come in the hospital room at his lowest ebb, he'd understood for the first time how someone could commit a crime of passion.

Who would have dreamed that after driving her out of the hospital room with his raging invective, she'd be right back with the son they'd created together? Their perfect child. Jean-Cesar...

Sarah was right. His mother would be crazy about her little Giovanni. Cesar knew his parents were suffering over his paralysis. Knowing their pain, he'd kept them away, unable to bear seeing it in their loving eyes. He couldn't deal with that yet.

Luc understood. He'd almost lost his leg in a ski tram accident a few years ago. The despair had almost driven him mad. Olivia had changed all that.

Cesar's hands flattened on the arms of the wheelchair. Once his family heard the news, there was going to be celebrating at the Falcon estate in Monaco. One look at Johnny and joy would mitigate their anguish for him. He'd phone them in a little while.

Right now he wanted to stay here and try to comprehend the wonder of his boy's reality. After Cesar was certain his wife had gone to sleep, he would ask Angelo to help him get in to bed.

Not quite the picture of two lovers on fire for each other, is it Sarah?

CHAPTER FIVE

SARAH stood hidden at the doorway to Johnny's room studying Cesar's profile. She'd been watching and listening the whole time. An unseen hand squeezed her heart to see his head thrown back with his arm covering his eyes.

Cesar—

She turned away and removed the robe over her nightgown before getting into their bed. When he finally came in to the room, she wanted him to believe she was unconscious to the world. Sarah loved him so much, his condition would never matter to her. In fact she loved him more because of it. But without the love on his part, the situation was repugnant to him.

She had to come to terms with the fact that he despised the very thought of sleeping in the same bed with her. Only for Johnny's sake would he steel himself to go through the motions and pretend they were a typical, happily married couple.

In that regard Cesar was displaying the same heroic fighting nature that had catapulted him to racing stardom and made him a beloved sports hero in the eyes of millions.

Everyone well intentioned or not wanted a piece of him. When the paparazzi got their first photos of Johnny accompanying the dashing man in the wheelchair, the relationship between them unmistakable, a whole new wave of public sentiment would spread.

How could it not? To see two utterly handsome men, one little, one big, enjoying each other's company as only a father and son could do.

She may have handled everything else wrong with Cesar, but with Johnny's watchful eyes and thoughts going into the making of the scrapbook to honor his father, she'd given Cesar a priceless gift he couldn't reject.

Before she turned out the lamp on her side of the bed, she placed Johnny's baby book on Cesar's pillow. Another gift assembled from those very first moments following their baby's birth up to last week when she'd put in a picture of him posing next to Carson with their soccer team. All of it to help his father catch up on the years he'd missed with his son.

Elaine had taken dozens of those first photos in the hospital room. Pictures of the nursery, Sarah's doctor, the family taking turns holding the new little bundle…

Bless you, Elaine.

Having done all she could for tonight, Sarah turned away from his side of the bed and pulled the covers around her head. With the air-conditioning on to shut out the intense heat of the day, they actually felt good.

When Cesar was convinced Johnny wouldn't wake up, he wheeled himself out of the room and through the villa. Knowing Sarah was getting ready for bed, he wanted to put as much distance as possible between them. He soon found himself on the terrace.

Like the sheerest bridal veil, twilight had fallen upon the face of Positano. It was the time of night when anything Cesar was feeling seemed to be magnified a hundredfold. Awash with emotions he couldn't ignore, he realized it was time to contact his parents. Though the doctor would have given them updates, he had orders not to let them know Cesar had left the hospital.

But now that he was a father, it was as if he'd been given second sight. How come it had taken something this earth-shaking for him to understand what a selfish bastard he'd been to shut them out? Since his decision to race cars, he'd put them through so much hell, they deserved to know before anyone else that he was no longer the bachelor they'd been worrying about all these years.

Without wasting any more time, he pulled out his cell phone to call them. They'd be in bed. His father answered after the first ring, which meant he'd been waiting. He would have seen Cesar's name on his caller ID.

"Mon cher fils—"

Cesar had to clear his throat. "Papa."

"Grace à Dieu!" He could hear his mother crying the same thing in the background.

"I'm sorry I haven't phoned before now. I couldn't. Forgive me."

"There's nothing to forgive. We understand." They always did. "What's important is that you're alive!"

He hadn't thought so until yesterday morning when he'd heard the shocking words, "Honey? This is your daddy."

"I realize it's late, Papa, but I wanted you to know I'm back in Positano. I can hear maman asking questions. Tell her I'm starting my physical therapy."

"That's the best news, *mon fils,* but you can't be expected to get through this alone. We'll be flying there tomorrow to help you."

Tomorrow would be too soon. Cesar needed another day to get into a routine with his son before the family descended en masse.

"I've got plenty of help, Papa. Why don't you and maman come the day after tomorrow. Bring Luc and his family with you. By then I'll be all settled. There are two people I want everyone to meet."

"Ah, oui?" The nuance in his father's tone meant Cesar had piqued his interest.

"Turn on the speaker so Maman can hear this, too." They were in for the shock of their lives.

Apparently Sarah had been more exhausted than even she'd realized because she never heard Cesar come to bed. When Johnny came running in to the room the next morning to wake her up, Cesar was nowhere in sight. Only the indentation of his head on the pillow and the disappearance of the baby book gave proof that he'd spent the night next to her.

Had he been able to sleep?

She hoped so. He needed his strength to begin the uphill battle that would restore life to his legs. She chose to remember the doctor's prognosis in the most positive light.

"Guess what, Mommy?"

"Did you already have breakfast with your daddy?" It was after nine o'clock.

"Yes. Juliana made me cinnamon toast and juice."

His favorite. "That sounds good." She sat up and kissed the top of his head. He'd dressed in his blue plaid shorts and blue shirt with a T-rex on the front. "Where's your father now?"

"In the gym with his thair-pust."

"You mean therapist." Thank God. The doctor had warned her that every day he refused to get help, the faster his condition would deteriorate. This had to be the best sign!

Johnny nodded. "She speaks French with daddy."

She?

Sarah slid out of bed and drew on her pink robe. "What's her name?"

"Daddy calls her Bibi. Isn't that funny?"

"Very." Sarah made for the bathroom. She had a sinking feeling about this Bibi.

"She kind of looks like Tinker Bell."

Did she really?

Tinker Bell was the fetchingly shaped blond fairy who loved the fictional Peter Pan. A surprising stab of jealousy attacked her.

Over the years Sarah had struggled to keep the green eyed monster from ruining her life. Cesar had insisted he wouldn't marry until his career was over. She'd kept that uppermost in her mind every time the tabloids hinted at him being in another serious relationship.

"Daddy told Bianca to put her in the blue bedroom."

That comment, said from outside the door, caused her to drop the brush in the sink. "She's going to stay here?"

"Yup."

"For how long?" Sarah put on underwear before joining him. He followed her into the walk-in closet where she'd hung her things the night before.

"Bianca said for a long time."

Sarah felt the ground shake. She really was going to have to get her jealousy under control. The other woman was here to help Cesar. Sarah ought to be getting down on her knees to her.

"Hurry and get dressed, Mommy. Daddy said we're going to get me some toys."

"I remember."

If they were going to be walking around Positano, she'd better wear something appropriate as befitted Cesar's wife. There was little to choose from in the small wardrobe she'd brought. The sleeveless lightweight jersey dress with its all-over navy and white print would have to do.

When they were in town she'd shop for a few new outfits. Maybe they could drop off the throwaway camera at the same time to get their wedding pictures developed. Since her family hadn't been present at the ceremony, they'd want to see them.

She quickly slipped on the dress, pairing it with navy sandals. As she emerged from the closet, she saw that Concetta had brought her a breakfast tray. Her breath caught to see corn-flakes with bananas and strawberries. It was the same meal she and Cesar had eaten after making love all night.

He remembered… No one else knew how to twist the knife to heighten her pain to such exquisite proportions.

"While I eat, let's phone your grandparents."

"Can I tell them we live with daddy now?"

"You can tell them everything."

Together they sat down at the table. She dialed the house phone and handed it to him. Even if it was midnight in Carmel, she couldn't put it off any longer.

While she started to eat she heard, "Hi, Papa! Guess what?" In the next little while her son gave his grandparents an amazingly comprehensive description of everything that had gone on. He'd always been a happy boy, but there were degrees of happiness.

Being with his daddy had increased his capacity for joy. Already he was more complete, more confident. She could hear it in his voice. Only a father who wanted his son as much as Cesar wanted him could have wrought this fantastic change in so short at time.

"Here, Mommy. They want to talk to you. I'm going to see if daddy's ready to go." With such an exciting day before him, naturally he couldn't sit still.

Sarah put the receiver to her ear with some trepidation. "Hi, you two. I'm sorry if we wakened you."

"You didn't. We've been lying here talking," her mother said. "Johnny's a new boy."

"I know."

"Now we can sleep." This from her father. "You've done the right thing, honey, even if we're going to miss you living so far away. What does the doctor say about Cesar's condition? We want the unvarnished truth."

Her hand tightened on the phone, fighting not to break

down. "The nerves weren't severed. He is hopeful that with enough therapy Cesar will walk again. So am I."

"Oh, darling—" her mother cried for happiness.

"Don't count on it," came her husband's forbidding voice. He'd wheeled himself into the bedroom so silently, she hadn't realized it. For once Johnny wasn't with him to announce their arrival. "Give me the phone, Sarah."

His forehead and eyebrows were beaded in perspiration. Whorls of damp black hair clung to the back of his neck. Large patches of sweat blotted his white T-shirt. Beneath his shorts, his hard-muscled legs glistened with moisture from his workout, the first since the accident. Judging by his grimace, it hadn't gone well. How could it have? This was only the beginning…

When she handed him the receiver, she knew he could feel her body trembling.

On his part he sounded comfortable talking with them. After all, he'd been a guest in their home many times. Despite everything that had happened, her father was in awe of Cesar and his accomplishments. But her husband made certain their conversation centered on Johnny.

"You'll have to fly over and visit us soon. I'll leave the arrangements to you and your daughter. Here she is."

Thrusting the receiver at her, he wheeled himself toward the bathroom. His mood was so grim, Sarah couldn't concentrate. She promised to call her parents back later, then hung up just as Angelo appeared. His arrival prevented any conversation. He nodded to her before following Cesar inside.

With a groan for what he had to face in order to facilitate his recovery, she picked up her purse and went in search of Johnny. His father needed privacy while he showered and dressed.

Since he wasn't on the main terrace, she went down another hallway until she heard voices. One of them was her son's, the other a woman who spoke English in heavily accented French. Sarah found them in the gym with its state-of-the-art equipment.

Though she'd love to scratch out the brown eyes of the attractive, toned blonde in her skimpy workout shorts and sports bra top, she knew it was a sentiment unworthy of her. *Bibi* was demonstrating the use of the barbells to a fascinated Johnny. Her ponytail swung back and forth.

"Mommy—look at me!"

It was impossible not to. "Great job!"

The other woman flashed her a smile. "Good morning, *signora.*"

"How do you do, *signora,*" she said in kind.

"Everyone calls me Bibi."

"That's what I understand. I'm Sarah." They shook hands.

"One day your son will grow to be strong like his handsome papa."

"I'm sure of it." After a hesitation she said, "Bibi? How did it go this morning?"

She stood there with her hands on her hips. "He struggled, but that is to be expected. At least he came. In the hospital, he told me to get out."

Bibi had been there? "H-have you known him a long time?"

"Four years. I worked on his brother, and later a racing colleague of his."

"Who was that?"

"Arturo Scorzzi."

"I remember. He was almost killed."

"Yes, but now he is fully recovered. Cesar's doctor showed me his X-rays. In time your husband will be, too."

The information along with her positive declaration filled Sarah with fresh hope. Cesar wouldn't have hired her if she weren't the best therapist for his kind of injury.

"His problem is not just his body, Sarah. It is up here." She tapped her own temple. "He must visualize each movement before he tries to make one, but he is too impatient. In the beginning that is natural."

"How can I help?" she cried softly.

"When you're in bed at night, help him to turn on one side part of the night, then turn him on the other side later."

"What about his stomach?"

"Fine if that's what he wants. But when he's on his side, put the little pillow I gave him between his knees like this." Bibi demonstrated. She clearly thought Sarah and Cesar had a conjugal relationship.

"I can do that," Sarah said, having no wish to alter that assumption. "Anything else?"

"A good backrub will ease a lot of tension. Arms, hands, fingers, neck. It all helps. And make sure he comes to every session."

"We will," Johnny piped up. He'd put the bar bells down to listen.

"How often are they?"

"Four times a day for the present. After breakfast, after lunch, before dinner and before bed. They are short in duration, but they will force the nerves to remember."

That was a strict regimen, but the other woman who looked to be Cesar's age knew what she was doing. No wonder she needed to live here. Sarah took back her unkind thoughts about Bibi.

"What will you do between sessions?"

She gestured with her hands. "I have a boyfriend. We do this and that when he's able to join me."

"I'm glad. And I'm thankful for you."

A look of speculation entered her eyes. "You are the new wife of the greatest racing champion alive. I think this is very hard on you."

Bibi understood a great deal.

"Johnny and I want him to walk again," she whispered tremulously.

"His sponsors and fans want the same thing. It is my job

to make that happen. *Courage,*" she said in French, reminding Sarah of the priest's words.

Courage was the operative word where Cesar was concerned. She nodded to Bibi, then grasped Johnny's hand.
"Come on, honey." They left the gym.

"Daddy said to meet him at the car behind the pool."

"Do you need to use the bathroom or get a drink first?"

"Nope."

"Okay. Let's go."

When they left the villa and walked through the portico,
they discovered Angelo helping Cesar from the wheelchair
into the back seat of a black luxury sedan.

He looked fabulous in a pair of tan chinos that covered his
powerful thighs. Dressed in a navy-blue sport shirt revealing
his broad shoulders and well-defined chest, the uninformed
person wouldn't know that a horrible injury afflicting the
spine was hidden within his spectacular physique.

Johnny ran around the other side of the car so he could sit
next to him. Sarah got in the front passenger side. After
Angelo had stowed the wheelchair in the trunk, he took his
place behind the wheel.

"Drive us to Fortuno's, Angelo."

"Bene." The older man reversed the car to the road, then
began the hairpin turns down to the town below. Flower
scented air filled the interior. The dazzling sunlight bathing
the villas and surrounding foliage almost blinded her.

"Is that a toy store, Daddy?"

"A big one. When I'm home I always get your cousins'
presents there. Have you decided what you want to buy?"
Cesar asked his son.

"Mommy wrote it down for me cos I don't write very good
yet."

"You don't write very *well,*" she corrected him.

"Let's have a look, Sarah."

It was the first time since yesterday evening that he'd spoken to her directly. She opened her purse and took out the list. Whenever she was around Cesar, her hands seemed to be permanently unsteady. When she turned to give the paper to him, their fingers brushed, fanning her fire.

Their eyes met as if he'd felt her heat and was scorched by it. Though the moment was only a fraction in time, she thought maybe he was remembering the way it used to be between them. But in a flash he pulled out his sunglasses and put them on, shutting her out more effectively than an eclipse of the sun.

She faced straight ahead again. It took time to negotiate the heavy traffic before Angelo pulled away from the stream of cars into an alley behind the store in question. He came to a stop next to a truck and got out the wheelchair.

While Johnny steadied it, the older man assisted Cesar from the car without problem. "I'll wait here for you."

"*Grazie,* Angelo."

The older man rang the buzzer at the side of the rear doors, then got back in the vehicle. Evidently Cesar had made prior arrangements with the management. Such heavy crowds out on Positano's main streets would have made it impossible for Angelo to find parking.

Johnny smiled at them while they waited for someone to answer. "Hey—we all look alike!" He spoke the truth. One way or another their clothes matched. Everyone in blue.

Cesar and son had come to town.

The moment the back door opened, their lives were no longer their own. Word had spread that the famous Cesar Villon, Positano's favorite son, was on the premises. After wheeling himself inside, he was besieged by staff and customers alike wanting to shake hands and get autographs. It was impossible to do any shopping.

Tourists with cameras or cell phones took pictures of the

three of them. Customers buying merchandise with his name on the packaging begged him to sign their purchases. Shouts in every language including English told him they were praying for him. His heart couldn't help but be warmed by the deep affection demonstrated.

For Sarah, it was a joy to see how much people cared. But Johnny on the other hand pressed against Cesar's legs, utterly bewildered by the near mob scene. Cesar noticed it immediately.

"I shouldn't have brought you in here," he muttered, squeezing Johnny's hand. Normally he handled the masses with calm and finesse, but this situation was different. He'd brought his son to do something special for him like any father. His frustration level had to be off the charts.

Sarah had been around screaming out-of-control fans at the racetrack for most of her life, especially when Cesar flew in for the big race. But this was Johnny's first experience with his father out in public. It was something he would never like, but would have to get used to. Now was the time to teach him his first lesson in dealing with his father's fame.

She looked at her son clinging to Cesar. "Don't be nervous, honey. This always happens when people see your daddy. That's why the security and police have arrived. They've posted themselves throughout the store to keep people away so you and your daddy can find the toys you want to take home. Ignore them.

"I'll push the cart along while you two get started. The racetrack games are down this aisle. This is going to fun!"

The anxious expression on his face turned into a smile. "Come on, Daddy."

With the crisis averted, they spent the next hour picking out the same kinds of toys he had at home but couldn't bring, plus some new ones. Enough to fill three shopping carts by the time they'd finished.

In excellent English the manager of the store asked Johnny if he wanted anything else. The clerk was ringing up the bill.

"Do you have any sunglasses like my daddy's?"

"I will find out." The other man snapped his fingers and called to another clerk in rapid Italian. Almost instantly a pair was produced.

Johnny put them on and turned to his father, oblivious to the fascinated audience hanging out in the store to watch from a distance. "Now we both look cool!"

Only recently had Johnny picked up that word from one of his friends who had an older brother. She heard Cesar chuckle. "You look very cool, *piccolo mio.*" They high-fived each other.

People started clapping. Out of the corner of her eye Sarah saw that several photojournalists had entered the store and were getting everything on tape for the evening news.

One of them shouted something in Italian to Cesar. Without turning to the man, Cesar called back in English, "If you want an interview, speak to my wife. She's my publicist now. Come on, Johnny," he whispered out of earshot. "Let's take our things to the car."

As they left the counter, the media converged on her like a swarm of bees. "*Per favore,* Signora de Falcon, when did you first meet Cesar? What's your name? What's your son's name? How long have you been married? Did you see the crash?" The questions came fast and furiously.

Cesar had dropped this squarely in her lap, hoping to embarrass her. Payback time for the way she'd exploded her bomb in front of him at the hospital.

By tonight the whole world was going to know everything anyway, so she decided to be as truthful as possible without getting into areas that were no one's business but theirs. Taking on a calm profile, she smiled into the video cams.

"As you can see, my husband's occupied at the moment. I'm Sarah Priestley de Falcon. We met when he came to race at the U.S. Grand Prix in Monterey, California, nine years ago.

My father, Edward Priestley, owns the track. After Cesar's spectacular world championship win, my parents hosted a party for him at our home. I was only seventeen at the time. It was love at first sight for me."

Her voice caught. "I discovered that it's a great responsibility to be in love with anyone who has such a rare talent. He's been gifted like few others in the history of racing. All this time I've had to share him with his fans. So has our son, Jean-Cesar, who came along five years ago.

"While Cesar's getting back on his feet to race in the first Grand Prix of the season at Monza next year, the three of us are going to spend some quality time together."

"Then he's not permanently injured?"

"You mean you believe the fairy tale your colleagues have been spreading?" But she smiled as she said it. "Can you actually imagine anything keeping the great Cesar Villon down? If you can, then your imagination is better than mine. He's already working out four times a day and will be back better than ever in no time. That's a heads-up for his competitors by the way.

"Now if you'll excuse us, our son is waiting for his daddy to put his new racetrack together at home." As she started for the rear of the store, there was a huge roar and a cheer from the crowd. People had come in from the streets.

The chants of "Cesar! Cesar! Cesar!" echoed until she exited the rear door.

When she reached the car, Angelo helped her inside. The two in the back seat were poring over Johnny's new PalmPilot. Cesar was showing him how it worked.

"Look, Mommy—" He put his hand over her shoulder so she could see. He'd used the metal stylus to print his name in his own irregular style. Big letters that couldn't fit on one line, all lower case.

j o h n

n y
p f a l c
o n.

"That's fantastic!"

"I know."

Spontaneous laughter rumbled out of Cesar. A sound of delight that started in the belly. Yesterday morning she couldn't have imagined hearing anything close to it.

Much as she wanted to do some other shopping, now wasn't the time. The hordes of people pouring into Positano made it almost impossible for Angelo to maneuver at the noon hour. Tomorrow would be soon enough. While Cesar worked out, Sarah would take a walk into town with Johnny.

At the moment, their son couldn't wait to get home and start playing with all his new toys. Being with his father was like having all his Christmases rolled into one.

As for Cesar, she imagined this outing had exhausted him emotionally. To face people after his injury took a tremendous amount of courage. But she had the satisfaction of knowing he'd made it through this morning's ordeal. With this hurdle overcome, it would be a little easier to face the next one.

Clearly he was willing to do anything for Johnny's sake. Just as she'd suspected, their son played *the* crucial role in his father's progress. She would milk it for all it was worth to get him walking again.

Once they'd returned to the villa, everyone including the maids helped take the packages inside. While Sarah freshened up in the bathroom, she soon heard cries and whoops of laughter coming from Johnny's bedroom. When she went to investigate she discovered Cesar had already assembled the new racetrack set on the table. With the giant packs of batteries purchased, they'd be able to play indefinitely.

Johnny was in ecstasy. Who wouldn't be with a father who

knew more about racing than anyone alive? She noticed everything else was still waiting to be opened and put away.

Sarah looked for the new bedding they'd bought. She pulled everything from the wrappers and started to make up her son's bed. Tonight he would sleep on sheets and pillows covered in his adored dinosaurs. As she was throwing the dinosaur comforter over the bed, Bianca came in to announce that lunch was ready on the terrace.

Several hours later, while Johnny and his father were swimming in the pool with Angelo and Bibi, Sarah put a superheroes lamp on his bedside table. A poster of the latest comic book hero movie adorned the wall above his bed. Those were the last finishing touches. The bedroom had been transformed and now resembled his room in Watsonville stuffed full with the treasures that made it home for him.

Anyone peeking inside would know a little boy lived here. Cesar's little boy.

Along with a soccer ball and a shiny red Italian scooter he could ride around the gym, his father had bought him some fairy tales published in Italian, French and Spanish.

Sarah had a feeling formal language lessons were about to begin with Cesar the teacher—required education for a Varano-de Falcon. She wasn't complaining. Sarah would need those lessons, too, the sooner the better.

When Bianca spoke Italian in Sarah's presence, she felt shut out. Cesar seemed to understand this because he stressed to the entire staff including Bibi that everyone speak English in front of Sarah and Johnny until they were acclimatized. Though she knew Cesar would always despise her, she appreciated his sensitivity.

By the end of their busy day she was worn-out. While Cesar disappeared for his final workout session with Bibi, Sarah put Johnny down, then took a long bath herself.

But unlike the night before, she was still awake when Cesar

wheeled in to their bedroom for his shower. Though she pretended to be asleep while Angelo helped him into bed, her body quickened to know he lay so close to her.

He'd brought the familiar smell of his soap with him. Combined with his male scent, her senses were instantly aroused. She crushed the edge of the pillow in her hands.

Even in the semidark Cesar must have seen the betraying gesture. "Sarah?"

Her heart began to thud. "Yes?"

CHAPTER SIX

"TURN around so I can talk to you."

For a moment Sarah had forgotten that Cesar had to lie on his back and couldn't move the bottom half of his body.

She rolled to her other side so she was facing him. Above the covers she could see his bare arms and chest with its dusting of hair. Her insides quivered in remembrance of the night they'd spent giving each other pleasure beyond comprehension.

"My family's coming tomorrow to stay through the weekend. They'll be arriving some time in the later afternoon."

Sarah had known it was going to happen, but she was frightened. "Do you wish they weren't coming this soon?"

"It's out of my hands." Over and above his frustration, he sounded resigned.

"Like any mother, she needs to see you with her own eyes and discover that her son is well on the road to a full recovery."

"What she sees is what it's going to be from here on," he bit out. "It's Johnny that has her sounding happier than I've heard her in years. She would have come tonight if I'd given the word."

"He can't wait to meet his other grandparents." She bit her lip. "As they're *your* parents, I know they'll treat me with every courtesy, but I have no illusions about their innermost feelings where I'm concerned."

He lay there with one hard-muscled arm over his eyes. "At

the moment they're too overjoyed to realize they're grandparents again to think about anything else."

It was a lot more than that. Fearing that Cesar would never be able to father a child period, this news had to mean everything to them. A child brought new life. Johnny had brought Cesar back from the edge. They knew he was the reason their son had left the hospital this fast, the reason he had started his therapy.

"W-what can I do to help?"

"You?" His voice mocked. "Nothing."

His curt response cut her to the quick. "Would you rather I made myself scarce while they're here?"

"Johnny wouldn't tolerate it."

"Of course he would."

"Lie to anyone but me. You're his mother. He knows where you are every second of the day and night, and if he doesn't, he goes to find you. That kind of bond takes years to develop."

Unshed tears stung her eyelids. "He has loved you since I showed him your picture from the first months of his life. From the beginning not a day has gone by that he hasn't brought up your name, wanting to know where you are, what race you're getting ready for. He goes to sleep with his daddy's name on lips.

"When you picked him up from your hospital bed, he launched himself into your arms with all the love he has in him. In case you've forgotten, when it grew tense in the store today he clung to *you*, not me. I'd be jealous if it were anyone but you."

A deep sigh escaped his throat. "Was it a normal delivery, or did you have complications?"

She couldn't keep up with his thoughts. "No complications. But there was a small time period right after the baby was born when I couldn't feel anything from my waist down because of the epidural. I had some anxious moments until it started to wear off.

"It's probably the closest I'll ever come to knowing something of what it's like for you," she whispered in pain.

His arm shifted back to the mattress. "How long were you in labor?"

"About thirty hours."

He stirred. "That long?"

"It's normal for a first baby."

"What about Johnny?"

"He was perfect in every way."

"Did you nurse him?"

"Yes."

"For how long?"

"Until he was nine months."

Trying to reassure him she said, "You can trust the pictures in his baby book. Our son has been a gift from day one."

She could hear his mind turning everything over. "His two-year-old photo looks like one of Luc at the same age."

"Your mother will probably tell you all the rest look like you."

After an uneasy silence he said, "My brother and Olivia will be coming with my parents. They're bringing Marie-Claire."

The news relieved her somewhat. "How fun for Johnny. He's very good around Lacey, Elaine's little girl. She adores her older cousin of course, and follows him everywhere. He pretends not to like it, but I know he *loves* being idolized." He's got all your charisma, Cesar.

"While he was brushing his teeth tonight, one of his bottom teeth came out in the front. It disappeared down the drain before I could catch it."

Sarah laughed gently. "I'm glad you were there. He hates blood."

"I noticed."

"I didn't hear him cry for me, Cesar."

Silence reigned before he said, "No."

"And you know why. Because he was with his daddy. That was all he needed. As long as we're on the subject of his fears, you should know that if he ever freezes on you for no apparent reason, it's because there's a fly somewhere around. He hates them. I made a mistake when I let him watch an animated film about flies. He wasn't ready for it."

It was Cesar's turn to chuckle. Always a beautiful sound she couldn't hear often enough.

"Cesar?" She raised up on her elbow, wanting to take advantage of this lull when he didn't seem so hostile. "Bibi told me you need to be moved to different positions during the night. I'd go crazy if I had to stay in the same position all the time. Why don't you let me turn you toward me now?"

"Angelo will come." His steely voice felt like a sudden blast of arctic air.

"There's no need with me right here."

She felt his anger. "There's every need."

Anger masked fear. It gave her an idea.

"What are you afraid of?"

"What in the hell are you talking about?"

"Whether you're wearing pajama bottoms or not, I've seen your body before. We made a baby together. It's no mystery to me." After the incredible night they'd spent together, he ought to know that.

"The doctor told me there's not a scratch on you. The injury's deep inside, so what difference does it make to you if I spare Angelo from having to get up in the night? Unless of course my touch is so repulsive to you, you can't bear the thought of my hands on your body. Then I understand and won't offend you again by offering."

The silence grew louder. "It's been a long day. Go to sleep, Sarah."

Before she turned away from him she said, "If you should change your mind, just whisper to me and I'll help you."

Half an hour later Sarah was still wide-awake. So was Cesar. His restlessness indicated growing discomfort.

This had gone on long enough. "When will Angelo be here?"

He didn't pretend to be out for the count. "At two, and again at four."

Her watch said midnight. "Neither of us can wait that long."

Whether she had his permission or not, she threw off the covers, revealing Cesar's long, powerful, pajama-clad legs to her vision. He was built like a Roman god.

Trying to focus on the task at hand, she got on her knees and reached across him. His warmth rose up to engulf her. With both hands on his left hip she carefully started to roll him toward her. It didn't seem possible he couldn't do it himself.

Their bodies brushed against each other in the process. He perforce had to adjust his head and arms to the new position.

"There! That *has* to feel better."

"It does," he admitted with telling reluctance.

"Good!"

She fit the small pillow lying at the end of the bed between his knees the way Bibi had shown her.

"In a little while I'll help you turn on your stomach. I know it's the way you prefer to sleep." The comment slipped out before she could stop it, but it was too late to call it back now.

Many were the times in the past when they'd lounged on the beach at Carmel. Sometimes after a race he would fall asleep from exhaustion and she would watch him. Inevitably he would turn on his stomach with his arms stretched beyond his dark head. A gorgeous specimen of manhood she longed to keep captive on her shore while she stood guard over him.

Would that she were one of those Sirens with the magic power to drive him mad with desire once more.

"Tonight when Angelo comes, tell him you won't need him anymore. I'm not only your new publicist. As of now I'm Bibi's new assistant."

So saying, she got out of bed and padded into the bathroom for her lotion. Feeling enabled since he'd told her he was more comfortable in the changed position, she intended to help make him even more relaxed.

After returning to the side of the bed, she poured some of it onto his left shoulder. Then she sat down next to him and began smoothing it into his beautiful, smooth olive skin stretched over hard muscle. She worked slowly, covering every centimeter of exposed flesh from his neck and back, down his arm to his left hand. A hand that had been gripping the steering wheel of various Formula 1 race cars since he was nineteen years old.

With another dollop of lotion she massaged his palm, finding the places in between his strong, ringless fingers. She loved the contrast of calluses only to find those tiny areas of soft skin. On her next trip to town she planned to buy him a wedding band. A simple one in gold. Whether he chose to wear it or not was immaterial. Inside the band she would have it engraved with a private message.

After keeping Johnny a secret from him for so long, he could accuse her all he wanted of not knowing the meaning of love. But he couldn't deny what had happened between them the night Johnny had been conceived. Theirs had been a union of fire. She still burned from the memories and craved to know his possession again.

It took the greatest strength of will not to put her lips to the skin she'd been touching and kneading. The urge to find his mouth with her own and make love to him for hour upon hour was fast becoming an obsession. If he was incapable of making love to her the old-fashioned way, none of that mattered. He was the love of her life. She would show him. Nothing was impossible.

Finally she heard the sounds of deep breathing and knew he'd drifted off. After four grueling workouts on top of everything else today, it didn't surprise her. She put the lotion on the bedside table and pulled the covers to his neck.

"Sleep well, my love," she mouthed the words. On impulse she tiptoed to Johnny's room and peeked inside. All was well. With both her men safely tucked in for the night, she could settle down. But there didn't seem to be any way to shut off her mind.

Tomorrow she'd be meeting Cesar's family. Another trial of fire.

Courage, the priest had said. Where did one go to find it?

"*Eh bien,* Bibi—looking as beautiful as ever I see. Haven't you finished torturing him yet?"

"*Tiens tiens!* If it isn't Luca de Falcon. The terrible two in one room," she teased.

From the exercise table Cesar eyed his tall, dark-haired elder brother who'd just walked in the gym. He looked good. "Bibi invented the word," he said on a groan.

Luc grinned. "Tell me about it. I've been where you are, little brother."

Once upon a time there had been a question whether Luc would keep his right leg, let alone ever be able to use it again. Bad news for a world-class alpine skier. Though he couldn't ski anymore, Bibi had been one of the therapists to help him walk again. A few years ago he'd been able to throw away his cane, the lucky devil.

"Five more knee-ups, then he's all yours, *mon vieux.*"

"You're all heart, Bibi," Luc muttered. "In that case I'd better do something ahead of time to counteract the effect of Juliana's cooking or Olivia will divorce me." He picked up a set of barbells and got started.

"Since when?" Cesar asked through gritted teeth. Bibi gave no quarter.

"Since I got on the scales last week and discovered I'm ten pounds heavier than a year ago."

"Your wife is right to get after you." Bibi entered into the conversation. "She wants you around for a long time."

Finally she gave a friendly pat to Cesar's shoulder. "You're done until tonight." She helped him from the exercise table to the wheelchair. "Now I'm off for a swim. *À toute à l'heure.*"

Cesar wheeled after her. Once she was out of the door, he locked it. When he turned around, Luc was right behind him. He glimpsed the compassion in his brother's eyes before he felt his arms go around him. They hugged while silent messages passed between them. But when he finally let Cesar go, those silver orbs similar to his own were dancing.

"You're so full of surprises, I still haven't recovered."

Cesar drew in a fortifying breath. "I'm afraid Sarah was the one with the surprise."

"She's *ravissante, mon frère.* You know what I mean," he said in a deep voice meant for no one else's ears but his.

Yes. Cesar knew. Last night his Siren had treated him to a new dimension of the word torture.

"Those eyes—it's no longer a mystery why there was a time when you found California more enticing than the usual grazing grounds closer to home. As for Johnny, I'm completely *bouleversé.*"

"So am I."

"After we were introduced, the first thing he did was show me where he'd lost a tooth. He then informed me that *you* weren't scared of anything, not even blood. That's high praise for a son to give his father." Laughter poured out of Luc.

Cesar laughed with him till the tears came. "He's so wonderful I can't find the words."

Luc nodded. "He has Maman enchanted. She can't stop crying. Marie-Claire is already his slave. But you should see Papa! He hasn't let go of Jean-Cesar's hand. At the moment your son is taking his *grand-père* on a tour of your house. Already he's playing the host. He's a Falcon all right."

They stared hard at each other. "He's one of us," Cesar whispered. "Incredible, isn't it?"

Luc cocked his head. "You couldn't have chosen a name to make papa prouder."

Cesar looked away from his brother. "That was Sarah's doing. She put it on the birth certificate five years ago."

"She's done a remarkable job of raising your son. You certainly met your equal in Carmel. She has all the right instincts." And all the right parts in all the right places. That's what he knew Luc wanted to say, but to his credit he didn't.

"Except for one fatal flaw. I don't want to talk about her."

"Then we won't."

Luc reached out to unlock the door. "Let's get you back to your room before Bianca bites our heads off that we're ruining Juliana's dinner."

"Johnny already has her wrapped around his little finger."

"Like father, like son. She always liked you better than me." Luc's eyebrows lifted. "Did I ever tell you I was jealous about that?"

"Did I ever tell you how jealous I was of my famous ski champion brother?"

"Those days are over for me. Let's thank God you'll recover in time to race again next year."

Cesar stiffened. *"Et tu, brute?"*

Luc shrugged his shoulders. "I'm only repeating your wife's words in front of the camera yesterday. Olivia and I happened to see her on last night's news."

A band constricted his breathing. He'd purposely not watched. "What exactly did she say?"

Luc gave him a verbatim report. "She was magnificent. To save face you *have* to get better now."

Cesar's gracious parents and brother shocked Sarah by hugging her the moment he made the introductions. She saw no censure in their eyes as they welcomed her to the family. Any strong feelings against her were lost in the joy they felt because Cesar had survived the crash and was looking so well already.

And of course, there was Johnny who took their hearts by storm. "Oh Cesario—he looks just like you at the same age!" his mother cried. "Come here and let me hug you again, Giovanni. You don't mind if I call you that, do you?"

The name Giovanni triggered something Sarah had said to Cesar in the hospital because he shot her a brief, narrow-lidded glance.

"I like it!" Johnny's comment caused everyone to laugh in delight. Like all Cesar's family, he had their charm.

Later that night Olivia leaned toward Sarah. "While everyone's still out on the terrace with the children, there's something I want to give you in private before we all go to bed. Come with me."

Intrigued, Sarah followed her sister-in-law through the house to the guest bedroom prepared for them. Olivia was one of the famous blond Duchess triplets from New York. The other two were married to Cesar's cousins.

Sarah found her warm and down to earth. After supervising their children throughout dinner and afterward, they'd already become good friends.

Once the door was closed, Olivia darted to the closet. "I put it in here." Sarah assumed it was a wedding present, or something for Johnny. To her surprise she produced a cane of all things. She hurried back to Sarah with it.

"You heard Cesar's parents talking about Luc's injury tonight, but you don't know the history behind this cane. When I first met Luc, he'd barely started using it to get around. He was in so much pain physically and emotionally, it was awful to witness.

"Seeing Cesar in that wheelchair tonight was like déjà vu. They're very much alike and so close. But there was a time when Luc thought Cesar had betrayed him with his fiancée."

Sarah stared at the floor. "I read about the scandal in the paper."

"None of it was true, Sarah. She'd had a secret affair with one of Cesar's mechanics and tried to pass off the baby as Cesar's whom she believed had more money than Luc because of his fame. What she did was evil. It almost destroyed both brothers because Luc believed her lies."

"I wish I'd known!" Sarah cried. "It's the reason I kept putting off calling Cesar. I thought—" She buried her face in her hands. "I thought if he already had a baby, he didn't need to hear about another one. How awful for them, for the whole family."

A groan came out of Olivia. "You have no idea how ugly things got, especially when Cesar had been going through a long, ongoing personal crisis of his own he wouldn't share with anyone. I think maybe you had something to do with that, Sarah."

"If I did," she said, lifting her head, "I was the last person to know it. Tell me everything."

"Luc refused to speak to Cesar who was totally innocent. To make matters worse, I went to watch Cesar race at Monza. Through a horrible misunderstanding, Luc thought I'd slept with him and wanted nothing to do with me. If you could have heard the things he said to me…"

Tears rolled down Sarah's cheeks. "Then you should have been in Cesar's hospital room the other morning when he found out he had a son I'd never told him about…"

Olivia put a comforting arm around her for a moment. "They're not brothers for nothing."

"No." Sarah sniffed, trying to gain her composure.

"Because of what happened with Luc's fiancée, Cesar has great reason to distrust any woman who tries to get close to him."

"He despises me, Olivia."

"He only thinks he does."

Sarah shook her head. "I did such a horrible thing to him, Olivia, there's no way I can expect his forgiveness. If only I could go back and rectify things." She sobbed. "When I see how much Johnny loves the family, how much he's needed all of you and his father, it kills me. I'm an evil person."

"No—" Olivia cried.

"Oh, yes, I am. After what I did to Cesar, it's a wonder he didn't sue for full custody of Johnny." Her voice shook. "He had every right to take him away from me."

"He would never do that to the mother of his son. He's a remarkable man."

"I know," Sarah whispered.

"Once I'd heard the truth from Cesar about Luc's fiancée, I went back to the sailboat to talk to Luc about it. I told him what Cesar had related to me. At the time, he wouldn't believe me. The next thing I knew, he'd left for Monaco.

"All that remained behind was a cruel note to me. I found the cane on the floor. It meant Luc could finally walk without help. It also meant he didn't want anything to do with me ever again.

"It was a nightmare because I loved him so much. Unable to get through to him, I went back to New York and took the cane with me. But there was a happy ending. Luc found the courage to face Cesar and they reconciled. Now they're closer than ever, and obviously Luc and I got together."

Olivia looked at the cane. "To me it represents the bridge between Luc's darkest hell and his journey back into the light.

"When I saw you on the news last night and heard your conviction that Cesar would be back next year to win another race, I knew you had to have the cane because in time I, too, believe he'll walk again. When he reaches a certain point, he'll need it for a while. Let it be your good luck talisman."

"What a priceless gift." Sarah reached out to hug her. "I'll hide it until the right moment." Cesar was in no state of mind to handle seeing it yet. "Thank you for telling me what I needed to know, Olivia. It helps me understand Cesar in ways I never could have done without your explanation."

"You're welcome. Let's be honest. We're married to the most fantastic men alive, but until every possible obstacle has been obliterated from their paths, they guard their hearts fiercely."

That's what the priest had said. He'd also promised that one day the sun would come out. Olivia had said much the same thing. Sarah gripped the cane tighter as a little frisson of hope chased up her spine.

"Excuse me for a minute while I find a place for it, then I'll join you and the others." She knew exactly where she would put it and headed for Johnny's room.

Once her mission was accomplished, she followed the noise of happy laughter back to the terrace. Earlier Johnny had brought out his game of twister. While the adults watched, he did amazing contortions.

Marie-Claire, with blond curls bobbing against her forehead, tried to imitate him and fell flat several times. Trying not to laugh too hard, Luc helped her get up and attempted to repair his daughter's wounded pride with words of encouragement.

Cesar on the other hand secretly aided and abetted his son from the wheelchair. The friendly spirit of competition between brothers would always be there, but Marie-Claire had worn herself out.

Olivia darted Sarah an amused glance before she said, "I think it's bathtime."

"Hey—she can swim in Mommy and Daddy's tub with me!"

Johnny's comment caused the family to roar with laughter. Cesar caught his son to him and pulled him onto his lap. "That's what the swimming pool is for. You can swim with her tomorrow. Right now it's time for bed."

"Okay," Johnny said with a long face.

Before she could say it, Cesar prompted his son to kiss everyone good-night. He jumped off his father's lap and did his bidding before leaving the terrace with him. Again, this was a proud moment for her husband, one in which Sarah didn't want to interfere.

Cesar's parents had decided to retire, too. While everyone said good-night, she gathered up the game and followed behind Luc who was carrying an overly tired, overwrought Marie-Claire in his arms.

While Cesar supervised Johnny's bath, Sarah straightened his bedroom, which looked like a disaster. Then she slipped into the other room to grant them their quiet time. Eventually he came running in to give her a toothpaste kiss, then hurried back to his daddy.

It was almost eleven before Angelo helped Cesar to bed. Though she was exploding with thoughts and feelings she'd been storing all day, she was too afraid of being rebuffed to initiate conversation. But as soon as they were alone, she turned to him only to discover him lying on his left side away from her.

"Cesar? Did you tell Angelo I'll help you in the night from now on?"

Though they weren't touching, she could feel the tremor that shook his body. "I told him to come at four."

Her pulse picked up speed. "Then I'll set my watch for two."

"If you sleep through it, don't worry about it."

"I won't." She bit her lower lip. "I—I like your family very much."

"Where did you and Olivia disappear to for so long?"

She moaned inwardly. Sarah had been waiting for that question, but he'd asked it without acknowledging what she'd just said. If she was hoping that seeing his family had done anything to ameliorate the tension between them, she could think again.

"Olivia didn't know how much I knew about Luc's accident."

"His wasn't anything like mine. Even if he'd lost his leg, he had another one."

"I know. Basically s-she told me not to give up hope."
Olivia had told her a lot of things that Cesar didn't need to hear.

He cursed softly. "The platitudes never end."

That made her angry and she sat up. "Would you prefer that
everyone tell you it's hopeless? How would you like it if your
family simply shook their heads and said, "You poor thing.
You're all washed up. You should have died out there." Her
body was shaking uncontrollably.

"It's what they're all thinking," his voice grated.

"No, Cesar—that's what *you're* thinking. It's pathetic!"

She threw her covers aside and jumped out of bed.

"Where in the hell are you going?"

Well, well. She'd made him fighting mad. That was good.
Would that he'd get so outraged, he'd leap out of bed to come
and strangle her.

"Away from you so you can wallow in self-pity. It's what
you want. I'll sleep with Johnny for the rest of the night.
Thankfully he has no idea the father he worships has given
up." At the doorway she turned to him. "Don't worry. I'll be
back at two."

CHAPTER SEVEN

THE night was endless.

Every time Cesar glanced at his watch, only five minutes had passed.

Since Sarah had swept out of the bedroom in a rage, memories of that day at the track had started coming back to him in flashes. The details weren't clear yet, but he relived that feeling he was careering to his death again and again. His body broke out in a cold sweat.

Whether he closed his eyes or kept them open, the horror of it left him gasping for breath.

"Cesar?"

He smelled Sarah's fragrance before she sat down next to him. Part of her flowing, lilac colored nightgown brushed against his arm. "What's wrong? I heard you cry out."

"It's nothing."

"Don't tell me that." She put a hand to his cheek. He felt her fingers brush the hair off his forehead. "You're hot, and you've been perspiring." She moved away. In seconds she came back with a cold, damp washrag and wiped his face with it.

"You've remembered the crash, haven't you. The doctor told me your mind would recall the moment of impact when it was ready. It means you're healing."

He groaned. If this was healing, he didn't want any part of it.

"I saw the whole thing. Is there anything you want to ask me?"

Cesar felt his eyelids sting. "How did Johnny handle it?"

She moved the cloth down the side of his jaw to his throat, giving him more relief. "Ever since the first time he saw you walk to your race car, he assumed you wore an astronaut suit. It's a good thing he considers them indestructible. When you crashed he said, "He won't die cos he's wearing his astronaut suit, Mommy.""

The blood pounded in his ears. "What did you say to that?"

"I told him, 'That's right. The great Cesar Villon is indestructible.'"

He inhaled harshly. "Is that what *you* thought?"

She stared down at him in the semidarkness. "No. Unfortunately I'm too grown up to believe in fairy tales. I just kept praying to God to preserve your life so you could meet your son and love him the way I do."

"It appears your prayer was answered."

"But not yours, right Cesar?"

Her salvo went straight to his gut. "I'll refresh the washrag. Then I'll be back to help you get in a different position."

He waited in agony for her return. In truth, he didn't want to be alone tonight….

"Which way do you want to lie next?" She'd put the cloth on the bedside table.

"On my back."

"Okay." She removed the covers. He was dressed in fresh pajama bottoms. "When I say three, you start to turn and I'll do the rest."

She put her hands beneath his hip and knees. "Ready? One, two, three—" Over he went on his back. She was strong when she had to be. As Luc had pointed out, Sarah Priestley had many attributes.

After putting the little pillow at the end of the bed, she made sure his legs were straight. "Does that feel better?"

"Yes."

Once she'd pulled up the covers to his waist, she sat down and began to wipe his bare chest and shoulders with the damp cloth. "Tell me when to stop."

Damn if he didn't want her to stop. "When I saw Johnny and Marie-Claire playing together, I realized how much he needs friends his own age. We need to get him into school right away."

"I was going to talk to you about that, Cesar. His kindergarten class in Watsonville started last week."

"We start a little later here. The family will be leaving Sunday evening. I'll inquire about it on Monday. He's going to have to be mainstreamed."

She nodded. "It's the best way."

"You agree?" He was relieved they wouldn't have an argument about that. Johnny wouldn't like it at first.

"When I was in grade school, the kids who came from other countries were tossed in at the deep end. Within a year they were spouting English as if they'd lived there all their lives. Children always pick everything up so fast. By this time next year we won't know Johnny from any of the other children here."

Exactly. "Except that with English his native language, he'll have an advantage."

"Yes. The best of you and me," she said in a raw tone, catching him off guard.

"Next summer we'll stay at the house in Monaco. Marie-Claire will be a year older."

"After a year of Italian, his French will come fast." She had read his mind. "Do you have a headache? Your ibuprofen is in the bathroom. If nothing else it might help you sleep now."

If he needed oblivion, it was to shut her from his thoughts for the rest of the night. In the face of her ministrations, it was impossible to maintain the same level of anger.

"Bring me four."

"Please," she corrected him the way she did Johnny. "Along with your desire to give up, you appear to have lost your manners, too. Being paralyzed is no excuse," came the sharp retort.

Cesar had no idea he'd married a woman with a biting tongue. The girl he'd made love to didn't have a mean bone in her beautiful body. But he had to admit that in six years that body was more alluring than ever. He also had to admit she was a perfect mother to their son. Cesar's mother had sung her new daughter-in-law's praises to him more than once since their arrival.

"*Per favore*, Signora de Falcon."

"That's better."

On that crisp note she withdrew the cloth and left him long enough to bring back his pills with a glass of water. After he'd swallowed them she started toward Johnny's door.

"If I ask you politely this time, will you read me a story so I can go to sleep?"

She swung around in surprise. Her nightgown swirled around her long, gorgeous legs. "What story?"

"Sleeping Beauty." Except that it was like he'd been the one asleep all the years they'd been apart and was just now coming awake. "It's in Johnny's room on his desk."

"It's in Italian!"

"I'll help you."

"In other words you're ready to start *my* lessons *now*. I guess it won't hurt to become proficient so I can understand my son when he curses in both languages like his father."

"Is that what I do?" he mocked.

"In four languages actually, depending on your mood. As you know, I'm awfully good at slaughtering Italian. But if you really want me to, it's your funeral."

"I'll chance it since it'll get my mind off the one I escaped in Brazil."

Her face closed up. "That's not funny, Cesar."

"It wasn't meant to be."

Before long she was back with the illustrated book in question. She turned on the lamp on her side of the bed and got in under the covers. Though she moved fast, it wasn't quite fast enough to hide the feminine contours of her silk-clad figure from his gaze.

In that instant he felt a stunning physical response of desire for her. Not just in his mind. *It affected every centimeter of his body, inside and out!*

Dear God— He'd thought he was dead in that part of his anatomy. Did that mean—

"Cesar? Your breathing sounds ragged all of sudden. Are you ill? Tell me the truth!"

His heart thundered in his chest. He needed to talk to his doctor as soon as possible. "I guess I'm still reliving the crash," he lied to give himself time to comprehend what was happening.

"Then let's get my lesson started." She opened the cover to the first page. *"La Bella Addormentata,"* she began, trying her hardest to pronounce the words so he'd understand them.

In one night he'd been in bed with two women, but it was his sweet, loving Sarah from that other life who lay next to him right now. Despite the terrible thing she'd done to him, his passion for her was back, stronger than ever.

It took all his strength of will not to reach out and pull her on top of his body. The need to feel her against him, to taste her mouth was such exquisite torture he groaned.

"Cesar—" she cried.

"Keep reading," he demanded. "Please…"

"Johnny, honey? Everyone's ready to leave." It was four in the afternoon. Cesar's family had a plane to catch.

He looked up at Sarah with a sad face. "Do they have to go?" That look brought searing guilt to the surface. For five years she'd deprived him of this.

"I'm afraid so, but you heard your father. We'll visit them next month."

Olivia walked over to them carrying her daughter who was inconsolable at having to leave. "Johnny? Do you know where Albert went? Marie-Claire can't find him. He's that little lamb that goes with her set of farm animals."

He lifted his eyebrows. "I don't know. She was playing with them everywhere."

"Maybe it's in your bedroom," Cesar suggested. "Let's take a look."

"I'll help, too," Sarah murmured. She eyed Olivia. "We'll be right back. If we can't find it, we'll keep looking and send it to you. There won't be any peace until she gets it back."

"You're right," Olivia said, sounding harried.

Sarah and Johnny hurried after Cesar who wheeled down the hall with greater energy than usual. Since Friday night when he'd had a breakthrough of memory, he seemed different. He wasn't quite so hostile with her for which she was grateful. The last thing she wanted was for Johnny to pick up on the tension between them.

Once they reached the bedroom, Cesar searched everything above the floor. Sarah leaned over the toy box in case it had been put inside. Johnny explored his closet, then lifted the bottom of the covers to look under the bed.

"I found it!" Johnny called to them.

"Bravo, mon fils."

"Hey—what's this?"

Too late Sarah remembered she'd hidden something there.

The moment Cesar glimpsed the cane, Sarah was afraid there'd be an explosion. Johnny handed it to him.

While Sarah held her breath, Cesar examined it. "This belonged to my brother when he needed help walking. I wonder what it's doing under *your* bed?"

Johnny hunched his shoulders in true Falcon fashion.

"Maybe Marie-Claire was playing with it and didn't want her daddy to know."

"Maybe," he said in a voice that sounded far away. Fearing the worst Sarah said, "Johnny? Will you please take Albert to Marie-Claire?"

"Okay. Do you want me to give Uncle Luc back his cane?"

"No," came the definitive response.

"Cos you don't want him to get mad, right?"

When his father didn't answer, he ran out of the room.

Nervous, Sarah turned to Cesar. "Olivia gave it to me," she admitted.

"I thought as much," he said in a gravelly voice.

"I-I realize that seeing it brings back memories of the time you and Luc were estranged. The thing is, Olivia thought it might bring you luck since you and Luc resolved your misunderstanding, and he was able to throw it away. Oh, Cesar, I'm so sorry." A sob rose in her throat. "I never meant for you to see it. Please forgive me. Where you're concerned, all I've ever done to you is the wrong thing."

His head reared. When she looked into his eyes they were a fiery silver. She'd forgotten they could look like that.

"The wrong thing? That's not strictly true. After six years, you could have continued to stay away and I would never have known. It took an extraordinary woman to brave me in that hospital room.

"It's even more amazing that you married me so I could have my son under optimum circumstances. You've had to make all the adjustments without any thought to your own needs. I'm not unaware that by marrying me, you've had to say goodbye to other men."

Oh, Cesar... Don't you know I said goodbye to them at the age of seventeen?

"Johnny's my life. He wants to be with you. His happiness is mine."

"Then we understand each other."

"Yes."

She understood that she'd killed any love he'd ever had for her, but for the love of Johnny he would find a way to make their marriage work. This was as close to an olive branch as she would ever receive from him, and was humbled by it.

"Tell the family I'll be out in a minute."

"I will."

Knowing he needed time, she rushed from the bedroom to join the others. When Cesar finally wheeled himself out to the back where everyone was loading up in the airport limo, there was no sign of the cane.

Olivia eyed Sarah knowing something was wrong. They squeezed hands. "I'll call you when we reach Monaco," she said in an aside.

"Please do," Sarah whispered back. Olivia was married to a Falcon. No one else could understand quite the same way.

Sarah waved goodbye to Luc and Marie-Claire before moving over to the other side with Johnny.

"We'll be expecting you next month." Cesar's mother kissed her on both cheeks before embracing her grandson one more time.

When Sarah turned away wet eyed, she almost ran into Cesar's father who was shorter than his sons, but every bit as attractive. He gave her a big hug and whispered in her ears. "You've saved my son's life. Bless you, *ma fille.*" He'd called her his daughter. In her wildest dreams she wouldn't have expected it.

"I've always loved him," she confessed so no one else could hear.

"Never stop, no matter what."

She'd just received pleading advice from the man who probably understood his son's emotional makeup better than anyone. Too soon the limo began to back out.

Johnny started crying. Cesar pulled him onto his lap. "We're going to miss everyone, aren't we?"

He nodded before throwing his arms around Cesar's neck. "I'm glad you're not going away."

"I'll never leave you."

Johnny squeezed him tighter. "I love you, Daddy."

"I love you, too, and I have an idea. How would you and your mommy like to take a boat ride on the Tyrrhenian Sea before dark?"

"The *what?*" His tears dried up in a hurry.

"That's the water we look out on from the terrace."

To Sarah's surprise Johnny frowned. "But what if we get too close to the Sirens?"

"Honey—there aren't any Sirens. That's just a story."

Cesar chuckled. "Don't worry. We won't go in that direction. Those islands are privately owned anyway. We'll take our boat to Capri. Since there are too many tourists walking around, we'll just enjoy a ride on the ocean and buy some *gelato* before we come back to the villa."

With Cesar in this mood, an outing to the famous Isle of Capri where he'd once promised to take her sounded heavenly.

"Juliana taught me that means ice cream."

"That's right. The very best there is."

"Um. I love strawberry."

"So do I."

"Hey, Mommy—Daddy likes strawberry, too!"

Sarah loved listening to them talk. "You must be his son."

"I *am!* You're funny, Mommy."

Rich, full laughter broke from Cesar. He sounded happy. After the incident with the cane she hadn't known what to expect. She would take this moment and savor it for the rest of the evening. But before they'd returned home, she noticed a change in Cesar. Johnny was doing all the talking while his father had gone quiet.

When she examined his features, she saw tension lines that hadn't been there earlier. Sarah sensed he was ill, but she didn't know if it was physical or emotional.

Maybe more memories of the crash were giving him a headache, one that made his complexion look like paste. Yet he hadn't said a word in case he alarmed Johnny.

The moment they reached the house she nodded to Angelo, signaling for him to take care of Cesar. He must have seen what she saw because the older man wheeled him straight down the hall.

Relieved they were back home, she put Johnny to bed without a bath. After his prayers she said, "I know you want to say good-night to daddy, but he's so tired he's already gone to bed and we shouldn't disturb him."

"Okay."

She tucked some toys in his covers and kissed his forehead.

"I can't wait till tomorrow. Daddy's going to help me build my Lego pirate ship."

"That sounds exciting." Every day with his father was a new adventure.

"Good night, Mommy."

"Good night, honey."

Anxious over Cesar, she hurried from the room into the master bedroom. Angelo had already put him to bed, hopefully with some pain medication. He lay on his back asleep. Moving closer to him, she saw how his hands clutched the sheet, as if he were in extreme pain.

As quietly as she could, she changed into her nightgown, then got next to him. After twenty minutes his breathing started to sound erratic. She could hear him muttering something unintelligible.

Her only thought was to give him comfort. Out of needs she couldn't suppress any longer, she wrapped her arm around chest and buried her face in his neck.

His body was damp with sweat. At first she couldn't make out what he was saying, but it was evident he was in torment.

Suddenly he crushed her against him with superhuman strength. "I'm a dead man!"

"You're not dead, Cesar!" She half-climbed on top of him, taking him by the shoulders. "You're alive, darling. You're alive. Come on. Wake up."

She began kissing his face, every centimeter of his skin and features. "You're all right, Cesar. You're here with me."

As fast as it came, the tension left his hard body. He opened his eyes. "Sarah?" He sounded dazed.

"Yes. You were reliving the crash. I heard you say 'I'm a dead man.' Tell me about it." He needed to talk about it. His doctor said it was vital.

Cesar blinked. "I was told to watch for debris coming around the turn. Rykert had taken a hit. Out of nowhere Prinz's car came flying at me." His powerful body shuddered. She felt it resonate to her insides. "When I was tossed through the air, I knew that was it."

How ghastly.

"But it wasn't the end. All three of you are alive and well. By next season you'll be out on the track again with Johnny cheering you on. *I'll* be cheering you on. I love you, Cesar. You have no idea how much," she cried before covering his mouth with her own.

Like someone coming out of a trance, he slowly began to respond until they were moving and breathing as one flesh. At last this was her Cesar in her arms. She needed his kiss the way she needed air.

While he put one hard-muscled arm around her back, he moved his other hand to the back of her head to keep her in place. Little did he know she wasn't going anywhere. All that she craved was right here with their mouths clinging to each other, tasting and savoring what had been denied them since that rapturous night years ago.

As his lips traveled to her throat, the white-hot heat of desire engulfed her. It had been so long since she'd known the feeling, she was burning with feverish needs.

"I'll help you get into a better position," she whispered into his vibrant black hair, aware he didn't have the same mobility and needed help. Aching for his love, wanting to show him he would always be desirable to her, she reached around to roll him on his side so he was facing her.

"There."

She smiled, wanting to help him get back his old confidence so they could recapture every glorious moment of the night they'd made love over and over again. Still on her knees, she started to lift off her nightgown. But she wasn't allowed to get any closer because his hand caught both of hers in a vise-like grip preventing movement.

A cruel smile broke out on his face. "This is as far as the show goes, *sposa mia*. You make an excellent mother, publicist and nurse, but your other talents need to be saved for a man who can service you."

He might just as well have squeezed every drop of blood from her heart. "Cesar— I only wanted to show you how desirable you are. We can work this out."

"If you mean *your* frustration, I'm afraid that's your problem, not mine. I did warn you."

After releasing her hands, he rearranged his pillow, then closed his eyes to let her know he wanted sleep and nothing else.

All she'd wanted was to make him realize he was still a man in every sense of the word. If she'd been any other woman, he might have allowed the experiment to continue. But there was no forgiveness for her. To ask for it was wrong.

She shrank from him and buried herself in the covers, realizing she didn't deserve more than his cold tolerance. You couldn't keep the secret of his son from him and expect anything else.

Much as she wanted to run someplace and cry out in pain where no one could hear her, she couldn't. He needed to be turned at two, and again at four. Furthermore tonight he'd had a complete breakthrough with his nightmare. In case he suffered another one before morning, she would be here to help bring him out of it again.

Cesar lay there writhing in physical and emotional turmoil. Sarah's perfume, the taste of her lips had intoxicated him almost to the breaking point. He despised himself for letting her get this close to him tonight. After her betrayal, how could he stand her touch?

It went to show what a fool he really was and always had been where she was concerned. The only good to come of their union was his wonderful Johnny. Surely for his son's sake Cesar could be stronger than her treacherous Siren's call—

He still had the rest of this night to get through, and all the other nights when she awakened to turn him. Never again would he allow himself to be caught off guard like helpless prey in her silken spider's web, one only she knew how to spin with those magic lips and fingers.

A car crash wasn't the only way to paralyze a man. She knew seductive methods as ancient as time itself.

He gritted his teeth. What he had to do was banish tonight's experience to the furthest regions of his mind and pretend it had never happened. When daylight rolled around, he would behave with the same detached civility he'd shown her since the wedding ceremony. Over time it would become a ritual he wouldn't have to think about.

By Monday of the following week, the de Falcon household had settled into a comfortable routine. Thankfully the bitterness of those first few days seemed to be gone for good. Sarah's tentative pax with her husband appeared to be holding.

There was no repeat of his nightmares for which she was thankful, no discussion of what had gone on when she'd overstepped her bounds to try to show him physical love. It might never have happened, except that she knew otherwise and functioned with shattered pieces of her heart to prove it.

Cesar allowed her to turn him several times a night. Angelo had stopped coming in. Sarah was glad about that. Though the older man was unobtrusive, she craved her privacy with Cesar. Nights were the only time she had strictly alone with him.

In between Cesar's workouts during the day, he spent his time with Johnny in the pool using special arm floaters, or simply playing with him. Since school would be starting the following week, this time was precious to them.

While they were thus occupied, Sarah had time each day to walk to town and get some much needed shopping done. She picked up the wedding pictures and stopped at a jewelers to pick out a ring for Cesar. With the engraving done, she would find the opportune moment to give it to him.

When she returned from town, she discovered both of them on the terrace eating a pasta lunch. Cesar's gaze scrutinized her before she sat down. Maybe he was relieved to see her wearing a different outfit for a change. One of her new purchases was this white skirt and silky orange blouse with the pointed lapels, both Italian designed.

"Ciao, Mama." Sarah blinked. "Daddy and I put the big puzzle of Italy together. Now I know where Positano is. Do you want to see it?"

"Where is it?"

"On the dining room table."

Since everyone enjoyed eating *al fresco*, they hadn't had a meal in there yet, but apparently the table had other uses.

"That sounds interesting. I'll take a look at it after lunch."

"Juliana made us *Scialatielli*."

His pronunciation sounded perfect to her ears. Their little boy was turning into his father before her very eyes.

She took a bite, then answered back with, *"Questa pasta è deliziosa!"* The only reason she knew a few words and phrases was because of Cesar. He used to call her "delicious" in Italian when he'd tease her and make love to her with his eyes.

Johnny giggled. "You sound funny, Mommy. Doesn't she Daddy."

"That's because you're not used to hearing your mother speak Italian. She pronounced that *perfectamente*."

With great daring Sarah flashed him a glance. "I had a good teacher." He could make of that what he wanted.

Cesar put down his glass of iced tea. "Speaking of teachers, it's time we talked about your school, Johnny."

Uh-oh. Sarah had wondered when Cesar would broach the subject. Since he'd missed out on so many firsts with Johnny, she was leaving this big step up to him.

Johnny had just finished his milk. It left a moustache. A scared look had crept into his eyes. "When is it?"

"On Monday. You go for a half a day in the afternoons. I've talked to your teacher. You'll like Signora Moretti. She speaks English, so you don't need to feel nervous."

Alligator tears poured down his cheeks. "But I don't want to leave you, Daddy."

That drooping, trembling lower lip got to Sarah every time, so she could just imagine how it was affecting Cesar.

"I didn't like to leave my parents, either, but everyone has to go to school."

"Why?"

"To learn things."

"But you know *everything!* You can teach me."

Sarah suppressed a smile. Even if Cesar was getting frustrated, he had to be thrilled with his son's confidence in him.

"At school you'll make friends."

"I don't want friends. I just want you." By now he'd slipped from the chair to climb on Cesar's lap. Over the shoulder of his son who'd thrown his arms around his neck, Cesar shot her worried glance. He needed some reinforcing about now. It had to be a first.

She wiped her mouth with a napkin. "Johnny? Did you know that's the same time Carson goes to kindergarten? But he isn't as lucky as you because his teacher doesn't speak Italian. You're going to learn twice as much. And do you know what else?"

Sarah had reached him enough that he turned around to look at her with a blotchy face. "What?"

"While you're at school, I'm going to be at my school learning Italian. We'll leave for class together, and come home together where Daddy will be waiting for you after his workout."

The idea had just come to her, but it made perfect sense. She needed to attend formal classes. Cesar expected it. This was something she could do for him and Johnny. For herself!

"Are you scared?"

"Yes. But do you know what? I don't want to be like Mrs. Lopez."

"Who's Mrs. Lopez?" Cesar questioned in a deep voice. His gray eyes were intent and curious as they studied her features.

"She lives in one of the town houses with her daughter," Johnny informed him. "She's from Mexico."

"Mrs. Lopez doesn't speak English, does she Johnny?"

"Nope."

"Guess how long she's been in California?"

"I don't know."

"Twenty years."

He frowned. "Twenty—"

"That's a long time to live in a country and not learn the language. She was probably scared, too. But just imagine if you and I lived with daddy twenty years and we still couldn't speak Italian? Think how much fun we'll have saying *Buon giorno* and *Ciao* to Nana and Papa on the phone. They won't believe it."

"I can say *Ciao* now!" He slid off his father's lap. "I bet Carson doesn't know any Italian." The wheels were spinning.

"Sure he does," Cesar murmured. "He can say pizza and spaghetti, can't he?"

Though Cesar kept a deadpan face, Johnny got the joke. He laughed and patted his father's cheeks. "You're funny, Daddy. Will you take me to my first class?"

"We'll all go," he announced. His eyes thanked Sarah in a private message. One crumb from his table and her insides turned to mush. "Now if you two will excuse me, Angelo's waiting to drive me to the clinic."

"What's wrong?" Johnny cried before Sarah could ask the same question.

"I'm taking the helicopter to Rome for my checkup. I have to keep my appointment with the doctor. It's been over a week since I left the hospital."

"Can't we go with you?"

"I won't be gone that long. He's going to do some tests. That's all. I'll be back before you know it."

"Promise?"

"I wouldn't lie to you."

Johnny stared at him, fighting more tears. "Okay."

Sarah got up from the table and put an arm around his shoulders. "Come on, honey. I want to see that puzzle."

Except that Johnny had other plans in mind. After walking his father out to the car, he returned to the terrace. Sarah stayed with him. Ten minutes later they both watched the helicopter lift above the other side of the mount and wing its way north. After the togetherness they'd all shared, it was agony to see the man they loved disappear into the blue.

Sarah knew Johnny wouldn't be himself until Cesar came back. In fact he probably wouldn't budge from the terrace watching for his return. She left him long enough to get some board games they could play while they waited.

As it turned out, he didn't come by dinnertime. He still hadn't arrived when it was bathtime.

"Do you think Daddy's okay?" he asked as she put him to bed.

"Of course. He would have called otherwise. Doctors always take a long time. Come on. I'll lie down with you."

After his prayer, which was all about bringing his father home safe, Sarah subsided next to him on top of the covers. She'd scarcely closed her eyes when she heard Cesar whisper, "Is he asleep?"

"You're back!" Johnny cried. He'd been awake the whole time. Like lightning he flew out of bed into his father's arms. "You took so long."

"The doctor had an emergency to take care of first."

Sarah didn't believe him, but it didn't matter. He was home now. She slid off the side and went into their bedroom to get ready for bed. Another hour passed before he was back with Angelo who helped him with his nightly routine.

Once they were alone she turned to him. He was lying on his left side away from her, a silent signal he didn't want to talk, but she wouldn't let him get away with it this time.

"Tell me what the doctor said. I can't wait any longer to hear."

"I don't know why." That cold, dismissive tone was back in his voice. Her spirits plunged. She'd almost forgotten. "I told you I have no expectations. To be blunt, I'm exhausted. *Buona notte*, Sarah. "

CHAPTER EIGHT

CESAR needed time to comprehend what he'd learned at the hospital. Two specialists besides his own doctor had run him through tests. After hearing that his bodily functions were returning to normal, and he'd been experiencing a tingling in his feet and legs over the last two days, their opinion was unanimous.

"The bruising wasn't as serious as we'd first supposed. The shock has worn off and the bundle of nerves injured is receiving those brain signals once more. That means you're going to walk again, Cesar. Perhaps not as perfectly as you once did.

"It's way too early to talk about getting back in a race car. Only time and hard work will give you the answer. It all depends on your physical therapy, which you will have to continue for a long time."

The miraculous news made him wonder if his heart could withstand the impact.

He could hardly believe it, yet the tingling sensations were growing stronger. They made him so restless he realized the nerves were coming back to life. Last night he could have sworn he felt Sarah's fingers on his hip after she'd turned him. They'd lingered for a moment, sending a shock wave through his nervous system.

For the time being he didn't want anyone to know except Bibi and Massimo. He'd sworn the doctors to absolute secrecy. Until he could at least get out of the wheelchair on his own power and prove he was a real man again, he preferred everyone remain in the dark, particularly Johnny and Sarah.

It was a good thing she planned to go to school at the same time as their son. Now that he knew the prognosis, there were rigorous new exercises to do. He wanted total privacy while Bibi helped him.

Once Johnny was asleep, he'd wheeled out to the terrace where he could be alone to ring Massimo. It was the middle of the night in the Peten jungle of Guatemala, but he didn't care and knew his cousin wouldn't, either.

After hearing the news, Massimo couldn't talk for a minute. Like Cesar, he was trying to wrap himself around the incredible news. "Miracles really do happen," he said in a husky voice.

"Incredible, isn't it?" Cesar had trouble swallowing. "I'm keeping it quiet for a while."

"I understand," Massimo said at last. "In your shoes I'd do the same thing. Julie would want immediate results and these things take time. Since you can't give your wife a definite date, I wouldn't want to put her through that, either. What Sarah doesn't know yet can't hurt her."

Thank God Massimo understood. *"Exactamente."*

"In three weeks Julie and I will be flying to Italy with Nicky."

"You're staying with us for the first week!"

"Capisce. I'll call you when it gets closer to our departure to make final plans. I'm dying to meet Giovanni de Falcon."

Cesar grinned. "Be prepared to answer a thousand questions. *Archeologo* is now a part of his vocabulary."

Massimo chuckled. *"A presto, Cesario."*

Two weeks later Sarah left the institute where she was taking Italian. Johnny's school was three blocks away. She had to hurry so she wouldn't be late to meet him. Normally they walked home together. The steepness of the vertical town with its unexpected steps and walkways was an endless source of fascination to both of them. But today when she rounded the corner, she noticed Angelo was out in front with the car.

After he had informed her Cesar was inside, she decided not to interfere and got in the passenger seat to wait. If there were anything wrong, Angelo would have told her. A man of few words, she couldn't tell if he liked her or not. Bianca didn't talk much more, but Sarah felt her antipathy.

Between them and Cesar's remote, standoffish behavior since his hospital checkup, she felt like a persona non grata in her own home. Technically it was her home now, but Johnny was the only one who acted as if he'd always lived there. That was because everyone adored Johnny.

His adaptation to his new school was nothing short of amazing. Cesar went over his lessons with him every night. Sarah sat in on them so she could learn, too. Johnny's quick mind had already picked up the days of the week. He could say his own address, phone number and could count to fifty. With the staff always helping him learn new words, he was absorbing Italian like a sponge.

Cesar's pride in him shone in his eyes. Would that he'd look at Sarah like that sometimes. But she'd forfeited the right to everything except to be Johnny's mother. Cesar needed her for that and nothing else.

Lately she could tell he disliked having her turn him in bed. He didn't want her touch any more than he wanted her presence. This was the price she paid for doing the unforgivable to Cesar. She would go on paying for it for the rest of her life. Some days she handled it better than others. Today wasn't one of them.

Unable to sit there any longer with her torturous thoughts, she told Angelo that she'd walk home and meet them there. For once he gave her a look that actually bordered on concern before he nodded.

The heat was pretty intense. She would stop at the shop where she always bought water for her and Johnny. But to her dismay, when she came to it, she discovered it was closed. That's how her day seemed to be going.

Three-quarters of the way up the hill a car pulled alongside while she was walking. "Sarah?" An attractive man with brown hair called to her from the driver's seat. She looked again. He was one of the Americans in her language class. She'd caught him smiling at her several times. He'd managed to learn her name, but she couldn't return the compliment.

"Allow me to take you where you need to go."

She shook her head. "Thank you, but I'll walk."

"In the middle of this heat wave?" He smiled again. "Please. My name's George Flynn. I've been transferred here from New York. I don't bite."

Sarah believed him. Too bad she was feeling so lightheaded. It showed obviously. She guessed she hadn't drunk enough today and was dehydrated. Perspiration beaded her brows and hairline.

"I only have a few more streets to go."

"Then let me take you the rest of the way. You look ready to pass out." He levered himself from the small car and went around the side to open the door for her.

"That's very kind of you."

After he'd helped her in and had come around to take his seat behind the wheel he said, "Tell me where to go." She glimpsed his language books lying on the back seat.

"If you'll drive to the end of this street, then turn left and continue to the top."

"The top?" As he took off, he winked at her. "Where only the titled and famous have their retreats. Is that what you are?"

"No," she answered honestly, "but my husband is."

"Ah! And here I thought my luck was finally going to change."

He was nice. It was her fault he thought she was single. They only used first names in class, and she hadn't been able to bring herself to wear the Alexandria ruby. Cesar could mock her all he wanted, but she knew that stone meant everything to his mother. She doubted anyone in class was wearing a king's ransom in jewels.

"Will I be allowed on the property to deliver you?" he teased.

She chuckled in spite of her discomfort. "The security guard will see me, so you don't need to worry."

"That's a relief."

"You're very nice to do this."

"It's my pleasure."

After giving him one more direction, he turned off the road into the private driveway…right behind Cesar's car. Oh, no—

Her heart beat a swift tattoo. Angelo had already helped him into the wheelchair. Johnny's hands were full of papers from school. He saw her and said something to Cesar whose dark head jerked around in her direction. The sunglasses hid his eyes, but not his disapproval. She saw his hands grasp the sides of the wheelchair as if he'd like to do damage.

"I don't believe it," George muttered before turning to her awestruck. "If it isn't Cesar Villon. When I pick them…"

"It could happen to anyone. Please keep it to yourself."

"Of course."

George needed to leave. Now! Taking advantage of his shock, Sarah jumped out of the car. "I'll think of a way to repay you. See you in class next week. *Grazie, signore.*" She used the words they'd practiced in class today, then shut the door and raced past her son and husband. She dove into the house and headed for the kitchen, surprising Bianca.

By the time everyone had gathered round, she was downing one of the bottles of water she kept stored in the fridge. Nothing had ever tasted so good before. She could feel herself reviving with every swallow.

"Who was that man?" Johnny wanted to know. Her little protector.

She finished the last drop. "A student in my class named George."

"Hey—like George of the Jungle." Laughing, he turned to his father. "I have a video game called Curious George, but it's back in Watsonville."

"I didn't know that." Cesar's features could only be described as grim. He'd removed the sunglasses. His eyes stared pointedly at her ringless finger.

Sarah couldn't handle the tension. "You know what's funny, Johnny? George is from New York. He saw me walking up the hill. Since it was so hot, he offered to give me a lift."

"Why didn't you wait for us?" Cesar demanded in a deceptively quiet voice.

"I didn't know how long you'd be. It's so lovely here I felt like walking."

"In hundred degree heat?" he bit out.

"I—I thought I'd be able to buy water on the way home, but the shop was closed today. By then I was wilting. He was kind enough to stop." She smiled at Johnny. "Let's go to your room. I want to see what you did in school today."

"Signora Moretti said I did a good job!" He skipped along next to her all the way down the hall to their suite of rooms. She assumed Cesar had disappeared to do his workout.

While she showered, Johnny told her all about his day. He kept mentioning one little boy named Guido. It sounded like he might have found a friend. She'd discuss it with Cesar later—that is if he was speaking to her.

She didn't blame him for being upset with her. Cesar spent thousands of dollars a year for much needed security. So what did she do? Let a near stranger drive right to the back of his private property. It was anyone's guess if she could trust

George to keep quiet about what he knew. She ought to be shot for her stupidity.

Or go back to Watsonville.

Of course she couldn't do that. There was no place to run from Cesar's acrimony.

Thank goodness for Johnny who chattered throughout dinner. Afterward, she took a lazy swim in the pool while Cesar spent time with him in his room.

When her son eventually came into their bedroom to say good-night, she was in her robe and had turned on a cartoon DVD. Though it was in Italian, Johnny had seen it enough times to know everything that was happening.

He climbed up on the bed and snuggled next to her. Certain words sounded so funny he laughed. Sarah wished she could, but the incident with George had put a pall over the situation with Cesar. He wheeled in to watch the movie with them. When Johnny showed signs of getting sleepy, Cesar told him it was time to go to bed and followed him into the other room.

Sarah quickly removed her robe and got under the covers. A minute later Cesar reappeared with Angelo. She knew what was coming. The second the older man had left them alone, her husband started in.

"Why in the hell did you leave the car?" She could tell he'd been rolled on his side facing her.

You don't want to know the real reason, Cesar.

"I told you earlier. I thought you might be a while and I wanted to walk."

"Did Angelo say something to upset you?" came his surprising question in a low voice.

She blinked. "If you want the truth, Angelo never speaks to me unless he has to."

"He's not disapproving, Sarah, just shy."

"That's not Bianca's problem though, is it?"

A sigh escaped his lips. "She and Angelo couldn't have

children because of an injury he received when he was in military service. They've always thought of Luc and me as their boys. Bianca became overprotective of me a few years ago…because of a certain incident."

"You mean the one involving Luc's fiancée."

When she turned to look at him, she saw his fingers torturing the sheet beneath his hand.

"I read about it at the time, Cesar. It made all the tabloids, but it was Olivia who told me what really happened."

After an odd silence he said, "Bianca lost her trust in women when Luc's fiancée entered this house as a friend and ended up intending to sleep with me. It almost cost me my brother."

With an ache in her voice she said, "After what I did to you, it's remarkable Bianca hasn't poisoned me yet. Maybe you don't believe what I told you in the hospital, but when news about the scandal broke, I'd just made reservations to fly to Monaco with Johnny to see you where you train at the track. You can check with the airlines or my credit card company. I'm sure both have a record of it.

"Johnny had just turned three and couldn't understand where his daddy was. I realized it was long past time for you two to meet. Whether you were at the top of your career or not, whether you would ever give him the attention he needed, that no longer mattered to me.

"But after hearing there was a question whether the baby involved was Luc's or yours, I—I thought you and your family didn't need any more on your plate, so I decided to wait until there was more word. But I waited in vain. My pain increased because nothing else was ever released to the press. I didn't know what to think."

Cesar made a strange sound in his throat. "Thanks to Olivia's intervention, Luc and I got things straightened out. At that point we made certain the story was quashed once and for all," he said in rasping voice.

"I wish I'd known the truth— I wouldn't have let anything stop me from coming. When Johnny and I saw you crash—" A little sob escaped. "Oh, Cesar, you'll never know my agony. If you'd died, it would have been my fault our son never knew his father, or you, your son. I thank God morning and night that you were spared.

"I don't know how you can bear the sight of me. Bianca has every right to despise me."

"Then it will interest you to know she thinks you are the ideal mother."

Wiping her eyes with the sheet she said, "You must have heard her wrong."

"No, Sarah. It's true. The reason Johnny is so remarkable has everything to do with you."

"And you, Cesar," she whispered. "His Falcon genes guaranteed he would be a very special little boy." Taking a deep breath she said, "Speaking of our son, I think he's made a friend at school."

"You mean Guido."

"Yes."

"His mother was there to pick him up. That's why Johnny and I were late coming out to the car. We talked about getting the boys together next Monday after class. I suggested we take Guido home with us first so Johnny will feel comfortable."

"That's perfect. If Juliana doesn't mind, I'll make them Johnny's favorite treat while they're playing."

"Why would she mind? You're the mistress of this house."

"Even after I unintentionally allowed an outsider to see where we live?" her voice throbbed.

"Angelo told me you looked pale when you got in the car. Even if George has been lusting after my wife, I'm glad he came to your rescue before you fainted. Since I'm aware you're terrified of losing the ruby, I'll see you get a modest wedding band to wear in public by tomorrow."

"Thank you."

Maybe this would be the right time for his gift. Or not.

After a slight hesitation she slid out of bed and went over to the dresser. Returning to his side of the bed she said, "I know you've never worn rings. I—I had to guess about the size," her voice faltered.

"You probably won't wear it, but I wanted you to have it." She placed it on his bedside table. He made no move to look at it which told her all she needed to know. Why would she have expected anything else?

Devastated by fresh pain she went back to her side of the bed and got in under the covers. Her mind was still on George. She fidgeted for a moment. "Cesar— I think I should withdraw from the institute and find another school."

His chest rose and fell visibly. "I'll take care of it so you don't have to go back."

"I'd appreciate it." She was glad she'd brought up the idea of changing schools before he did. It wouldn't do for Cesar to think she'd encouraged the other man's attention.

"The Galli Language School isn't as close to Johnny's, but it has an excellent reputation. Angelo will enjoy driving both of you to and from the villa. The heat's too oppressive to walk up the hillside right now. In the fall it will be different."

"I agree." Thankful to have that settled she said, "Tell me about Guido."

"He's the last of three children and seems well behaved. His parents run the Vittori florist shop in Positano. The teacher paired them up for a game on their first day. She told me they've been fascinated by each other ever since. While Johnny's been filling him with envy about surfing, Guido's entranced our son over his father's sport bike. Johnny can't wait to take a ride, too."

Sarah groaned. "Before long he'll want one of his own. It's already beginning."

Cesar eyed her frankly. "If he comes to you one day and tells you he's going to race cars, what will you say?"

She'd been thinking about that since the day she learned she was going to have a boy. Cesar's boy.

"My father wanted to race but never did because he said he wasn't good enough, so he built a track for those who were. Between the two of you I'd be surprised if Johnny turned out to be a dentist."

Cesar let out a laugh that resounded off the walls of their bedroom. When it subsided he said, "In other words y—"

"I would tell him to make us proud."

In the next instant she felt his hand grasp hers. She'd never expected to feel his touch again for any reason. "You really meant that, didn't you?"

"Yes. In this life we have to do what makes us happy, or what we *think* makes us happy."

Before letting her go, he squeezed her fingers so hard she realized he couldn't possibly know his own strength.

Anxious to try out what she'd learned in class already she whispered, *"Buona notte, sposo mio. Sogni belli."*

She really did hope he had sweet dreams. After the way he'd cried out in the night a few weeks ago, she never wanted him to relive the crash again. It had been too horrifying. Without thinking of the consequences, she'd covered him with her body to try to take away his terror.

Then her desire had taken over. All it had accomplished was to earn more of Cesar's revulsion. He would never welcome her into his arms again. She didn't have the right to expect it.

Hot tears trickled out of the corners of her eyes. Sarah knew better than anyone her comfort would always be abhorrent to him.

Bibi's eyes probed his. "I keep telling you, Cesar. If you want to try getting out of that wheelchair, you have to visualize it first!"

"You think I don't know that?" Since his visit to the hospital, his impatience bordered on panic because he wasn't making any progress.

"Physically we know you can do it now, but your mind must tell your legs."

The wall served as the brace for the back of his wheelchair. The parallel bars were directly in front of him, tantalizing him. All he had to do was get up. That's what he'd been telling himself for days now.

As he gripped the arms of the wheelchair, the sweat poured off him. "Is the door locked?"

"*Oui.*"

"I don't want Johnny to come bursting in." Or Sarah. Except that she had never come near the gym while he was working out.

"*Sois tranquille.* Now close your eyes and concentrate. You can do it."

He hadn't been able to yet!

Damn how he would have loved to fly out of the wheelchair two weeks ago and deck George of the Jungle. The white-toothed predator had been stalking the gorgeous American female who by some miracle had landed in his class.

The man must have thought he'd died and gone to heaven. Cesar figured he'd seen Sarah walking home every day with Johnny and had been salivating while he waited for the opportune moment to make his move.

"*Eh bien—* Cesar— *Regarde!*" Bibi cried.

When he opened his eyes and looked down, he was halfway out of the wheelchair. The shock caused him to drop back down.

Bibi threw her arms around his neck and gave him the bear hug of his life. "Whatever diabolical plot you were hatching just then, keep it up, *mon vieux.*"

He was trembling like a man with palsy. "I did it, Bibi."

Cesar had always heard of drowning victims whose whole

lives flashed before them on their way down. Right now that's what was happening to him except that instead of drowning, he was flying around the track pulling four g's.

She stood there with her hands on her hips. "There was never any doubt *le grand Cesar Villon* would be back."

His eyes smarted. "Not without you helping me."

"You know what? You're going to be walking by the end of the week. Come on. We've got work to do."

This was Monday. Massimo would be coming on Friday night. That gave him five more days. When his best friend pulled in to the driveway, Cesar intended to get up out of the wheelchair in front of Sarah and Johnny to hug him man to man. He was living for the moment when his wife realized she hadn't married half a man after all.

She was in for a shock!

Somebody on the Falcon race team had sent him a copy of the news clip showing Sarah in the toy store. When he'd watched it in private, her defiant stance in front of the camera on his behalf had stunned him. But he knew that in her heart of hearts, she didn't really believe he'd walk again.

If she *had* believed it, she would have worked out any compromise for them to parent Johnny short of becoming Signora de Falcon. It was his utterly helpless situation that had driven her to lock herself in marriage for the sake of their son's happiness.

The truth was the truth. After the night they'd slept together, she'd lost interest in him.

Before he'd called with the news that he'd purchased her an airline ticket to join him in Positano, her desire for him had died. At the time he hadn't bought her reasons for not being able to accept his invitation. Much more recently he hadn't bought her explanation that she hadn't wanted to ruin his career by telling him about her pregnancy.

He wasn't like his brother who, though he'd been unconscionably cruel to Olivia, had instilled such overpowering emotions in her, she'd walked through fire to win his love.

Cesar might have broken all previous racing records, but he hadn't possessed what it took to inspire that all-consuming kind of love in Sarah. He wasn't capable of producing those feelings in her. He'd inspired nothing *until* the crash. Only then had her guilt taken over, sending her to Cesar's side with their son.

The last thing he wanted was her pity. He would never wear the ring she'd felt compelled to buy him, a supposed visible token of her love and fidelity.

Up until she'd come to Italy, he believed she hadn't been involved with another man. Johnny would have told him. There would have been signs of Mick trying to make contact with her. It hadn't happened. But things were different now. Already she was looking further a field.

You couldn't convince Cesar that she hadn't sent out signals to George on some level the other man had picked up on. She'd covered up by saying she wanted to change schools, but he didn't buy that, either.

Cesar had a hunch that with everything settled where Johnny was concerned, she'd finally given herself permission to start feeding her own desires. With him shouldering part of the responsibility for their son, that freed her to look at other men who appealed to her.

When Cesar could walk in their bedroom and have a conversation that meant she had to look *up* into his eyes, then he'd talk to her about their nonexistent sex life and what they were going to do about it.

In the beginning he'd been obsessed with the determination to get his revenge on her. Could anything be sweeter than forcing her to marry him so she would be deprived of an outlet for her sexual drive for the rest of her days?

"That's quite a talk you're having with yourself," Bibi said, jerking him from thoughts about his wife and how he wanted her to make her pay for not loving him. "I'm feeling sorry for your competitors already."

His head reared. "Not a word about this to a single soul. *Tu comprends?*"

"Not even your wife?"

He ground his teeth. "Especially not my wife or son."

She flexed her shoulders. "If I were Sarah I w—"

"But you're not—" he cut her off. "I'm paying you well to help me get back on my feet. Nothing else!"

Her eyes narrowed. "For a man who has just found out he's been given a second chance to live a full life in every sense of the word, I find your bitterness *extremement alarmant*. It's my opinion you need a psychiatrist, but as you said, I'm only here for one reason. Let's get to work."

CHAPTER NINE

SARAH was just leaving her classroom when she heard a male voice call to her in the hallway. Fear seized her when she turned around and discovered it was George Flynn. He was walking through the crowd of students toward her. If Cesar found out about this…

When he came up to her she had to say something to him. "Hello, again. What brings you to this school?"

"When you stopped coming to class last week I got worried. Since then I've gone to several other schools in the area looking for you to make certain you're all right."

"I'm fine."

"Obviously. Look— I'm a huge fan of your husband's. If I were he, and you were my wife, I'd be nervous about a stranger approaching you. What I'm trying to say is th—"

"I know what you're trying to say. I should have known better than to walk home in the heat, and I did appreciate the ride." I should have worn the ruby ring to class. It was my fault. "But to make my husband feel more comfortable, I switched schools, that's all."

He nodded. His gaze took in the new wedding band Cesar had left on her pillow before leaving for his morning workout last Saturday. She had a feeling Angelo had picked it out.

What woman had ever been given a ring of that significance with such cold calculation?

"I promise you'll never see me again. For what it's worth, I'm sorry for what happened to him."

She felt his sincerity. "Thank you. So am I."

"He was the greatest."

"He *is* the greatest," she corrected him. "One day he'll race again."

His lips pressed together in acknowledgment. "With you behind him, I have no doubts. *Arrivederci*, Signora de Falcon."

Sarah watched him leave the building. After waiting five minutes she decided it was safe to do the same. Once outside she was surprised that Angelo wasn't there waiting for her.

While she stood in front, a Russian student from her class stepped out of the building and approached her. He was an aggressive type. She hadn't liked the way he'd been looking at her since she'd enrolled. "If you need a ride, my car is just around the corner. I'm available just for you."

This time she wasn't taking any chances. "I'm not," she said succinctly. "There's my husband now."

To her relief she saw the sedan headed her way in a stream of heavy traffic. Angelo was a little later than usual. Something must have held him up. She hurried toward the car and got in, hoping the Russian got the point. Otherwise it meant another transfer.

"*Buona sera*, Angelo." She greeted him slightly out of breath. After Cesar had told her Bianca's husband was shy, she'd been trying to practice small conversations with him. They were part of her daily assignment. He went along with it and seemed more friendly of late. It was a beginning.

"*Buona sera, Signora. Come va?*"

"*Va bene. Grazie.*"

Suddenly she started to laugh because she couldn't say

anything else. He laughed, too. The warmth of it broke the ice a little more.

"Tomorrow I'll have something new to say."

His eyes smiled. *"Bene."*

They drove the rest of the way to Johnny's school in companionable silence.

When she entered his classroom, he ran over and hugged her. "Mommy? I have to ask you something."

She leaned down to hear. He whispered, "Can Guido come home with us? We want you to make us scones again."

Her eyes flicked to his friend. "Is it all right with his mother?"

"Yes. She'll come and get him after her work. You can ask Signora Moretti."

"Okay."

Once everything was cleared, the three of them left the school and climbed into the car. She turned in the seat. "Be sure you strap yourselves in."

"We already did," he said in a tone of voice that reminded her of Cesar. Since starting kindergarten, she was already noticing subtle changes in her son. He wasn't her baby anymore.

The minute they arrived at the villa, the boys ran to Johnny's room while Sarah headed for the kitchen to make roll dough. Juliana wouldn't start dinner until later, so Sarah had the place to herself.

Within fifteen minutes she called to the boys who dragged the kitchen chairs over to the counter to help her cut the dough into different shapes. They made a mess, but she loved it.

"Cut out some dinosaurs, Mommy."

Sarah fashioned half a dozen very rough facsimiles of stegosauruses before frying them. The boys got all excited to watch them puff up like pillows. After draining them, she put them on a plate and carried it to the table.

"Two milks coming up."

While they were enjoying their treats, Cesar wheeled into

the kitchen dressed in his workout clothes. He'd just come from another session with Bibi. Though she could tell he'd been put through it hard, she thought he'd never looked in better shape. Several damp black curls clung to his forehead. Cesar exuded a virility that was breathtaking.

He asked the boys about school and ruffled their hair affectionately. What she'd give to feel those same fingers run through hers.

"Daddy! Mommy's made scones! Tell her to make you one."

"Maybe later when I'm hungry." Without looking at her he wheeled over to the fridge and pulled out a bottle of water. Something was wrong for him not to acknowledge her in front of company. It hurt. Thankfully the children seemed to be unaware.

"Can I show Guido your trophies? He wants to see them. *Per favore, Papa?*" he added at the last second. He sounded like he'd been born here. If that didn't melt his father on the spot, nothing else would.

Cesar drained all the liquid in one go. "Tell you what. After you're through eating and have washed your hands, bring him to the den."

On that note he left the kitchen giving her the impression he couldn't get away from her fast enough. Though torn apart inside, she managed to finish feeding the boys without breaking down. When they declared themselves full, she made certain they visited Johnny's bathroom on the way to the den.

As Sarah was putting the last dish in the cupboard, Juliana appeared. They discussed the menu for dinner. In this heat they decided on a light meal of fish salad and fruit. With that accomplished she went out to the pool where Bianca was watering some plants. Sarah asked her for Luc's phone number.

For once the older woman obliged her without eyeing her as if she'd just crawled out from under a rock. Relieved on that point, she sat down in one of the deck chairs to call

Olivia. She needed a friend to talk to. Unfortunately her sister-in-law was out, so Sarah left the message for her to call back when she could.

Needing something to occupy her mind until dinner, she retraced her steps to the kitchen and sat down at the table to do her homework. Within another half hour Guido's mother came to pick up her son.

Considering that neither of them spoke the other's language beyond a beginner's proficiency, they communicated well enough. Luckily his mother had a friendly disposition that put Sarah at ease. They made arrangements for Johnny to go to their house after school on Wednesday when Guido's mother didn't have to work.

Later, through the dinner hour and Johnny's bedtime that followed, Sarah got the distinct impression Cesar was angry with her about something specific. A problem that was over and above what he could never forgive her for. But she had to wait until Angelo had helped him to bed after his last workout session before she could get to the bottom of it.

As soon as they were alone, she sat up and turned on the light. He was lying on his back. She'd come to think of it as the position he used when he had something to get off his chest. Well, for once she was ready and waiting for him.

"Whatever's wrong, please tell me now and I'll attempt to remedy it if I can," she said without preamble.

He didn't pretend not to understand. "While Angelo was waiting for you today, he saw George pull up in his Fiat and go inside your school."

George again. She might have known.

"When George came back out alone, Angelo followed him to an apartment building before returning to school. That's when he saw another man bothering you."

She sucked in her breath. "I didn't encourage either of them."

"I'm not accusing you, Sarah. You're a beautiful woman.

Every man has the right to look. He wouldn't be a man otherwise. However, if George is stalking you, then that's something else again."

If she was so beautiful, why didn't he ever look at her like she was? Except that she knew the answer to that question. Beauty was in the eye of the beholder. All Cesar beheld was a woman who had betrayed him in the worst way a woman could. She should be getting used to their situation by now, but if anything, her guilt seemed more acute than ever.

She shook her head. "George caught up to me inside to apologize for causing me to change schools."

"How did he know where to find you?" Cesar used a conversational tone with her, but it covered emotions boiling below the surface.

"I don't know. He said that when I didn't show up for class anymore, he decided to look at several other schools in the hope of finding me again to make certain I was all right."

"He certainly did that."

"The point is, he wanted to apologize. He didn't know I was married. The second he saw you, he recognized you and told me he's one of your biggest fans. I could tell he felt terrible when he realized what you must have thought.

"H-he told me I'd never see again. I believed him. That's all there was to it. The other man Angelo saw was some obnoxious foreign student. He's in my class and couldn't have helped but see my wedding band, but that didn't stop him.

"When he asked if he could take me somewhere, I told him my husband had come for me, and I hurried to the car. If he bothers me again, I'll report him. But if you'd rather I never went out and were tutored at home, tell me now."

He swore softly. "Angelo and I talked about it. I'm going to triple the security on you and Johnny. You'll hardly know they're around, but it's necessary. I'm afraid you'll always be a target, but after your appearance on television, it has increased the risk to you. I'm not willing to take any chances with your lives."

Sarah took back some of the negative thoughts she'd been having.

"I think it's a good idea as long as you triple the security on yourself, too. While the boys were playing in the bedroom, I guess Guido said something to Johnny about famous people getting shot."

Another curse escaped his lips.

"After Guido went home, Johnny broke down to me in the bathtub. He loves his daddy and doesn't want anything to happen to you. Maybe you should tell him about the security men. I know it will make him feel better."

"After my workout in the morning, I'll have a talk with him."

She bowed her head. "I'm sorry about the George situation."

"I'm not," he fired back. "Because of him we've added precautions that are going to make everyone sleep easier at night. In case you haven't noticed, Angelo has become attached to you and Johnny. You couldn't ask for a better watchdog."

"He's been helping me with my Italian."

"That's what he told me. He said you have a good ear. That's high praise coming from him."

Much as Sarah loved hearing that, she craved approbation from the one man who couldn't give it to her.

"I like him a lot." His devotion to Cesar made her a fan for life.

Needing the darkness to hide her tears, she turned off the light and lay back down on her side away from him.

"I've heard from Massimo."

Surprised he still wanted to talk, she turned her head toward him. "Are they already in Italy?"

"No. They'll be arriving in Positano on Friday and will stay with us for a week before going on to Bellagio."

"I bet you can't wait to see him. The two musketeers together after such a long time."

"Make that four. Johnny and Nicky have joined us."

All the satisfaction of a proud father was contained in his deep voice. It spoke volumes. Once again guilt stabbed her for depriving him of the joy of his son before the crash.

"Have you met Julie?"

"No. We've only talked on the phone. I'd planned to attend their wedding in Milan, but they called it off. Later on Massimo rang me from Guatemala to tell let me know the ceremony had taken place there."

Sarah could hear a story behind that, but she knew Cesar would never share it with her.

"They e-mailed me some pictures. You and Johnny can look at them on the computer in the den."

"We'll do it tomorrow. Which one of them does their baby resemble the most?"

"Oddly enough both of them, even though they're not the biological parents."

"What?"

"Nicky's the son of her brother, and Massimo's sister. They were killed in a car accident. In the will they drew up before he was born, my cousin was named the legal guardian in the case of their deaths. No one could have foreseen that day coming, least of all Massimo.

"He flew to California before the funeral. I wanted to attend, but it was on the eve of a race. With my sponsor depending on me, I couldn't pull out. So I missed being there for him.

"It seems that's where he and Julie met for the first time. To my shock, and that of my bachelor cousin, he fell deeply in love. While he was in Sonoma, one thing led to another and she ended up flying to Bellagio with him to help take care of Nicky. Now they're a family and have adopted him legally."

"How amazing and marvelous for the three of them. Is there anything special you'd like to plan while they're here?"

"After coming from the jungle, they'll probably want to laze around the pool for the first few days and relax."

"That makes sense with a baby." It would also be easier on Cesar who had to stay on top of his therapy. "Johnny can't wait to ask him if he's seen any boas. He learned about them in class the other day."

"I have no doubt Massimo will be able to tell him some tales guaranteed to give him nightmares. I'll have to screen them first."

"That's the problem with Johnny. He loves to talk about all the scary things, but then he scares himself to death."

"Sounds like someone else I know," he drawled.

Sarah gasped quietly. For just a moment Cesar had become the charming tease she'd fallen madly in love with at seventeen. She couldn't believe it.

"If you're referring to my fear of sharks, I wouldn't have developed a phobia if you hadn't pretended one was circling us."

"I really had you going there for a while and couldn't resist. It served you right for watching *Jaws* too many times."

She'd clung to him out of fear until he'd started roaring with laughter. By then it was too late to be mad at him because he'd begun kissing her with a passion she could never have imagined. With the sun shining down on them in the middle of the swells, the taste of his mouth and the salt spray had ignited her inside and out.

Sarah had thought she'd die from the thrill of being in the arms of Cesar Villon, the racing sensation who'd become the world's greatest heartthrob. Back then he'd been bigger than life to her.

He was much bigger to her now in an entirely new way. Not only had Cesar proven to be a superb father, but he was also a man who, like the mythical phoenix, had risen from the ashes.

He reminded her of that great bird who was said to regenerate when hurt or wounded by a foe, thus being almost immortal.

Fate had wounded her husband, yet his work ethic in the face of soul-destroying odds was the stuff that gave rise to legends.

"Has our son seen it?"

His low voice stirred her out of her thoughts. "Seen what?"

"Jaws."

"No," she whispered. "Not yet."

"I'll go through my CD collection tomorrow and Johnny-proof it. After the way Guido and Johnny went through all the stuff in my den, I've a feeling nothing's going to be safe around this house."

"I think you're right," she murmured, but her mind wasn't on Guido. She'd just experienced an adrenaline rush because that meant Cesar possessed a copy of the *Jaws* movie. But the sensation quickly subsided when she realized that if he ever watched it and remembered their time in the sea, the memories hadn't driven him to get in touch with her.

She wouldn't be lying in this bed if she hadn't come to him with a gift he couldn't refuse.

Cesar's feelings for her were as dead as the driftwood that washed up on the beach at Carmel. You could do a lot of things with driftwood for decoration, but you could never make it go back to be a living tree.

She was thankful he couldn't read her mind, or he'd use the analogy to mock his present physical condition. He didn't believe he would ever walk again, but being the hero he was, he would give it his best shot anyway.

Having a son who idolized him had inculcated Cesar with the desire to be the right role model no matter what.

Sarah loved him with a ferocity that continued to grow in quantum leaps. As she buried her face in the pillow, she heard a noise on the other side of the room.

"Mommy? Daddy?"

"What is it, *piccolo*?"

"There's something in my room."

Cesar patted the space between him and Sarah. "Come up here."

Johnny needed no urging from his father to climb onto the bed and get under the covers. This was a first for him. "It made a scary sound."

She kissed his forehead. "I'll go check."

Sure enough when she crossed the floor to his room, she heard a buzzing in the window. Afraid of sharks, not bees, she gave it a swat with one of Johnny's school papers. On her return to the master bedroom, she turned on the overhead light.

"You were right. Here's our culprit."

"Is it dead?"

"This bee is deader than a doornail."

"A doornail's not dead, Mommy."

Cesar laughed.

"I know, but that's what people say because a doornail never moves."

Johnny sat straight up. "Let me see." Taking great care, she showed him the proof lying on top of the paper without getting too close. He clung to Cesar. "I thought it was a fly."

"I'll put it down the toilet."

When she came back she discovered Johnny deep in conversation with Cesar. "I want hair on my chest like you when I grow up."

His father had a spectacular chest Sarah would do well not to look at or think about. She turned off the light and got back in bed.

"Don't worry. All the Falcon men have it."

"Papa Priestley hardly has any."

She tried not to laugh. Out of the corner of her eye she could tell Cesar was struggling, too.

"Mommy doesn't have hair on her chest. How come?"

The blood poured into her cheeks making them so hot she feared they were glowing.

"Hair makes men look tough. God created women to look beautiful."

Cesar—

"Mommy's beautiful, isn't she Daddy?"

"In Italian we say she's very *squisita*."

Johnny tried the word out on his tongue. Perfect pronunciation.

Sarah could hear Cesar's mind working. Your mother is *squisita* and deadlier than the Sirens.

She leaned closer to him. "Come on, honey. It's late. Let's get you back to bed. We've got another fun day ahead of us tomorrow."

"Okay." He gave his father a kiss before following her to his room. When he was under the covers he said, "Do you think there are any more bees?"

"No, but if there are, come and get me."

"I love you, Mommy." He pressed a big one against her lips.

"I love you, too, darling."

"Are you going to have a *bambino*?"

Startled by his line of questions for the second time in one night she said, "I don't think so. What is it?"

"You *know* what it is."

"I do?" she teased.

"It's a baby. You're funny, Mommy."

She gave him another kiss. "Why do you ask?"

"Guido said his mommy's having one."

That Guido.

"How exciting. Good night, honey."

Once she was back in bed Cesar wanted chapter and verse of the conversation in Johnny's bedroom. When she told him he said, "In some ways Guido's too precocious for his own good."

"I agree, but he's a darling boy."

"Darling is as darling does," Cesar growled without any bite to it. She loved it when he was like this. Let it last for a little while.

"Johnny's picking up a lot more Italian by playing with him."

"I caught a word or two I didn't like."

She smiled to herself. "I don't suppose you said those words at the same age."

"With Luc and my older cousins around all the time, I probably said a lot more."

"Well, he's our first, so we don't have to worry about him being corrupted quite so fast."

Until the words flew out of her mouth, she didn't realize what she'd just said.

"Y-you know what I meant," she stammered.

"I'm afraid I do." The icy mockery was back. "You *will* insist on your fairy tales. Be very careful they don't become your ruination, Sarah."

By Wednesday Sarah had employed Bianca's help to have a crib for Nicky delivered from town. She'd asked Angelo to set it up in the guest bedroom Luc and Olivia had used. Up until now, Cesar's Positano home had been his bachelor retreat from the world and didn't contain such things.

He couldn't have made it more clear on Monday night that there would never be one of *his* babies in residence, but with all his extended family having children, Sarah felt a crib for them had become a necessity when they came for visits.

She and Johnny had sat at Cesar's computer to view the pictures of Massimo with his wife and their baby. Years earlier he'd shown Sarah wallet-size photos of his cousin. He was dark and handsome like Cesar, but the other two were golden blondes who looked out of place among the natives.

They lived in a real jungle among ancient Mayan ruins. Johnny couldn't wait for them to come. Sarah was excited, too. Yet oddly enough, as the time grew closer Cesar's behavior around her grew more remote than ever. She hated the tension between them.

Since Massimo was his favorite person, she couldn't understand his brooding mood…unless he was dreading the moment when his cousin would first see him bound to a wheelchair. They'd both been so adventurous all their lives, it had to be killing Cesar now.

To heighten her pain, when she and Johnny got home from school on Thursday, they discovered he'd flown to Rome for another checkup at the hospital without warning them in advance. Johnny handled it much better than he'd done the first time. Not so Sarah who grew alarmed when Bibi was nowhere to be found to give her input on his condition or state of mind.

Maybe his appointment had always been scheduled. Sarah just wished he hadn't excluded her from something so important. In truth she wanted to go to his checkups with him. Where was it all going to end? Contrary to his accusations, she wasn't living in a fairy tale.

Sarah had gone into this marriage with her eyes wide-open. She could put up with anything except his unnecessary cruelty to her when it came to his physical health. If he was suffering from headaches or more flashbacks of the crash, she would be the last person to know about it. Where he was concerned, the only way she found out anything was by accident.

When he came to bed that night, he refused to discuss his visit to the doctor with her. Lying on his side turned away from her, no one could shut her down faster than Cesar delivering one of his wintry rebukes. With the assertion that all he wanted to do was go to sleep, he might as well be living on a distant planet.

Angelo brought her and Johnny home from school on Friday. To his disappointment their company still hadn't arrived. After the sleepless night she'd been forced to live through suffering in silence, she experienced some apprehension about the weekend ahead of them.

Normally Cesar was there to greet Johnny and take a swim with him in the pool. Not today. According to Bianca, Cesar was still in the gym. Sarah thought of it as his man-cave, a place where he could go to be totally alone. She didn't dare bother him there. Only Bibi had that privilege, and even she was off-limits when she wasn't actually running him through his exercises.

Her heart ached for him. For him to behave like this, she began to think he'd been dreading Massimo's visit all along. It wasn't any different from the way he'd shut out his family at the hospital. Not even his brother had been welcome.

Cesar's pain was all tied up with his pride. She wished she could help him, but how? Johnny had definitely been the catalyst to make him get out of that hospital bed and start living again. But what kind of living was this if he couldn't enjoy his best friend?

Luc had called several times wanting to see him again on a quickie visit, but Cesar had come up with excuses to prevent it. Friends and colleagues from his racing team deluged him with phone calls and e-mails. Except for taking his parents' phone calls, he wasn't having any of it.

Johnny was the only one he allowed inside his heart. Cesar was fast becoming a recluse, even from Sarah who shared his bed every night. She couldn't bear it. The pretense that everything was fine would be hard to keep up in front of Massimo who would see right through it.

She was almost tempted to tell him not to come yet, but she couldn't do that. Cesar wouldn't forgive her for interfering in what he would consider none of her damn business.

Together she and Johnny got ready for their guests. He put on his favorite T-rex shirt and shorts, and his new shoes that Cesar had bought him. They flashed red lights when he walked. Sarah chose to wear one of her new purchases. It was a kelly-green silk blouse and tan pleated pants, another Italian designer outfit that made her feel casual yet elegant.

Wanting to look especially good for Cesar's closest friend and his new wife, she took time applying her coral lipstick and black eyeliner. Slowly she brushed her hair until it glistened like dark mink in the light. Being in the sun every day had given her skin a golden glow.

After putting on her favorite mango scented lotion, she gathered Johnny from his room where he was playing with his miniature race cars. The metallic black Faucon was already looking rather the worse for wear. Together they went out to the terrace, leaving the suite empty for Cesar when he chose to get ready for their company.

Cesar suddenly wheeled out to the patio. Sarah's breath lodged in her throat.

With his black curly hair a little longer, and his olive skin clean-shaven, he looked fantastic in a new pair of white cargo pants and a tight fitting, navy and white striped cotton sport shirt. The kind with the short sleeves that emphasized his powerful arms. His clothes fit him to perfection, revealing broad shoulders and hard-muscled thighs and legs.

She couldn't help but compare him to the bearded, depressed man she'd walked in on at the hospital weeks ago. Yet she had to admit that both men filled her eyes and heart so there was no room for anyone else.

He was the epitome of the Italian male that women the world over fantasized about. He always smelled so good. Cesar lacked for nothing but the wedding band she'd bought him. The one he still hadn't started to wear and probably never would.

His dark fringed eyes, shot with silver in the late afternoon light, zoomed in on his son. If he'd even glanced at Sarah, it would have been a covert regard. He'd managed to make her feel invisible.

"I just had a call from Massimo. They'll be arriving any minute now. Come with me, *piccolo,* and we'll greet them."

"Hooray!"

Sarah followed them through the rear of the villa to the outside portico. Knowing how bittersweet this reunion was going to be, her soul cried out for her husband. She would gladly take on his suffering if she could.

When she caught up to them, Cesar had pulled Johnny onto his lap. Seconds later the airport limo pulled in to the driveway and came to a stop. Sarah watched a tall, dark-haired Massimo emerge from the back first.

"Ciao, Cesario!"

So much deep emotion was conveyed in those two words as he raced to greet her husband.

Sarah's glance flicked to Johnny who had slid off Cesar's lap to stare up at the brilliant archaeologist his father had told him about.

Then the strangest phenomenon happened.

As if it were the most natural thing in the world, Cesar got up out of the wheelchair and took half a dozen careful steps toward his cousin to embrace him.

Surely she had to be dreaming. This had to be one of those out-of-body experiences, only it had happened to Cesar, not to her.

"Daddy—you can walk!"

CHAPTER TEN

JOHNNY had just said the words Sarah hadn't been able to articulate because her mouth and body felt like they were stuffed with cotton.

Soon Massimo's blond wife, Julie, approached carrying their son. She stared in shock at the two men hugging each other while tears started to stream down her lovely face.

Johnny jumped up and down hugging his father's legs. His shrieks of joy brought Bianca running outside.

The minute she saw Cesar standing there, she, too, cried for joy and broke into a paroxysm of tears. That summoned Angelo who put a hand on his wife's shoulder and wept.

Juliana wasn't far behind him. One look at what was happening and the cook crossed herself before burying her face in her apron, sobbing.

Sarah's prayers for her husband had been answered in such a quick, drastic fashion, she feared she was dreaming. She seemed to see and experience everything as though she were looking through a frosty pane of glass. Shock had made her slow to react.

In the periphery she noticed Bibi who had unexpectedly emerged from the foliage. But the solemn-faced therapist was looking at Sarah, not Cesar. It was a dead giveaway that she'd been part of Cesar's conspiracy to keep this a secret from

Sarah. She had no doubts her husband had sworn the other woman to secrecy.

Cesar's miraculous recovery had to have been ongoing from the day they'd come home from the hospital. Her mind went back over the nights she'd lain at his side, helping him to turn because he couldn't.

How long had he been able to do it by myself?

As late as Monday night when he'd told her he would never have a baby of his own, he'd already known he could walk. That's why he'd gone to Rome again. His doctors and staff had to be overjoyed for him.

But he'd been adamant about keeping *her* out of the loop.

She could still hear the things he'd said to her to quash any hope that he would ever have a normal life.

You will insist on living your fairy tales. Be very careful they're not your ruination.

Those words had been a warning. It was evident he'd been planning this moment for weeks. When he sprang his surprise on everyone, he didn't want her getting any ideas that now he was better, anything was going to change between them.

Standing there with Massimo while he celebrated his return to a full life, she realized this was his revenge for what she'd done to him.

She understood it. She deserved it. She would keep her pain to herself and live with it, but right now she couldn't hold back her joy at his recovery. This was what she'd been praying for since seeing the crash on television.

Sarah ran blindly toward him, uncaring of her tears. She threw her arms around his waist from behind, hugging him hard.

"Thank God, Cesar. Thank God," she whispered against his strong, warm back.

His body stiffened at the contact. She knew she repulsed him, but she was also aware he was probably too unsteady to handle anyone's weight against him just yet.

By now Bibi had pushed the wheelchair over to him so he could hold on to the handles. Naturally his balance would be a little off until he grew stronger.

"Look, Mommy! Daddy can push *me!*" To everyone's amusement, Johnny had climbed into the wheelchair Cesar had recently vacated.

She let go of her husband and leaned over Johnny to hug him. "Can you believe it?" she cried, delirious with happiness. "Your daddy can walk again! Pretty soon you'll be able to go swimming in the ocean together."

He looked over his shoulder at his father. "I knew you'd get better cos mommy said your astronaut suit would protect you."

Everyone laughed at his comment.

"That it did," Cesar said in a thick-toned voice.

Her husband's eyes met Sarah's in recognition of an earlier conversation before he began pushing the wheelchair. He took slow, deliberate steps. Bibi hovered in case he needed help, but Sarah could have told the other woman to leave well enough alone. Cesar was on his feet now. The phoenix had definitely risen and would do the rest of this by himself.

Suddenly aware of their guests, she hurriedly turned to Massimo and his wife who were following everyone into the villa. The three of them hugged.

"Forgive me for ignoring you."

Massimo's eyes were suspiciously bright as they smiled into hers. "We're all in shock."

Sarah nodded before her gaze darted to Julie. His wife's attractive features glistened with tears. She was shaking her head. "Things like this just don't happen."

"I know. I still can't believe it. It's going to take me time to absorb the wonder of it, yet there he is. Walking!"

"It's incredible."

"So's this little boy of yours. He's absolutely adorable. Can I hold him?"

"Of course."

Trembling, Sarah reached for Nicky, needing to feel his warm, compact body in her arms. "We have a crib set up for you."

"Bless you."

They both laughed through their tears.

"I know how hard it is taking a child on a long flight. To think you've come all the way from Central America."

"I must admit we're glad to be here at last."

"Cesar and I don't want you to do anything more than relax around the pool. Johnny and I will help take care of this little guy."

"That sounds heavenly."

"Come on. While our husbands catch up, I'll show you to your room."

When they reached it, Julie turned to her. "Isn't it amazing that our husbands married California girls? I feel like I know you already."

Sarah nodded. "I have the same feeling. Someone from home, someone familiar." She rocked Nicky in her arms. He seemed content as long as he could see his mother. "Carmel and Sonoma aren't that far from each other. To think we grew up so close, yet unaware."

Julie put her handbag on the dresser. "Who would have dreamed we would meet in Positano of all places? Cesar's home is so fabulous I can't take it in."

"I understand Massimo's villa on Lake Como is to die for."

"It is."

"Yet you live in the jungle."

She smiled knowingly at Sarah. "You do what you have to do when you love your husband."

"Isn't that the truth," Sarah said in a sober voice.

Compassion shone from Julie's eyes. "You've been through hell."

"It's been nothing compared to what Cesar has had to live

through. I can't comprehend his terror when he woke up and realized he couldn't move from the waist down."

"That *is* a nightmare, but I'm talking about the years you forced yourself to stay away from him while you were raising his son."

A little sob rose in Sarah's throat. "What I did was wrong. I'll go to my grave paying for it."

"You know what?" Julie murmured. "If I'd been in your shoes, I would have done the same thing."

"No you wouldn't."

"I beg to differ." Julie wouldn't let it go. "The first time Massimo talked me into marrying him, I canceled it at the last minute because he was only doing it to legitimize my living with him and Nicky. I knew he wasn't in the market for a wife.

"His childhood had been drastically marred by the fact that his parents never married. It caused untold grief. As a result, he grew up intending to remain a bachelor. The last thing I wanted was to be his wife unless he loved me beyond anything in existence. Since I knew he didn't, I proposed we live together instead for Nicky's sake.

"When we left for Guatemala, I didn't care what people thought. They didn't know we'd never slept in the same bed. I went with him because I loved him and Nicky. But I wanted Massimo to stay a free agent, able to walk away at any time because that's what I knew *he* wanted.

"You think I don't know how you felt being in love with a race car driver like Cesar? The rolling stone who gathers no moss? With his background and breeding, men like him only come along maybe once in a century.

"According to my husband, Cesar never intended to marry, or if he did, it would be after he walked away from his career. I fully understand your terrible dilemma. If I'd gotten pregnant by a man who belonged to the world and made no bones about it, I would have done exactly what you did.

"What kind of a life would that be for your son? He'd suffer from only seeing his father once in a while. That's no life for a baby. That would be no life for you knowing you'd trapped him into marriage."

Sarah gazed at her. "You *do* understand."

Julie took a big breath. "You know something? Massimo thinks God had a hand in your decision because He saw how much Cesar would need both of you further down the road. He's convinced your surprise visit to Rome gave Cesar the will to fight back."

She bit her lip. "Well, now that he's done that, he doesn't need me anymore. All he wants is Johnny."

"But he can't have him without you," Julie said. "I understand where you're coming from because I've been there. But remember one thing. Massimo told me Cesar wanted you enough to invite you to Positano. *You're* the one who turned *him* down.

"It may interest you to know Cesar's home has always been off-limits to other women. My husband said you're the only one he ever bought an airplane ticket for. Think on that before you decide everything's hopeless."

"Mommy?" Johnny came bursting in the guest bedroom. "How come you're still in here? Daddy wants all of us to get on our bathing suits."

"Coming, honey."

Sarah handed the baby back to Julie. "Thanks for the talk," she whispered. "It has meant more than you know."

"Anything to help," she whispered back. "Cesar's situation has torn my husband apart. He wants to see him happy again. You deserve the same happiness." She reached out to hug Julie before running to catch up with Johnny.

Quiet reigned throughout the villa. All children were accounted for. Everyone had gone to their rooms except Cesar and Massimo who'd been sitting out on the terrace enjoying a vintage bottle of wine while they talked.

Cesar glanced at his watch. "It's after eleven. Don't let me keep you up any longer. I'm sure Julie's waiting for you. Time for all good husbands to be in bed with their wives."

His cousin slanted him a curious glance. "Let's go."

Massimo got up from the chair, but Cesar remained seated. "I'm going to sit here a while longer."

"You mean *your* wife's not waiting for you?"

Cesar knew what he was asking.

"I'd rather not talk about her."

"You're going to have to sometime."

A shudder rocked his body. "She kept Johnny from me for five years!"

"*Cugino mio*—when she didn't come to Positano, why didn't you go back to California and find out why? If you can ever bring yourself to answer that question, maybe you'll be able to forgive her."

He poured himself another glass of wine.

"Keep that up and you'll have to call for Angelo to put you to bed tonight. I thought those days were over."

His fingers grasped the stem of the glass so tightly, it almost snapped in two. "I didn't ask for a lecture from you."

"Have you forgotten I'm your friend who loves you? *Buona notte.*"

After Massimo melted into the darkness, a too late repentant Cesar pushed the glass away, spilling some of the golden liquid on the table. He used a napkin to mop it up.

Grinding his teeth, he slowly got out of the patio chair and reached for the handles of the wheelchair to help support him on his walk through the villa. By the time he entered the bedroom, exhaustion had taken over.

After a glance at the bed to ascertain Sarah was asleep, he stripped down to his boxers leaving everything on the floor.

She'd pulled his covers aside to make it easier for him. He visualized rolling onto the mattress before he actually did it.

Once he felt it give beneath him, his body felt like a dead weight, but it didn't matter. For the first time since the crash he'd gotten to bed on his own power. The sooner he saw the last of that wheelchair, the better. When all of them went out for dinner tomorrow evening, he'd use the cane. Johnny couldn't wait to see him in action with it.

During his conversation with Massimo, he'd hoped to drink enough to dull his senses. The imprint of Sarah's body against his back had lit a fire he couldn't put out on his own. Cesar needed total oblivion of the woman sleeping next to him to get through the night.

He might have achieved his objective if his body didn't have its own built-in alarm clock that wakened him at two for his first turn of the night. Despite his mind willing it otherwise, his body waited to feel Sarah's hands rearranging his hips and legs. Ever since the numbness had worn off weeks ago, the craving for her touch had grown stronger. He lived for the twice nightly ritual.

Cesar held his breath and studied the ceiling while he waited for her watch alarm to go off. When it didn't, he shouldn't have experienced such fierce disappointment. It came in a close second to the pain he'd felt when she'd told him she wouldn't be able to fly to Positano. She hadn't wanted him then. She didn't want him now.

He should be thanking providence he'd just gotten past his first hurdle. At this point he was in training to wean himself from her nightly ministrations.

If he kept this up long enough, his body would learn how to lie near her without listening to every breath and sigh. When she changed positions, it would no longer come alive with the need to take her in his arms.

He waited another ten minutes before shifting onto his left side. Bibi had helped him practice the maneuver on the exercise table. Turning his body while he lay flat was a difficult ordeal, but not impossible.

As he reached around to grab the side of the bed with his right hand, he felt Sarah's hand on his upper arm. The contact brought on instant weakness that attacked his body so thoroughly, he rolled back in place, helpless at her touch.

His jaw hardened. "I don't need your help anymore."

"I know you don't." She sounded breathless.

He closed his eyes tightly. "Then what is it?"

"Today I wanted to show you how I really felt about your recovery, but I couldn't do it front of everyone. Now that we don't have an audience, I can't wait any longer."

She moved with stunning speed until she was half lying across his chest with her arms partly around his neck. It was like déjà vu.

"I love you, Cesar. I always have, and I always will. I know you've lost any affection you once had for me, but please don't reject me right now. I couldn't take it if you did."

The last part she whispered against his mouth before her lips roved his face and throat.

Engulfed by her scent and the press of her beautiful flesh against his, Cesar could feel himself spiraling out of control. Her mouth covered every inch, moving enticingly closer until it fell on his. She was trying to coax his lips apart.

Thrilling memories of the night they made love swamped him. He'd been the initiator then. She'd followed his lead, giving him the response his body and soul had craved beyond all else. But her feelings for him had been ephemeral.

Now the tables had turned. She was making celebratory love to him in the heat of the moment. Pity had a lot to answer for. Her avowals of love were nothing more than simple window dressing. They were the kind that would sound good to a man who'd believed his days of making physical love to a woman were over for good.

If he hadn't been through this experience with her weeks ago, he would probably buy her act. But he could see past her motives. Tonight she was out to let him discover for himself he was still a man who could perform.

"I'm tempted, Signora de Falcon," he murmured, carefully easing her away from him. "You're a luscious package. I've tasted all of your delights before. But you only offered them for a season, a contingency I never saw coming. I learned my lesson."

Even in the semidarkness he could see her normally colorful complexion had lost color.

"You never said you were in love with me."

The blood pounded at his temples. "After coming back to you year after year until you were old enough for your father to consider giving you to me in marriage, I didn't think I needed to. Without action to back them up, words don't mean that much in my world."

He felt her body shiver. "In my world they would have meant everything. When you invited me to Positano, I didn't know it was in your mind to propose. If I'd had any idea, nothing would have stopped me from flying to you. School was just an excuse to salvage my pride.

"You've seen the scrapbook," she cried. "I started keeping it the day after daddy introduced me to you. As young as seventeen I wanted to be your wife, Cesar. I spent four years plotting and scheming how I was going to get you to propose to me despite your determination to remain a bachelor.

"But without the words to help me, I was terrified I'd end up like all the other women who dreamed of winning your love, and failed.

"When you told me you'd bought me a round-trip ticket, that was like a death sentence. It meant you wanted me with you during your downtime between races, but the second you had to be back at the track, I would have to leave. If I'd come, I would never have left you, and then it would have gotten ugly."

"I wouldn't have let you leave, Sarah. I made it round trip to give you breathing room I had no intention of honoring."

"But I didn't know that." Her lower lip trembled like Johnny's when he worried that he'd done something wrong. Liquid caused her eyes to glisten.

"The reason I didn't tell you about Johnny was that I was convinced you weren't in love with me. It takes two people madly in love to raise a happy child. When you never phoned or came back to Carmel to see me, I had to love you in silence. After Johnny was born, I poured out my love on him. He was all I had of you."

That well of bitterness rose up in his throat once more. "While I had none of him, you had him five long years."

She moved away from him. "We'll never get past that, will we? What are we going to do, Cesar? Now that you're walking again, we can't go on like this."

"I agree. But right now isn't the time to talk about it. Soon we're all going to Monaco for a few days to be with Luc and the family. Nic and Max will be bringing their families, too. Following that, Massimo wants us to stay a week at the villa with them in Bellagio.

"It'll mean that Johnny misses five days of school, but we'll ask Signora Moretti to give us material he can work on while we're away. After our return and we're strictly alone, you and I will deal with our problem."

Without saying anything, Sarah slid off the bed.

"Where are you going?"

"Where I always go when I need comfort." The next thing he knew she'd disappeared into Johnny's room.

Cesar walked past Luc's secretary and opened the door to his private office in Monaco where his brother was working at the computer with the utmost concentration.

"To be here at eight in the morning, you must have turned

into a workaholic. What kind of fantastic robot are you designing now?"

Luc lifted his dark head. At the sight of Cesar standing there, his eyes filmed over. He shook his head. "Look at you."

"Bonjour, mon frère." Cesar moved closer. Within seconds the two of them were hugging again, man to man this time.

"We all heard about the miracle." Luc stepped back to look him up and down. "I'd say you've returned to the world better than ever."

"Hardly," Cesar murmured, "but it's coming."

"Coming?" He punched his shoulder. "There's not so much as a scratch on you. I think you're a fraud."

Cesar smiled. "Recognize this?" He held up the cane he'd been hiding behind his back. "I came to return it. Don't get me wrong. I've been grateful for it, but—"

"But you never want to see it again. I know exactly how you feel. Once upon a time I threw it away. My wife has a lot to answer for." They both grinned as Luc took it from him. "I didn't think you'd be in Monaco until this afternoon so I hurried in here early to finish something I've been getting ready for you. Have a look."

Cesar did his bidding.

His brother had designed a new prototype of the Faucon. Humbled by his devotion to him, Cesar couldn't talk for a minute. Luc had always been his number one racing fan. It was because of his brother's interest in Formula 1 racing that Cesar had decided to become a driver in the first place.

"I've made a lot of new improvements. The other day I talked to Giles. This car can be ready for testing in January. When Sarah announced to the world that you'd be back to race next year, I thought I'd better get busy."

He propped himself against the desk before studying his elder brother. "She did do that, didn't she."

"With you barely out of the hospital, too. A wife's love is its own miracle."

"You ought to know."

Luc's brows lifted in surprise. "And you don't?"

"Come on, Luc. Olivia was always there for you. Let's not pretend. I don't have what you have and I never will, but it's okay. The crash helped me to understand a lot of things. I'm finally over my jealousy of you."

He frowned. *"Jealousy—"*

Cesar nodded. "You were my hero. You had it all. I wanted to be just like you, but that wasn't possible, so I decided to drive cars in an attempt to make you proud of me."

Luc looked shaken. He put a hand on his arm. "I've always been proud of you."

"I know. That's what makes you the best, and Olivia knew it, too."

"You don't know what the hell you're talking about. After I hurt her so unconscionably, I lived in fear I'd lost her for good. Ask Nic. He'll tell you how bad it was. With an ocean between us, I knew I'd never see her again unless I did something drastic to get her back. I had to do a lot more than get down on my knees."

"But deep down she always loved you. I'm afraid in my case, my marriage to Sarah isn't going to work."

A sound of incredulity escaped Luc's throat. "Wait just a minute. What am I missing here? Are you trying to tell me she hasn't been there every second for you?

"Who was always there waiting for you when you flew to California? What do you think that scrapbook Sarah made was all about? You're the one who kept her a racing widow for five years. Who else but the woman who loved you beyond all else dared to enter your hospital room after you'd put the fear into everyone including your doctor?

"She didn't have to come, you know. When all the chips

were down, *she* was the one who showed up without any encouragement from you in six years.

"Who's been raising your son all this time? After five years
I still don't see any stepfather around. If she hadn't always
kept you alive in her heart, why in the hell do you think Jean-
Cesar was already bonded to you the moment he climbed up
onto the chair to watch you shave?

"She didn't have to marry you the same day you made your
demand. Sarah agreed because she's always wanted *you*." He
thumped Cesar's shoulder again.

"The fact is, she never knew if you always wanted her. It
took real love for her to come to Italy still believing you were
involved with my ex-fiancée."

Cesar blinked. It appeared Sarah had told Olivia everything.

"Since we're putting every card on the table, there's something you still don't know about Olivia and me."

He stared at Luc in puzzlement.

"I had to resort to kidnapping her to make her listen to me."

"Kidnapping?"

"It's true. With Nic's help we got her back to Spain on false
pretenses. When she thought she was getting into a limo at
the hotel, it was one of my experimental robot cars. I locked
her in it, then made it drive to Nic's villa."

On hearing that, Cesar burst into laughter and couldn't
stop. "She must have been terrified."

To his surprise, Luc wasn't laughing. He wasn't even
smiling. "Not as terrified as I was, believe me. If she'd turned
me down then, I didn't have any more tricks in my bag. From
what I can see, you don't need any tricks to win Sarah's love.
She's always been yours for the taking."

That's what Sarah had told him in bed ten nights ago, but
he hadn't listened. Since then the wall between them had
grown even higher.

A surge of adrenaline coursed through Cesar's body.

"You're so right big brother, and I've been the greatest *cretino* alive. Your confession has just given me an idea. I'm going to need your help."

Luc's eyes ignited with the devilry of former days. "I'm all ears, little brother."

Sarah and Johnny were just finishing breakfast with Cesar's parents when Luc entered the dining room. Cesar had left before anyone was up. She'd assumed he'd gone to see his brother. Since the night she'd discovered he could walk, there'd been next to no communication between them.

"Darling," Luc's mother cried. "Come and join us."

"I'd like to, but Olivia and Julie sent me to whisk Sarah and Johnny away to our house for a little while. Marie-Claire can't wait any longer to play with Johnny. I promise I won't be long. Then we'll all be back."

"That's good. The rest of the family will be arriving anytime now."

"Where's Cesar?" This from his father.

"I don't know. I thought he'd be here with you."

His mother looked pained. "That means he went straight to the track." She turned to her husband. "I can't believe he'd do this today of all days. Surely after his accident…" She couldn't finish the rest and buried her face in her hands.

Sarah's heart went out to her. She'd learned from Massimo how much Cesar's beautiful black-haired mother had suffered over his choice of careers.

Johnny got down from his chair and went over to pat his grandmother's arm. "Don't cry, *Nonna*. Daddy likes to race!"

She laughed through the tears. "I know he does. Just don't *you* get any ideas about being a race car driver. One in the family has been quite enough, my little Giovanni." She gave him a big hug. "Now you need to run along with your uncle, but hurry back."

"We will," he promised. After giving both grandparents a kiss, he joined Sarah and they walked out to Luc's blue sedan. Everyone buckled up before he started the engine.

They'd barely started to drive away when Johnny said, "How come we're not driving up the hill? Daddy says that's where you live."

"You're right, but we're not going to my house right now. Your daddy asked me to drive you to the track, but I didn't want to say anything in front of your grandmother."

Johnny gave Sarah a sheepish look. "*Nonna* gets upset, doesn't she?"

"I'm afraid she'd get really upset if she knew your daddy was going to take you for a ride in one of his race cars," Luc confided.

"Hooray!" Johnny cried. In his excitement he tried to sit forward, but the seat belt held him back. Sarah was excited for him. To ride in his father's race car had been his childhood dream.

Though she'd never been here before, Sarah knew the track where Cesar did his training lay on the outskirts of Monaco City. Luc drove them past the main building where they were let through the gate to the speedway. No one appeared to be out on the track right now. Nothing was quieter than a track minus the whine and scream of the engines.

"I see a race car!" Johnny shouted.

Sure enough, a flashy red one was sitting in a pit stop area surrounded by half a dozen crew members.

"Where's Daddy?"

"I'll take you to him." Luc drove closer and stopped the car.

"There he is!"

Sarah's son saw him before she did. Johnny scrambled out of the back seat and ran toward the Formula 1 car. She hurried after him, followed by Luc who carried his video camera. The pit crew separated for them.

Cesar was already inside the cockpit. The sun shone down

on his black curly hair. He wore no helmet today. His hands gripped the steering wheel that had just been locked into place. Something glinted at her. She let out a slight gasp to discover he was wearing the wedding ring she'd given him.

While she was trying to work out what it meant, she saw the white smile her husband flashed Johnny. Quick as a wink Luc picked him up and laid him across Cesar's strong arms.

In a seat built like a jet fighter's, there was no room for anyone but the driver. Johnny lay there and held on to his father's arm with a combination of joy and nervousness written on his precious face. This was a supremely special moment between father and son.

Her breath caught as Cesar turned on the engine. While he talked to Johnny, he let it idle for a minute. Sarah could feel the vibrations. It drowned out his voice.

Soon she saw Johnny nod his dark head, and then they took off. Carrying such precious cargo, Cesar couldn't be driving more than twenty miles an hour, but to a little five-year-old boy, it had to be the thrill of a lifetime. It was for Sarah whose eyes grew blurry as she watched their progress around the track.

"Quite a sight isn't it," Luc murmured while he filmed everything.

"Johnny's been waiting for this moment forever."

"I can't tell who's having more fun, my nephew or my brother."

They eventually came around the final curve and pulled in to the pit stop.

"Mommy!" Johnny cried to her. "It was awesome!"

One of the crew who was all smiles reached for him and set him on the ground so Sarah could hug him.

"Your uncle got pictures of you. We'll go home later and look at them with the whole family."

"What if *Nonna* sees them?"

"Don't worry. She'll love these."

As she stood up to look at Cesar and thank him, the same pit crewman suddenly picked her up. Her cries of protest went ignored as he laid her across Cesar's arms like a bride being carried over the threshold.

The position itself was awkward enough. Unfortunately she'd put on a blouse and skirt this morning, which now meant she was revealing an embarrassing length of bare leg to the men's view. If only they knew how precarious things were between her and Cesar, they wouldn't have done this.

"Whoa, Mommy—"

How humiliating.

Sarah was caught with no place to go. She had nowhere to look but up. No eyes to look into but his. Beneath jet-black brows, they gleamed like newly minted silver. His eyes only went that particular color when he was at the height of excitement.

Her arm had to snake around the back of his head to give her some support. "Please tell one of your crew to lift me off you, Cesar!"

He started the engine.

"Luc—help!"

Before she could inhale again, they began moving. He was taking it carefully, like he'd done with Johnny.

"No one else can hear you, *bellissima*. It's just you and me taking a final victory lap around the track."

She swallowed hard. "What do you mean final?"

Halfway around he slowed to a stop so he could give her his full concentration. "This is the last time I'll ever drive a Formula car again. I thought we'd enjoy it together."

Sarah couldn't comprehend what he was saying. "But you can walk now. That means you can drive again. You only have two more world championships to win. You're almost there."

"Five is more than enough for any man. I'm a father now, and a husband who's madly in love with my *squista* wife."

She couldn't take it in. "D-don't say that if you don't mean it, Cesar."

"It's what I should have told you on the phone when I invited you to Positano. When you told me you couldn't come, I should have jumped on the next plane to California to get the truth out of you. But I was younger then, full of self-doubts.

"The man you're looking at has finally grown up. Having been given a second chance at living, I have no intention of wasting any more time. What matters is our being together day and night, and all the hours in between. When I told you our marriage wasn't working, that was because of me, not you. It's confession time, Sarah.

"I'm afraid you fell in love with a man who didn't have enough self-confidence to believe a woman like you could love me. I always lived in Luc's shadow, wishing I could be like him. I didn't have enough faith in myself.

"I don't blame you for not telling me about Johnny. With hindsight I can understand why you felt you were making the right decision for him. Back then I rarely had time for you in my life. Why would you think I'd make any more time for Johnny?"

She was trembling. "I know *now* that you would have," she cried.

"We both know things now we didn't know before. Every time I've castigated you for what you did to us, I realize I've really been blaming myself for my tunnel vision. Will you forgive me? I want to put the past behind us where it belongs."

His pleading came from a soul laid naked before her. She was humbled by it.

"Oh, darling—"

She felt his eyes burning with love for her. "That's what

you called me the night Johnny was conceived. I want to hear you call me that again and again, and never stop."

Sarah groaned with longings still unassuaged. "How come you've chosen this moment to say these things to me when we're both trapped and can't do anything about it?"

A smile broke the lines of his compelling mouth. "Are you saying you want to do something about it?"

"Cesar de Falcon— I've tried to make love to you twice since we flew home from Rome!"

"Don't I know it? If it were humanly possible, I'd be more than happy to accommodate both of us right here, right now. How about we go back to Luc's and take a little nap before we have to go over to *les parents?*"

"Yes, please—hurry!"

Deep laughter rumbled out of him as he revved the engine, then they were moving.

"Did I tell you Massimo's going to let us enjoy a mini-honeymoon on his cabin cruiser? They'll tend Johnny for a couple of days while we're gone."

"I've always wanted to see Lake Como."

"I'm afraid you won't see most of it this trip. The bedroom's below deck. But if you're a good girl, I might let you up long enough to peak out of the porthole once a day."

"Sounds like you've got plans."

His expression sobered. "I had plans six years ago. They've been percolating ever since. I'm in love with you. I need you, *sposa mia.*"

"I need you, too, Cesar, but can we talk about it when we're in a more comfortable position?"

He chuckled. "The Formula 1 wasn't designed for lovers."

"No." She groaned once more. "It's for men who want to fly free."

"Not *this* man. Never again."

* * *

"Darling?" she murmured.

Cesar crushed his wife more fiercely against him. After making passionate love to her until he'd lost count, he wanted to keep her safely locked in his arms where nothing would disturb them.

"I can't hear any noise. I think everyone left for your parents hours ago. Look—the sun's at a totally different angle in the sky."

He buried his face in her fragrant hair. "I'm afraid all I can see is you, *amorata,* looking totally ravished. Did I ever tell you your mouth drives me insane with desire?"

To prove his point, he devoured it again. He loved every part and particle of her. Making love to her was ecstasy such as he'd never known. She held nothing back. "My sweet, wonderful Sarah. Thank God it wasn't too late for us after all."

"I love you, Cesar. I love you—" she cried over and over. "I can't believe you've forgiven me. I'm the luckiest woman on earth."

"We're the two luckiest people alive," he murmured against her throat.

Once again they were swept away by a ritual that became new every time their mouths and bodies entwined.

Finally sated for the moment, she reached for his left hand and pulled the ring off. "Did you know I had this band inscribed?"

The delights were never ending.

He kissed the palm of her hand before lifting it so he could see what was inside.

"King of my heart," he read aloud.

"I had it done in English so you'd remember that while everyone else in California crowned you the King of speed, I'd already given you another title."

He crushed it in his fist before closing his mouth over hers. He couldn't drink long enough or deep enough. When he eventually lifted his head he said, "I should have believed in us, Sarah. What we had was magical from the moment we met."

She raised her hands to his cheeks and pulled his head down to kiss his moist eyes. "It's still magical, my love."

"What a son we made together!" he cried into her scented neck. "I swear when I saw the two of you in my hospital room, my heart nearly failed me."

"Let's promise each other no more heart failures ever again. Well, except for the things Johnny's going to put us through as the years roll by."

"And maybe a Jane."

She laughed. "Where did you come up with that name?"

"In my first English reader. You know. Dick and Jane." His smile turned her heart over.

"You made that up." He chuckled. "For our next child I was thinking something brilliant like Octavia Priestley de Falcon."

"I think we can come up with a better name than that."

"But not now. We've got to get up. You can't ruin your mother's party. She's been living for this day."

"You're right. Just one more kiss."

"No, Cesar. It won't be just one."

She whipped out of bed, but he caught her around the waist and pulled her back on top of him. They clung feverishly to each other. "We can't do this to your family, Cesar."

"I know," he said huskily, "but first I have to do this to you. I've only recently come back to life because of you. Humor me, beloved."

* * * * *

THE ITALIAN
DOCTOR'S PERFECT
FAMILY

Alison Roberts

Alison Roberts lives in Christchurch, New Zealand. She began her working career as a primary school teacher, but now juggles available working hours between writing and active duty as an ambulance officer. Throwing in a large dose of parenting, housework, gardening and pet-minding keeps life busy, and teenage daughter Becky is responsible for an increasing number of days spent on equestrian pursuits. Finding time for everything can be a challenge, but the rewards make the effort more than worthwhile.

CHAPTER ONE

THE nudge from a small elbow demanded attention.

'Pip?'

Philippa Murdoch turned her head swiftly. 'Sorry, hon—I was miles away.'

In the emergency department, no less, where she'd had to leave a patient who hadn't been overly impressed by the disappearance of his albeit junior doctor.

'I think they're calling me.'

'Alice Murdoch?'

Everyone in the packed waiting room of the paediatric outpatient department was looking at each other with a vaguely accusatory air. Maybe they'd all had the same kind of hassle as Pip in fitting in their appointments and they didn't appreciate the possibility of further delay due to a less than co-operative patient.

'Here!' Pip stood up hurriedly, wishing she'd left her white coat downstairs. The woman who'd been trying to negotiate a truce between three small children fighting over the same toy in the corner gave her a suspicious look that made her feel as though she was somehow jumping the queue by means of professional privilege.

As if! They'd probably waited as long as anybody here

for an appointment with the most popular paediatrician in the city. Which was why Pip had been forced to abandon her own duties to make sure the consultation wasn't lost.

Had she missed something in that initial assessment of her last patient? The symptoms had been non-specific and unimpressive and too numerous to find one that seemed significant, but maybe she should have taken more notice of that toothache he'd mentioned? What if Pip had left him under observation while he was busy having a heart attack? She should have ordered a twelve-lead ECG and some bloods rather than more routine vital sign observations.

She and Alice were ushered into a small room with three chairs in a triangle on one side of a desk and a couch against the opposite wall. The nurse deposited a plain manila folder with Alice's name on the front onto the desk.

'Have a seat,' she invited. 'Dr Costa won't be long.'

Alice raised her eyebrows. 'Funny name, isn't it?'

'It's Italian.'

'Why can't I just go back to Dr Gillies?'

'Dr Gillies is our family doctor. Part of his job is to get someone else to see his patients if he's not sure what's wrong. It's called referral.'

Alice absorbed the information with a small frown. Then her face brightened.

'Knock, knock,' she said.

'Who's there?' Pip responded obligingly.

'Dr Costa.'

'Dr Costa who?'

'Dr Costa lotta money.'

Pip's grin faded with astonishing rapidity as she realised she wasn't the only one to have heard Alice's joke, but the tall, dark man, whose sudden presence seemed overwhelming in the small consulting room, was smiling.

'I don't really cost much at all,' he said to Alice as he eased his long frame into the remaining empty chair and leaned forward slightly. 'I'm free…and I'm all yours.'

Alice was staring, open-mouthed, and Pip could sympathise with the embarrassed flush creeping into the girl's cheeks. She would have been thoroughly disconcerted to have a dose of masculine charm like that directed at *her*. Poor Alice would have no idea how to respond.

The soon-to-be-teenage girl was currently the sole focus of attention from a man who had to be far more attractive than any one of the pictures of the movie-star and pop idols that Alice and her friends already enjoyed discussing at length.

With hair and eyes as dark as sin, a killer smile and that intriguing accent, it was no wonder that one of the senior ED nurses had sighed longingly when Pip had explained the necessity of accompanying Alice to this appointment.

'I wouldn't miss that opportunity myself.' Suzie had laughed. 'In fact, I wonder if I could borrow someone's kid?'

'It's only because my mother's got some kind of horrible virus that's making her vomit and Alice is too young to go by herself.'

'It's not a problem,' Suzie had assured her. 'Your voluble Mr Symes has probably only got a virus as well. I'll keep a close eye on him while you're gone.' She waved Pip towards where Alice was waiting patiently on a chair near the door. 'Go. Enjoy!'

And with that smile from Dr Costa now coming in her own direction, it was impossible not to feel a curl of very feminine pleasure. Philippa could hear an echo of Suzie's sigh somewhere in the back of her head as she returned the smile.

'And you must be Alice's...sister?'

The noticeable hesitation was accompanied by a spark of curiosity in those dark eyes, but who wouldn't wonder about such an obvious age gap between siblings? There was also a subtle frown that suggested the doctor was puzzled by the somewhat unorthodox situation of a sibling accompanying a new patient to a medical consultation.

That inward curl shrivelled so fast it was a flinch, but Pip managed to keep her smile in place for another heartbeat. About to correct his assumption, she was interrupted by Alice.

'Mum's sick,' Alice informed Dr Costa. 'Isn't she, Pip? She couldn't come with me today 'cos she's got some horrible bug that's making her throw up all the time.'

'I'm sorry to hear that!'

He really sounded sorry, too. Pip took a deep breath.

'We didn't want to miss this appointment.' She didn't need to catch the meaningful glance from Alice that pleaded with her not to make any corrections. It could be their secret, couldn't it? Dr Costa wasn't the first person to assume they were sisters and it was much cooler than reality as far as Alice was concerned.

It seemed perfectly reasonable. Secrets were fun after all, and if they were harmless, they only added to bonds between people.

'There's quite a waiting list to get into one of your clinics, Dr Costa,' Pip added calmly, as she shot Alice just the ghost of a conspiratorial wink.

'Call me Toni. Please.' He was eyeing her white coat. 'You're on staff here, Pippa?'

'It's Pip. Short for Philippa.' Though she liked *Pippa*

rather a lot more, especially delivered with that accent. 'And, yes, I've just taken up a registrar position here. I'm a month into my run in the emergency department.'

Alice was watching the exchange with keen interest.

'I thought you were supposed to be Italian,' she said to her doctor.

'I am. I come from Sardinia, which is a big island off mainland Italy.'

'Tony doesn't *sound* very Italian.'

'It's Toni with an "i",' she was told. 'Short for Antonio. Will that do?'

Alice returned the smile cautiously. 'I guess.'

It was Pip's turn to receive another smile. 'Thank goodness for that. What would I have done if I couldn't have established my credentials? Now…' He reached for the manila folder on the desk. 'Tell me, Alice, how is it that you've come to see me today?'

Alice looked puzzled. 'I came on the bus from school. I often do that now so that Pip can give me a ride home in her car. I used to have to catch *two* buses.'

Pip caught the unspoken appeal as the paediatrician opened the file. He wasn't getting the short cut he might have hoped for in this consultation.

'Alice's GP made the referral,' she said helpfully. 'He's been trying to find a cause for recurrent abdominal pain with associated nausea and vomiting and some general malaise that's been ongoing for several months now.'

Toni Costa was nodding as he skimmed the referral letter. 'No evidence of any urinary tract infections,' he noted aloud, 'but your doctor's not happy to settle for a diagnosis of childhood migraine or irritable bowel syndrome.'

'Mmm.' Actually, it had been Pip who hadn't been

happy to settle for an umbrella diagnosis, but she didn't want to have anyone else thinking she was interfering because of her training.

The swift glance she received from her senior colleague conveyed a comprehension of her thought that was instant enough to be unsettling, but his expression suggested a willingness to respect her opinion that Pip appreciated enormously. The invitation to say more was irresistible.

'Mum had a cholecystectomy for gallstones a few years ago,' she told Toni. 'And she had an episode of pancreatitis last year. The symptoms were rather like what Alice seems to experience.'

Pip paused, waiting for the kind of reaction Dr Gillies had made to the suggestion. The unsubtle query of how soon after Shona's illness Alice's symptoms had appeared. As though Alice was disturbed enough to be suffering from Munchausen's syndrome and had latched onto a known condition. As if you could fake the symptoms like tachycardia and pallor and vomiting that could come with real, severe pain!

'And you're concerned about a possibility of an hereditary condition?'

'Yes.' The tension in Pip evaporated. Toni Costa was going to take her concerns seriously. Her opinion of this man shot up by several notches.

'What's a hairy-de-tairy thing?' Alice demanded. She gave Pip a suspicious glare. 'You never said I might have *that.*'

Toni was smiling…again, and Pip decided that was just the way his face naturally creased all the time. Did smiling always make those almost black eyes seem to dance? No wonder he was so popular with his patients.

'Hereditary just means it's something you were born

with,' he was explaining to Alice. 'You get a whole parcel of genes when you born and some of them come from your parents and grandparents and something hereditary means it came in the parcel.'

'Is it bad?'

Toni shook his head, making sleek waves of rather long, black hair move. 'It doesn't mean anything by itself, Alice. It's like catching one of your buses. If it's hereditary it just means you already had your ticket. If it isn't, you're buying the ticket when you jump on the bus instead. It's the bus we're interested in, not the ticket.'

Was he always this good at explaining things to children? Further impressed, Pip watched the satisfied nod that made Alice's ponytail bounce.

'So what's my bus, then?' she asked. 'Where's it going to take me?'

'That's what we're going to try and find out.' Toni Costa folded his hands on his lap and leaned forward a little. 'Tell me all about these sore tummies you've been getting.'

It was a relief to slide into a routine initial assessment of a new patient. Toni could now completely ignore the slightly odd atmosphere in his consulting room.

'And how often do you get the sore tummy, Alice?'

The young girl screwed up her nose thoughtfully. 'The last time was the same day as Charlene's party because I couldn't go.'

'And how long ago was that?'

'Um…well, it's Jade's party this weekend and she's exactly a month older than Charlene.'

'Older?'

'I mean younger.'

Toni nodded. 'So the last episode was a month ago. And the one before that?'

'I had to miss school and they were going on a trip to the art gallery that day.'

Toni raised an eyebrow at Alice's sister and could see the smile in her eyes. She had to know exactly what it was like, chasing the information he required, and how frustrating the process could be sometimes.

'They're happening at four-to-six-week intervals,' she supplied readily. 'And it's been ongoing for nearly six months now.'

With a quick, half-smile by way of thanks, Toni turned his attention back to his patient. 'It must be annoying to miss special things like your friends' parties,' he said sympathetically.

'Yes,' Alice agreed sadly. 'It really is.'

'So the pain is quite bad?'

'Yes. It makes me sick.'

'Sick as in *being* sick? Vomiting?'

'Sometimes.'

'Is the pain always the same?'

'I think so.'

'How would you describe it?'

The girl's eyes grew larger and rounder as she gave the question due consideration. Pretty eyes. A warm, hazel brown with unusual little gold flecks in them.

Her sister had eyes like that as well. Very different.

Intriguing.

Toni cleared his throat purposefully. 'Is it sharp?' he suggested helpfully into the growing silence. 'Like someone sticking you with a big pin? Or is it dull, like something very heavy sitting on you?'

Alice sighed. 'Kind of both.'

Toni gave up on getting an accurate description for the moment. 'Is it there all the time or does it go away and then come back—like waves on a beach?'

'Kind of both,' Alice said again. She bit her lip apologetically and then tried again. 'It doesn't really go away but it gets worse and then not so worse.' She shook her head. 'It's really hard to remember.'

'I know, but it's important you tell me everything you can remember about it. Does it stay in one place?'

'Yes. In my tummy.' Alice gave him a long-suffering and eloquent look. Did he really expect a tummy pain to go somewhere else—like her head, maybe?

Toni smiled. 'What I meant was, does it stay in *exactly* the same place? Does it get bigger and go to more places in your tummy, or does it make your back feel sore?'

Alice's face brightened. 'Sometimes it helps if I put the hottie on my back instead of my front. Is that what you mean?'

'Yes. Knowing that sort of detail is very helpful.'

Radiation of abdominal pain to the back could well point to something like pancreatitis and the thought automatically took Toni's gaze back to the older woman sitting in front of him.

She had to be quite a lot older than her sister. Late twenties probably, which was why he had been initially hesitant in querying their relationship to each other. Far better to assume they were siblings than to insult a woman by suggesting she looked old enough to be someone's mother.

The resemblance was certainly marked enough to make them believable siblings. Pip had those same astonishing eyes. Her hair was a lot darker—a real chestnut instead of red-gold—but the genetic inheritance in the soft waves was also apparent.

And should be of no interest whatsoever in this interview.

'Any associated symptoms other than the vomiting?' he found himself asking steadily. 'Diarrhoea, headache, temperature?'

Pip shook her head.

'And no family history of migraine?'

'No.'

'Peptic ulcers? Gastrointestinal reflux?'

'No. And she's been trialled on antacid medications.'

'Any unusual stress factors or family circumstances?'

Pip looked startled. Almost taken aback.

How curious.

'I don't have an ulcer,' Alice said firmly. 'That's silly. Only old people get ulcers. They thought Nona might have one once.'

'Nona?'

'Mum's name is Shona,' Pip put in quickly. 'For some reason, that's what Alice started calling her when she learned to talk, and it stuck.'

'Oh?' The extra distraction from professionalism was unavoidable. 'How strange!'

Pip's gaze was shuttered and her tone guarded. 'Is it?'

'Only to me, maybe.' Toni smiled reassuringly. 'I was largely brought up by my grandmother. Nonna.'

'Was *her* name Shona, too?' Alice sounded fascinated. 'How weird!'

Toni shook his head. 'No. *Nonna* is Italian for grandmother.'

And that was more than enough personal stuff. So odd that sharing something so private had seemed compelling. Almost as odd as the glance now passing between the Murdoch sisters. Toni stood up in an attempt to get completely back on track.

'Now, *cara*, it's time I had a good look at this tummy of yours. Can you climb up onto the bed for me?'

But Alice was staring at him now. 'Why did you call me Cara? My name's Alice.'

'Sorry, it's Italian. It means…sweetheart.'

'Oh…' Alice dropped her gaze shyly as she moved to climb onto the examination couch. 'That's all right, then.'

There weren't many people that could have won Alice Murdoch's full co-operation so easily. Pip stayed where she was, seated by the desk, while Toni began his examination. Close enough for support but far enough away to allow closer interaction between doctor and patient. Pip was more than happy to observe an examination that was thorough enough to be both impressive and a learning experience for her. She would make sure she remembered to apply the same principles for her next paediatric patient.

Toni did a head-to-toe check of Alice with astonishing efficiency, covering a basic neurological, cardiovascular and respiratory assessment before concentrating on Alice's abdomen. He also fired questions at Pip. Fortunately, the focus of his attention and the distance across the consulting room meant he probably didn't notice anything unusual in her responses.

But, then, he wouldn't be expecting her to be able to answer them easily, would he?

'Do you know if there were any difficulties associated with Alice's birth and the pregnancy?'

'Ah…' Pip had to stifle a kind of incredulous huff of laughter. 'Difficulties' couldn't begin to cover the emotional and physical trauma of a sixteen-year-old girl discovering she was pregnant.

Having the father of that baby abdicate any kind of responsibility or even acknowledgement of his child.

Being forced to burden her own mother who was still trying to get her life back together after the tragic loss of her husband and Pip's father only the year before.

Suffering a labour that had been so badly managed, prolonged and horrendous that Pip had known ever since that it was an experience she could never face repeating.

Her hesitation was interpreted as a negative response, but Toni's nod indicated it was only to be expected. 'I imagine you would have known if there had been anything seriously amiss.'

'Yes, I think I would have.'

'Normal milestones?' he asked, after listening to Alice's chest and heart with a stethoscope. 'Do you remember what age Alice started walking, for instance?'

'She was just over twelve months old.'

Twelve months that had been the hardest in Pip's life. The responsibility and practical skills of caring for a baby would have been totally overwhelming and dreadful if it hadn't been for Shona. In a way, though, it had been a wonderful twelve months because Shona had forged an even closer bond with her daughter and then rediscovered her joy in life through her granddaughter. That she had become more of a mother to Alice than Pip had been gradual but inevitable as Pip had been encouraged to finish her schooling and even chase her dream of going to medical school.

'What about talking?' Toni asked, as he let down the pressure from the blood-pressure cuff around Alice's arm.

'I'm not so sure about that. Around two, two and a half.' Hard to confess her lack of certainty but it was true—she wasn't sure. Alice hadn't been stringing more than a few single words together when Pip had headed away for her first term at university, but she had been chattering by the time she'd headed home for her first holiday break.

'Childhood illnesses? Measles, mumps, chickenpox and so on?'

'She's fully vaccinated. She had chickenpox when she was…oh, about four. The whole kindergarten class came down with it, I seem to remember.'

Not that Pip had been there to help run baths with soothing ingredients or apply lotion or remind Alice not to scratch. The letters and phone calls from her mother had made her feel guilty she hadn't been there to help and share the worry. Worse than the poignancy of missing the joy of other milestones. But, as Shona repeatedly said, it wasn't because she didn't love Alice. She was doing what was best for both of them. For their futures. It couldn't be helped that she had to be away so much.

No wonder their relationship worked so much better as sisters now. They all knew the truth, of course, but it worked so well for all of them the way it was.

Pip had the niggling feeling that Dr Toni Costa might not think it was an ideal arrangement. He already thought it strange that Alice called her mother 'Nona' and there had been something hidden in the tone which with he'd shared the information that he'd been raised by his grandmother. She wasn't about to try and analyse why she didn't want to be thought less of by Alice's paediatrician but it was enough to prevent her correcting his initial assumption that was now making answering his questions rather uncomfortable.

It was a relief when he concentrated totally on Alice again for a few minutes.

'Show me where you feel the pain in your tummy.'

Alice pointed vaguely at her midriff.

'Does it hurt if I press here?' His hand was on the upper middle portion of Alice's abdomen.

'A little.'

Pip could see how gentle he was being, however. How sensitive his touch was. It was hard to look away from that hand, in fact. The olive skin with a dusting of dark hair. Long fingers and neatly manicured nails. Movements that were confident but careful.

'What about here?' He was trying the upper right quadrant now. The area that pain would be expected if Pip's suspicions had any grounds.

'Yes,' Alice said quickly. 'That hurts.'

'A little or a lot?'

'Not too much. But that's where it gets *really* sore when I get sick.'

The strident beeping at that point made Toni glance at the pager clipped to his belt. Then he raised his eyebrows in Pip's direction.

'Sorry. I think ED's trying to contact me.'

'Feel free to use the phone on the desk if you wish.'

'Thanks.' Pip was embarrassed to interrupt the examination but she couldn't not take the call. What if her Mr Symes was busy having a cardiac arrest in a side room or something?

Suzie sounded apologetic as well. 'I'm sure it's nothing, but Mr Symes is complaining of chest pain now. Says it's a crushing, central pain that's radiating to his left arm.'

Classic symptoms. Almost too classic. 'Any associated symptoms?'

'Not really. He's been complaining of nausea since he came in, along with all those aches and pains, but he's not vomiting or sweating or anything. He reckons this came on suddenly.'

'I don't suppose he gave you a pain score without being asked, did he?'

Suzie laughed. 'Ten out of ten. Do you think he's been reading the right textbooks?'

'We can't afford to make assumptions. Can you do a twelve-lead ECG and put him on telemetry?'

'Sure.'

'What's his blood pressure?'

'One-fifty over ninety.'

'Safe to try a dose of GTN, then. Put him on oxygen as well. Six litres a minute.'

'OK.'

'We'll do some more bloods, too, and add in cardiac enzymes. I can do that when I come down. I shouldn't be much longer.'

In fact, Toni was sitting down to share his findings with her as she hung up the phone, and Pip was aware of a vague feeling of disappointment that the consultation was almost over.

'Cardiac patient?' he queried.

'Probably not, but we'll have to rule it out.'

'I won't keep you too long. Alice seems like a normal, healthy little girl on first impression. The only finding I can make is mild and rather non-specific abdominal tenderness.'

That feeling of disappointment grew. Were her instincts misplaced? And would there be no reason for Alice to see Dr Costa again?

'Mind you, that's not an unexpected result and it certainly doesn't mean I don't wish to make any further investigations.'

Pip nodded, listening intently.

'I'd like to do some further blood tests and another

urine culture and microscopy. I think a general abdominal ultrasound examination would be a good idea. Maybe even an MRI scan.' Toni was ticking boxes and scribbling notes on request forms.

'We might like to consider a carbon-labelled urea breath test and possibly endoscopy to rule out the gastritis and duodenal ulceration that *Helicobacter pylori* can cause.'

Pip nodded again. This was more than she had expected.

'Alice hasn't been hospitalised with any of these episodes, has she?'

'No. I came close to bringing her in the first time because she was so miserable, but it only lasted about half an hour.'

'It would be ideal if we could see her and get a blood sample while she was having the pain. To check liver function for elevated blood amylase levels.'

'So you think pancreatitis is a possibility?' Pip caught Toni's gaze and held it. To voice the unthinkable—that Alice could have a tumour of some kind—was unnecessary. The eye contact told her that he already knew her deepest fear.

'I'm not ruling anything out at this stage. We'll find out what's causing the problem and then we'll deal with it, yes?'

'Yes.' Pip dropped her gaze, embarrassed to show how grateful she was. 'Thank you.'

'And you'll bring her in if it happens again? And call me? I'd like to see her myself if it's at all possible.'

The warm smile that curled around the words made Pip think that this consultant might even get out of bed and come into the hospital at 3 a.m. if that's when the attack happened to occur.

And that he was really going to do whatever it took to make a diagnosis and then fix whatever was wrong with Alice.

Did all the relatives of his patients feel so cared about? So…safe?

Pip was smiling back as Alice finished getting dressed and plopped into the chair beside her. She glanced from Toni to Pip and then back again.

'OK,' she said. 'Where's my bus off to, then?'

Alice was less than impressed with all the tests she might have to undergo.

'Why can't they just take an X-ray or something? You know I *hate* needles.'

'An ultrasound test is completely painless and it's better than an X-ray. And an MRI scan is even better. It's like having photographs taken of what's inside your tummy. It's incredibly detailed.'

'Ooh, gross! Can you see, like, what you had for breakfast?'

Pip laughed. 'Almost, but I wouldn't worry about any of it. You might have to wait for weeks to get an appointment for something like an ultrasound. We'll do what Dr Costa suggests and bring you into hospital next time you get a sore tummy.'

'Will you come with me?'

'Of course.'

'What if you're working?'

'Then I'll stop working to look after you. Like I did today to go to your appointment.'

'Do you get into trouble for doing that?'

'Of course not.' Pip almost managed to convince herself as well as Alice. 'I just have to make up for it later. Like now. Are you OK to sit in the staffroom and read magazines while I go and look after the patients I still have?'

'Sure.'

'You can get a hot chocolate out of the machine. You know how to work it, don't you?'

'Yeah.'

They bypassed the main area of the emergency department to reach the staffroom.

'Hey, Pip?'

'Yeah?' When had she picked up Alice's speech patterns that now came so automatically?

'Dr Costa's nice, isn't he?'

'Very nice.' Her agreement was deliberately casual. What an understatement!

'Is he married?'

'I have no idea.' Liar! Pip knew as well as most women on the staff of Christchurch General that Toni Costa was single.

'Maybe you should find out.'

'Why?'

''Cos it's about time you got a boyfriend and *I* think Dr Costa's hot.'

Pip wasn't about to engage in that kind of 'girl-talk' with any twelve-year-old but most especially not her own daughter. 'I'm way too busy to fit a boyfriend into my life.'

'If you leave it too long, you'll get old and crusty and no one will want you.'

'Oh, cheers!' But Pip was grinning. 'For your information, kid, twenty-eight isn't *old*!'

They had reached the staffroom now but, as usual, Alice had to have the last word.

'Well, he likes *you*. I could tell.'

* * *

Toni sat back in his chair and sighed with relief as the shrieking toddler who had been the last patient in today's clinic was removed from his consulting room.

He eyed the pile of manila folders and patient notes on his desk and pulled a pen from his pocket. While it would be nice to escape the hospital completely and revel in the peace and quiet of his home, he never left a clinic until he'd expanded his rushed notes to make a detailed summary of each visit. It wouldn't take long.

When he got the Alice Murdoch's file, however, he found himself simply staring into space, fiddling with the pen instead of writing efficiently.

How long would it be before he saw the Murdoch sisters again? Not that he'd wish an episode of acute abdominal pain on Alice, of course.

He could always find another reason to visit the emergency department, couldn't he? A consult that he didn't send a registrar to do, for example.

It wasn't as though he intended to ask Pippa out or anything. Good grief, she was the relative of one of his patients.

Only the sister, though, not the mother. Did that somehow make it more acceptable?

But what would be the point of starting something that would go nowhere? He'd done that too many times already. And she was a doctor. A career-woman. Toni wasn't about to break his number-one rule. However ready he might be to find his life partner, the mother of his children was going to have to be as devoted to them as he intended to be.

As devoted as his own parents had always failed to be.

But he was going to have a career, wasn't he? Wouldn't

any intelligent woman also want a career—at least part time?

Maybe this Pippa Murdoch was planning to go into general practice some time.

Part time.

Toni tried to shake off his line of thought. Tried, and then failed, to complete the task waiting for him on his desk.

There was just something about the bond between those sisters that was very appealing. It was something special. Unusual.

Her family was clearly very important to her. She had left a patient who sounded as though he could be having a heart attack to accompany Alice to the appointment, and she was concerned enough to be determined to get a more definitive diagnosis than her family doctor had supplied.

He respected that.

And there was no getting away from the fact that she was a beautiful woman.

Different.

Stunning, in fact.

Toni reached for the phone and punched in an extension number.

'Ultrasound Reception, Marie speaking.'

'Hello, Marie. It's Toni Costa here, Paediatrics.'

There was a small noise on the other end of the line. Almost a squeak.

'You'll be getting a request for an abdominal ultrasound on a twelve-year-old patient of mine, Alice Murdoch.'

'Yes?' Marie sounded keen to be helpful.

'I'd like you to let me know when you schedule the examination. If I'm available, I'd like to come and watch.'

'Really?' Marie recovered from her surprise. 'Of course, I'll let you know as soon as it's in the book. Is it urgent?'

Toni considered that for a moment. 'It's important rather than urgent,' he decided aloud. 'But it would be very nice if it could happen within the next week or two.'

And it would be very nice, albeit unlikely, if he happened to be free at the time of the appointment. That way, there was at least a chance he might see Pippa again in the not-so-distant future.

He went back to finishing his paperwork.

Quite oblivious to the half-smile that occasionally played at the corners of his mouth.

CHAPTER TWO

THE child looked sick.

Pip had gone past the mother, sitting with a boy aged about two on her lap, twice. They had been there for nearly half an hour and should have been seen before this, but a major trauma case had come in and a significant percentage of the senior emergency department staff were tied up with several badly injured patients in the main resus bays.

The department had been crazy all day. Pip currently had three patients under her care and they were all genuinely unwell. Seventy-five-year-old Elena was having an angina attack that was much worse than usual and could herald an imminent myocardial infarction. Her investigations were well under way and adequate pain relief had been achieved, but Pip was trying to keep an eye on her ECG trace as she waited for blood results to come back and the cardiology registrar to arrive.

Doris, in cubicle 3, was eighty-four and had slipped on her bathroom floor to present with a classic neck of femur fracture. The orderlies had just taken her away to X-Ray and then she would most likely need surgical referral for a total hip replacement.

Nine-year-old Jake had had an asthma attack that

hadn't responded well to his usual medications and his frightened mother had rushed him into Emergency just as the victims from the multi-vehicle pile-up on the motorway had started arriving. Judging the attack to be of moderate severity, Pip had started Jack on a continuous inhalation of salbutamol solution nebulised by oxygen. She had also placed a cannula in a forearm vein in case IV drug therapy was needed, but his oxygen saturation levels were creeping up and the anxiety levels dropping in both mother and child.

Pip was about to check on Jake again and consider whether he needed admission to the paediatric ward.

Toni Costa's ward.

Seeing another child waiting for assessment made her think of Toni again, but Pip was getting quite used to that. It wasn't just Alice's fault for making that unwarranted but rather delicious suggestion that he'd been attracted to her. Pip preferred to think the explanation was because she'd been so impressed with the man as a paediatrician. How good he was with interacting with his young patients and what a good example he'd set in making such a thorough assessment of a new case. How he'd taken Pip's unspoken concerns seriously and made her feel that her daughter was in safe hands.

Toni wouldn't leave an obviously unwell child just sitting to one side of an emergency department and waiting too long for assessment because of pressure on resources, would he?

The small boy looked febrile. His face was flushed and appeared puffy. What bothered Pip more, however, was how quiet the child was. With the alien bustle of an over-worked emergency department flowing past in what should have been a frightening environment, the boy was just lying limply in his mother's arms and staring blankly.

Even from several metres away Pip could see that the little boy was in respiratory distress. A small chest was heaving under a thin T-shirt…way too fast.

Pip moved towards him, pausing for a moment beside the central triage desk.

'Doris has gone to X-Ray so we've got an empty cubicle for a while. Could you find me a bed, please, Suzie? I think I should take a look at that little boy over there.'

'Oh, would you?' Suzie sounded relieved. 'That would be great. I was just going to upgrade him for an urgent assessment. He's looking a lot worse than he did when he came in.' She sent a nurse aide to find a bed in the storage area off the main corridor to the hospital. 'Put it in cubicle 3. Hopefully we'll have another free space by the time Doris comes back.'

A stretcher was coming through the double doors from the ambulance bay. Another one was lined up behind that.

'What's the history?' Pip queried briskly, before Suzie could get distracted by the new arrivals.

'Just became unwell today. Running a temperature, off his food. Family's new in town so they didn't have a GP to go to.'

'Cough? Runny nose?'

'Apparently not. Temp's well up, though—39.6 when we took it on arrival.' Suzie was moving to intercept the first stretcher. 'His name's Dylan Harris. Turns two next month.'

Pip smiled at a mother who was probably her own age. What would life be like for herself, she wondered briefly, if she had a two-year-old instead of a twelve-year-old? She certainly wouldn't be doing what she was doing now—a job she loved with a passion.

'Mrs Harris?'

'Yes…Jenny.'

'I'm Dr Murdoch.' The thrill of saying those words had never worn off. Worth all those long years of hard work and heartache. 'Follow me. We're just finding a bed so I can check Dylan for you.'

'Oh, thank goodness! I think he's getting sicker.'

The bed wasn't needed immediately. Pip carried the chair Jenny had been sitting on as she led the way to cubicle 3.

'Keep Dylan sitting on your lap for the moment, Jenny. It'll keep him happier and help his breathing as well.'

'He's started making funny noises.'

'Mmm.' Pip was listening to the soft stridor on expiration and a gurgle on inspiration with mounting alarm. 'And how long has he been dribbling like that?'

'Is he?' Jenny looked down at her son. 'I hadn't noticed. It must have started just now.'

Something that could compromise a child's airway this quickly was extremely serious and Pip already had a fair idea of what she might be dealing with. She signalled Suzie to indicate the need for assistance but the senior nurse was still occupied with a patient on an ambulance stretcher. Her apologetic wave and nod let Pip know she would do something as soon as she could. Pip reached for an oxygen mask.

'Hold this as close as you can to Dylan's face without upsetting him,' she instructed Jenny.

Pip could see the way the skin at the base of his neck was being tugged in as Dylan struggled to breathe and the retraction of his rib-cage when she lifted his T-shirt to place the disc of her stethoscope on the small chest.

An empty bed was being pushed into the cubicle behind her.

'Get me a nurse, please,' Pip told the orderly. 'Preferably Suzie, if she's available.' She took another glance at Dylan's face. 'You're being such a good boy. You're not feeling too good, are you, sweetheart?'

She got no response. Not even eye contact from the toddler. Pip looked up at Jenny.

'Has he been talking much today?'

'He hasn't said anything since we got here. He's not even crying, which is weird. He usually cries a lot. Does that mean it's not that serious?'

'Not necessarily.' Pip wasn't going to alarm Jenny by telling her that it was the quiet children that were usually most at risk. With the oxygen mask held close to his face, Dylan was leaning back on his mother's shoulder, his chin raised. The 'sniffing the air' position that indicated an instinctive method of maximising airway calibre.

'And he hasn't been coughing at all?'

'No. This came on really suddenly. He seemed fine except he wouldn't eat his toast this morning. I wondered if he might have a sore throat.' She cast a worried glance at her son. 'It's getting worse, isn't it?'

It was. Dylan's eyes drifted shut and his head drooped. Pip touched his face.

'Dylan? Wake up, love. Open your eyes.' She got a response but it wasn't enough. 'I'll be back in a second,' she told Jenny. Slipping through the curtain, Pip nearly collided with Suzie.

'Any of the consultants free at the moment?'

The nurse shook her head. 'One of the trauma cases has arrested. It's a circus in Resus.'

'I need a paediatric anaesthetist here,' Pip said. 'And we need to get Dylan to Theatre. I'm pretty sure he's got epiglottitis and his level of consciousness is dropping.'

Suzie's eyes widened. 'I'll find someone.'

'Get me an airway trolley in the meantime?'

'Sure.'

Pip could only hope that intervention could be avoided until Dylan was safely under the care of an expert anaesthetist.

'I think Dylan has something called epiglottitis,' she told Jenny a moment later. 'It's a nasty bacterial infection of the epiglottis, which is at the back of the throat. If it gets inflamed it can interfere with breathing, which is why Dylan has started making these noises.'

'What will you do?'

'We treat it with antibiotics but we have to protect the airway in the meantime. I'm going to get Dylan taken to an operating theatre if possible to have a tube put down his throat.'

'He needs an *operation*? Oh, my God!'

'Not an operation,' Pip said reassuringly. 'Not unless it's difficult to get a tube in place. In that case, it might be necessary to create a temporary external airway by—'

Suzie was back with a trolley. 'Someone's on the way,' she interrupted Pip. 'Shouldn't be long.'

It was going to be too long for Dylan. The small boy's eyes suddenly rolled and then closed. Jenny felt him go even floppier and when she moved the oxygen mask to look at her son, they could all see the blue tinge to his lips.

'Dylan?' Pip rubbed his sternum. 'Wake up!'

There was no movement to be seen. Including the chest wall. The toddler was in respiratory arrest. Pip plucked him from his mother's arms and laid him on the bed.

'Oh….*God*,' Jenny gasped. 'He's not *breathing*, is he?'

'No.' Pip was pulling on gloves and hoping she sounded much calmer than she felt. Where on earth was that consultant? 'We're going to have to put the tube in here. Could you hyperventilate him, please, Suzie?'

While the nurse used the bag mask to try and pre-oxygenate Dylan, Pip pulled the tubing from the suction kit and switched the unit on. She clipped a straight blade to the laryngoscope and picked out the smallest, uncuffed endotracheal tube from the sterile drape she had opened on the trolley.

'Hold his head for me, Suzie.' Pip peered over the blade of the laryngoscope moments later. 'Can't see a thing,' she muttered.

'Secretions?' Suzie asked.

'Yes. And the epiglottis is very swollen.'

'I'll give you some cricoid pressure.' Suzie pressed on Dylan's neck and Pip tried to take a deep breath and banish her mounting alarm. She knew how critical it was to get this airway secured and it was not going to be easy.

Jenny was sobbing loudly enough for another nurse to put her head around the curtain.

'I can't bear to watch,' the young mother gulped.

'Come with me for a moment, then,' the nurse said. 'I'll look after you while the doctors look after your little boy.'

Pip was barely aware of Dylan's mother being led from the cubicle due to her intense concentration on the urgent task, but even with the pressure on the neck, the secretions sucked away as much as possible and her best efforts, there was no way to get the tube past the obstruction of swollen tissue.

'It's no go,' Pip said tersely.

Suzie sounded just as tense. 'What do you want to do?'

Pip had to think fast. She couldn't rely on a senior doctor arriving in time to take over. If she didn't do something herself, now, this little boy could die.

'Ventilate him again for me, Suzie.' She ripped open another kit on the trolley. 'I'm going to do a cricothyrotomy.'

Stripping off her gloves and reaching for a fresh pair, Pip had to fight a moment of pure panic as the consequences of not succeeding with this next procedure forced themselves into her mind.

Then, for some strange reason, she thought of Toni Costa.

Well, not so strange, really, because Dylan would probably end up being the paediatrician's patient.

And she had been thinking of Toni at rather disconcertingly frequent intervals over the last week anyway.

For whatever reason, Pip could almost sense his presence in the cubicle right now, and it brought an underlying confidence to her determination to succeed. So that Dr Costa would be impressed at the emergency care a patient of his had received.

Her fingers were as steady as a rock as she palpated the cricothyroid membrane on Dylan's neck. There was no need for local anaesthetic as the child was deeply unconscious, and there was no time in any case. Pip stabilised the ring of cartilage with one hand and made a single, decisive incision with the scalpel.

Part of her brain registered the movement of the cubicle curtain and the fact that someone had entered the space and was now standing behind her. A large figure. Maybe it was Brian Jones, one of the emergency department consultants, answering her plea for back-up. She couldn't look up at this point, however, or hand over to anyone else, even if they were far more experienced.

Reversing her hold on the surgical instrument, Pip inserted the handle of the scalpel and rotated it ninety degrees to open the airway. Then she slid the tube into the incision, removing the introducer and replacing it with the tip of the suction apparatus tubing.

She attached the bag mask to ventilate Dylan and listened with her stethoscope to make sure both lungs were filling adequately with air. Then she checked for a pulse and looked up just as the curtain twitched back for the second time, allowing herself an audible sigh of relief.

A sigh that was abruptly terminated. It was Brian Jones who had just entered the cubicle, so who had been watching over her shoulder for the last few minutes? Pip's head swivelled for a second to find Toni Costa standing behind her.

'What's been happening?' Brian queried.

'Epiglottitis,' Pip informed her senior colleague succinctly. 'Respiratory arrest. Intubation failed due to the amount of inflammation.'

Dylan was making a good effort to breathe on his own now and was stirring. He would need sedation and the assistance of a ventilator urgently, but the consultant took a moment to nod with satisfaction.

'Well done, Pip' was high praise from a doctor known for being taciturn. 'Let's get him on a ventilator. Where's his family?'

'I'll find his mother,' Suzie offered.

'And I'll make sure they're ready for this young man in ICU.' Toni moved to follow Suzie but turned a second later. 'Bravo, Pippa,' he said quietly. 'You certainly didn't need my assistance.'

Warmth from that single, unusual word of praise stayed with Pip until she ended what had been a memorably long day. When her last patient, Elena, had finally been admitted for observation in the chest pain ward and Doris was in

Theatre, having her hip joint replaced, Pip took a few minutes to visit the paediatric intensive care unit. She wanted to check up on Dylan and, if she was honest with herself, she wanted to enjoy that sensation of having done something special. And if she was *really* honest with herself, the possibility of meeting Toni Costa again had to be a distinct bonus, so she was more than happy to find him talking to Jenny and a man she assumed to be Dylan's father.

'Oh…it's you!' Jenny's face lit up. 'He's going to be all right. Darling…' She turned to her husband. 'This is the doctor I told you about. The one who saved Dylan's life when he'd stopped breathing.'

'Really?' The man stepped forward and gripped Pip's hand with both of his. 'What can I say? How can I thank you enough? It was…'

It was clearly too much to articulate further. Dylan's father was overcome by emotion.

'Sorry…' he choked out.

'It's OK,' Pip reassured him with a smile. 'I totally understand. It was a frightening experience.'

For her as well. What would Dr Costa think if he knew that he'd provided the confidence Pip had needed to succeed, even before the surprise of his genuine presence? She didn't dare look at him.

'I'm so pleased to hear Dylan's doing well,' she added.

'He's doing very well.'

Pip had to look up as the paediatrician spoke. She found herself basking in a smile she could remember all too easily.

The warmth of this man!

'And I must congratulate you again,' Toni added. 'I didn't get the chance to tell you how impressed I was with what I saw. I couldn't have managed that procedure any better myself. You did, indeed, save young Dylan's life.'

Pip had never felt so proud of herself. It had taken so much hardship to cope with the long training and compromises in her personal life to get to precisely this point, but Toni's approval and the gratitude of Dylan's parents made it all seem worthwhile. More than worthwhile.

But then Pip's gaze was caught by the sight of the young parents moving to sit with their son. They were holding hands with each other and they both used their free hands to gently touch their child. The bond between the three of them was palpable and Pip was aware of a sense of loss that took the shine off her pride. Life could be so complicated and there was no doubt that sacrifices had been made for her to get to where she was. Sometimes things got lost that could never be replaced.

'Don't look so worried,' Toni said. 'He is going to be fine.'

Pip nodded. And smiled—happy to let the paediatrician assume she had been thinking of the child they could see. The return smile gave no hint that he might have guessed her real thoughts, although his words were startling.

'How's Alice?' he queried.

Nobody could read minds that well, Pip reassured herself. 'She seems fine at the moment.'

'Have you received the appointment for the ultrasound examination?'

'Yes, it's next Thursday. Faster than I would have expected.'

Toni didn't seem surprised but then his attention was being diverted by a nurse approaching with a patient's chart.

'Could you sign off these medication adjustments, please, Dr Costa?'

'Sure.' But Toni was still looking at Pip as she turned away with a nod of farewell. 'I'll try and drop by to see what they find on ultrasound. Ten o'clock, isn't it?'

Pip's nod slowed and she left the unit feeling oddly dazed. How on earth had Toni known the time of the appointment? And why would he want to interrupt what had to be a gruelling work schedule in order to attend?

For one, extremely disconcerting, moment, Pip thought that maybe Alice was right. Maybe Toni Costa was attracted to her and was looking for an opportunity to see her again. She couldn't deny that the possibility of seeing *him* again had not gone unremarked in her decision to follow up on Dylan Harris's progress.

How would she feel if that *was* the case? Pip walked through the hospital corridors barely noticing the people or departments she passed. If the tingling sensation in her body right now, coming in rather pleasurable waves, was anything to go by, she would feel very good about it.

Very, very good!

Alice was not feeling very good. Pip entered her home that evening to find her daughter looking downright mutinous.

'Nona's taken my phone,' she announced by way of greeting for Pip. 'It's not *fair*!'

'It's perfectly fair.' Shona appeared in the kitchen doorway. 'You spend half your life texting your friends. You'll get it back when you've finished your homework.' She smiled at Pip. 'You're home, finally! Wash your hands, love, it's almost dinnertime.'

The tone Shona used to speak to both Pip and Alice had been…well…motherly. Caring but firm. Possibly a little close to the end of a tether. Alice and Pip exchanged a glance. They both knew it would be a good idea to smooth potentially troubled waters. Alice disappeared upstairs, to at least look like she was doing some homework. Pip followed her mother to the kitchen.

'You OK, Mum?'

'I'm fine. Bit tired, I guess.' Shona pushed strands of her greying hair behind her ears as she bent to open the oven. 'It's just casserole and baked potatoes. Hope that'll do.'

'It'll be fantastic,' Pip said sincerely. How many other overworked and stressed junior registrars could bank on going home to a warm house and delicious hot meal? Or having their laundry done or messages run when time simply wasn't there for mundane chores?

But, then, how many twenty-eight-year-olds would want to be still living in their childhood home?

It wasn't that Pip resented the security and comfort of being mothered. It was just that—sometimes—it would be nice to choose entirely for herself. To maybe sit down and chill out with a glass of wine instead of being immediately sucked into a predictable family routine.

A routine that had been the only way she could be doing what she was doing, Pip reminded herself. And look what she'd achieved today. A life saved. A family who would be only too happy to return to a normal routine. Pip gave her mother a one-armed hug as Shona stood up to place a tray of hot baked potatoes onto the bench.

'What's that for?' But Shona didn't sound displeased.

'Just because I love you,' Pip responded. She grinned. 'And because I had a great day today. I had to do a really tricky emergency procedure on a little boy, Mum. He'd stopped breathing. He could have died but he's going to be fine.'

'Well done, you!'

Shona's smile was proud but Pip could detect an under-tone. 'You sure you're all right? Is that pain back again?'

'No, not really. Just a bit of an ache.'

'Have you made another appointment with Dr Gillies yet?'

'No. I'll do it tomorrow.'

'That's what you said yesterday. And last week.' Pip eyed her mother with concern. She looked a bit pale. And tired. 'Is Alice giving you a hard time about doing her homework?'

Shona smiled again. 'No more than usual. We'll get it done.'

That 'we' didn't need to include Pip, but she brushed aside any feeling of being left out. 'Anything I can do to help in here?'

'Have you washed your hands?'

'Mum, I'm twenty-eight! If I want to eat dinner with dirty hands, I'm allowed to.' Pip sighed fondly. 'OK, I'll go and wash my hands.'

'Good girl. Tell Alice to wash hers as well. Dinner will on the table in five minutes.'

Alice was brushing her hair and staring at herself in the bathroom mirror.

'Dinner in five,' Pip told her. 'Wash your hands.'

'Hey, Pip—can we watch "Falling Stars" after tea? In your room?'

'Sure.' Although half an hour of watching a gossip show about Hollywood celebrities wasn't Pip's cup of tea, time cuddled up on her double bed with Alice, watching the tiny screen of her portable television, had to be a highlight of any day. It was usually after Shona had gone to bed and often with illicit bowls of popcorn or a packet of chocolate biscuits to share.

Their time—with no parental type obligations to fill, for either of them.

Alice bolted her dinner with one eye on the kitchen clock.

'It's nearly 7.30,' she announced finally, with a meaningful glance at Pip.

'I know. I'm sorry I was a bit late today. Things got really busy.'

'"Falling Stars" is on at 7.30.'

'I know. You can go and watch it if you like, and I'll come after I've done the dishes.'

Shona was only halfway through a plateful of food she had been picking at without enthusiasm. 'Have you finished that assignment you have to hand in tomorrow, Alice?'

'I'll do it later.'

'No, you won't. You never do. You'll have to get it done before you do anything else, and that includes watching television. *Especially* watching television.'

'But it's my *favourite* programme!'

'It's a load of rubbish.'

'*Mum* said I could watch it.'

Alice only called Pip 'Mum' when she wanted to play one of the adults in her house off against the other, a habit that had formed over the last few months—ever since she had decided it was cool to call Pip by her given name.

Pip took one look at her mother's drawn face and knew it had been the wrong button to push tonight.

'Mum's right. You have to get your homework done, Alice. I'll tape the programme and we can watch it later.'

'But I want to watch it *now*! I've been looking forward to it *all* day!' Alice looked at Pip with the face of someone unexpectedly betrayed.

Shona said nothing but her lips were a tight line.

'Please, Pip?'

It was tempting to give in to that plea and maybe negotiate a compromise, like supervising the homework being done later, but Pip could sense a disturbing undercurrent to what should have been an average family-type wrangle. Roles were being challenged.

Alice expected her support but maybe she was too used to getting her own way by pulling the 'friends' card out.

Shona expected her support as well. Pip was Alice's mother after all, and maybe Shona was feeling too tired or unwell not to play the 'mother' card.

Pip was caught in the middle but it was perfectly clear which way she had to jump.

'No,' she said firmly to Alice.

'But you *said*—'

'I know what I said, but I didn't know you hadn't done your homework.'

'Yes, you did! You heard—'

'That's enough!' Shona's fork hit the table with a rattle. 'I'm sick of this.'

Alice jumped up and stormed from the room, slamming the door behind her.

'Sorry, Mum,' Pip said into the silence that followed. She sighed. 'I'm not very good at the parent bit, am I?'

'We're getting to the difficult stage, that's all.' Shona echoed Pip's sigh. 'I'd forgotten what it was like, living with a teenager.'

'Was I so awful?'

'No.' Shona smiled wearily and reached out to touch her daughter's hair. 'You were great.'

That touch took Pip instantly back to childhood where the gesture could have provided comfort, communicate pride or been as loving as a kiss. The love she had for her mother welled up strongly enough to bring a lump to her throat.

'I wasn't that great. Remember the fuss I made when you wouldn't let me get my ears pierced? I kept it up for a week.'

'It wasn't your ears I minded—it was the belly-button ring you wanted.'

'And what about that first rock concert I was determined to go to?'

'I seem to remember you getting your own way in the end that time. Thanks to your dad.'

They were both silent for a moment. The memory of that terrible wrench when Jack Murdoch had died so suddenly was still painful. A period neither of them liked to dwell on. Pip skipped it entirely.

'And then I got pregnant.' She snorted softly. 'I have no idea how you coped with that so well, Mum.'

'When you have to cope, you do. That's all there is to it, really.'

'And you're still coping. Far more than you should have to at your time of life.' Pip couldn't brush aside the pangs of guilt. 'I should be taking full responsibility for Alice by now. I should have a house of my own and not make you live with all her mess and angst.'

'And how would that help while you're still finishing your training?' Shona straightened visibly in her chair. 'I wanted to do this, Pip. I still do. I want to see you settled into the career you've always dreamed of. Into a relationship, even.'

Pip rolled her eyes. 'Yeah, right! Just what every man my age wants—a woman who's still living at home and relying on her mum and a package deal with an angsty teenager thrown in.'

'Don't judge all men on what James thought. He was an idiot.'

'An idiot I wasted four years on at medical school. I'm in no hurry to go back there.'

'It might have helped if you'd told him about Alice a bit earlier.'

'Getting pregnant at sixteen isn't something I'm proud of, Mum.'

'Maybe not, but Alice should be,' Shona said quietly. 'You can be very proud of her.'

Shona's words stayed with Pip as she tidied up after dinner. They could both be proud of their girl, but the credit had to go largely to Shona for the successful up-bringing of Alice. Imagine what a disaster it would have been if it had been left entirely to *her*? But she was much older now. Hopefully wiser. And it was way past time she took more of the burden from Shona's shoulders.

The silence from her daughter's room had been deafening and, having finished her cup of tea, Pip left Shona in the living room and went and tapped on Alice's door. It might be a good time to try and have a real 'mother-daughter' type talk. To start a new phase in their relationship.

'Alice?'

There was no response.

Pip tapped again and opened the door. Alice was curled up on her bed and had her face turned away from the door.

'Alice?' Pip stepped closer. She could see that Alice's arms were locked tightly around her slight body. 'We should talk, hon.'

Alice rolled and Pip saw that her face was scrunched into lines of what looked like severe pain. Reaching to smooth the hair from her forehead, Pip felt the damp skin and then Alice groaned.

'Oh, no!' Pip took hold of her daughter's wrist, knowing she would feel the tattoo of an overly rapid heart rate. 'Is it your tummy again? Why didn't you come and tell me?'

'It just started.' Alice broke into sobs. She didn't look anything like her twelve and a half years right now. She looked like a sick frightened little girl. And along with her maturity had gone any desire for a 'cool' relationship with her mother. 'It hurts, Mummy. Make it go away...*please*!'

'Right.' Pip pulled the duvet around Alice. 'Put your arms around my neck. I'm going to carry you to the car and then I'll take you into the hospital.'

'No-o-o!'

Shona had heard the noise. 'What's happening?'

'Tummy pain again. I'm going to take her into Emergency.'

'Should I call for an ambulance?' Shona asked anxiously.

'It'll be quicker if I take her.'

'I'll get the car out,' Shona offered. 'I can drive.'

'You don't have to come. It could be a long night.'

'Of course I'm coming.'

'I don't want to go,' Alice sobbed. 'I don't want to *move*!'

'I know, hon, but we have to. We need to do what Dr Costa asked us to do. When you're in the hospital you'll be able to have some medicine that will take the pain away completely.'

Alice's arms came up to lock around Pip's neck. She braced herself to take the weight.

'You promise?'

'Yes.' Pip lifted the girl. 'I promise.'

'Will Dr Costa be there, like he said he would?'

'I don't know, hon. Let's hope so but it's late and he's probably gone home by now.'

Alice was still sobbing. 'But I *want* him to be there.'

'Mmm.' The strength of her own desire to have Toni Costa there was overwhelming. Pip had to close her eyes and try very hard to sound casual. 'Me, too.'

CHAPTER THREE

THE triage nurse took one look at Alice and sent them straight to a resus bay.

The registrar on duty, Graham, was right behind them.

'Let's get some oxygen on,' he ordered a nurse, 'and I want some vital sign baselines. What's going on, Pip?'

'This is Alice, she's twelve,' Pip responded. 'She's got acute epigastric pain radiating to her back with associated nausea and vomiting.'

'First time this has happened?'

'No. She had an appointment with Toni Costa recently because we want to find out what's causing it. He asked me to bring her in when it happened again so we could get bloods to check amylase levels.'

'Right. I'll get a line in straight away.'

But Alice jerked her hand away from the registrar. '*No,*' she said fiercely. 'I want Dr Costa.'

'He doesn't work in Emergency, love,' Graham said patiently. 'Come on, this won't hurt for more than a moment, I promise.'

'No.'

'We'll be able to give you something for that pain after I've put this little tube in your vein.'

'No!' Alice's sobs turned to a choking sound and Pip held her daughter's head as she vomited yet again. Shona took a dampened towel from the nurse, ready to wipe Alice's face.

'Sorry,' Pip said to Graham, 'but Toni did ask us to call him if we came in acutely. Alice was expecting to see him, I guess.'

'It's 9.30 p.m. Not much chance of him being in the building.'

'I know.'

Graham looked at the sobbing, unwell child on the bed and his expression revealed his reluctance to force treatment on someone who was very unlikely to be co-operative. He looked down at the IV cannula in his hand and then glanced at Pip.

'I could try beeping him—just in case.'

'Good idea.' Pip smoothed damp strands of Alice's hair back from her face. 'It's worth a try.' At least that way Alice would know they had tried to get the person she wanted to look after her. When she knew it was impossible, she might be prepared to let Pip put a line in her hand if Graham still wasn't acceptable.

She wasn't prepared for the look of surprise on Graham's face when he reappeared less than a minute later. 'He was in ICU. He's on his way down now.'

'Hear that, Alice?' Pip could allow herself to sound delighted on her daughter's behalf. 'Dr Costa's coming to see you.'

Alice hiccuped. 'Good.'

It *was* good. Better than good. Pip had no disagreement with Alice's conviction that Toni was the top of the list of desirable people to care for her. The worry that the paediatrician might have been in the intensive care unit because Dylan had taken a turn for the worse was dismissed with only a small pang of guilt. Pip's attention had to be focused much closer to home for the moment and she wanted the best for her own daughter.

Their confidence did not appear to be misplaced. Toni took over the resus bay from the moment he arrived and managed to exude an air of authority tempered with a charm that reduced the stress levels for everybody concerned. He actually managed to both reassure Alice and gain the information he wanted at the same time. Pip could see Alice visibly relax when the doctor smiled at her and patted her hand before his fingers rested lightly on her wrist.

'Heart rate?'

'One-twenty,' Graham supplied.

'Respirations?'

'Twenty-eight.'

'Temperature?' The touch on Alice's forehead was hardly necessary but Pip could see that it was appreciated. Alice closed her eyes and, just for a moment, the lines of pain on her face almost vanished.

'Thirty-seven point four.'

'Blood pressure?'

'Eighty over fifty.'

'Bit low. Postural drop?'

'We haven't tried assessing that.'

Pip was still watching quietly, enjoying the sensation of having an expert take over. As a doctor, it was a good learning experience, being on a parent's side of this equation. Her anxiety was actually receding to the point where Pip could register how impressive Toni's clinical skills were. He was able to palpate an invisible, tiny vein in Alice's forearm and then slip a small-gauge cannula into place without eliciting more than a squeak from his patient.

Worry kicked in again with his latest question, however. A drop in blood pressure from a change in posture could be serious and the paediatrician seemed to be looking for signs of hypovolaemic shock. What could Alice be bleeding internally from? A perforated peptic ulcer? Something as nasty as acute haemorrhagic pancreatitis?

'She said she felt dizzy when she had to sit in the car,' Pip told Toni as he taped the cannula into place.

'We'll get these bloods off and then I'd like some fluids up,' Toni said to Graham. He smiled at the nurse who was holding a page of sticky labels already printed with Alice's details and hospital ID number, ready to label test tubes.

The smile was warm. Appreciative of her readiness and inviting the junior nurse to consider herself a valuable colleague. For an idiotic moment Pip actually felt something like jealousy.

'We need amylase levels, haemoglobin and haematocrit, electrolytes...' The list seemed to go on and on as the nurse plucked tubes with different coloured stoppers from the tray. 'And we want blood cultures as well,' Toni finished.

'Goodness!' Shona's eyes had widened at the mounting pile of test tubes.

That smile appeared again. 'Don't worry, Mrs Murdoch. It looks like we're taking a lot of blood but it's less than a teaspoonful in each tube.'

'Why the cultures?' Pip queried. 'Wouldn't Alice be running more of a temperature if this pain was caused by infection?'

Toni nodded. 'We still need to rule it out. We'll do a dipstick test on her urine as soon as we can as well.' The quick smile was almost a grin this time—faintly conspiratorial. 'I like to be thorough,' he confessed.

Thorough.

And gentle.

Pip watched Toni's hands as he carefully examined Alice's abdomen. She had watched him doing this once before and, unbidden, the memory had already returned more than once.

If only Alice hadn't planted that absurd suggestion of Toni as potential boyfriend material. If only Pip hadn't found herself remembering those hands and their touch in the middle of the night. Wondering how it feel to have them touching *her*.

It had been all too easy to imagine. And highly inappropriate, given the current setting, so it was easy to dismiss. It evaporated more than convincingly as Alice cried out in pain. Toni's voice was now as gentle as his touch but excited no odd tingles in Pip. Her focus was firmly on her daughter as she stepped forward to take the small, outstretched hand.

'It's OK, hon,' she said. 'I'm here.'

'I know it hurts, *cara*,' Toni added in an equally soothing tone. 'We're going to do something about that very soon. It's a bit mean, isn't it, but we need to try and find out what's causing it before we take the pain away.' He turned to the registrar who was adjusting the flow on the IV line attached to a bag of fluids. 'I think we could get some pethidine on board now.'

'Why not morphine?' It was the standard analgesic to use in situations such as this.

'There's some evidence it can cause sphincter of Oddi spasm.'

Graham nodded. He eyed Alice thoughtfully and Pip

could tell he was trying to assess how much she weighed in order to calculate a dose of the narcotic. Toni picked up the hesitation as quickly as Pip did but showed none of the impatience some consultants might have displayed. Instead, he smiled at his young patient.

'Do you know how much you weigh, Alice?'

'No.'

'I'm sure Mum knows.'

There was a tiny pause as Shona blinked at being the focus of attention. 'Ah…' She flicked a puzzled gaze at her daughter. 'Actually, Pip's—'

'She's about thirty-two kilos,' Pip interrupted quickly. This was hardly the time or place to correct Toni's assumption about her relationship with Alice, was it?

'We'll start with 25-mg IV,' Toni told Graham. 'I'd like to get an abdominal X-ray and then admit Alice to the ward overnight.' His gaze found Pip. 'We'll restrict her fluid intake and make sure we get the pain under control. I want to do an arterial blood gas as well and we'll see if we can get that ultrasound done first thing tomorrow. We'll have the blood results back by then, and then we'll look at what else we need to do.'

A lot seemed to be happening with extraordinary ease as Toni calmly issued instructions and made more than one phone call. Even when everything was sorted to his satisfaction, he didn't take his leave.

'How's the pain now, Alice?'

'Getting better.' Alice smiled for the first time since they had arrived and then she yawned.

'We'll get you to bed as soon as you've had that X-ray and then you can have a proper rest. Would you like your mum to stay with you in the hospital tonight?'

Alice nodded slowly. 'Mummy?'

Pip gave no thought to the fact that she was about to let Toni learn of the deception she and Alice had allowed to occur. Or that she had complications in her life that were enough to scare most men firmly away. The only thing that mattered right now was Alice. Providing any comfort possible. She squeezed Alice's hand.

'What is it, hon?'

Toni's glance slid from Shona to Pip, a puzzled frown appearing between dark brows.

'Will you stay with me?' Alice asked plaintively. The question was clearly directed at Pip rather than Shona.

'Of course I will, chicken.'

Toni merely raised one eyebrow. 'If you'd rather have your sister stay with you, Alice, that's absolutely fine.'

'Pip's not *really* my sister,' Alice mumbled drowsily. 'She's my *mother.*'

The timing of the radiologist's arrival to take the abdominal X-ray Toni had ordered was fortunate. He could cover up his reaction to Alice's startling revelation by moving abruptly to go behind the protective glass screen in one corner of the main resus area. And then he was able to concentrate on the first results coming in from the blood tests.

Or appear to concentrate, at least. Toni was shocked, he couldn't deny it. Pip had been less than honest with him, hadn't she? Yes, he had to concede that he had made the assumption they were sisters himself, but she hadn't made any attempt to correct him, had she?

But, then, he knew that women couldn't be trusted, didn't he?

His grandmother would hold the prize of a visit from his parents over him to extract co-operation. He soon

learnt, however, that the reality of the reward was so intermittent it could never be completely trusted. Or dismissed.

His mother had always been so believable in her
promises that one day—soon—she would take him away
with her. That they would be a real family and he would
see more of the adored but shadowy figure of his father.

Promises that were never kept.

And there had been Ellen, of course. The woman he had
begun to really love. The one who could have restored trust
and instead had betrayed him the moment her former boyfriend had called for her to join him in his new life
overseas.

Had he expected something different simply because
this particular woman was so damned attractive?

If so, he was a fool.

Even more foolish was his decision to stay in the
hospital a little longer, knowing that it wasn't due entirely
to a desire to see Alice settled and to try and obtain a definitive diagnosis for what was causing her discomfort.

Something other than shock was also undeniable.

Curiosity.

The compulsion to watch, covertly, the way the three
generations of this family interacted. To see if it bore any
relevance and would thereby confer some understanding
of the effects his own, less than usual upbringing had had
on his life. Because, if he could understand, maybe he
would be able to forgive.

And if he could forgive the two women who had created
such misery, maybe he could move on. He might even be
able to find what was so painfully lacking in his own life.

On first impression, it was easy enough to equate the kind
of matriarchal status his grandmother had wielded within

the Costa villa to the position Shona filled. She fussed around Pip with almost the same level of concern she displayed for Alice.

'I'll stay with Alice,' she told her daughter, when the X-ray had ruled out a perforating ulcer or major abdominal bleed. 'You've got work in the morning and you need your sleep.'

'There's no way I'm leaving Alice.' Pip had her arm around her mother's waist as they prepared to move Alice's bed to the paediatric ward. 'Besides, you need rest more than I do. I'm worried about you, Mum. You've got to stop trying to do everything. And you've *got* to go and see Dr Gillies. Tomorrow.'

The conversation was muted but Toni's senses were tuned to more than the verbal exchange between the two women. There was love and support there. A closeness that had never existed between his mother and her mother-in-law. Was that what made the difference?

'I'll come up to the ward with you,' he announced.

'You don't have to,' Pip responded quickly. 'I can see her settled and try to get that urine sample for testing.'

'I do have other patients I intended to check on before I leave.'

'Oh...of course.'

She sounded embarrassed, Toni decided. He hadn't meant the response as any kind of put-down but maybe the tone had been defensive because he wouldn't want her to guess the real reason for his interest. He'd never had much patience with people who could lay the blame for any lack of success in their lives at the feet of an unhappy childhood. You dealt with what life threw at you and you coped if you had any kind of strength.

Toni had that kind of strength.

Maybe Pip did as well. She wasn't exactly unsuccessful, was she? There were a set of parents in the paediatric intensive care ward right now who would be grateful for her skill for the rest of their lives. Being a single mother could be viewed as adversity but she had come through with flying colours. It was quite possible they had something very basic in common, which could explain the attraction.

Having checked on his other patients, Toni went back to the single room Alice had been allocated and once again covered his observation of Pip and her family by apparent absorption in recording his notes.

Alice seemed equally content to receive comfort from both Pip and Shona as they helped her into a hospital gown, persuaded her to provide a urine sample for analysis and then made her as comfortable as possible for the night. It was as though the child had two mothers, and there was no way Toni could relate to abundance like that.

He hadn't even had one, really.

He'd had a grandmother who'd done her duty, however inconvenient it might have been, and had never hidden her disapproval of her son's choice of wife. The number of times he'd seen his father could easily have been counted on his fingers and even Toni's mother, Elizabetta, had been a stranger. A beautiful visitor who arrived in a cloud of perfume and gifts, created extraordinary tension in the household and then left, never failing to leave behind a sensation of emptiness.

In the short space of less than two hours with the Murdochs, Toni had gained more of an impression of a family bond than he'd ever known himself. It was a compelling warmth that he was standing away from. It was like being in the rain, looking through a window to a room that was filled with firelight and laughter and the smell of something baking. Irresistible.

What made this family unit work when his own had been such a miserable failure? In both cases, the pregnancy had to have been accidental. Elizabetta would never have chosen the disruption to such a successful modelling career and Pippa—well, she couldn't have been more than in her mid-teens. She wore no wedding ring and Alice's surname was the same as her mother's and grandmother's, so presumably there was no father in the picture.

Toni watched Pip fill a glass with iced water from the jug on the bedside table. Her movements were graceful, her hands managing to look elegant even while performing such a mundane task.

The thought of her being sexually active at such a young age was distasteful and Pip must have felt his stare because she glanced up suddenly. Maybe something of what he was thinking showed on his face, which would explain why she looked away so suddenly, her cheeks flushing uncomfortably.

Except it didn't fit. Something about this woman made the thought as insulting as it was distasteful.

Toni's curiosity reached a new high point.

Had she been raped?

Involuntarily, he sucked in his breath, confused by the strong emotion the idea provoked. Disgust? Not really. Anger? No. He watched the way Pip smoothed Alice's hair as she laid her head back on the pillow, having taken a sip of the iced water.

There was such tenderness there. The kind of caring Pip should have been shown herself. Maybe that odd emotion was, amazingly, regret that she could have been shown something so very different.

And how ridiculous was it to be imagining scenarios and feeling for somebody when he had no idea what the real story was? His voice, when he spoke, was uncharacteristically gruff.

'I'll be back in the morning. We'll arrange whatever other tests need to be done when we get the rest of the blood results.' Toni avoided meeting Pip's gaze as she thanked him, in the hope of avoiding any more disturbing sensations. He turned abruptly. 'Sleep well, Alice. Tell the nurses if your tummy gets sore again and they'll give you some more medicine.'

He found himself holding the door for Shona when she decided to take her leave at the same time.

'I'll get some sleep,' she told Pip, 'and then I'll be back first thing so you can sort things out with your working hours.'

The temptation to escort this exhausted-looking older woman to her car was something Toni tried to dampen. If he did that, he knew he might not be able to resist asking questions that would be satisfying a less than professional curiosity.

If he couldn't shake this desire to learn more of Philippa Murdoch's story, he could at least be honourable enough to find a way to do so face to face.

The summons to Toni Costa's office late the following afternoon was unexpected, and Pip was distinctly nervous as she weaved through the traffic of a busy hospital's corridors.

Her day had been broken on more than one occasion as she'd accompanied Alice to the various investigations Toni had ordered in the wake of the abnormal liver function test results. Investigations that must have been comprehensive enough to give him a good idea of what they might be dealing with.

To have called her to his office instead of catching her in Alice's room or coming to find her in the emergency department suggested that it was something serious he wished to discuss.

He looked serious. Disconcertingly, there was almost an air of discomfort as he ushered Pip to a chair and then hooked a long leg up to perch on the corner of his desk as he reached for the set of patient notes. His first words, however, were reassuring.

'We've been able to rule out any indication of a possible tumour.'

'Thank God for that,' Pip breathed. 'I really was worried.'

Toni's smile revealed that he had shared her concern. 'We've also cleared her for liver disease, peptic ulcer and gastroesophageal reflux.'

Pip was watching his face intently. There was something he was undecided about telling her. 'Not much left to worry about, then, is there?'

'I'm happy to discharge her this afternoon.' Toni nodded. 'Theoretically, we should wait for a second occasion in which the pain and abnormal liver tests are consistent, but I'm confident that Alice has sphincter of Oddi dysfunction.'

Pip frowned as she searched her memory banks.

'It's not that common,' Toni told her. 'I'd be surprised if it's caught your attention yet.'

'It's got something to do with the flow of bile from the pancreas, hasn't it?'

Toni nodded again. 'The sphincter is a small complex of smooth muscle surrounding the bile ducts. The dysfunction is a benign, noncalculus obstruction, most commonly hypertonic. It can affect people of any age but typically it's middle-aged females, especially after cholecystectomy.' He raised an eyebrow. 'It can be hereditary.'

Pip mirrored his earlier nod, filing the information away. Was it possible that Shona had a similar condition that could explain her own episodes of abdominal pain?

'What's the treatment?' she queried. 'If this *is* what Alice has?'

'There are trials going on for medical therapy that affects smooth muscle structure like nitrates and sublingual nifedipine but, at present, the definitive treatment is endoscopic sphincterotomy with surgical therapy as backup.'

'What about dietary modification? I know Mum found it helpful to go very low fat and avoid alcohol when she had problems initially.'

'Alice isn't drinking alcohol yet, surely?'

'I hope not,' Pip agreed fervently, 'but you never know with teenagers these days. She's already talking wistfully about the parties some of her friends are allowed to go to.'

'But she's not allowed to go?'

'No.' Pip smiled fondly. 'Mum's always been very strict about things like that.'

There was a moment's rather thoughtful silence and Pip watched, fascinated at the play of emotion on Toni's face. Indecisiveness which looked totally uncharacteristic and then the beginnings of a smile that played at the corners of his mouth.

'And you, Pippa?' The question was spoken softly. 'Are *you* allowed to go out?'

Pip's jaw dropped a fraction. 'Excuse me?'

The hand movement Toni made was nonchalant, as

though the startling query was of little importance. The intensity of the gaze Pip found herself subjected to, however, suggested something very different.

'I'm going to refer Alice to one of our paediatric surgeons, Greg Murray,' Toni said. 'He's going to look in on her and possibly have a chat to you about her management before she goes home this afternoon.'

Pip waited, her bewilderment increasing.

'Which means,' Toni continued, 'that…professionally speaking Alice isn't strictly *my* patient any longer.' He cleared his throat. 'Which also means that you, Pippa, are not—strictly speaking—the mother of one of my patients.'

She loved the way he continued to call her Pippa unless he caught himself. It went with that delicious accent that made everything he said sound somehow exotic and more interesting.

Not that she was sure what he was talking about right now. She knew what she *hoped* he might be talking about, but what kind of idiot would she appear if she was coming to a wrong conclusion? She felt obliged to say something in the short pause that followed his reasoning.

'Ah…yes. I suppose it does,' she managed lamely. 'Does it matter?'

'Oh, yes.' Toni let out an audible breath that was almost a sigh. 'I think it does matter.'

'Why?'

'Because it means I can ask you out. For a drink, perhaps. Or dinner.'

'You mean…on a *date*?' Pip felt faintly dizzy. Her blood sugar must be really low, she decided. If she'd found time to have lunch, she might have coped with something this unexpected without this peculiar physical effect.

'Yes,' Toni said calmly. 'That is precisely what I mean.'

Oh, Lord! Echoes of those fantasies Alice had stirred rushed to fill Pip's brain and she could feel herself blushing.

This had to be unprofessional on some level, surely? Should she say no?

But was it the stuff of long-forgotten teenage dreams, not to mention more recent ones? Should she say yes as decisively as possible?

In the end, neither word emerged. Pip opened her mouth and surprised both of them by saying, 'But...*why*?'

It was Toni's turn to look astonished. 'I'm sure a woman as attractive as you are doesn't need to ask such a question! You must be well used to being asked for dates.'

Well, no, but Pip wasn't about to admit to how many years it had been since someone had asked.

'I meant,' she said quickly, 'why *you* asked. I just...ah...wasn't expecting it.'

What an understatement! That look she had caught last night, well after Toni had had time to get used to the information regarding her real relationship to his patient, when they had been settling Alice in her room for the night, had been almost—and hardly surprisingly—one of something akin to disgust.

He was giving her a mildly amused look right now and Pip realised how ungracious she was being. It was probably a first for Toni Costa to have his motives for asking a woman out questioned.

But he didn't seem fazed. 'That's easy to answer,' he responded smoothly. 'You interest me, Pippa.'

His expression had an edge to it that Pip had not seen any hint of before this. An edge that had probably made many women in his past go rather weak at the knees.

His tone had the same silky, seductive quality as he added just another couple of words.

'A lot.'

CHAPTER FOUR

'A *date*!'

'You don't need to sound so surprised, Mum. I am female and single and reasonably presentable, I hope.'

'A *date*!' From the back seat of the car, Alice echoed her grandmother's exclamation with much greater evidence of approval. 'With Dr Costa? Oh…*man*!'

Pip looked over her shoulder with an it's-not-that-big-a-deal kind of expression that was supposed to deny sharing her daughter's underlying delight with the development. Alice just laughed.

'What are you going to wear?'

'I have no idea.'

'Where are you going?' Shona asked cautiously.

'Out for dinner.'

'Upmarket?'

Pip thought about that as she slowed down for a red traffic light. With his impeccably cut pinstriped suit and that elegant Rolex watch, Toni gave the impression he could be well used to expensive venues. Could she imagine him out of hours in faded denim jeans and a leather jacket? Perched on a bar stool at a casual bistro maybe? With those waves of black hair a little tousled and those long fingers curled around the stem of a wine-glass?

Oh…*yes.*

Pip felt a powerful lurch of what could only be reawakening lust curling deep inside her belly. Shifting gear and pressing the accelerator to get the vehicle moving again was a rather necessary distraction. And hadn't Shona asked her a question? She dragged her wayward imagination back into line.

'I have no idea,' she repeated, 'but I don't have anything to wear in any case so I'll have to go shopping, I suppose.'

'Cool,' Alice said approvingly. 'Can I come with you?'

'I don't think so,' Shona said. 'You've just been in hospital overnight, young lady.'

'But I'm fine now.' Alice did look so much better, with colour in her cheeks and a sparkle back in her eyes. 'And that Dr Murray says that if the pain comes back, I can have that sort of operation thing and I'll be cured.'

'Hmm.' Shona didn't sound much happier. 'I still don't think gallivanting around town on a shopping spree is a sensible idea.'

'But I haven't had any new clothes for ages!'

'That is true.' Pip cast a sideways glance at her mother. Shona had always taken care of most of the shopping for Alice and there had been a few arguments recently over what was deemed suitable. Maybe this was something Pip could take over. It could prove to be enjoyable, quality 'girl time' together. 'Let's see how Alice is feeling tomorrow, Mum. It's late-night shopping and I'll have to go because the date's on Friday. You could have an evening to yourself and a bit of peace and quiet.'

'Hmm.' This time the sound indicated the suggestion might be welcome, which made Pip think of something else that might please her mother. She flicked on the indicator and pulled the car in toward a small group of shops. 'We're going to pick up some Indian or Chinese food,' she said firmly. 'No cooking tonight.'

Shopping with Alice had been an excellent idea, Pip realised when she opened the door to Toni's knock on Friday evening.

The chosen outfit had seemed a rather radical departure from normal—a skirt that clung to her hips and then swirled around her knees and a camisole top that looked far more like underwear than outerwear.

'It's what *everybody* wears now, Pip,' Alice had stated knowledgably. 'You're so old-fashioned!'

It had been a long time since Pip had taken much notice of fashion and she had been persuaded by Alice's criticism, helped considerably by finding a gorgeous jacket she could keep on to cover her bare shoulders. Pip had fully intended to keep the jacket on all evening but the look in Toni's eyes as he took in her appearance undermined that resolve.

How long had it been since she had felt this attractive? Certainly even longer ago than the purchase of any fashionable clothes.

A slight awkwardness prevailed when Toni accepted the polite invitation to come inside for a minute while Pip collected her handbag, but maybe she was the only one to sense the approval—excitement even—radiating from both her mother and her daughter.

An excitement that Pip was trying, very hard, not to catch. This was merely a first date after all. She would be stupid to read anything more into it than an interest.

A mutual interest.

How sad that that was enough to spark something like excitement.

Hope, even, if she was really honest with herself.

A hope that looked rather likely to be crushed as soon as the small talk was abandoned after choosing their meals from the menu at the small French restaurant Toni had chosen.

'You have a wonderful family, Pippa.' Toni smiled. 'You are very lucky.'

The undertone of sadness was unmistakable and any hope Pip might have had of avoiding painful subjects went out the window. She wanted to know what had caused that sadness and—more dangerously—was more than willing to share her own.

And all it took to start the ball rolling was a single, tentative query.

'You weren't so lucky, Toni?'

His headshake was poignant. 'I've never told anyone about my upbringing. I was startled to find myself confessing that my mother had abandoned me to the less than willing care of my *nonna* when I first met you.' Toni toyed with the stem of the wineglass in front of him. Candlelight caught the ruby glints of his chosen wine but Pip was more transfixed by the sight of his fingers—straight out of that brief fantasy she'd had driving home the other night, only far more effective because they were *real*. And moving. One tapped the stem, as though Toni was undecided, or puzzled, about something.

'It wasn't as though I was aware of your own circumstances at the time,' he added. 'Of anything we might have had in common.'

'I'm sorry I didn't make it clear.' Pip kept her gaze on the play of light on the crystal glass. And on how still

Toni's fingers now were as he listened carefully. 'I guess I prefer not to be judged on my past by people who don't know me.' She glanced up, her tone becoming a little defensive. 'And I didn't *abandon* my daughter.'

'I know that.' Toni's gaze held hers. 'And that is partly why you impress me so much.'

Pip felt a small glow of pleasure at those words. She impressed him? A *lot*?

'It's very obvious how much love there is in your home,' Toni continued. 'You—and your family—have made a success out of what could have been a disaster. What *was* a disaster in my own case because there was none of that kind of love.'

How amazing to find a reaction that engendered pride in what had shaped Pip's life to such an extent. The shame that James had magnified so destructively could, finally, be vanquished.

'It nearly was a disaster,' Pip admitted. 'It was my mother who kept everything together.'

'Tell me about it,' Toni invited. He touched Pip's hand when she hesitated briefly. 'Please.'

The plea in his touch as well as his tone was all the encouragement Pip needed.

'My father was a doctor,' she told Toni. 'A general practitioner. He was a wonderful man and I grew up wanting to be just like him—and to be a doctor who cared so much and was loved by his patients as much as he was.' Pip paused to mirror Toni's action and take a sip of her own wine. 'One day, when I was fifteen, he went out to mow the lawns and had a massive heart attack.'

The food arrived at that point and there was at least a minute of subdued silence. The waiter looked anxious.

'Is everything all right with your meals, sir?'

'It looks wonderful,' Toni assured him, but he didn't pick up any cutlery even after the waiter had gone. He was watching Pip.

'He died?' he asked quietly.

'Instantly.' Pip could smell the truffles and chicken on her plate. She picked up her fork but couldn't start eating. She put it down again. 'I saw it happen from my bedroom window. Mum called an ambulance and they tried their best but it was too late.' Pip tried to smile and lighten the atmosphere a fraction. 'It was so sudden! The engine on the lawnmower was still running when it was all over. Nobody had thought to turn it off.'

Toni seemed to have forgotten his dinner. 'What a dreadful thing to have happened. Especially when you were so young!' Toni's face was such a picture of sympathy, Pip could almost imagine the shine of tears in his eyes. 'Girls need their fathers, especially when they're in their teens.'

'It *was* awful. Mum and I were both devastated. Even now I try to avoid thinking about what it was like for the first few months.' Pip shook her head as though to clear the memory and a wisp of hair escaped her loose French plait. 'Anyway.' She tucked the strand of hair behind her ear. 'Please, eat, Toni. I'd hate this lovely food to get cold.'

For a minute they both tasted their food but Pip's unfinished story hung between them. What Toni really wanted to know about was Alice, wasn't it? When the waiter walked past their table moments later, with a nod of approval at the fact they were now eating, it gave her the opportunity to start talking again.

'I was so unhappy,' Pip said slowly. It was easy to look back and realise how badly she had behaved but it was much harder to admit it—especially to someone she would prefer to impress. 'And I was a self-centred teenager. I needed support and attention and I couldn't see that Mum needed it as much as I did. I set about trying to get what I wanted in totally the wrong way which only made everything worse, of course.'

Toni was nodding. It was more than nonjudgmental. 'I understand,' he said with a wry smile. 'I tried that myself for a while.'

'Did you ignore your schoolwork?'

'Only until I realised that using my mind was actually the only way I could control my own life.'

'Did you hang out with bad friends?'

'As much as it was possible in the kind of boarding schools I was sent to.' Toni's smile was broader. 'It was probably just as well I didn't have much freedom.' His face stilled then, ready to listen and accept whatever Pip wanted to tell him. 'You had more freedom?' he prompted.

Pip nodded sadly. 'Too much. I chose a new group of friends simply because I knew my mother would not approve of them.' She took a half-hearted mouthful of food but then put her fork down again. 'One in particular, Catherine, was bad news but she had the reputation of being "cool". We got into trouble at school and she got me into parties with her older brother's friends from uni. There was a lot of alcohol and I discovered it could make me forget for a while.'

'How unhappy you were?'

Toni also seemed to have forgotten his food. He reached out and touched her. Just a stroke of a finger on the back of her hand, but it conveyed so much that it almost brought tears to Pip's eyes. He knew what was coming in this story and he understood. He accepted it. Pip had only told this tale to one other man and Toni's gesture couldn't be more different to the disgust she had seen in James's face. It gave her courage.

'Not just my unhappiness. I could stop feeling guilty about hurting my mother by how badly I was behaving. It was at the last one of those parties I went to that I let things get completely out of hand. Realising what I'd done was a wake-up call and I started to get my act together, but I'd left it just a bit too late.'

'You were pregnant?'

Pip nodded. 'I didn't figure it out for a while and then I was too terrified to tell anyone. I realised how much harder I'd made things for Mum and I was way too scared to make it worse by telling her I was pregnant. By the time I did, it was too late to even consider any option other than having the baby, and Mum was just as horrified as I knew she'd be.'

'She was angry?'

'The anger would have been easy to handle. I deserved it. What really got to me was how sad she was. She thought I had ruined my life. The father couldn't be traced easily. He'd only been in town on holiday from Australia and when Mum finally caught up with him he denied everything and refused any responsibility. We were on our own.'

'But you coped.' It was a statement rather than a question and Pip could hear the undertone of approval. Respect, even. Not that she could take the credit.

'Thanks to Mum. She refused to let me ruin my chances of having a career. She made me finish school and then persuaded me to follow my dream of medical school. She said it's what Dad would have wanted for me as well, and if she didn't do anything more with the rest of her life than making that possible, she would be as happy as she could ever be again.'

They finished what they wanted of their meals in a

rather thoughtful silence. It wasn't until the waiter appeared to collect their plates that Toni nodded.

'She's a strong woman, your mother,' he said approvingly. 'But she does seem…less than well at the moment.'

'I know. She's finally been to see our family doctor and he's referred her back to the surgeon who looked after her when she had the problem with gallstones.'

'That's good. I'm sure she will be fine.'

'Mmm.' Pip was happy to agree. 'I'm not going to let her do so much for me any more, though. It's funny, but it's only recently that I've realised how much more of a mother to Alice she is than I am.'

'And you don't like that?'

'I suppose I was flattered that Alice wanted to start calling me by my given name. To pretend we were sisters.'

'From my experience with working with families, I think that a lot of people aspire to being a friend to their children. It just needs to be balanced with the guidance a parent needs to provide.'

'And I've let Mum do most of the hard bits. She shouldn't have to do that twice in a lifetime.'

'But she loves it?'

'Yes. I can't just push her aside.'

Toni nodded. 'And you need to be able to do the job you're so good at.' Then he smiled. 'But you still need a life of your own outside working hours. What sort of things do you like to do for yourself, Pippa?'

He raised his eyebrows at the silence.

'Have you ever put what you wanted or needed just for yourself above the duty to your family or your studies?'

I tried that once, Pip thought. When she had believed she'd had a future with James. And that had been a disaster, hadn't it?

Toni nodded again at what he apparently read from her expression. 'I thought not,' he murmured. 'Maybe now is the time. You enjoyed eating out?'

'Oh, yes. But I'm afraid I spoilt it for you, talking about *my*self too much.'

His smile was nothing less than gorgeous. 'So, we'll redress the balance. Next time, I shall talk entirely about myself.'

Pip smiled back, unable to put a lid on the joy the words 'next time' had sparked.

'Do you like to dance? Go for walks in a forest or on a beach? Watch a movie?'

Pip's smile broadened. 'All of the above.'

Toni inclined his head in a satisfied nod. 'Then that's what we shall do,' he announced. 'All of the above.'

If he hadn't been so distracted by catching a glimpse of Pippa at the end of the corridor, Toni wouldn't have bumped into the edge of the meal trolley and found himself in the undignified position of having to collect the papers that had spilled from the folder he was carrying.

This was more than embarrassing. Toni Costa had never let a woman get under his skin to this extent since the heartbreak of Ellen walking out on him. To creep, unbidden, into his thoughts almost constantly. To have his heart pick up speed and his awareness of his immediate surroundings fade at the mere sight of her at some distance.

It was disturbing.

Then again, when Pip stopped to help him, it no longer seemed to matter that her significance in his life was increasing exponentially. Or that there were others to witness the effects of his clumsiness. It was simply too good to be this close to her. To smell her perfume. To feel the brush of her hand as she passed him the pink 12-lead ECG trace.

'They're a traffic hazard, those meal trolleys, aren't they?'

Dio! Her smile was gorgeous. Toni wanted to kiss those curving lips and never mind who was watching. He'd wanted to kiss her last week when they'd been to dinner for a second time and even more last night when they had been to the movies. Why had it seemed so important to restrain himself? To decide that, for the first time in his life, he wasn't going to rush things. To let physical passion—or worse—the possibility of falling in love undermine rational thinking. He knew only too well how that could lead to disaster.

But it was *so* hard! Toni stood up so that he wasn't on the same level as those eyes but Pip's attention, fortunately, had been caught by a sheet of paper. She was still staring at it as she straightened and unconsciously followed his move to step to one side of the corridor and stop disrupting traffic.

'Good grief! This doesn't look very healthy.'

'No.' He may not be able to kiss her but Toni couldn't resist the opportunity to talk and keep Pippa close for just a little longer. 'Do you know what it is?'

'Supraventricular tachycardia?'

'How do you know it's not ventricular?'

'The QRS complexes are too narrow for that.' Pip was touching the paper as she counted. 'And it's fast enough to be a pretty impressive tachycardia. The rate must be over two hundred beats per minute.'

'Two hundred and thirty.'

'There's ST depression but it's probably rate-related. I

wouldn't think a patient of yours would be suffering angina. If it *is* a patient of yours?' Raised eyebrows and the expression of such keen interest made Toni smile. Or was it the pleasure of an excuse to admire those curious gold flecks in the most beautiful eyes he'd ever seen?

'It's a trace from a twelve-year-old I've got in the ward. Unsuccessfully trialled on anti-epileptic medication by his GP.'

'For blackouts? Or was he having hypoxic seizures?'

Pippa's intelligence was just as sexy as everything else about this woman, Toni decided as he nodded. 'It's quite a common mistake, especially in this age group. What is that saying? About hoofbeats?'

'When you hear hoofbeats, think of horses, not zebras?'

'Yes. Only, in this instance, it is a zebra. You'd expect a convulsion in a child to be a disruption of the brain's electrical signals, not a lack of oxygen because the heart is not functioning properly.'

'Will he need a pacemaker?'

'I'm just on my way to discuss that with a cardiologist and refer him. Then I'll speak to the parents and preferably the boy as well.'

'He's young to have to face something as serious as this. Only Alice's age.'

'I don't like being anything less than honest with my patients. Often they cope better than their parents.'

'I'd better not keep you.' Pip looked pleasingly reluctant. 'But I'd better head back to the salt mine of Emergency. My lunch-break seems to be vanishing way too fast.'

'I'd better not keep you either, then.'

'No.' But Pip was smiling and neither of them moved. The days were disappearing way too fast for Toni at present, thanks to their busy and often clashing work-loads. They'd managed only three dates in the last two weeks.

'I enjoyed the movie last night.' It wasn't hard to sound sincere but the enjoyment had come more from holding Pippa's hand than anything he'd seen on the screen. He could almost still feel the delicate length of her fingers and the smoothness of her palm.

'So did I.'

'You cried.'

'It was a sad movie.' Pip grinned. 'And I saw you wiping your eyes so don't try to deny it!'

'Hey, I'm Italian—what do you expect?' Toni allowed himself to relax into the pleasure of Pip's company for just a second longer. It couldn't last, of course, as they were both expected elsewhere. 'Are you busy tonight?'

Pip grimaced. 'I'm on till 11 p.m.'

'Tomorrow night? Ah, no!' It was Toni's turn to look frustrated. 'I'm on call. Friday?'

Was it wishful thinking that made Pippa's face light up with pleasure?

'Yes, I'm free on Friday night.'

'Well, we've done the eating out and the movies. I think it's time to go dancing.'

It had to be the most sensual activity Pip had ever experienced.

They were both fully clothed and in public but the touch of Toni's hands and body couldn't have been more arousing.

Or more frustrating.

Pip had to exert enormous self-control not to simply drape herself over the man she was dancing with, close her eyes and think of nothing but the feel of him. She didn't dare raise her face to look at Toni in case he guessed what she was thinking.

What if he didn't share this level of attraction?

He hadn't made any attempt to kiss her yet, so maybe he didn't.

The chill that ran down Pip's spine at the thought made her realise just how close she was to falling in love with Toni…if it wasn't already too late. Memories of the agony in the wake of the failed relationship with James sounded a warning, but Toni already knew about Alice, didn't he? He liked her.

And Alice thought Toni was 'hot,' although she had been disappointed at news of the relationship's progress at breakfast-time today. Pip let herself twirl to the music and used the memory of the conversation to try and distract herself from the unnerving level of desire the activity was generating.

Shona had smiled at the news that Pip was going out for an evening of dancing. 'I think you're being swept off your feet—in more ways than one.'

'Hmm.' Pip had unsuccessfully tried to hide a smile. 'Maybe it's got something to do with that Italian passion. It *is* kind of irresistible.'

Alice's jaw had dropped and her eyes had been like saucers. 'Are you and Toni…you know…like, *doing* it?'

'*Alice!*' Shona had been shocked.

'That wasn't what I meant,' Pip had said reprovingly. 'You can be passionate in ways that aren't physical, Alice.'

'Like what?'

'About things. Values. Toni's passionate about what he does for a job, which is why he's so good at it. And he's passionate about the importance of families.'

'Why?'

'I think a lot of Italian people place more value on their families than other cultures.' But Pip understood where a lot of Toni's passion in that area came from by now. She couldn't imagine how hard it must have been, growing up feeling such a lack, but it said a lot about Toni's personality and strength that he had chosen to dedicate his medical career to the care of children.

'So you're not doing it, then.' Alice sounded bored.

'Mind your own business,' Shona scolded. 'It's time you got ready for school, in any case.'

She gave Pip a curious glance when Alice stomped from the room.

'It's good if you're not rushing things,' she said. 'If something's worth having, it's worth waiting for.'

Pip's response had simply been a noncommittal sigh. It was none of Shona's business either, and Pip wasn't about to confess her growing frustration to anyone. Imagine if her mother could read her thoughts right now, as Toni's hand slid to the small of her back and pulled her even closer.

'So…' His voice tickled her ear. 'What shall we do next, Pippa Murdoch?'

'Ah…' Oh, God! Had her thoughts been transparent in her body language, even though she had tried to dampen them? Pip shuddered to think what Toni might think of her if she told him exactly what she thought they should do next.

She could swear his smile was knowing as the music finished and he led her back to their table, but his tone was perfectly innocent.

'On our next date,' he added belatedly. 'Assuming you want one, of course?'

'Mmm.' Pip had to quell the disappointment of knowing this one was nearly over. 'Of course,' she echoed.

'What's left on our list?' Toni leaned forward so that, for one heart-stopping moment, Pip thought he was about to kiss her. Then he smiled. 'Ah…yes. The walk. Forest or beach?'

'Ah…a beach would be nice,' Pip said faintly.

'Then again—' the look Pip was receiving made her wonder if Toni shared her thought that a beach might not be private enough '—maybe you could come to my house. I could cook for you.'

There could be no mistaking the underlying invitation. Toni could do a lot more than cook for Pip. What he was really asking was whether she was ready to take their relationship to the next level.

Pip was more than ready.

'I'd love that,' she said.

So the invitation had been issued and accepted. Something new came into the atmosphere between them and Pip knew exactly what it was. Anticipation. The kind of anticipation that gave her a peculiar feeling deep in her abdomen, like a lift dropping far too quickly. Was it possible that the reality could be a disappointment?

Not if the kiss she received when Toni took her home that night was anything to go by.

As a first kiss went, it couldn't have been more perfect.

Toni had climbed from the driver's seat to open her door, as he always did, and he had taken her hand to help her from the low sports car. What had not become customary was the way he kept hold of her hand to keep gently pulling until she was in his arms. So close, it was inevitable that his head should dip and their lips graze.

And then he let go of her hand and cradled her head instead, renewing the contact and taking it deeper.

So deep that Pip felt herself drowning in that kiss, her lips clinging to his as though they were the only solid object that could save her. Melting inside at the first silky touch of his tongue.

Wanting more.

So much more.

The invitation had not only been issued and accepted. The agenda for the evening had just been clarified.

'You cooked pasta?'

Toni's shrug was eloquent. 'Hey, I'm Italian—what did you expect?'

'I had no expectations,' Pip responded. Which was perfectly true in regard to food at any rate. 'It looks delicious.'

'An old family recipe. Let me get you a glass of wine, Pippa.'

'Thank you.'

'Are you happy to stay in the kitchen? I may need to stir things occasionally.'

Pip sat down on an old spindle-backed wooden chair. 'I love kitchens,' she said warmly. 'They're the heart of a house.'

'They *are*!' Toni's smile gave Pip a very pleasurable glow at having said exactly the right thing. 'A place for family and food. What more could anyone need?'

Pip wasn't going to answer that one. She had been waiting days for this evening. Days in which the impossible had happened and the level of anticipation had heightened until Pip was as nervous as she had ever been on any date. 'This kitchen is gorgeous,' she said hurriedly, looking around at the old furniture with its polished wooden legs on a slate floor. At the row of gleaming copper pans hanging in front of an old, coal range. 'Your house is gorgeous.'

'Not what you expected?'

'No.' Pip had parked in front of the stately old home in a well-established suburb with some trepidation. 'I had imagined you in a townhouse, for some reason. All modern and sleek and low maintenance.' Not in a house with a huge garden that was crying out for a whole family.

'I love old things.' Toni was pouring two glasses of red wine. 'Traditions. I'm not sure of the word I need. Solidarity, perhaps? Things that have stood the test of time. That you can depend on.'

'Trustworthy?'

'Yes.' Toni handed Pip her glass and their hands touched. Pip's glance flicked up just as he ran his tongue over his lower lip. 'Are you trustworthy, Pippa Murdoch?'

The question seemed important enough to give Pip a frisson of something she couldn't identify. Or maybe it had been the glimpse of the tip of Toni's tongue that had undone her completely. Strangely, it had vanquished her nerves but her voice still sounded a little wobbly.

'Completely,' she said.

'I thought you might be.' Toni bent his head and kissed her. A lingering kiss that promised much more than it had time to deliver. Then he smiled at her. 'Are you hungry?'

Pip had never felt less like eating but Toni seemed to accept her vaguely strangled assent and turned back to the stovetop.

'How is Alice?'

'She's fine. Gone to a sleepover birthday party she was very excited about being invited to. Apparently Dayna is one of the "cool" girls at school.'

'Like your friend Catherine was?'

'Lord, I hope not!' But Pip smiled. Fancy Toni remembering a detail like that from a conversation that was now weeks old. He really did listen, didn't he? As though whatever she said was important to him. She liked that. Very much.

'And your mother?'

'She's OK. I think she's lost a bit of weight recently. I'm watching her colour carefully, too, because I thought I caught a hint of jaundice, but she hasn't mentioned any abdominal pain. She's gone out tonight, too, with a friend. To a movie, I think.'

'Not a sleepover?'

'No.' Pip laughed as she watched Toni grinding black pepper over the saucepan. He swapped the grinder for the bottle of red wine, sloshed a good measure into the sauce and then moved to top up Pip's glass.

Maybe it was the mention of sleepover parties that had increased the electricity in the air—reminding them both of that unspoken agenda. Or maybe it was the combination of red wine and the rich aroma of a creamy pasta sauce. Pip found herself holding her breath as she watched Toni slowly put the bottle down on the table. With his hand free, he touched the loose waves of Pip's hair, lifting the weight from her shoulder and letting it drift through his fingers.

'Beautiful,' he said softly. 'It catches the light.' He lifted another handful but this time he didn't let it spill. Instead, he held it clear as he reached down to kiss the side of her neck. '*You* are beautiful,' he murmured.

Any hope of being able to eat a single mouthful of the food Toni was preparing evaporated. Somehow Pip found her arms around Toni's neck, being lifted to her feet, a trail of kisses leading from her neck to her lips.

It was several minutes before she could take in enough air or the inclination to speak.

'I think,' she whispered then, 'that you should turn that stove off for a while.'

The sauce did not get reheated that night.

Hours later, when Pip returned to the kitchen to collect her car keys, the sight of the abandoned meal reminded her she hadn't eaten. She was not remotely hungry, however. How could she be when she had never in her life felt this kind of satisfied glow?

The knowledge that every conceivable desire she might have had just been so completely fulfilled.

Toni had surpassed every fantasy of what he would be like as a lover. His kisses...his touch...his ability to take control and yet to be so astonishingly gentle at the same time had been a revelation.

It had only been with the greatest reluctance that Pip had finally extracted herself from the bed with the antique brass bedhead.

'Stay, *cara*.'

'I can't. Not tonight. I'm expected home and it's too late to ring.'

'Your mother won't approve?'

'It's not that.' Pip fastened the catches of her bra that felt curiously too small. The lacy fabric grazed oversensitised nipples and made it impossible not to remember exactly what it was like to feel the caress of Toni's lips and tongue. Even his teeth. 'Next time, I'll stay,' Pip promised. She picked up her jeans. 'That is, if you invite me again.'

Her wrist was grasped so fast Pip gasped. Then she let out a small shriek as the ensuing tug had her tumbling back amongst the rumpled bedclothes. Against the smooth skin of Toni's chest where she could feel his warmth and smell the sheer maleness of his body.

'How could you possibly think you wouldn't be, after *that*?'

'Oh, I don't know,' Pip murmured mischievously. 'Maybe it wasn't so good for you.'

'Then you weren't listening to a word I said,' Toni growled.

Pip grinned. 'You were talking in Italian.' And how sexy had *that* been? Pip hadn't needed any expertise in another language to guess the meaning of those phrases, but Toni wasn't to know that.

'Then next time,' he announced, 'I will speak in English.'

'No.' Pip returned a final, lingering kiss. 'I don't want anything to be different. It was just perfect the way it was.'

The echo of those lyrical phrases was still with Pip as she let herself quietly into her house. She could have stayed with Toni. She supposed. Shona would have understood. But what if Alice had become ill during the night and she had been absent? Selfishly ensconced with a lover? The idea of being in a relationship intense enough to include overnight visits needed a bit of time to get used to. For all of them, she suspected.

Was that why Shona was still up? Pip hadn't expected to see the kitchen light still on. Or to hear her mother call.

'Pip? Is that you?'

'Yes, I'm home. Are you all right, Mum?'

The silence made her frown. Pip dismissed her plan of going straight to bed where she would have used the darkness to relive every moment of the last few hours and keep that satisfied glow alive. Instead, she moved towards the kitchen.

'Mum?'

Shona was sitting at one end of the table. She looked as though she had been crying.

'Can you sit down for a bit, Pip? I need to talk to you.'

CHAPTER FIVE

THE sensation of fulfilment vanished utterly.

'What's wrong?' Pip asked sharply. 'Has something happened to Alice?'

Shona shook her head. To Pip's horror, a tear escaped and rolled slowly down her mother's cheek.

'You're not upset that I've been out with Toni, are you?'

Shona smiled through her tears. 'Oh, no! How could I be? This is the best thing that could have happened. For all of us. Especially now.'

There was an undertone to Shona's words that Pip didn't like. She sat down on the chair closest to her mother.

'I don't understand, Mum. What's upset you so much?'

The brightness in Shona's voice was forced and made her words sound anything but casual. 'I had an appointment today. At the hospital.'

'What? Why didn't you tell me?'

'I did tell you that I was being sent to see the surgeon again.'

'You didn't say *when*. I would have come with you.'

'I know. I didn't want you to, love. And, anyway, that was a couple of weeks ago. I've had lots of other tests since then.'

A sense of foreboding took hold of Pip. 'But why didn't you *say* something?'

'I didn't have all the information. And you're so happy at the moment. I didn't want to spoil things.'

Foreboding became dread.

'Tell me,' Pip said slowly, 'what the surgeon said.'

Shona wiped away the last traces of her tears as she took a noticeably deeper breath. 'They found something on the ultrasound and I got referred to another doctor. In oncology. I had an MRI scan today.'

'Oh, my God!' This was unbelievable. Pip had floated through her day at work, in excited anticipation of what she had known would happen between herself and Toni tonight, totally oblivious to something major happening in her own family. How selfish was that? 'And?' she prompted her mother.

'And I have cancer,' Shona said calmly. 'Of my pancreas.'

The bottom was falling out of Pip's world. She could hear an odd buzzing in her head and she felt faintly nauseated. She could never have anticipated being blindsided like this. To find her mother had exactly what she had feared most when she'd taken Alice to that first appointment with Toni. The fear had been dismissed. It *couldn't* be happening again—to Shona instead of Alice.

'It's at something they call Stage llA. I'm not sure exactly what it means, although they did tell me. It went over my head a bit. Apparently it's past the stage where I could expect any kind of cure, though.'

'*No!*' The word was torn from Pip. Fear had replaced dread. Mixed with it was a very uncomfortable level of guilt. She closed her eyes. 'You've known about it for most of the day and you didn't tell me. You let me go out on a…a *date*!'

'I needed a bit of time to get my own head around this,' Shona responded. 'And I had to wait until Alice was out. I don't want her to know.'

'She'll have to know.'

'Not yet,' Shona said urgently. 'Promise me, Pip—you won't tell her until *I'm* ready.'

Pip's silence was taken as acquiescence, which was hardly surprising if her expression reflected what she was thinking. She would have promised Shona anything right then, if it could have made a blind bit of difference to the outcome.

'Things are changing,' Shona continued thoughtfully. 'And I really don't want to spoil them.'

She had said that earlier. She had allowed Pip to be selfish enough to revel in the start of a promising romance and, by doing so, she had taken away Pip's right to choose. As though she was still a child who needed important decisions made *for* her. Unexpectedly, resentment bloomed amongst a maelstrom of even darker emotions.

'I can't believe you didn't tell me. That you've been dealing with this for weeks by yourself. That you let me go out tonight of all nights, when I should have been here. With you.'

'That's precisely why.' Shona patted Pip's hand. 'You would have stayed if you'd known and I had the feeling tonight was going to be special with it being the first time you've been to Toni's house.'

Pip might have been embarrassed if she'd focused on how accurately her mother had interpreted the significance of tonight's date. Or if she had given a second's thought to what had happened over the last few hours. Funny how something that had seemed so incredibly special had suddenly become insignificant. Something she could even feel ashamed of.

'You wouldn't have gone if you'd known, would you?' Shona prompted.

'Of course I wouldn't.'

'And that would have changed things. It might have been enough to stop them completely.'

Would it? Toni would have understood if she had cancelled the date due to a family emergency. He would have approved of where her loyalties lay. But what about the weeks or months ahead? Would the start of any physical relationship have been given any priority in what was likely to be a time of intense family commitment?

Probably not. But because they had become so close tonight, it would be far more difficult to shut Toni from her life than it would have been if she'd stayed home and had this conversation with her mother so much earlier. Not telling her—keeping even a hint of the news away from her—had been an unselfish act on Shona's part. While Pip could feel resentful at having had her free choice removed, she could understand the motivation. The love it was based on.

'You're far more important than anything else I have going on in my life, Mum. *This* is far more important. I'm going to help you fight this.'

Shona smiled sadly. 'Don't think I don't want to fight it, love, and I will...but we need to be realistic.'

'I'll go and talk to your doctors tomorrow. Find out exactly what we're dealing with. I can't believe you went to this appointment today by yourself.'

'I wasn't really expecting to find out what I did.'

'Did they mention treatment options?'

'They told me so much that most of it went over my head. I can't remember a lot.'

'Which is why I should have been with you.'

'I asked for another appointment on Monday. So that you could come and hear everything and then help me decide on what's going to best.'

'Did they say anything about the possibility of surgery?'

'Yes. They talked about surgery and radiotherapy and chemotherapy and even clinical trials I might like to consider. What I did understand was that anything done might buy me a little more time or make me more comfortable but it's not going to change the outcome. I may only have a few months.'

Pip couldn't hold back her tears now. Or the fear. Or the feeling that she was a child again—no older than Alice. The comfort of being held in her mother's arms was indescribable. And *so* poignant. It was some time before either woman could control their grief.

'If I need surgery,' Shona said eventually, 'I'm going to tell Alice it's the same as the gallstone operation I had.'

'Why?'

'I don't want her to make a connection between what's wrong with me and what's wrong with her. It would be scary.'

'Alice doesn't have cancer.'

'No, but she has an abnormality in her pancreas. It could be that there's a genetic link, couldn't there? That she might be more at risk herself?'

'I don't know,' Pip admitted. 'But I do know that Alice is going to be fine. It's you we need to concentrate on at the moment.'

'I do want more time.'

'Of course you do. *I* want more time for you as well. As much as possible.'

'I don't need too much. Just enough to see if Toni is the one for you. Whether you can make a family together when…when I'm not here.' Shona stroked Pip's hair. 'That's all I need to know, Pip. That you and Alice are both going to be safe…and happy.' She gripped her daughter's hand. 'He's a wonderful man, darling. Alice thinks so, too, although I think the words she used were "hot" and "cool"—which don't seem to be contradictory for teens these days.'

They both smiled.

'He seems totally smitten with you,' Shona added, 'and I've never seen you as happy as you've been in the last month. Don't let this change things, Pip. Please!'

How could it *not* change things?

The first, and possibly most unexpected, change occurred well before the appointment Pip was dreading on Monday when the official confirmation of her mother's prognosis would come.

If she had given any thought to Toni during the sleepless hours of that first night, it had been poignant. Their relationship was so newborn and fragile and there could be no room in her life for romance now. Not when her emotional energy had to be focused on the needs of her mother and her daughter.

The time she had spent with Toni that evening had been too good to be true. Magic but selfish. A gift her mother had wanted her to have, but in some ways it might have been easier if Pip hadn't experienced what Toni had to offer as a lover. She wasn't going to be desirable as a romantic companion for the foreseeable future, and it was too much to hope that Toni cared about her enough already to take this in his stride.

He wouldn't drop her immediately, of course, he was far too nice for that, but the baggage she brought with her had suddenly become much heavier, almost too heavy to lift, and it would have to start making a difference. It would become too much and their relationship could falter and die, inch by inch.

Maybe it would be better to let him escape now before things became miserable.

But Toni had other ideas.

The fact that he could tell something was wrong simply by the way she said hello when he rang the next day was a surprise. The depth of concern in his query about what was wrong that went unanswered was almost enough to reduce Pip to tears and the way he took control was irresistible.

'Be at your gate in five minutes,' he ordered. 'I am coming to take you for a drive and you will tell me what is upsetting you, *bella*.'

Shona had waved her off. 'Be as long as you like, love,' she instructed. 'Alice and I need time to argue about what take-aways we want to order and what we're going to watch on television tonight.'

Normal Saturday night family stuff when normality was no longer a real option. Pip waited at her gate with confusion thrown into the maelstrom of her heightened emotions.

Sliding into Toni's car and accepting his kiss could have been an exciting new normality after last night, but Pip had to pull away. At least, she tried to, but Toni held her—his fingers gripping her shoulders with determination.

'Whatever is wrong? Is my kissing so bad?'

Pip tried to laugh. Instead, she burst into tears.

'Drive…' she managed to choke out. 'Please… I don't want Alice to see me crying.'

Toni drove the shortest distance. Just around the corner until they were out of sight of her house. He pulled the car to a jerky stop, snapped open both his own and Pip's safety belts and then pulled her into his arms.

For the longest time, he said nothing.

Demanded no explanations.

He simply held her and let her cry, and if Pip hadn't realised she was in love with this man before, she could have no doubt about it now. He had no idea what she was so upset about but he was still prepared to hold and comfort her. It was like the way he accepted Alice as part of her life. Whoever she was and whatever baggage she brought with her was made to feel acceptable.

And when she was finally ready to talk, he listened with the same kind of attentiveness with which he had heard the story of her past. He held her as she spoke and every subtle movement of his body and hands implied willingness to be there. To support her.

'And she waited to tell you this because she knew it was our…first time together?'

'Yes.'

'She is a wise woman.'

'You think so?' Pip couldn't help the seed of new hope being sown. A hope that this wouldn't be enough to drive Toni from her life.

'I know so. She knew that you would have shut yourself away from me if you'd known. You care too much for the people you love to allow something as selfish as a lover at such a time.' Toni kissed Pip's hair gently. 'But you cannot do that now, can you, *cara*?'

'No.' There was no way in the world Pip could voluntarily give up what Toni was giving her.

'I can help. I can give you strength.'

'It's not very romantic.' Pip felt obliged to at least issue a warning. 'I won't be able to swan off for things like dinners and dancing and walks on the beach for a while.'

'Romance can come in many forms,' Toni said seriously. 'Maybe this will be the most important one.'

'It's a lot to ask of you.'

'It's what friends are for.' Toni kissed her hair again. 'And we are more than friends, aren't we?'

'Yes.' Pip turned her face and received another kiss, this time on her lips. It was a kiss that carried all the strength of passion and yet there was nothing overtly sexual about it. It was like nothing Pip had ever experienced. More than sex. More than friendship. It conveyed hope. The possibility that Toni had fallen in love with her to the same degree she had with him. It was enough to cause the sting of tears again. Was that what reminded Toni of why she was sitting in his car?

'And you have an appointment to go to with your mother on Monday?'

'Yes. She was, understandably, a bit hazy on the medical details and options for treatment. I want to make sure we have all the information we need so I can help her decide the best next step.'

'Would you like me to be there as well?'

'That's sweet of you, but, no, I think it would be better if it was just me and Mum.'

'You'll come and talk to me afterwards?'

'Of course.'

'I will be at home on Monday evening. I will be waiting for you.'

'Stage llA is where the tumour extends beyond the pancreas but there's no involvement of the celiac axis or the superior mesenteric artery.' The oncologist showed Pip the pictures from the MRI scan. 'No regional lymph node metastasis and no distant metastasis.'

Which sounded as though things could have been a lot worse, but Pip had done some research of her own over the weekend and was all too aware of how difficult it was to control this type of cancer. And how fast it could progress if you were one of the unluckier victims.

'I need you to go over the treatment options again,' Shona said. 'So that Pip can help me choose what to do.'

'As we discussed, there's surgery. It's the only form of therapy with any potential for cure and even with a tumour like yours, situated in the head of the pancreas, we could expect good results. Palliation of symptoms at the least and a life expectancy greater than the average for inoperable pancreatic cancer.'

'Which is?' Pip asked tightly.

'Approximately ten months.'

'What about follow-up treatment?'

The surgeon nodded. 'Of course. We'll look at radiation and/or chemotherapy and we'll treat anything else as it crops up.'

Like pain, Pip thought miserably. 'What's involved with the surgery?'

'It's a pancreaticduodenectomy.'

'Goodness!' Shona actually smiled. 'It must take as long to say that as do the surgery.'

But it was no laughing matter. 'We remove the head of the pancreas,' the surgeon continued soberly. 'And the adjacent duodenum plus the lower bile duct and a portion of the stomach. This will take out the tumour and the adjacent lymph nodes.'

'That's major,' Pip murmured.

'But with very good statistics as far as mortality and morbidity are concerned.'

'How will I eat?' Shona sounded stunned. 'How much of my stomach gets taken out?'

'About half. You'll be able to eat normally though not in large quantities. Your diet may need some adjustment but the dieticians will help you with that. It can be more difficult to digest food so you may need replacement pancreatic enzymes or hormones after the surgery. You may also develop diabetes and need to take insulin.'

'How soon could you schedule the surgery?' Pip asked.

'As early as next week if that's the route you want to take.'

'I'm not sure about that,' Shona said. 'I need to think about it. How long would I have to be in hospital for?'

'At least a week.'

'And it would mean weeks of recuperation on top of that, wouldn't it? As long as it took after I had my gallbladder out?'

'Maybe longer, if you're starting other treatments in that period.'

'So that might represent a significant percentage of the time I have left. I'm not sure I want to spend it in and out of hospital.'

The short silence underlined the fact that there would be no escape from hospital and medical intervention in the near future if Shona wanted to put up any kind of fight against what was happening.

She sighed deeply. A resigned sound. 'Well, that's going to need careful planning,' she said heavily. 'We've got the care of a house and a young child to take into account.'

'We'll manage,' Pip said, yet again, that evening. 'I'll take care of everything, Mum. I'll juggle my shifts so I can drop Alice off at school. She can come to the hospital after school and wait for me. Or she's old enough to come home by herself and be alone for a while.'

'Why am I going to be alone?' Alice breezed into the kitchen, heading straight past the table towards the pantry. 'Have we got any chocolate biscuits, Nona?'

'You've just had your dinner.'

'Yeah, but I'm still hungry.' They could hear packages being rustled in the depths of the large cupboard. 'So why am I going to be by myself?'

'I might need to go into hospital for a few days,' Shona said casually. 'For an operation.'

'Oh…' Alice shut the cupboard, having extracted a new packet of biscuits. 'Like last time?'

'Yes.' Shona gave Pip a warning glance. 'Just like last time.'

'Do I have to go and stay with that friend of yours? The one with the false teeth?' Alice gave a visible shudder. 'It was gross!'

'No,' Pip said. 'I'm going to look after you.'

Alice looked surprised and then pleased. 'Cool.' She ripped open the packet of biscuits. 'Can I go to the movies with Dayna tomorrow night?'

'No.' Pip couldn't believe how callous Alice was sounding. She opened her mouth to say something to that effect, but caught another look from her mother.

'Not on a school night,' Shona said evenly. 'Maybe at the weekend.'

Pip watched her daughter leave the kitchen, her mouth full of chocolate and wafer. Her eyebrows rose. 'Aren't you going to tell her to go easy on those biscuits?'

Shona shook her head. 'It doesn't matter. And don't be

angry because she doesn't seem to care. She doesn't know the truth and that's the way I want it for the moment.'

'The fact that you even need to go to hospital should be enough to wake her up into thinking about someone other than herself.'

'She's a teenager.' Shona smiled. 'The job description is to think of no one but yourself, isn't it? Besides, we've been here before. She stayed with Mary of the false teeth for a few days and then everything was back to normal. No big deal.'

Except that nothing was going to be back to normal this time. Not ever.

'Are you sure you can cope?' Shona sounded worried now. 'On top of working? There's more than just supervising Alice and being a taxi. There's all the housework and cooking and shopping and washing and—'

'I'll manage,' Pip assured her. 'You'll see.'

Her mother nodded. 'I'm sure I will. I've never given you the space to try managing everything yourself, have I? Not the best way of parenting, but I guess I got used to feeling needed.'

'You'll always be needed, Mum. Just not as a house-keeper or babysitter.'

'It'll help to know you can manage without me.' Shona tried, but failed, to summon a smile. 'One less thing to worry about, anyway. And, Pip?'

'Yes?'

'You're to go and have at least one more date with that gorgeous boyfriend of yours before I go into hospital.'

The date was low key. A coffee and a talk in a kitchen that held no delicious aroma of a meal that would go uneaten because passion intervened.

'Surgery is definitely the best option,' Toni agreed, still

holding Pip's hands after listening to her account of the interview. 'The only option.'

'It's going to be hard on Mum, having to go through the pain and recuperation period without knowing whether it'll make much difference to the outcome.'

'Far better than not going through it and thinking it *could* have made a difference.'

'I'm not going to be able to get out much. It's going to be difficult keeping the house going and looking after Alice and keeping up with work. I don't want to take time off before I really have to because it could mean waiting another year or more to get into the GP training scheme.'

'I can help,' Toni said decisively. 'We can take Alice out at weekends to let your mother rest. I can cook for you at your home.' His thumbs were stroking her palms. 'I can be here whenever you need to escape. To have someone to talk to. To hold you. Whatever you need, Pippa.'

The kind of things any good friend would offer at a time like this. Was it so wrong to want more?

'I need you.' Pip confessed. 'I think I would like you to hold me, Toni. Is that all right?'

Toni said something in Italian as he pushed back his chair and helped Pip to her feet. Into his arms. Whatever it was, the tone made her feel as though it was her giving something to him instead of so completely the other way round. He still made it feel like that when he took her to his bed a short time later.

Their love-making had a quality that could never have been there the first time. Could never have been there at all, if not for the sadness Pip was having to deal with. It was about far more than physical attraction or release. It was a confirmation of intent. A willingness to be there no matter what. To provide comfort.

Love, even? The kind of love that could endure and last a lifetime?

Maybe. But it didn't matter if it wasn't because right now Pip was living from moment to moment.

And this moment was perfect.

'You are supposed to come *straight* home after school. It's nearly six o'clock! Where the hell have you *been*?'

'At the mall. With Dayna.'

'Why weren't you answering your phone? I've been worried sick.'

'My phone's dead. I forgot to charge it last night.'

'That's not good enough, Alice. I've got more than enough to do right now, without having to worry about where you are.'

'Who said you had to worry? If I'm old enough to be home by myself, I'm old enough to go to the mall if I want to. It's only ten minutes' walk away. You can't stop me!'

'Don't bet on it!'

They were so alike, Toni thought as he watched Pip and Alice facing each other off across the kitchen table. Pip had probably been just as independent and determined when she had been Alice's age. He couldn't imagine Pip treating Shona with such disdain, however. Was it a generational thing or was it that the dynamic between this particular mother and daughter was flawed? Despite nearly two weeks of trying to establish new routines and roles, Pip was clearly still struggling to find her feet.

From Toni's perspective, it was easy to see where the problem lay. Due to circumstances entrenched over many years, Pip was firmly cast in the role of a big sister. Much closer to being a friend than a parent. A dynamic that worked brilliantly on some occasions, such as the hilarious afternoon last weekend when Toni had offered to give Alice her first driving lesson and Pip had supervised from the back seat of the car. Or the night at home when Alice had tried to teach both Pip and Toni the dance moves she had picked up from the new music video she had borrowed from Dayna.

At other times, though, like now, Pip had no idea where to put boundary lines. It suggested a total lack of confidence in her ability as a parent. Of being prepared to risk popularity to provide the kind of control and guidance a child needed. And if she didn't take the plunge now, it wasn't going to get any easier as Alice headed into adolescence. The shadow of having to take on this role permanently had to be weighing heavily on Pip's mind, but Toni was holding back from making any promises of being there to help.

It was a privilege, being allowed inclusion in this family at such a time. A chance to show Pippa how deeply he cared but also a chance to make sure his trust in her was not misplaced. He couldn't afford to make a mistake. Not just for himself. Or for Pippa. Alice was important, too. It was a trial by fire for this romance but Toni wasn't put off. Not at all. In a curious way, he was enjoying the argument. The dynamics of being on the inside of a normal family-style dispute that could be heated but the underlying love was never lost. Just the kind of interaction that had been missing from his own life.

'Just don't do it again,' Pip was saying. 'In future, you let me know where you are and what time you'll be home.'

'OK.'

Toni wasn't surprised at how readily Alice agreed to such a minor restriction to her freedom. Text messages could easily be less than honest, couldn't they? He had the horrible feeling Pip was buying into a whole lot more trouble but it wasn't his place to intervene. As much as he would like to be more, he was still merely an observer. Moral support for Pip. Only included because it was what Pip wanted.

'That's cool.' Alice sounded placating now. 'What's for dinner?'

'Spaghetti Bolognese,' Toni told her.

Alice groaned. 'I think I'm turning into an Italian.'

'Don't knock it.' Pip's tone was short. 'It's only thanks to Toni that you're getting fed at all tonight.'

'Don't stress,' Alice commanded. 'How's Nona?'

'A little better. Are you going to come and visit her tonight?'

'Nah. I've got a heap of homework to do. She's always asleep when I come in anyway.'

'She still knows when you're there.'

'She's been in hospital for ages.'

'There were some complications after her operation. Now they need to work out the best diet for her when she gets home.'

'Oh.' The unspoken complaint that the visits and someone else being the centre of everybody's attention were becoming tedious hung in the air, and Toni found himself gritting his teeth.

Alice had no idea how sick her grandmother was and Toni was convinced it would be better for her to know the truth despite Pip's acquiescence to Shona's wish of keeping it from the child. He wasn't about to push the issue, however. Pip was dealing with more than enough, without him adding to her stress levels. She was looking even more pale and tired this evening and what Toni wanted to do was to take her in his arms and look after her—another argument was the last thing she needed. What if she really disagreed with him? Would she ask him to step aside and let her manage her own family in her own way? Toni wasn't ready to test those boundaries. He didn't want to step aside.

'When's she coming home?' Alice was looking at her phone—the half-smile suggesting she had received a welcome message.

'In a few days.'

'That's good.' But Alice's attention was now on the screen of her mobile phone as she responded to a text message. Did Pip not notice the blatant discrepancy of batteries that were no longer flat?

'You should get on with that homework. Dinner won't be for half an hour and if you get it done, you could come into the hospital with me later.'

Pip turned to Toni when Alice left the kitchen and he was only too willing to accept her kiss.

'Sorry,' she murmured.

'What for?'

'Having to listen to us scrapping. Just what you need after a long day at work.'

'You don't need it either.' Toni kissed her again. 'I wish I could make this easier for you.'

'You are. I wouldn't have coped so far without you. You're a rock.'

'I could do more.' He could talk to Alice. Maybe tell her a few home truths and explain the necessity for making her changed relationship with her mother more positive. It was quite possible she would appreciate the opportunity to make her own, real contribution to this family in a time of crisis.

'You don't need to,' Pip assured him. 'It'll be better when Mum's back at home. Things will settle down then.'

* * *

'Time of death.' Pip looked wearily at her watch. 'Three forty-five p.m.'

The frail body of their ninety-three-year-old patient was a silent testimony to failure. Pip had spent nearly two hours trying to hold back the inevitable after this elderly woman had come in with severe heart failure exacerbated by pneumonia. She gently closed the woman's eyes and then stripped off her gloves. 'Are any relatives here?'

'No.' Suzie was starting to pick up wrappers and discarded equipment. They had known they were probably fighting a losing battle when faced with heart failure bad enough to cause the bloodstained froth the woman had presented with around her mouth, but Pip had tried everything.

Oxygen, nitrates, morphine, diuretics. Continuous positive airway pressure via a face mask and a raft of other drugs to try and combat the ensuing cardiac rhythm abnormalities. They had gone through the protocol for the subsequent cardiac arrest but Pip had called it well before the time they might have spent on another patient. It had been clearly pointless but at least they all knew they had given it a shot.

'It was a neighbour who called the ambulance,' Suzie said. 'And there's no next of kin listed in her notes.'

No family to talk to, then. Nobody to mourn the loss of a mother or grandmother. There were still things Pip needed to do for this patient, however. Forms to fill in. Did she have enough information to complete a death certificate herself or would she need to refer the case to the coroner?

'I need to have a word to Brian before I do the death certificate,' she told Suzie. 'You OK to finish up in here?'

'Absolutely.' Suzie touched Pip's arm. 'Are *you* OK?'

'Sure. She was ninety-three after all and she'd been battling increasing heart failure for a while, by the look of her notes. I guess any death just comes a bit close to home at the moment.'

'How *is* your mother?'

'Picking up. She's able to get out of bed for part of the day now and I don't feel so bad leaving her when I'm at work.' Which wasn't quite true. Pip was carrying a sense of guilt with her on a permanent basis but she couldn't afford to interrupt her training programme for too long and Shona wasn't about to let her. How would she support Alice if she let herself slip too far back? 'She's got a good friend who comes every day to stay with her and she has been taking her to some of the radiotherapy appointments. I'll have to take leave if she deteriorates, though.'

Or should that have been 'when' not 'if', Shona deteriorated. With a last look at the patient on the bed in Resus 2, Pip moved to find her senior colleague to check on death-certificate requirements. It was hard to try and shake off the weight of sadness that still caught her out at times but it was hardly unexpected just now, having tried and then failed to prevent someone dying.

'The notes are pretty comprehensive,' Brian told her a short time later. 'And you got a chest X-ray done, which confirms the pneumonia. See if you can get hold of her GP, but I think the background we've got here and the length of time you were treating her in ED means there's no reason for you not to complete certificating the cause of death.' He gave Pip an intense glance. 'You look done in.'

'It hasn't been a great day,' Pip admitted. 'And this wasn't the best way to finish.'

The GP's receptionist promised to return the phone

call as soon as the doctor was between patients. Pip stayed sitting beside the telephone at the central desk, filling in what she could on the forms.

Thank goodness her working day would soon be over. It hadn't been all that great even at its beginning, but whose fault had that been?

Staying up until the early hours, preparing a casserole for tonight's dinner so that all Shona needed to do was turn the oven on. Making a school lunch for Alice and ironing the horrible pleats into the skirt of her school uniform. It could all have been done at a much more reasonable hour if Pip hadn't spent the evening with Toni.

It had been the first time they had been alone together at his house in longer than she cared to count, and Pip wouldn't have gone if Shona and her friend, Mary, hadn't virtually pushed her out the door.

'We're going to play Scrabble,' Shona had said. 'And I intend to win.'

'I'll be here until you get home,' Mary had added. 'And I don't expect to see you this side of midnight. Shona's told me all about that gorgeous young man of yours.'

Alice had been on the computer, instant messaging her friends, and had seemed completely disinterested in the fact that Pip had been going out.

'Have fun,' had been all she'd said.

'Fun' wasn't exactly in Pip's vocabulary these days, but the time with Toni had been like a temporary release from prison. An escape into paradise.

And she hadn't felt guilty. Well, not much, anyway. Surely she owed Toni that little bit of time and undivided attention? He'd been amazing ever since the news of Shona's diagnosis. If she'd needed a test to see whether she'd found the man she wanted to spend the rest of her life with, she couldn't have devised a better one. A trial by fire, no less, that he was passing with flying colours.

Being overtired to start her working day had been a small price to pay for the reprieve last night had given her.

In response to the beeping and message on her pager, Pip lifted the telephone receiver to take the incoming call, fully expecting to find herself talking to her patient's GP.

But the name wasn't right.

'Bob Henley, did you say?'

'That's right. I'm the headmaster at Alice's school.'

Pip drew in a quick breath. 'Is she all right?'

'She's not unwell.' The headmaster cleared his throat. 'We do have a bit of a problem that we need to discuss, though, and I'd rather not do it on the phone. Would it be possible for you to come to the school?'

'Of course.' It was just another aspect of parenting she was going to have to get used to. What on earth had Alice done to get herself into trouble? 'When? I'm almost finished work for today. I could come almost immediately.'

'That might be best. I've got Alice here in my office at the moment. We'll both be waiting for you.'

CHAPTER SIX

ALICE was sitting, all alone, on a seat outside the headmaster's office.

Pip finally slowed her pace. 'What's going on, Alice?'

'Nothing.'

Which turned out to be precisely what the headmaster was concerned about.

'Alice just isn't doing anything at the moment,' he informed Pip. 'No work in class, no homework, no effort in any direction that we can detect. We're worried about her.'

'Oh.' Pip looked at Alice, who was now slumped in a chair beside her in front of Bob Henley's desk. She was staring at the floor and gave no indication that she was at all bothered by the fact she was in trouble.

Where had the child gone, who had rushed home from school eager to share the day's accomplishments or bathe in the glow of parental pride engendered by a good end-of-term report?

Pip couldn't also help wondering where those pleats she had painstakingly pressed into Alice's school uniform last night had gone. Melted by the large splodge of green paint, perhaps? Her gaze travelled swiftly over her daughter as though seeing her from Bob's point of view. A lot of hair had escaped the ponytail, a thread dangled from a drooping hem on the stained uniform and socks that should have been knee-high were slumped around ankles. From head to toe, Alice looked scruffy. And supremely bored.

'We've had to confiscate her mobile phone and separate her from her friend, Dayna. Their behaviour in class has simply become too disruptive.'

'I had no idea,' Pip sighed.

'Of course not. We thought it would be helpful to bring you into the picture sooner rather than later.' Bob made a steeple of his fingers. 'This has been a rather dramatic change for Alice over the last couple of months. I wondered if you knew of anything going on outside school that could be making the difference.'

Pip sat up a little straighter. Had she been neglectful as a parent in not informing the school of Shona's illness? She hadn't even thought of doing so, thanks to Shona's insistence that things remain as normal as possible for Alice's sake.

To give her time to get used to changes.

Like the change her relationship with Toni was causing.

If the school had noticed a difference over a period of nearly two months, that meant the deterioration in Alice's behaviour coincided with Pip's relationship with Toni and predated any hidden tension she might have picked up since the diagnosis of Shona's illness. But it had been Alice who had encouraged Pip to find a boyfriend. Did she now resent the fact that Pip had someone else of significance in her life?

And if that resentment was enough to cause the negative change in attitude at school, how much worse would it be

in a few months' time—or however long Shona might
have left?

A clear flash of her own resentment towards her mother
in initially withholding the truth about her condition swept
through Pip. As well as another resentment that Toni had
sparked by suggesting Shona was wrong in trying to
protect Alice like this. That children had as much right to
honesty as adults did. That they might find that trying to
protect her would only make things a lot worse in the long
term.

This seemed to be a clear warning that Toni was right.

'Things *are* a bit unsettled at home just now,' Pip told
the headmaster. 'Alice's grandmother isn't well.'

'I'm sorry. Is it serious?'

Pip gave a single, brief nod. Bob Henley looked taken
aback and his gaze flicked to Alice, but she was still
staring at the floor and gave every impression of not listening to a word being said around her.

'I'm sorry,' Bob repeated. 'Is there some way the
school can help?'

'We're managing,' Pip assured him. 'At least, I thought
we were. I guess I haven't been taking as much notice of
Alice as I should have been in regard to homework and so
on.'

'Let's see how things go now that you're aware of the
situation,' Bob suggested. 'And, please, keep in touch and
let us know if you need any support.' He opened a drawer
in his desk and extracted a pink mobile phone. 'I'll give
this to you,' he said to Pip. 'It might be a good idea if Alice
restricts its use to out-of-school hours.'

'Can I have my phone back?'

'Not right now. I want to talk to you.'

'It's *my* phone!'

'Alice.' Pip's tone was a warning. She had no intention of being deflected from having a proper discussion with Alice on the drive home. 'This isn't like you. What *is* your problem?'

'School sucks,' Alice declared. 'Nona's sick and you've got a boyfriend. It's *boring*.'

The confrontational tone angered Pip, which made it easy to override the warning bell that suggested she should investigate any effect her relationship with Toni might be having.

'So you thought you'd make life more interesting by getting into trouble at school?'

'It's not as though I've been suspended or anything. It's no big deal.'

'It felt like a big deal to me.'

'Dayna's mother gets called into school all the time. For nothing!'

Bob Henley was hardly likely to waste his time like that. Pip listened to that warning bell this time. She had ignored it when Toni had jokingly suggested that Alice's new friend might be 'cool' in the way Catherine had been 'cool'. Trouble. 'I've never met Dayna, have I?'

'Why should you?'

'You get to meet *my* friends.'

'You mean Toni? Like he'd be hard to miss! He practically lives at our house.'

Pip bit back a defensive comment about how much help Toni had been in the last few weeks. Making him seem more important to her than Alice at the moment wasn't going to help.

'Why don't you ask Dayna round one day? For dinner, perhaps. You could both get some homework done and make your teachers a lot happier.'

Alice snorted. 'Yeah…like *that* would be fun.'

Pip had had enough. 'None of us are having much "fun" at the moment, Alice. Especially Nona. You might like to start thinking about someone other than yourself for a change.'

'Are you saying I'm selfish?'

'I'm saying that it would be nice if you tried helping, instead of trying to make things harder. I'm trying to do everything right now, Alice. My job, the housework, looking after Nona, looking after *you*, and you're not exactly helping. It's hard enough, OK? *Too* hard, even.'

'It's not *my* fault Nona's sick.'

'I'm not saying it is.'

'And it's not as if she's going to *die* or anything.'

Pip steered the car to the side of the road and pulled to a halt. She sat there, aware of Alice's surprised silence, her hands gripping the top of the steering-wheel.

'Actually,' she said, very quietly, turning her head to make eye contact with her daughter, 'she *is*.'

The look in Alice's eyes was awful. Shock. Mistrust. The silence ticked on and on and then Alice gave a strange sort of hiccup.

'But…but she's just had an operation. Like last time.'

'Not like last time.' Pip steeled herself to maintain the eye contact. 'That's what Nona wanted you to think but she's a lot sicker this time. She's got cancer, Alice. Of her pancreas.'

'Her pancreas!' Pip could see the pupils in Alice's eyes dilating. 'But *I* might have to have an operation, too. Is that what *I've* really got? *Cancer?*'

'No.' She couldn't blame Alice for instantly relating this news to herself. Or for being so afraid. Shona had been right in thinking she would. Had Toni been wrong in advising that she needed to hear the truth? 'You definitely don't have cancer, Alice,' Pip said firmly. 'That's one of the first things they looked for in all those tests you had.'

Alice's eyes were swimming with tears. 'Is Nona really going to die?'

The tears were contagious. 'I'm afraid so, hon.'

'When?'

'We don't know. I hope she'll still be here when you start high school next year, but there are no guarantees. It'll depend on how well the treatment she's getting at the moment works.'

Pip undid her safety belt so she could lean over and hug Alice. 'We need to be as brave as we can,' she said brokenly, 'for Nona's sake. She doesn't want us to be sad. She's wants us all to make the most of whatever time we've got left together. And I…I need your help, hon.'

Would appealing to Alice in a more mature way make any difference?

'Can you do that? Try and help?'

Alice was sobbing now, her face buried against Pip's shoulder.

'I'll…try…'

'Good girl.' Pip kissed the top of her head. 'Love you.'

'You did the right thing.'

'I'm not so sure. She's been so quiet for the last couple of days and she's avoiding spending much time with Mum.'

'Has she been in any more trouble at school?'

'Not that I'm aware of.'

'And she's doing her homework?' Toni could see that some of the tension was leaving Pip's body. She took another sip of her wine and nodded.

'Seems to be.'

'And helping?'

'She did the dishes last night without even being asked.'

'That's better.' Toni traced the outline of Pip's cheek with the back of his index finger. 'You almost smiled then, *bella*.'

'Oh-h.'

Toni loved the way that line of consternation appeared between Pip's eyes. A line he could almost always smooth away.

'Do I seem that miserable?' Pip asked anxiously. 'I'm not, really. Mum's feeling so much better at the moment.'

'That's good.' And it was, but Toni hadn't seen Pip for three days and he had some other things on his mind. Like getting her to relax. Taking her to his bed, finding that magic place where they were so close—body and soul— that he couldn't imagine ever wanting to be anywhere else.

'She's wondering why Alice is so quiet, though.'

'Shona doesn't know that Alice knows the truth?'

'No. I've been scared to tell her. I didn't exactly promise not to but I think Mum assumes I did.'

'You still did the right thing.' Toni picked up Pip's hand and pressed his lips to her palm. 'The only thing you could do as a responsible parent.'

'I wish I felt more like a parent. Like I *knew* that I was doing the right thing.'

'No parent knows that for sure. You just have to do the best you can. What feels right.'

As he would. How many times in the years to come would he sit with Pip like this and reassure her that she had done the right thing? That *they* were doing their best as parents? It would depend entirely on how many children they had, of course.

Toni wanted a lot. At least four. Even six. A happy,

noisy tribe of youngsters like some of his schoolmates had had. Theirs would be lucky enough to have a much older and probably adored sister in Alice. Increasingly, Toni had felt the empty space around him in his house and garden. He had imagined it filled with the sound of children's voices and laughter. Had imagined coming home each night knowing that Pip would be there.

Waiting for him.

Loving him.

Not that he was about to rush into proposing marriage or anything. It was enough, for now, to know his trust in Pip had not been misplaced. That the recent weeks, while hardly romantic in the way he would like them to have been, had cemented the depth of how he felt about this woman.

How much he loved her.

It wasn't the right time to talk about their own future. To make plans for a wedding or their own *bambinos*. Not while Pip had to deal with such a crisis in her life. Toni knew he had no right to feel impatient or to put any pressure on Pip, but he couldn't prevent the smile that crept onto his face or resist the need to hold eye contact with the woman he loved and communicate the deep emotion warming his heart.

Pip smiled back. 'You look happy, anyway. Did you have a good day?'

'No, it was terrible! Far too busy. A case of meningitis, two cases of gastroenteritis, one of whom was severely dehydrated. And a little girl with periorbital cellulitis who couldn't even open her eyes, poor thing, so everything was even more terrifying.'

'*Staphylococcus aureus* infection?'

'Yes. And I got called in because my registrar couldn't

get near her to get an IV line in. The mother was just as distressed as the child by then.'

'I'm sure you sorted it out.' The way Pip was looking at him made Toni feel on top of the world. Capable of achieving anything and being damn proud of it.

'We gave her some sedation,' he admitted.

Pip's smile broadened. 'Who—the child or the mother?'

'Are you suggesting I need to sedate the relatives in order to treat my patients?' It was so good to see Pip smiling properly. To make her happy. Maybe she was finally in a mental space where he could ease her away from her family responsibilities, at least temporarily.

'I'm sure it would make life a lot easier.'

'My life is exactly the way I want it.' The moment Toni had been waiting for ever since Pip had arrived at his house that evening was finally here. He could lean close enough to kiss her still smiling lips. And he did. Slowly. Tenderly.

The need to say something else was an unwanted distraction so he barely pulled back. He could still feel the softness of Pip's mouth beneath his as he spoke.

'*Exactly* the way I want it,' he whispered.

With a sigh of pure contentment Toni focused completely on making love to the first woman who had ever captured his soul as well as his mind and body. Minutes later, with no protest from Pip, he scooped her into his arms and carried her away to his bedroom.

'Are you seeing Toni again tonight?'

'He's coming round soon. He said something about a challenge you'd issued regarding Scrabble?' Pip eyed her mother suspiciously. 'Since when did you become a Scrabble fanatic?'

'Since I found what a good distraction it is,' Shona responded. She grinned. 'I'm such a good speller. I can cane everybody.'

'Hmm. Do you need another cushion?'

'No.' Shona was stretched out on the couch in the living room. 'This is perfect.'

'Are you warm enough?'

'I'm fine. Stop fussing, love.'

'Have you taken all your pills?'

'It's a wonder I had room for any dinner after that lot.'

'You didn't have room for much.' Pip glanced at her watch. It was only 6.30 p.m. They had eaten earlier than usual because Alice had been hungry. 'It's about time for your insulin.'

'Bring me the box. I'd like to do it for myself tonight.'

'You'll need to test your blood-glucose level first so we can check the dose.'

'I can do that.' Shona sounded irritated now. 'I'm not stupid, Philippa.'

'I know that.' Pip backed off. 'You wouldn't cane everybody at Scrabble if that were the case.' She went to the kitchen, returning with the container of drugs, syringes and the testing kit. 'You might even beat Toni later.'

'As long as he doesn't claim international privilege and throw in Italian words, like he did last time.' Shona took the container. 'Where's Alice?' She didn't like her granddaughter having to see her have injections.

'She's in her room, doing her homework.'

'She seems to be working very hard lately. She didn't even argue much when you said she couldn't go to the mall with Dayna.'

'There's no way I'd let her wander around the mall for no reason on a school night. It's just asking for trouble.'

'I agree, but it does seem to be what most teenagers want to do these days. Especially on late-shopping nights. And Alice has seemed very keen to spend as much time as possible with her friends lately.'

'Maybe getting into trouble at school was just what she needed to pull her socks up.'

'Hmm.' Shona wasn't convinced. 'So why am I getting the impression it's a good excuse to avoid *me*?'

'I don't know.'

'Yes, you do.'

The tone was one well remembered from childhood and with a small, defeated sigh Pip lowered herself to sit on the arm of the couch. 'I had to tell her the truth, Mum. I'm sorry. Things were just getting out of hand.'

Shona was silent for a long moment. 'I suppose she had to know,' she said eventually.

'Yes. Toni thought it was the right thing to do.'

'A shame it had to be this soon, though. When I'm starting to feel a bit better. Like I might even win this battle for a while, anyway.'

'I know. But she asked, kind of, and I couldn't lie.'

'No.' Shona leaned back on her cushions, her eyes closed. 'I'll talk to her so it's all out in the open. I knew there something going on that I didn't know about.'

'I should have told you. I'm not dealing with any this particularly well, am I?'

'You're doing just fine. None of it is easy—for any of us. We'll get used to it.'

'I'm not so sure about that. About managing this parenting bit by myself. I just don't feel, you know, maternal enough, I guess.'

Shona smiled. 'It takes practice.'

'I'm not sure I can do any of it without you to back me

up,' Pip said sadly. 'I was a complete failure as a parent right from the start with Alice, wasn't I?'

'You were sixteen,' Shona said, as though that explained everything.

But it didn't. Plenty of sixteen-year-olds had babies and felt the kind of instant bond you were supposed to feel with your baby, didn't they? They wouldn't have been so relieved that someone more maternal was there to fill the breach and gradually take full responsibility.

'It'll be different next time,' Shona said. 'You'll see.'

'No, I won't,' Pip said fervently. 'There's not going to be a "next time".' Even now, the terror of those long, pain-filled hours of labour was a memory clear enough to make the hairs on the back of Pip's neck prickle. And that had only been the start. The feeling of inadequacy—of failing to be a good parent—had been unpleasant and ongoing. It seemed to be surfacing with a new regularity all over again now—like during that interview with Alice's head-master.

'Doesn't Toni want children?'

'He's never mentioned it.'

'He seems very happy to include Alice in your relationship.'

'Yes. He's great with children, which is partly why he's such a brilliant paediatrician. Plus, he's Italian. They all seem to adore kids and realise how important families are.' Pip felt a familiar wave of gratitude. How many women in her position would be lucky enough to find a lover who would take on board an older child and a sick mother they weren't related to?

'So don't you think he's going to want a family of his own?'

'Maybe not. He didn't have a very happy childhood

himself. That can be enough to stop people wanting to have their own children.'

'And it can make others want to undo the damage by making sure it doesn't happen to the next generation.' Shona was watching Pip now, her expression anxious. 'You're still so young, darling. You could easily have more children.'

'But I don't want to.'

And she didn't want to talk about it any more. It wasn't just the thought of being expected to have more children that was disturbing, it was that the thought hadn't occurred to her prior to this. Maybe it was an issue she should have discussed with Toni right at the start of their relationship. But then, how could she have known how intense things were going to get? On her part, at any rate. She still didn't know how Toni really felt. Whether he was considering a real commitment to a future together. This wasn't the time to be thinking about it, anyway. She had far too much else going on in her life.

'Sometimes you have to be prepared to compromise if you want a relationship to work,' Shona said.

'Hmm.' The sound was noncommittal but it wasn't an area that was up for negotiation as far as Pip was concerned. She wasn't about to prove herself a failure all over again. It was time to change the subject. 'Are you sure you don't want some help with that insulin?'

'I'm sure.' But Shona wasn't about to let Pip close the subject quite yet. 'Talk to him about it, won't you, Pip?'

'Of course I will. Sometime. It's early days, Mum.'

'Not for me,' Shona said quietly. She summoned a smile for her daughter. 'Don't take this the wrong way, love. It's just that I'd like to think I'm going to be around long enough to help plan a wedding rather than a funeral.'

* * *

Why couldn't life be simple?

The information contained in the article Pip was reading in an emergency medicine journal on the management of secondary deterioration in level of consciousness wasn't really sinking in.

She had declined another game of Scrabble, having been soundly beaten by both Toni and Shona, who were happily engaged in another epic battle. The Scrabble board sat on a small table beside the couch and Toni's long frame was lounging on the floor on its other side. Pip could see he had way too many vowels on his letter rack but he seemed undaunted.

'Axe,' he said aloud. 'Ten points.'

How homely was this? All it needed to complete the picture of happy domesticity would be to have Alice doing her homework on the dining table in the corner of the room, instead of being shut away in her bedroom at the other end of the house.

Inclusion couldn't be forced, though, and the niggling worry that Alice resented Toni's inclusion in her mother's life was just one of the underlying tensions that made the happy picture only superficial.

Pip tried to return her attention to the article. Constant reassessment of level of consciousness was mandatory, she read, as changes in the Glasgow coma score were more important than any static assessment. Faced with deterioration, the first objective was to confirm oxygenation and ventilatory adequacy. Then to ensure adequate volume status and haemoglobin. And to check BGL.

The mention of a blood-sugar level was enough to make Pip glance towards the couch again.

'Extra,' Shona was pronouncing with satisfaction. 'I used your "x", Toni, only I got it on a triple word.'

'Very good,' Toni said with a feigned level of grudging admiration. 'What's the score?'

'Twenty-two.'

'Really? It should be more than that.' He leaned over the board. 'It's more like thirty-six!'

It was so good to see her mother looking this happy. The tension of worrying about her condition and managing all the hurdles they were bound to face in the coming months was the biggest reason that life was nowhere near simple. It occurred to Pip that Shona might be looking this happy right now because she was with someone who wasn't as emotionally involved as she was herself. Someone who could operate better in that superficial picture and treat Shona as though she was going to be around to play Scrabble for many years.

Was it a reprieve for her mother—in the way that it was for Pip when *she* spent special time with Toni?

Like last night had been.

Impossible to concentrate on information about criteria for consulting a neurosurgical team and ordering urgent cerebral scanning for someone whose level of consciousness was dropping. Pip's head was firmly where her body had been last night. Being loved so thoroughly—so *amazingly*—by Toni Costa.

Thanks to that earlier conversation with Shona, however, a new tension had been added to the complexity of Pip's life. Was her mother's notion, that Toni would definitely want his own children something she should add to her list of worries? Or could it be shelved, in the same way as that niggle about Alice resenting her attachment to someone new?

If it wasn't broken, don't try and fix it, she told herself.

Things were fragile enough without searching for cracks, weren't they?

Maybe managing life was the same as being a parent. You dealt with things when you had to. You did what felt right and you did the best you could. Addressing issues that weren't an obvious problem and could be potentially destructive certainly didn't feel like the right thing to do.

Pip discarded her journal. 'Anybody feel like a hot drink? Tea or coffee?'

'Please.' Toni had his gaze on the board. '"Predom" is not a word,' he said to Shona. 'Sorry.'

'It is, too.'

Pip laughed. 'Of course it isn't. Do you want the dictionary, Mum?'

'Don't need it. I can spell.'

'Do you want a cup of tea?'

'Yes. Go away.'

'I'll come and help you.' Toni pushed himself up off the floor. 'You can have another go while I'm gone, if you like, Shona.'

'Don't need it.'

'Is she serious?' Toni asked when they had reached the privacy of the kitchen. 'I'm right, aren't I? Or is "predom" some English word I haven't learned yet?'

'It's not a word,' Pip assured him. 'Mum's just getting stroppy. She's probably tired.' She filled the electric kettle and switched it on.

'Are you tired, *cara*?'

'Not really.'

'Good. Come here, then.'

Pip was only too willing to go into his open arms. To raise her face for one of the kisses she was coming to know so well. Kisses that she couldn't imagine not receiving on a very regular basis.

It took some time for them to complete the task of setting a tray for supper, but Pip felt happier than she had all day by the time they returned to the living room.

'Here's your tea, Mum. Do you feel like a biscuit?' Pip peered at her mother before turning to Toni. 'I think you tired her out. She's too sleepy for a hot drink.'

'Hmm.' Toni came closer. 'Shona?'

'Don't wake her,' Pip advised. 'She needs a rest.'

'Hmm,' Toni said again. He laid his hand on Shona's forehead. 'She's very clammy,' he said. This time Pip said nothing as he shook Shona's shoulder. 'Shona? Wake up!'

'I'll get her blood-glucose monitor,' Pip said. 'Maybe she wasn't just being stroppy with that strange word.'

'She certainly looks like she could be hypoglycaemic,' Toni agreed. 'She's diaphoretic and tachycardic and she's quite deeply unconscious. I'm going to call an ambulance.'

Pip was back with the kit rapidly. 'She insisted on doing her insulin herself tonight.'

'What was her BGL reading?'

'It says 8.4 on this but that's what it was this morning. It's been so unstable lately I'd be very surprised if it had been the same this evening. Maybe she forgot to take it.' Pip had inserted the test strip. She used a lancet to prick the end of her mother's finger and then collected a drop of blood on the end of the strip.

The wail of an ambulance siren could be heard in the distance by the time they got proof that Shona's blood-sugar level was dangerously low.

While the paramedics established IV access and started a glucose infusion running, Pip sped down the hall and knocked on Alice's door.

'Alice?'

She opened the door to find Alice lying on her bed with headphones on. Compact discs were scattered all around her and even from where she stood, Pip could hear the music. Alice jumped at the intrusion and peeled the headphones off.

'What?' she demanded. 'I've finished my homework.'

'Nona's sick,' Pip said tersely. 'We're going to take her into the hospital by ambulance. Do you want to come with us?'

Alice went very pale. 'Is she…?'

'No, hon, it's OK.' Pip's heart squeezed painfully as she saw the level of distress in Alice's face. 'It looks like she might have had too much insulin tonight but it should be easy enough to fix. We just need to have her in hospital to make sure we get it right and an ambulance is the most comfortable way for her to travel.'

'Will you be gone all night?'

'No. I'll come home as soon as things are stable.'

'Then can I stay here? I don't like hospitals and I want to watch TV later.'

'Would you be all right by yourself? I could ask Mary to come over.'

'I'll be fine.' Alice sat up on the edge of her bed. 'I'm not a kid any more, Pip. I don't need a babysitter.'

'OK.' It was much easier to relate to Alice when she wanted to be treated more as an adult than a child. 'I'll call you soon, then.'

The phone call went unanswered an hour later when Pip was finally happy to leave her mother's bedside.

'I'm perfectly all right,' Shona was insisting. 'But I'm not hungry. I really don't want that sandwich.'

'You need to try and eat it, Mum. It's part of the management for an insulin overdose.'

'It wasn't an overdose. I just had a bit of trouble with the monitor. I couldn't get it to beep when I put the test strip in.'

'It was probably the wrong way round.'

'I'll get it right next time.'

Pip thought that her phone call home would be answered the next time she tried, but it wasn't. She tried Alice's mobile phone but it went straight to voicemail.

'She's probably got her headphones on again,' Toni said. 'With the music loud enough to deafen her.'

'I'm still worried. I think I'll call a taxi and head home. They're going to keep Mum in overnight to monitor her blood-glucose levels.'

'I'll come with you.'

It wasn't late when they arrived back at the Murdochs' house—a little after 9 p.m. and Pip fully expected to find Alice curled up in her bed watching television.

She could hear the telephone ringing as she unlocked the front door, but it stopped as soon as she stepped into the hallway.

'I wonder who that was at this time of night?'

Toni was close behind her. 'If it was important, they'll ring again.'

'I hope it wasn't the hospital.'

'They'll have your mobile number.'

'Yes.' Pip stopped talking, aware of how quiet the house was. She couldn't hear the sound of a television. She couldn't hear anything.

'Alice?' she called. 'We're home.'

The silence was more than just a quiet house. It felt...empty.

The living room was empty, the Scrabble board with its unfinished game a reminder of how much the evening's peace had been disrupted. Pip kept moving. The bathroom light was on but the small space was deserted. An open mascara wand lay beside the basin. Pip's bedroom was in darkness, the screen of the portable television blank, but there was a light showing under Alice's door.

Pip knocked once and opened the door. 'Alice?'

Seconds later, she entered the kitchen where Toni was busy making coffee.

'Toni?'

He turned swiftly. 'What's up, *cara*?'

'Alice isn't here.'

'She must be,'

Pip shook her head in bewilderment. 'I've checked everywhere. She's not here.'

'Where could she have gone?'

'I don't know.' A dreadful sensation was gripping Pip. She shouldn't have left Alice at home alone. She was really only a child still. What kind of parent would do something like that?

Pip had no idea at all of where Alice might be or who she might be with. She had failed—yet again—to do the right thing as a parent, and this time she might have put her daughter into real danger.

'Oh, my God, Toni,' Pip breathed. 'What am I going to do?'

Toni's touch was reassuring. At least she wasn't going to be alone in tackling whatever new crisis was about to present itself in her life. He opened his mouth to say something but, at exactly the same moment, the telephone began to ring again.

Pip froze. This was going to be bad news, she just knew it.

Toni looked at her face. 'I'll answer that,' he said. He touched her cheek. 'I'll be right back.'

CHAPTER SEVEN

'WE'LL be right there.' Toni put the phone down and turned to Pip. 'She's safe.'

'But where *is* she?'

'With the police.'

'*What?*' Horrific images of abduction and potential violence crowded the back of Pip's mind.

'She's safe,' Toni repeated. 'She's at the mall.'

'I don't understand.'

'She and her friend—Daisy, is it?'

'Dayna?'

'Yes. They were caught shoplifting.'

'Oh, no!' Pip groaned. 'How *could* they?'

'They're too young to be arrested but apparently the mall's policy is to involve the police. They want you to go and collect Alice.'

Pip nodded tersely. She scooped up her car keys from the bowl on the end of the kitchen bench. ' I'll go straight away.'

'I'm coming with you.'

'You don't have to do that, Toni.' Pip's half-smile was rueful. 'As if you haven't had enough of my family's dramas for one evening.'

'I'm not going to let you cope with this by yourself, Pippa.' Toni patted the pocket of his jacket and Pip heard the rattle of keys. 'I'll drive.'

The strength that Toni's company imparted was dented as soon as they entered the mall management's offices.

'What's *he* doing here?' Alice demanded.

'Who is he?' The girl sitting beside Alice had bleached, blonde hair, too much make-up and a top that exposed several inches of midriff and a large jewel in a belly-button piercing.

'My mother's boyfriend.'

'Oh-h. So that's the Italian stallion.'

The derogatory tone and the innuendo was too much for Pip. So was the sullen expression on the girl's face. At least Alice had the sense to look frightened beneath a thin layer of defiance, faced as she was with the presence of a bored-looking security guard, an angry mall management representative and two police officers.

Pip would have expected her to be looking relieved with the arrival of someone prepared to defend her, but Alice didn't look any more pleased to see her mother than Toni.

'You're Alice Murdoch's mother?' The policewoman looked surprised.

'Yes.' Pip was in no mood to provide an explanation for looking too young for the part.

'She's been spotted in the mall on several occasions, so we're told—with Dayna here. The security guard followed up his suspicions tonight and kept a close eye on the pair of them.'

The nod from the burly security guard was satisfied.

'These items were found in Dayna's bag as they were trying to leave the mall at closing time.'

Several items of clothing were lying on the office desk, the labels advertising their newness.

Toni raised his eyebrows. 'So Alice hasn't actually stolen anything?'

'She was aware of what was going on. A willing accomplice.'

Alice wasn't meeting Pip's gaze so she turned to the policewoman. 'What's going to happen to her?'

'At this stage, probably nothing more than a warning, but we wanted you to be aware of what your daughter's involved in, Mrs Murdoch. It's not the first time we've had trouble with her friend, Dayna, and we intend to deal with her a lot more severely. If you don't want future involvement with the police and Social Services, I suggest you take your daughter home and have a very serious discussion with her.'

'Oh, I will,' Pip said heavily. 'Don't worry.'

Extra stress like this was the last thing they needed at this time. The thought of having to explain all this to Shona was horrible. Why was Alice choosing now to make trouble? To emphasise *her* failure to meet the demands of taking over as a full-time parent? Pip felt as though she was under siege.

'How long has this sort of thing been going on?' she snapped as they marched Alice towards the car a short time later.

Alice shrugged.

'Those CDs and videos and everything that Dayna's been lending you lately—are they all stolen property?'

Another shrug was infuriating.

'Do you *want* to get into real trouble?' Pip's voice rose. 'End up in juvenile court and get suspended from school?'

Alice's silence continued as they climbed into the car.

It was Toni who broke it as he started the engine. 'I think the problem might be one of association rather than intent,' he said mildly.

Pip was hoping that was true. She could deal with that. 'You're not to have anything more to do with Dayna,' she informed Alice crisply. 'She's bad news.'

'She's my *friend*.'

'What kind of friend sets out to get you into big trouble?'

'Why should you care?'

'Because I'm your *mother*, that's why!'

'No, you're not.'

Shocked by the vehement tone, Pip turned to look at Alice. The intermittent light from streetlamps couldn't conceal a very adult anger on the young girl's face.

'You've never been my mother,' Alice continued bitterly. 'Not really. You never wanted me. You couldn't even look after me by yourself. Nona had to do it.'

Pip could sense the glance she was getting from Toni without meeting it. He was as shocked as she was. He might want to help but there was nothing he could do or say. This was between Pip and Alice and it was private. He was probably embarrassed to be a witness. Pip was certainly embarrassed. Mortified, even. She'd always felt a failure as a parent but she'd never expected such blatant confirmation of her inadequacy to come from her child.

The despair in Alice's voice filled the car. 'Now Nona's going to die and she's the only person who ever cared about me.'

'That's *not* true, Alice.' The despair her daughter was feeling was an abyss that Pip had no idea how to reach across. The distance felt impossible. 'I love you. I've *always* loved you.'

'You gave me to Nona. You went back to school and then you went away to university. For years and years and *years.*'

What could she say to that? It was true. They had discussed moving so that they could live in a city that boasted a medical school, but it would have meant all the upheaval of selling and buying a new house in a far more expensive area, and finances had been tight enough as it was. Alice would have been taken away from the play centre she'd loved. From the GP who had cared for her since birth. Shona would have lost her own friends, who'd provided a network of support. And they'd decided against it because Alice had been so happy.

Pip had been so sure that she had been the only one to suffer because of the prolonged absences.

'I missed you,' she told Alice. The words sounded totally pathetic. 'I always told you how much I missed you.'

'Ha!' The sound was derisive. 'It's not as if anything changed even when you came back. You're always working now. You still don't want me. I'm just in the way.'

'That's *not* true!'

'You've got Toni,' Alice said accusingly. 'You'll get married now and have babies that you *do* want. You'll forget all about me.'

'No!' Pip put all the conviction she could into the word. She had to ignore the sharp intake of breath from Toni. This wasn't the time to try and explain she was denying a lack of interest in Alice rather than the prospect of marriage or babies with Toni. 'That's not going to happen, Alice.'

'And I'll have no one.' Alice either hadn't heard or didn't believe her.

* * *

The car had stopped. They were home. And it had never felt less like home.

Toni switched off the engine and spoke for the first time since they'd left the mall car park. 'You're not going to lose your mother, Alice. She loves you. I know you're going through a tough time at the moment and I understand how you feel. I—'

'Shut *up*!' Alice shouted. 'You don't know anything. This is *your* fault, anyway.'

'Alice!' Pip couldn't help the remonstrative exclamation but, it was lost in Alice's continued shouting.

'We were fine before you came along. Now Nona's going to die and Mummy doesn't have time for me any more and…and I *hate* you.'

Pip tried again. 'Alice, you can't say that.'

'I can, too.' Alice was fumbling with the door catch. 'It's true. And I hate you, too. Go away. Go and live with Toni and have babies and see if I care.'

'I'm not going to do that, Alice.'

'I don't *care*!' Alice flung the door open and jumped out. She was crying now but still managed to shout between the racking sobs. 'Have *lots* of babies. Sing them all the special ottipuss song. I. Don't. *Care*!'

Stunned, Pip got out of the car. Alice had left the front door wide open and she heard her daughter's bedroom door slamming as she entered the house.

'Let her go,' Toni advised quietly. 'She's not going to hear anything you want to say to her until she's had time to calm down a little.'

He was probably right but it went against every instinct Pip had. She needed to hold her child. To rock her. To reassure her that she was deeply loved. And wanted. And she *would* do that—just as soon as Alice would let her close enough.

Until then it seemed to be Pip's turn to be held and comforted but, for the first time, it didn't feel right to be in Toni's arms. There was something a little stiff and awkward about the embrace—almost as if they were strangers. His body felt tense. Clearly, he was upset as well. When Pip went to pull away, Toni released her instantly. So fast, in fact, that Pip had to wonder if he'd let go even before she'd started to move.

Was he upset at simply being involved in this horrible conflict between her and Alice? More than that? Oh…yes. Pip remembered that shocked sound from him when he'd taken more than she intended from her words of reassurance to Alice. But he couldn't really expect her to want to think about or discuss the future right now, would he? Whether it was possible she would ever want another child when this had to be the time she'd felt more of a failure as a parent than ever before?

'I had *no* idea,' she said slowly, closing the front door behind them, 'that Alice felt anything like that.'

'I do understand where she's coming from, even if Alice doesn't believe me,' Toni said soberly. 'I've always hated my own mother for not wanting me.'

'But I *did* want Alice.' To have Toni taking Alice's side was almost as shocking as her daughter's attack had been. She turned swiftly to face him. 'I know I needed a lot of help looking after her, but I was only sixteen, for God's sake! And it wasn't my idea to go back to school and then to go to university. I got talked into it and there didn't seem to be a good enough reason not to go. Alice was too young to understand the difference between the people who loved her and looked after her. She was *happy*.'

'She's not very happy at the moment.'

Rubbing that in was cruel. And unnecessary. Pip could suddenly understand Alice shouting at Toni. She barely stopped herself doing the same. The bubble of responsibility she felt for upsetting Toni evaporated. So did any intention of trying to discuss this from his perspective. Of telling him she hadn't meant to deny the chance of a future together. She couldn't think of anyone but Alice right now.

'Of course she's not happy,' she said with tight control. 'Her grandmother's dying. She's trying to find a way of dealing with that and it's too much for her. She's sad and angry and looking for someone to blame. *Me.*'

Pip's control slipped and she buried her face in her hands. 'I shouldn't have told her the truth. Not yet. Mum was right—she's got too many things changing all at once.'

Alice wasn't the only one with too many things changing all at once.

Toni stood there in the hallway near the front door, wanting to take Pip in his arms to try and reassure her, but what if she just pulled away like she had only moments ago?

It was hard not to feel rejected with that vehement declaration of Alice's still ringing in his ears.

She hated him.

And a phrase Pip had uttered was vying for equal prominence.

'That's not going to happen,' she'd said.

What wasn't going to happen? At the time Toni had dismissed the shock of her words and assumed Pip was reassuring Alice that her daughter was still going to be important in her life, no matter what. A part of her new family if she did marry Toni and they had their own children.

But right now, as Toni stood with his arms by his sides, miserably checking the impulse to hold Pip—in the wake of her pulling away from his comfort—that first meaning that had occurred to him seemed far more likely to be the correct one..

What wasn't going to happen was a future with him.

Was it possible he had made a terrible mistake?

That he'd given away so much of his heart to Pip that it could never be whole again if she wasn't in his life and that she didn't feel the same way about him? And never would?

The seconds ticked past. Awkward seconds. Pip had taken her hands from her face and had been staring in the direction Alice had taken down the hallway towards the bedrooms. When she looked up at Toni, her expression was desolate.

'She blames me for everything. I've messed things up completely, haven't I?'

'No.' Toni's smile was wry. 'It's all *my* fault, remember? Alice hates me.'

'She hates me, too.'

For bringing Toni into her life on top of everything else Alice perceived that Pip had done wrong as a parent.

A flash of something akin to amusement showed in Pip's eyes. They were both hated, which could actually deepen the bond between them. Except that Pip couldn't afford to let that happen, could she? Not if she didn't see a future together. Not if she wanted to repair the damage in her relationship with her daughter.

'No.' Toni spoke more seriously this time. 'It's me that

Alice is really resenting. She needs you and she sees me as competition. Me being here is making things harder…for you all.'

Would Pip try and reassure him in some way? Perhaps even give them the chance to discuss that damning denial of the future he'd been dreaming of with the sound of small feet and happy laughter filling his house?

He wanted to touch her. To remind her how much he loved her, but that would be begging for reassurance, wouldn't it? For the sake of his pride as much as not wanting to force the issue, Toni had to make himself wait for Pip's response.

A response that was slow in coming.

Too slow.

She certainly wasn't inclined to grasp the opportunity to silence that negative little voice in his head that was re-playing things said under duress. He was upset as well and Pip's silence stirred the unpleasant emotion enough to make him go a step further.

'Maybe you need some time as a family. The way you used to be. Without me.'

Pip was staring at him but he couldn't read her expression. Couldn't find the reassurance that his offer might not be welcome. And it hurt.

She must know that he was doing more than offering her some space. That he was really asking if she wanted him as part of her life.

If she wanted *him*.

Pip opened her mouth to speak but then had to close it again. What could she say? She had feared this moment would come. That her baggage would become too much of a burden and that Toni would want to distance himself.

This was the perfect opportunity, wasn't it? Alice had made it very clear that she resented Toni and his relationship with her mother. He would have to be very determined that he wanted a future with her to weather a storm like this.

If she told him what she wanted to say—that she couldn't imagine being able to cope without the kind of strength he gave her—would it come across as being needy and scare him even further away?

Or, worse, would it open the can of worms regarding how he saw their future if he did stay to help her through yet another family crisis? If he told her that having his own family was paramount, it would add a new pressure. An additional facet to the emotional forces laying siege to her life. Pip couldn't handle that.

Not tonight.

And maybe Toni was offering this space because that was what he wanted himself. An escape. And why wouldn't he? Pip could see this from his point of view so easily. His own mother had failed him miserably. He was currently in a ringside seat to observe Pip's failure with her own daughter. Would he wish that on any children of his own? Not likely.

But could Pip summon the dignity to let him have that escape if that was what he was really asking for? Could she do it in a civilised fashion even?

'I do need to talk to Alice,' she said finally. 'To try and make her understand.'

'Of course. I'll go home.'

'I'll see you tomorrow?' Pip couldn't help sounding hopeful. 'At work?'

'Of course.' Toni paused, his fingers gripping the door-handle. His smile seemed different. Distant. Then he raised an eyebrow. 'What did Alice mean?' he asked, 'by the "special ottipuss" song?'

'I used to sing to her to get her to sleep when she a baby,' Pip responded softly. 'It was a Beatles' song—"The Octopus's Garden". Only she was too little to be able to pronounce it.'

'How old was she?'

'Less than two.' Pip had stopped singing that song after she'd gone away to medical school. 'I'm amazed she remembers it.'

'Some things are never forgotten, Pippa.'

So true. Like the look Toni was giving her right now. An uncomfortable look as though he was upset because he knew he might be hurting her by walking out like this but couldn't help himself. He needed to escape.

She had to be strong.

She had to think about Alice right now.

Her *daughter*.

Part of herself. A part that was torn and bleeding right now. A part that had nothing to do with Toni, no matter how much she loved him.

Why hadn't she heeded those warnings that Alice resented how quickly and deeply Toni had become part of their lives? No wonder she felt shut out and unable to cope with Shona's illness. How selfish had Pip been, letting her relationship become so important?

As selfish as she'd been pursuing the career she'd dreamed of and letting her mother shoulder ninety per cent of the upbringing of her young child?

No wonder Alice had felt the need to attack her.

For being an inadequate mother.

For appearing to abandon Alice for the second time in her short life. For choosing an education and now for choosing a lover—at the worst possible time—when Alice needed her more than she ever had.

It felt wrong to Pip to be standing here like this, debating whether there was anything else she could say to Toni that would make him—and herself—feel better. She had almost made a joke of Alice hating them both equally—as though they were both her real parents. She should be trying to get through to Alice even if there was no hope of succeeding just yet. Otherwise, Alice could accuse her of not caring enough to even try.

Something else was hurting, too, quite apart from the thought that Toni was pulling away from their relationship. His query about that long discarded song had evoked a powerful memory. Another one of those things that could never be forgotten.

The memory of holding a tiny, warm, sweet-smelling body. The tickle of soft red-gold curls as Pip bent into the cot to kiss her daughter goodnight.

The feeling of the bond that had always been there but had been buried under layers of unwelcome feelings. Of being inadequate. Too young. Too alone. Too uneducated.

None of those excuses held water any more.

Except maybe being alone because Toni was leaving now with no more than a nod of parting.

The click of the front door closing behind him had a finality that completed the downward slide of an evening from hell. One that seemed to have been scripted purely for the purpose of breaking Pip's heart.

CHAPTER EIGHT

THE children's ward had never looked so festive.

The paediatrician heading for the treatment room had never felt so bleak.

'Dr Costa! Look at *me*!'

A tiny child was propelling a custom-built wheelchair at speed along the central corridor of the paediatric ward and came to a halt, barely missing Toni's toes.

The small boy was wearing a Superman costume. The mask was far too big, covering most of his face, but the misshapen body in the chair would have been instantly recognisable in any case.

Toni sounded as puzzled as possible, however. 'Goodness me, who can this be?'

'It's *me*!' The mask was dragged upwards. 'Nathan. See?'

'So it is! I'd never have guessed.'

Nathan beamed at him. He knew perfectly well that his doctor was being less than honest but it was the correct response. The familiar broad grin of this long-term patient was welcome. Nathan had spent far too many of his six years in and out of hospital to deal with the management and complications of his physical abnormalities but he never seemed to resent any of it. His mission in life was clearly to have as much fun as possible and nobody could resist the uplifting effect of his personality.

Even Toni, the way he had been feeling for days now. Ever since Pip had apparently accepted his offer to step out of her life.

'It's Hallowe'en,' Nathan informed Toni. 'And I'm going in the *parade*!'

'So am I.' Eight-year-old Jasmine, sporting a pair of sky-blue fairy wings and wielding a glittery wand in a rather menacing fashion, emerged from the nearby bathroom.

'Cool bananas,' Toni said, still smiling.

This celebration had been planned for weeks. Parents, nurses, physiotherapists, occupational therapists and everybody else concerned with the wellbeing of the children in this ward had been using the calendar date as inspiration to keep their young patients motivated, distracted or just amused. Masks and costumes had been made or hired and all those well enough were going to go on a pre-planned 'trick or treat' parade through carefully primed areas of the hospital such as the geriatric wards, cafeteria, pharmacy, the waiting area of the emergency department and even the chapel.

A baby with a pumpkin hat that took attention away from the dressings covering a recently repaired cleft palate and hare-lip was carried past, and an older girl with a nasal cannula supplying oxygen from a tank she pushed in front of her had the cylinder disguised with a large bunch of straw that had a stick poking up from the centre.

'It's my broom,' she told Toni when he raised his eyebrows.

'You're going as a sweeper, Jodi?'

'No, silly.' Jodi had to catch her breath. The chest infection complicating management of her cystic fibrosis was not yet conquered. 'I'm going to be…a witch. Mum's bringing…my costume.'

Another wheelchair came to clutter the part of the corridor Toni had stopped in and a nurse carrying one of their young arthritic patients, who was looking extra-cute in a tiger suit, shook her head.

'I might have known,' she said. 'If there's a traffic jam of kids anywhere, it'll be Dr Costa in the middle of it.'

Toni eyed her headband that had sparkling red devil's horns attached. 'Very appropriate, Mandy.' He nodded approvingly.

The nurse sniffed. 'I'll find a costume for you, don't worry.'

'That won't be necessary.'

'What? You're not coming on the parade?' Several sets of horrified eyes were glued on Toni.

'Of course I'm coming.' He may not feel anything like as enthusiastic as he managed to sound but the delight displayed by Nathan and his fellow ward members made the effort worthwhile.

'What are you…coming as?' Jodi asked.

'Hmm, let me think.' Toni kept up a thoughtful silence but was uninspired. 'Maybe I could come as…a doctor?' He waggled the end of the stethoscope hanging round his neck but the children all shook their heads sadly.

Mandy giggled. 'You'll have to do better than that.'

Toni was spared any further efforts by another nurse appearing in a nearby doorway.

'We're ready for you, Toni.'

He escaped to the relative security of the treatment room where an anxious mother was waiting, holding a ten-month-old girl.

'You've had this procedure explained to you?' Toni queried.

'Yes. I wish there was a different way to get the urine specimen, though. It seems horrible, having to stick a needle through Emily's stomach.'

'It's a very fine needle,' Toni assured her. 'And a quick procedure. I'll be very gentle.'

'Is it really necessary?'

Toni nodded. 'It's important that we find the source of Emily's infection so we can make sure we've got her on the right antibiotics. This won't take long but she's not going to be happy about us doing it. Would you rather the nurse looked after her and you waited back in Emily's room?'

Relief and worry vied to take over Emily's mother's expression. 'Would that be all right? I'd feel terrible leaving her.'

'If it's going to upset you, then it's probably better for Emily if you're not here. We'll get another nurse to help us and we'll take very good care of her, I promise. You'll be able to give her all the cuddling she needs as soon as it's over.'

The woman burst into tears as she left the room and Toni could sympathise. Most mothers would far rather have a procedure themselves than witness their children suffering. Some, like Emily's mother, found it unbearable, whereas others refused to be parted from their children no matter how dreadful the procedure might be.

The bond between mothers and their children had always fascinated Toni. Perhaps he was more conscious of it than most because the lack of experiencing it personally had always haunted him. He was confident that the awareness had made him a better doctor. He approved of the bond. He went out of his way to support the parents of his small patients.

So he had no right to feel rejected because Pip was putting Alice's needs ahead of his own, had he?

Or to feel resentful of Alice. To feel that she was knowingly depriving him of what he most wanted.

A family.

She wasn't even prepared to acknowledge her mother at the moment. She had no idea how lucky she was to have someone who loved her that much. Someone who was prepared to sacrifice something as important as a relationship with a lover to make things better for her child.

Toni scrubbed his hands at the basin in the treatment room while the nurse jiggled baby Emily, who was grizzling loudly in the wake of her mother's disappearance.

'Could you poke your head out the door, please?' Toni asked. 'See if Mandy or someone is free to help us for a minute. We'll need two people to keep Emily still enough.'

He dried his hands and tried to shake off the downward spiral of his spirits that had begun yet again by thinking about Pip and Alice, but day by day a negative interpretation of their current situation seemed to become more prominent and there didn't seem to be anything he could do about it.

Toni couldn't take the first step, no matter how much he might want to. He couldn't force his way back into Pip's life. What would be the point? She had to *want* him.

If Pip felt anything like the same level of emotion he did, she would find it impossible to exclude him, no matter how powerful the bond with her child was. He could have helped to find another way through this impasse but he hadn't even been given the opportunity. As each day had passed, the feeling of being less than significant in Pip's life had increased.

And something even more negative than the sensation of rejection had blossomed. Betrayal. The kind of betrayal he had sworn never to make himself vulnerable to again. For the first time in his adult life Toni had totally trusted a woman. Had given himself heart and soul. He was missing Pip terribly. A dozen times he had picked up his phone, intending to call or text. Compelled to jump over that boundary line and find out if she was all right and whether there was any way he could help. Each time, something had stopped him.

And he knew exactly what it was.

The echo of her vehemence in assuring Alice that she had no intention of marrying him or having his babies refused to fade. If anything, it got louder every time it clawed its way back into his head.

'It's not going to happen,' she'd said.

It's *not* going to happen.

Surely Pip would realise the interpretation he could have put on those words? The damage they could have done? Toni was quite prepared to believe the more positive spin of it being a promise to include Alice in their lives, and even the smallest gesture on Pip's part would have been enough to make him feel wanted and repair the damage. Just a phone call. Even a text. Just…contact.

There hadn't been any.

This was the fourth day since Alice had confronted Pip with those awful accusations of being less than a real mother. Shona had been discharged the next day and must be doing well enough for Pip to continue working because he'd seen her car in the car park on more than one occasion. Probably because he'd been looking for it.

Mandy came into the room as Toni snapped on some gloves. 'Thanks, Mandy. We've just got a suprapubic aspiration to do on Emily for a urine sample. Shouldn't take long.' He leaned over the baby as the nurses positioned her on the table, keeping her body and legs as still as possible.

Toni swabbed the crease in the skin above the symphysis pubis with an alcohol wipe. He inserted the fine, 23-gauge needle to its full length and then drew it back, aspirating with the attached 2-ml syringe at the same time. Urine flowed into the barrel of the syringe almost immediately, and by the time Emily had gathered enough lung power to express her outrage, the procedure was virtually completed.

'Looks pretty cloudy,' Toni commented. 'I'd like a result back on this as soon as possible.'

'I'll take her back to Mum,' Mandy offered, scooping the baby up for a cuddle. 'It's the only thing that's going to cheer you up, isn't it, button?'

Toni dropped his gloves into the bin. The only thing that would cheer *him* up would be time with Pip and finding out that she *did* want a future with him. A family. But that obviously wasn't going to happen in a hurry, was it?

Maybe it would never happen.

It was no wonder they said that timing was everything. If Shona hadn't become ill when she had, things would be very different. None of those wounding words would have been uttered. It had been cool for Pip to have a boyfriend until the prospect of losing the head of their small family had been revealed. Alice could have shared a 'sister' but not a mother. And why should she? Her need for Pip's love and attention was much greater than Toni's.

It just didn't feel like that.

'Heaven's above, what's all that commotion?'

'It's all right, Mrs Evans. Try and keep still while I get this dressing in place.' The frightened twitch had been enough for paper-thin skin to slough away from the raw flesh Pip had been trying to re-cover.

'But the noise!'

There certainly was something happening in the corridor near the cubicle Mrs Evans was occupying. It sounded like a busload of children had been deposited around the waiting area for the emergency department, except they sounded far too happy to be unwell or injured.

'I'll go and see what it is in a minute. There…' Pip smoothed the wrinkles from the skin flap and reached for a dressing to hold it in place. 'You'll have to be careful of this for a while.'

'Oh, I know, dear.' Mrs Evans sighed wheezily. 'It's such a curse, having skin that tears like this. I barely touched that cabinet door.'

'It's the medication you're on that makes it like that. You've been using steroids for your breathing problems for a long time, haven't you?'

'I have a terrible chest,' Mrs Evans agreed. 'I was trying to get my puffer when I knocked my arm. Never seen so much blood! I had to call an ambulance.'

'How's your breathing feeling at the moment?'

'Terrible! I'm as tight as a drum.'

'I'll have a listen to your chest.' Pip wound a crêpe bandage over the dressing to avoid having to use anything sticky on her elderly patient's fragile skin.

The noise in the corridor had subsided but started again as Pip was trying to sort out the significance of the various wheezes and crackles she could hear in Mrs Evans's lungs. She hooked her stethoscope around her neck and slipped through the curtains to see what was going on.

The sight made her smile and it felt like the first time her lips had moved in such a direction for many days.

A procession of children in bright costumes was coming back through the double doors that led to the main reception and waiting area. They carried bags and were shouting 'Trick or treat' at regular intervals. They were obviously paediatric inpatients as a lot of staff were accompanying them and some of the children were in wheelchairs or being carried. One was in a bed decorated to look like a rowing boat and the child was waving a set of cardboard oars. He was being pushed by a pirate.

A large pirate with a jaunty hat and a patch over one eye, who was laughing as he tried to cope with other children who wanted to be so close they were making the task of pushing the boat somewhat hazardous. Pip recognised him well before she heard him say, 'Shiver me timbers,' in that delicious accent and she had to catch her breath as she watched.

He looked to be completely in his element. Surrounded by children and enjoying every moment of it. Shona had been right, hadn't she? Toni would want to have his own children and he *should* have them. A whole tribe of them. He'd be the most amazing father.

Did he look this happy because of his small companions or was there something else that could be contributing? The fact that she was allowing him his freedom perhaps? The chance to quietly distance himself from the baggage and inadequacy she brought with her and find someone else who would be far better mother material for his own children? He looked so much happier than Pip thought she could ever feel again.

Toni must have felt her stare because he looked in her direction and her heart twisted painfully at the way his smile faded so rapidly. The way his face emptied of that happiness cut into her like a knife. Only a week ago, seeing her would have had the opposite effect on his features. Pip hadn't seen him for days now. She'd been hoping he would come down to Emergency or at least ring her.

It was proving a lot more difficult than she'd imagined, sticking to her resolve of putting Alice first and giving Toni the opportunity to escape the dramas her family situation represented. She missed him desperately and had to remind herself repeatedly that putting her own wishes first would be reinforcing Alice's impression of her selfishness. If she made any move to contact Toni it would be the thin edge of a wedge she would never be able to control. An admission of defeat. But if he contacted her, it would be different. Pip wasn't quite sure of her reasoning, she just knew it could somehow be justified. That if he thought enough of her to put up with the kind of stress her family represented, the chance of a future together would be virtually guaranteed.

He hadn't rung. Pip hadn't even received a text message to ask how she was.

'What's going on, dear?' Mrs Evans sounded querulous.

'It's Hallowe'en,' Pip said over her shoulder. 'The children's ward is having a procession. They're all dressed up.'

'Lot of nonsense,' Mrs Evans pronounced. 'And they're far too noisy. There are sick people in here.' She coughed, as if to prove her point.

'Mmm.' Pip was waiting until the procession passed her. If Toni glanced her way again, she was going to smile. To say hello. Maybe even suggest they meet for a coffee. It was too hard, this staying away from him. There had to be a way to work something out that wouldn't undermine the repair work she was trying to accomplish with her daughter.

'Trick or treat!' a small fairy said.

'Sorry, hon, I haven't got anything I can give you.'

Toni and the boat were almost level with her now, a large island in a slow-moving sea of small children.

'Hey,' Pip called softly. 'You look like you're having a good time.'

'We are indeed.' Toni's return smile was brief. Detached. It had less warmth than a new patient would receive. Pip knew that because she'd seen that kind of introductory smile. She'd also seen the kind of smile he gave someone he loved and this one couldn't be less like it. 'How are you, Pippa?'

'I'm fine.' Such an automatic response but to say anything else would barely give lip service to the tip of the iceberg that had undermined Pip's life to such an overwhelming extent. A stressful job. A hostile daughter. A potentially broken relationship...a dying mother.

'Good.' The word was clipped. Part of an exchange that was going to be fleeting because the forward movement of the procession had not ceased. Fleeting—and painful. The few seconds of eye contact so far had been searing.

'And your mother? How is she?'

'Doing well.' For now. 'We've got her insulin levels under control.'

Toni's nod was as brief as his smile had been. 'And Alice?'

'Still not talking to me.' Pip had to blink quickly. Tears she had been holding back successfully for days were alarmingly close. 'And you? How are you, Toni?' The words were rushed. A desperate attempt to keep a line of communication open. They were too formal. Totally inadequate.

'Oh, I'm fine, too.' Toni broke the eye contact, turning his head. 'You OK, Jodi? Keeping up? Want a ride on the boat, *cara*?'

Pip's gaze followed his to the girl pushing the oxygen cylinder, who did look out of breath. Then it slid further. How many more children would need to be waited for? How much longer would Toni be this close? Was she going to have a chance to say anything else? But what *could* she say?

A nurse carrying a small tiger was bringing up the rear of the procession but Pip's eye was caught by the figure right behind the nurse.

Alice. Arriving, as arranged, for her lift home after school.

Looking as sullen and uncommunicative as she had for the last four days. She was staring at the unusual spectacle in the corridor ahead of her and seemed to be focused on the pirate. Had she recognised Toni? Had she seen Pip and guessed that she was talking to him?

Suddenly her daughter's expression didn't strike Pip as being sullen. It was more like being desperately unhappy. When she caught her gaze, Pip smiled and waved.

Toni turned his head as though wanting to see what had caught her attention. Then he shoved the bed onwards.

'Good to see you, Pippa,' he said, without turning his head.

And then he was gone.

Pip went back to her patient. Alice knew the way to the staffroom and would be engrossed in her homework by the time Pip went to collect her. The distraction of treating a patient was exactly what Pip needed right now. Alice's timing had been perfect, hadn't it? Especially just after her realisation that Toni should have his own children—with a mother who was a lot more capable of parenting than she was. Maybe their relationship would have foundered without the crisis in her family. Maybe Alice had done them all a favour with her pre-emptive strike.

Wishing things could be different was a waste of emotional energy and Pip was tired enough to realise her store was not inexhaustible. What strength she did have had to be reserved for her mother and her daughter. She wasn't going to let either of them down, no matter how hard it was.

'I haven't seen Toni for days,' Shona remarked. 'Must be almost a week. And you've been home every evening you're not working, Pip. What's going on?'

'Nothing.'

'Philippa!' It was exactly the tone Pip adopted with Alice when she knew the answer was way less than truthful.

Pip let out a resigned breath. 'I'm not seeing him just at the moment.'

'Why on earth not?'

'I need to show Alice she's more important than a boyfriend, I guess.'

'Is *that* what all these "no-speaks" are about? I thought it was just that shoplifting business.'

'I'm talking to Alice. She's the one who's not speaking.' Pip started clearing the table. 'At least she's not avoiding you any more, Mum.'

'Quite the opposite. She's gone all clingy. She'll be waiting for me now in the living room, I expect, wanting to show me all her homework.'

'Are you up to it? You don't want an early night?'

'I'm fine. I want to make sure she's all right. I thought she was looking a bit pale, didn't you?'

'She's been looking like that for days. Unhappy.'

'She hardly touched her dinner.'

'No. Maybe she didn't like it. Ask her if she wants a sandwich.' Pip smiled at her mother. 'How are you feeling, anyway? You're actually looking a bit brighter.'

'I'm feeling a lot better. And I intend to make the most of every moment I have left with my family, you know. Sleeping's a waste of time.' She was watching Pip rinse the plates. 'And you shouldn't waste time either. You should talk to Toni and patch things up. You can't let him think *he's* not important. Unless you've changed your mind about him.'

'No, I haven't changed my mind. I still love him. But I think it might be too late. I think he might be relieved to be away from *me*.' Pip sighed heavily. 'And it hasn't really helped with Alice. I don't seem to be able to the right thing whichever way I turn.'

'Welcome to parenthood.' Shona smiled wryly. 'Seriously, though, love—you can't put what Alice wants above what's going to make you happy. Self-sacrifice never works in the long term. It just builds resentment. It's a ticking bomb.'

'Look who's talking! How much did you give up to help me raise Alice?'

'It wasn't purely altruistic, as you well know. I did it because it made *me* happy. It gave me a reason to carry on after Dad died and…and maybe it wasn't the right thing to do.' Shona pushed her chair back, got slowly to her feet and went to hug her daughter. 'Maybe it's my fault that things are difficult between you two at present, with neither of you having the kind of relationship you should have had.'

'Don't say that, Mum.' Pip hugged her mother back,

hating how thin Shona was now. 'It worked. It was a wonderful thing to do and I love you for it. And Alice adores you.'

'Yes. I've had something not many grandmothers are blessed with, that's for sure.'

'It's just the wrong time to let someone else into my life.'

'No.' Shona almost pushed Pip away so that she could see her face. 'It's the perfect time. You can't give up on it just because Alice is disgruntled. On top of everything else, she's a teenager almost. She'll get over herself eventually. She loves you, Pip. She wants you to be happy.' Shona's smile was amused now. 'She just doesn't realise it yet.'

'But I can't give Toni what he wants anyway. It would never work.'

'Why not? What is it that you can't give him?'

'Children. A family.'

'What's Alice, then? Chopped liver?'

'You know what I mean. You said it yourself. He'll want his own children and I can't give him that.'

'Are you sure about that?'

What was Shona asking? Pip wondered. Whether she might change her mind about having more children? Or whether she was sure that that was what Toni wanted in his future? How could she be so sure when they hadn't even talked about it? Hadn't talked about anything at all in days.

Pip had to close her eyes and take a deep breath to deal with the wave of misery that came with the strength of missing Toni this much.

'I guess I'm not totally sure,' she admitted finally.

'Then talk to Toni,' Shona said. 'Always talk about everything, love. It always worked for your father and me and it's the best advice I can pass on. Not talking will make a mountain out of a molehill every time.'

Maybe the mountain was finding the courage to initiate such a conversation with Toni in the first place. Or finding the time to make any contact at all.

Having thought about her mother's advice all night, Pip had come to work determined to find a way to talk to Toni. A phone call had been deemed too impersonal but when she used her break time to visit his office, she found it empty.

It was even harder to summon the courage to make another attempt. Far easier to allow herself to be swept into the controlled chaos of an unusually busy afternoon in the emergency department.

Patient after patient to see. Assessments to be made, tests ordered, results reviewed and treatments decided on and initiated. The ambulance service was being run off its feet as well. Stretcher after stretcher rolled in. People were having heart attacks and strokes. Asthma attacks and accidents.

Pip barely registered the call for a paediatric consult from the neighbouring resus bay as the department dealt with the aftermath of an MVA involving two carloads of mothers and their young children. She was looking after one of the mothers and she had barely finished her primary survey of airway, breathing and circulation adequacy when her patient screwed up her face and groaned in an alarming fashion.

'What's wrong, Stephanie?' Pip queried sharply. 'What's hurting?'

'I think…it's the baby.'

Stephanie was pregnant with her third child. Her oldest was in the next-door resus bay and sounded like he'd been concussed badly enough to warrant a specialist consult. With the pregnancy being almost full term, Pip had included a foetal check in her primary survey but there had been no sign of imminent labour and the baby's heartbeat had sounded strong and regular. Pip had been about to order an ultrasound examination in any case, because of the possibility of abdominal trauma for the mother after the driver's airbag had been deployed in the collision.

'Try not to push.' Pip was pulling on a fresh pair of gloves. 'I'll see what's going on.'

It was immediately apparent that there was a lot going on. The bed was soaked with amniotic fluid and the bulge that was about to become a baby's head was growing rapidly.

'You're right,' Pip told Stephanie. 'Your baby doesn't want to wait any longer.' She caught the attending nurse's startled gaze. 'Grab a birth kit for me, please. And some entonox.'

Stephanie groaned again and, as always, the undertone of agony triggered unpleasant memories for Pip. She knew exactly how excruciating the pain of labour could be but at least Stephanie wasn't going to have to endure hours and hours of it. By the look of how fast this labour was progressing, it could well be over before they could even set up the entonox for pain relief.

'How long did your last labour go for?'

'About an hour. *Ah-h-h!*' The sound became strangled. There was no point in asking Stephanie not to push. The force was clearly well beyond her control.

Pip held her hands ready to catch the baby. There was no time to call for assistance. Or even to check the position of the umbilical cord or use suction to clear the nasopharynx as the head emerged. It seemed that one moment the head was crowning and the next Pip was holding the slippery bundle, keeping it head down to help drain any fluid in its airways.

'Oh!' Stephanie seemed as stunned as Pip had been by the precipitous birth. 'Oh, my God! Is he all right?'

'He's a she,' Pip responded. 'You've got a little girl, Stephanie.'

The baby's warbling cry was a huge relief. An emergency department resus bay was probably not the ideal facility to resuscitate a limp newborn. There wasn't even a paediatrician within shouting distance.

Or was there? The nurse had just arrived back with the birthing kit and an entonox cylinder. Her jaw dropped.

'Can you see if anyone from Paeds has arrived next door yet?' Pip asked.

'I'm right here.' The tall figure of Toni loomed behind the nurse. 'I heard the cry. What's the Apgar score?'

'I haven't done one yet.' The baby was pinking up nicely, though. She was moving in Pip's hands and her cry was increasing steadily in volume.

'Here, let me.' Toni held out his arms. 'I'll hold her while you cut the cord.' He smiled at Stephanie. 'I love babies,' he told her.

The third stage of Stephanie's labour was not going to be as fast as the rest had been. Pip waited, running a check of Stephanie's vital signs and trying to watch Toni at the same time as he examined the baby, checking its muscle tone, heart and respiration rate, colour and movement.

'She's perfect,' he pronounced. 'We don't have any scales here so we'll weigh her as soon as we get you up to the ward.'

He wrapped the baby in a clean, fluffy towel the nurse had ready but he didn't give her back to Stephanie immediately. He stood there, the tiny baby in his arms, smiling at it.

And something inside Pip simply dissolved.

He was born to be a father, this man. And she wanted him to be able to hold his own child like that one day.

Their child?

Was it actually possible that her love for this man was strong enough for her to overcome the massive block she had set in place after Alice's birth and cemented into place a little more firmly every time she considered herself to have failed as a mother in some way? Was her reluctance really a memory blown out of all proportion because of the other circumstances surrounding it? Like being so afraid of being a mother. Of ruining her life. Alice had been a noisy, demanding, terrifying little bundle and Pip had always felt desperately out of her depth.

Maybe things would be very different now she was older. If she had a child who had a father.

If that father was Toni.

In a totally unexpected flip, Pip realised how sad it would be if Toni *didn't* want children of his own. How sad it would be if she never had the joy of seeing him hold a child of theirs like that. Of having the chance to try again as a mother after all she had learned and do things differently. Better.

As he moved to hand the infant to her mother, Toni looked up and caught Pip's gaze. She tried to smile but her lips wouldn't co-operate. They wobbled. Worse, Toni didn't even try to smile back. It was impossible to interpret the expression in those dark eyes.

Was he still upset with her?

Remembering those words that denied him the chance of having children if she was his partner?

Was there some way she could communicate, with just a look, what she was feeling right now? That her love for him was strong enough to overcome any obstacles—as long as he felt the same way?

No. There was no chance. Pip's name was being called. She turned to see that Suzie had her head through the gap in the curtains.

'What's up, Suzie?'

'There's an ambulance coming in. Twelve-year-old girl who collapsed at school.'

'You want me to take it?' Pip was puzzled. It was taking a moment to refocus on a professional level. They must be very busy if she needed to leave a patient before she could arrange transfer to the next step in her care.

'Not exactly…' Suzie bit her lip. 'I just thought you should know. I'm sorry, Pip…but it's Alice.'

CHAPTER NINE

'ON THE count of three. One, two…three.'

Pip couldn't get near Alice just yet. They were transferring her from the stretcher to the bed in Resus 4, the only highly resourced area not in use following the influx of patients from the car accidents, and the paramedic was doing the handover to the only consultant available. Toni.

'She's febrile—temperature of 39.4. Tachycardic at 120, tachypnoea at 26 and hypotensive—75 over 45. GCS 13—she's been drowsy and confused.'

'What happened at the school?'

'She started vomiting and complained of severe abdominal pain and then collapsed. Apparently unconscious for about a minute. She was rousable but confused when we arrived.'

'Keep that oxygen on,' Toni directed the nurse. He looked at the IV line in Alice's arm. 'Is that patent?'

'Yes.'

'Fluids?'

'We've run a bolus of 500 mils 0.9 per cent saline,' the paramedic responded.

'Any change in blood pressure?'

'No.'

'Blood-glucose level?'

'Didn't get a chance to do one—sorry.'

Toni was at the head end of the bed. 'Alice? Open your eyes, *cara*. Do you know where you are?'

Alice opened her eyes but turned her head instantly and closed them again, emitting a groan that cut through Pip like a knife.

'It's OK, Alice.' Toni's voice was like a reassuring caress. It wasn't that he knew Alice—he would have been like that with any young patient. 'We're going to look after you.' He touched her cheek. 'Is it your tummy again? Is it hurting?'

The incoherent sound from Alice seemed to indicate agreement. Toni's hand went to her stomach and Pip saw the frown that coincided with another groan from Alice.

'Abdo's rigid,' he said.

This was bad. A rigid abdomen had to mean something serious. Internal bleeding or infection. Pip stepped closer as the barrier the stretcher had made between her and the bed was finally removed.

'I'm here, Alice,' she said, trying to sound calm and as reassuring as Toni had. 'It's OK, hon. You're going to be OK.' She caught the small hand lying on the bed, confident that this crisis would have done what no amount of talking had been able to do in the last few days and would have overcome the barrier Alice had erected between them. She had always turned to Pip as a mother whenever she was hurt or frightened.

But not this time.

Alice dragged her hand out of Pip's grasp. 'Go *away*,' she said clearly. 'I don't want you here.'

The paramedic at the foot end of the stretcher that was disappearing through the curtains turned to give Pip a startled glance, as though she had no right to be there. Already upset at Alice's public and very unexpected rejection, it didn't help.

'I'm her *mother*,' Pip snapped.

The paramedic shrugged, steering to one side to allow registrar Graham to enter the space.

'I don't want you here,' Alice sobbed. 'I want *Nona*.'

She was obviously becoming more distressed. Her breathing rate had increased until she was gasping between sobs. Her arms moved wildly enough to threaten the security of the IV line and Toni caught the hand before it hooked the plastic tubing coming from the bag of fluids suspended overhead.

'Take it easy, *cara*,' he said. 'It's all right. Everything's all right.'

Amazingly, Alice did start to settle, either because of Toni's words or the fact that Pip had taken a bewildered step backwards. She didn't understand. Why was Toni's attention acceptable when hers wasn't? Wasn't it Toni that Alice held at fault for the disruption to their lives? Had Pip put him at arm's length for no good reason and just suffered herself under the mistaken belief she was doing what Alice wanted?

Fear mixed with confusion took Pip back to a response she would never normally have considered acceptable as an adult.

It wasn't fair!

'Oxygen saturation is dropping.'

Toni looked up at Graham's observation. 'Right. I want an arterial blood gas and two sets of blood cultures,' he ordered. 'And urinalysis. Full blood count, urea, creatinine, electrolytes, and a coagulation profile.' He looked at the nurse. 'Let's do a bedside BGL and a 12-lead ECG. I want a chest X-ray and someone here with a

portable ultrasound machine, stat. Page a paediatric anaesthetist, too.'

He was unhooking his stethoscope as he moved around
the bed to speak to Pip. He put his hand on her elbow and
guided her towards the curtains.

'This looks like septic shock,' he said quietly, 'You should
be prepared in case we need to put her on a ventilator.'

Alice was *that* sick? Instinctively Pip tried to move
back towards her daughter but Toni's grip on her elbow
tightened. His tone was apologetic.

'She's sick,' he said sympathetically, 'which is
probably why she's decided she doesn't want you here.'

'But I—'

'I know.' The hand squeezed her arm, conveying more
than words could. 'But if it's upsetting her, it would be
better if you weren't here just for now. I'm sorry, Pip.'

He'd called her Pip, instead of his special 'Pippa'. It
didn't feel right. Toni was being so professional here.
Understanding and caring but…distant. Was that why
Alice was prepared to accept him treating her? Could she
sense the authority and skill and lack of personal attachment under the current circumstances?

He was doing exactly what Pip was failing to do.

Toni seemed to sense what she was thinking. 'Be
strong,' he said softly. 'I'll look after her.'

Pip knew that he would and his words, or perhaps just
that personal encouragement, were enough to give her
strength. She knew he was right. If Pip's presence was
going to distress Alice further when she was already in
trouble, she would be doing harm by insisting on staying.
However heart-breaking it was, she had to take herself out
of this. The only reason she could find that strength was
in knowing that Toni would be caring for her daughter.

'Thank you,' she whispered. She cleared her throat and spoke with more certainty. 'I'll call Mum. You can tell Alice I'm sure she'll be here as soon as it's possible.'

By the time Shona arrived at the hospital, Alice was deeply unconscious in a drug-induced state to allow mechanical ventilation.

Shona gasped with shock. 'Oh, my God, what's happened to her?'

There was no need for Pip to be excluded from the area now. Her patients had all been handed to the care of other staff members and Shona needed her support. Her shocked gaze had gone from the paediatric anaesthetist, who was adjusting controls on the ventilator, to Toni, who was scrubbed and gowned and using forceps and a swab to clean the side of Alice's neck in preparation for inserting a central venous line.

'What's happening?' Shona asked in distress.

'Alice's blood pressure is still too low,' Pip told her. 'Toni's putting a line into one of the bigger veins, which means they can administer fluid faster and also measure the pressures more accurately.'

'But why is she on a machine?'

'She's got some fluid in her lungs, which means she's not getting as much oxygen as she needs. The machine can improve that.' Pip watched as Toni felt Alice's neck with his gloved hand, identifying the carotid pulse so he could insert the needle into the internal jugular vein that ran parallel to the carotid artery.

'But why? I thought you said she had an infection.'

'She does. It's got out of hand. She's got something known as septic shock.'

'What sort of infection is it?'

'That's what we're trying to find out,' Toni said. 'Her abdomen is rigid so that's what we're focusing on right now. We're about to get a urinary catheter in place to get a specimen for analysis and we'll be doing an ultrasound examination next. Graham, have you got all the blood you need for cultures?'

'Yes.'

'We'll start antibiotics stat, then. Flucloxacillin 50 mg per kilo and Cefolaxime, also 50mg per kilo. She's about thirty-two kilos, isn't she, Pippa?'

'She was but I think she's lost a bit of weight in the last few days. She hasn't been eating well.'

'I thought she looked a bit pale last night,' Shona said. 'I asked her if she felt all right and she said yes.'

'How did she seem this morning?'

'Quiet.' It was Pip who answered this time. 'She didn't say a word to me during breakfast but that's hardly unusual at the moment.'

Nobody seemed to think the comment was strange but the staff members were concentrating on stabilising a very sick young girl.

'I'm still not happy with this blood pressure,' Toni said. 'We'll start infusion of an inotropic agent as soon as I've got this line secured.'

Dopamine, Pip thought. That's what they needed to try and get the blood pressure up. Not that she could say or do anything medical here. She was reduced to the status of a relative, nothing more. She hadn't been expected to even try finishing her shift in the emergency department. Any patients that had been under her care had been transferred by Suzie to other staff before the ambulance carrying Alice had arrived, which was just as well because Pip was in no state to treat anybody. Especially her own daughter.

'She didn't want me anywhere near her,' she had told Shona. 'She only wants you.'

'She doesn't know what she wants at the moment,' Shona had said matter-of-factly. 'We're both here for her and she knows that.'

They both stood close to the head of Alice's bed. Her eyes were shut and her mouth disfigured by the tube and mouthguard and the ties that were keeping them in place. Red-gold hair fanned out over the white pillow and the small face was almost as pale as the pillowslip.

'I can't believe this is happening,' Pip murmured. 'How could she get *this* sick this fast?'

The abdominal ultrasound gave them a provisional diagnosis.

'There's what looks like a pseudocyst here,' Toni pointed out.

'What's that?' Shona asked.

'It can be a complication of acute pancreatitis,' Toni responded. 'It's a collection of fluid and necrotic debris with the walls being formed by the pancreas and other surrounding organs. It can subside spontaneously or it can develop into an abscess. This area here…' Toni scrolled back to put another saved image onto the screen '…looks like it could be an abscess that's burst, which could explain the peritonitis and septicaemia.'

'What needs to be done?' Pip asked. 'Could that other pseudocyst be infected as well?'

'We'll do a CT scan and a guided needle aspiration. If it is the source of infection, surgery may be necessary to clean things up. In the meantime, we'll be monitoring Alice closely in the paediatric intensive care unit.'

'How long will she need to be on that machine?' Shona's anxiety was obvious.

'It depends on how well she responds to the antibiotics and what her lung function looks like. We should have a better idea in a few hours.'

Those few hours stretched into a few more. Late that evening, Alice was taken to Theatre.

Pip, Shona and Toni accompanied the entourage as far as the theatre anteroom, where the anaesthetist and surgeon were waiting.

'The good news,' the surgeon said, 'is that we'll be able to do the division of the sphincter of Oddi at the same time, which should make sure nothing like this happens again. Toni, do you want to come in and observe?'

'Yes. I'm on call but I don't think I have any other patients who will need me for a while.'

'Give your pager to one of the nurses. They can take any calls.'

Pip bent over the still unconsciousness Alice. She blinked back tears as she smoothed tendrils of fine hair from her daughter's forehead and kissed her gently.

'See you soon, hon,' she whispered. 'Love you.'

Pip and Shona went back to the ICU to wait. Shona eventually fell asleep in the armchair beside Alice's empty bed. Pip paced until the night staff took pity on her, made her hot chocolate and suggested she try to watch a late movie on the television in the unoccupied relatives' room.

'It might distract you for a bit. We'll come and let you know the second we hear anything.'

But it wasn't the night staff who came to find Pip later as she sat staring at a blank television screen, her hot drink forgotten and cold. It was Toni.

'It went well,' he said as he sank wearily into the chair

beside hers. 'Everybody's happy. She's in Recovery for the moment but they'll bring her back here soon.'

Pip started to get up. 'I'll go and tell Mum.'

Toni put his hand on her arm. 'Shona's asleep. I checked when I went looking for you. It might be a good idea to let her have a few minutes more rest, yes?'

Pip nodded and sat back again. 'I still can't believe this is happening,' she said slowly. 'We're not out of the woods yet, are we?'

'We'll get there.' Toni's voice had that same reassuring note he had used with Alice when she'd arrived in the ED. 'She's stable. Her blood pressure has come up a little and there's no deterioration in her lung function. We've just got to be patient and give the antibiotics a chance to get on top of things.' He rubbed his temple with his fingers and closed his eyes for a moment.

'You're tired,' Pip observed. 'You wouldn't be here all night like this if it wasn't Alice, would you?'

'I am on call.' A half-smile appeared. 'But even if I wasn't, I would be here, Pippa. For you.'

'I don't deserve your support. And I don't blame you for being angry with me. For wanting out.'

Toni opened his mouth as though to protest, but Pip didn't give him the chance.

'I thought I was doing the right thing. That it wasn't the right time for us to talk. That I shouldn't be putting any pressure on you if you didn't want to be there.'

Toni opened his mouth but again, he didn't get the chance to say anything as the words spilled from Pip.

'The only thing I could do was try and repair the damage as far as Alice and I were concerned, but nothing helped. I don't think it would have made any difference if you'd still been around or not. I've never done the right thing as far as Alice goes.' Pip sighed unhappily. 'I don't think I've ever been a good mother.'

'You're a wonderful mother,' Toni said with conviction, as Pip finally paused. 'I watched you with Alice when she was going into Theatre. I think that even unconscious she would have been aware of your love. It filled the room.' His smile was poignant now. 'I would have given anything to have my mother feel like that about me. I would have forgiven every forgotten birthday, every lonely night…everything.'

'Alice isn't about to forgive me. I feel like I've failed her. This shouldn't be happening. She must have been feeling unwell for days. I noticed she was pale and not eating much and I put it down to her being so angry with me. How self-centred was that?'

'You can't blame yourself.'

Pip ignored the comfort. 'I was always self-centred. I let Mum take over caring for her when she was a baby because it all seemed too hard.'

'You were sixteen. No more than a child yourself.'

'I was so scared of her,' Pip admitted with a rueful smile. 'I couldn't even bath her because I was scared I'd drop her or drown her or something. She screamed every time I tried to dress her. It was weeks before I could even get her to take her bottle when I was holding it. We used to both sit there and cry.'

Toni took hold of Pip's hand. 'Wasn't there someone there to help you?'

'Of course. Mum was there for me every minute. Alice wouldn't have survived otherwise.' She loved the fact that Toni was there with her. Touching her. Holding her hand. But he'd probably be doing this for any distraught mother with a child in the intensive care unit, wouldn't he?

'No, I mean professional help. Your family doctor or someone.'

'I didn't have postnatal depression or anything. I just couldn't cope.'

'Are you sure about that? Sounds like it was a pretty miserable experience.'

Pip was silent for a moment. 'I've never thought of that, even with the hindsight of medical training. When I have thought of that time, I decided I had made it the way it was. I felt like I'd failed Alice from the moment I found out I was pregnant. I hated it. The way people stared at me—knowing they knew far more about my private life than I wanted them to. I hated being fat but then I wanted to stay that way for ever because I was so terrified of actually *having* the baby. It must have contributed to the bad labour.'

'It was really bad?'

'Horrendous. I had a midwife who didn't think much of teenage mothers. She told me to toughen up. That people had babies all the time without making the kind of fuss I was making. That I'd had my fun and now I could grow up and deal with the consequences.'

'That's appallingly unprofessional.'

'That's what the consultant thought when he was finally called in, thanks to Mum's demands. I'd been in labour for about fourteen hours by then and I got terribly sick on entonox.'

'The woman should have been fired.'

'I think she was. Or she resigned when Mum made a formal complaint afterwards. The doctor was furious. I had marginal cephalopelvic disproportion. A trial labour shouldn't have gone for more than about four hours. It was too late for a Caesarean by then but the forceps delivery was dreadful and I ended up going to Theatre anyway. I had a post-partum haemorrhage and lost so much blood I needed a transfusion. I didn't even see Alice for three days.'

'Hardly the best start to something you weren't ready for anyway.'

'I was so sure I could never face it again. I avoided childbirth during my training as much as I could. Even hearing the pain Stephanie was in today was enough to send a shiver down my spine.'

Toni was still holding her hand. His thumb traced a gentle circle on her palm. 'I saw the way you were looking at that baby,' he said slowly. 'You looked...very sad.'

'Did I?' Pip had been trying to communicate the breakthrough in the way she felt about having another child. What message had Toni received? She had been sad for a second, though, hadn't she? Thinking about never having the opportunity to see him holding his own baby. *Her* baby. 'You looked so happy, Toni.' Pip couldn't help smiling. 'You were born to be a father, I think.'

'I would like to have my own family more than anything,' Toni agreed. His hand tightened on Pip's. 'But—'

The door to the relatives' room opening cut off what he was about to say.

'Alice is on her way down,' the nurse informed them. 'And Shona's awake. She's asking where you are, Pip.'

What had Toni been about to say? Was he going to qualify his wishes by suggesting that Pip could be part of his future without having to give birth again? That they could adopt children or not have any at all? Or perhaps that he loved her but he understood that it was enough to make their relationship unworkable and therefore he would have to keep searching to find the mother for his children?

There had been no opportunity for Pip to explain how she'd really felt when she'd seen him holding Stephanie's baby. That miraculous hope that she could put her past behind her and move on to a new life in more ways than one.

Right now, part of her past and her future was pulling her in. All Pip's emotional energy had to be spent supporting Alice. If Toni was right, and there was even a possibility that Alice was aware of her love, then her daughter was going to have it—in spades—whether she was awake and responsive or not.

With the resilience of youth and the aid of antibiotics, Alice's condition improved steadily over the next twelve hours. Her blood pressure crept up until it was within normal limits and the function of vital organs like her kidneys and lungs became acceptable enough to consider taking her off the ventilator.

Armed with a new sheaf of test results, Toni was making his way back to the intensive care unit early the next afternoon. Despite his lack of sleep, he had just completed a full ward round and was impatient to get back to the unit and pass on the good news. Annoyingly, the lift doors reopened before any upward movement but the latecomer was none other than Alice's grandmother.

'I went home for a few things,' Shona told Toni. 'Pip thought Alice might like her own pyjamas and music and old Ted.' She showed him a battered soft toy on the top of the items in the bag she held.

Toni hit the button for the third floor. 'I'm just on my way up to see Alice myself. The last blood tests are looking much better. I think we'll be able to take her off the ventilator this afternoon and let her wake up.'

'Oh, that's wonderful!' For a moment the deep lines of anxiety on Shona's face relaxed, leaving her looking drained and exhausted.

'How are you holding up, Shona?'

'I'm OK.'

'Really?'

Shona smiled at the undercurrent of doubt in his tone. 'Really.' She patted his arm. 'I think I'll be around for a while yet, Toni.'

'I certainly hope so.'

'Yes.' Shona adjusted her hold on the bag. 'My girls still need me for a bit, I think.'

'Of course they do.'

'Not that I'm afraid of dying. Love has an amazing power to conquer fear.' Shona was watching the numbers change on the lift floor display. 'I believe my spirit is going to connect with Jack's somehow. I've been missing him for thirteen years now, you know.'

'You must have loved each other very much.'

Shona smiled again. A very private smile. She said nothing as the lift doors opened but gave Toni a very direct glance as they stepped out.

'You look tired,' she said. 'Did you get any sleep last night?'

'Not much.'

'Have you eaten?'

'Kind of.'

'You need to look after yourself, Toni.' The instruction was issued with all the sternness any mother would summon. Then she softened the tone. 'My girls need you, too, you know, even if Alice doesn't realise it yet.'

Toni stopped by the central desk in the unit to collect Alice's notes as Shona went behind the glass wall that screened the area Alice occupied. He saw her hug Pip and then bend to kiss Alice. She took the teddy bear from the bag and tucked it gently under the covers so that Alice's arm was over the toy.

For a moment it was hard to concentrate on filing the new test results and checking his conclusions on Alice's progress.

Toni had been initially drawn into his relationship with Pip partly due to curiosity. He'd wanted to know why this small family unit worked when, on the surface, it had appeared to mirror some of the dysfunction of his own upbringing.

Now he knew what the difference was. The strength of the bond between the three generations of Murdoch women that held them together was love. A kind of love he had never had himself and had always wanted.

Marrying Pip would include him in that family. He would have a mother caring for him in the way Shona had just demonstrated she did. Sadly, it might not be for long but Toni would treasure every gesture.

He would gladly become a father for Alice. He could cope with any of the flak generated by any adjustments she needed to make in attitude and he knew they would win through in the end.

Both were compelling factors but they paled in comparison to the real reason Toni wanted to marry Pip. The insight he'd gained from their conversation last night had been enough to dismiss any lingering hurt from recent days. He understood why it was impossible for Pip to face the prospect of motherhood again. He'd seen the sadness in her face when she'd seen him holding that baby and realised it could be because she knew how important he'd always considered having his own children to be and that was something she didn't feel capable of giving him. Had allowing Alice to force the break in their relationship at least partly been due to that belief?

He had to find a way to tell her she was wrong. Yes, he had wanted his own children. To be able to give them the kind of love the Murdoch family possessed. The kind he'd never had. But there was another kind of love that was even more powerful and that was what Toni wanted more than anything else.

He wanted to love Pippa. And to have her love him back.

CHAPTER TEN

ALICE was asleep.

Peacefully asleep, without the aid of sedation. The wires and tubes connecting her to the life support equipment had been left behind in the intensive care unit when Alice had been transferred to the paediatric ward a few hours ago.

Toni was somewhere on the ward, too, despite it being well past his expected working hours today. A case of suspected meningitis in a two-year-old girl had been rushed in and he was doing the lumbar puncture and supervising the start of an antibiotic regime himself. He'd been gone for nearly an hour and during that time the lights had been dimmed and the ward had settled into a relatively calm period. A time for rest and maintenance. A time to heal or prepare for what a new day would bring.

Shona was asleep in the armchair by the window but Pip sat on a much less comfortable chair pulled up right against Alice's bed. She held her daughter's hand as she slept and watched the steady drip of the fluid keeping a forearm vein open, ready to administer her continued antibiotics or more pain relief if Alice chose to press the button of the attached pump.

The small fingers tightened a little as Alice stirred in her sleep and Pip squeezed them gently. As tired as she was, she had no desire to sleep herself. She wanted to enjoy this feeling of peace. Of knowing that the crisis for Alice was over and that when she'd woken up that afternoon, she had accepted Pip's presence as automatically as that of her grandmother. Her rejection of Pip appeared to have been forgotten.

Had being with her for every minute of this ordeal made a difference? Maybe, as Toni thought, Alice had been somehow aware it had been Pip caring for her alongside the medical staff. Smoothing salve onto dry lips, wiping her face gently with a warm, damp cloth. Talking to her. Singing endless repetitions of the 'Ottipuss' song.

Pip was humming it again now, which was enough to prevent the faint, fractious wail of a baby somewhere on the ward disturbing the bubble of contentment this private room contained. She was into the second chorus when Alice's eyes opened.

'Hi, hon.' Pip smiled. 'How are you feeling?'

'OK, I guess.'

'Are you sore? Do you need any medicine?'

'My tummy hurts a bit.'

'Press the button there. It'll give you some more morphine.'

'Will that make me go to sleep again?'

'Probably, but that's a good thing. You need to sleep so that you can rest and give your body the chance to get better.'

'*Am* I going to get better, Mummy?'

'Of course you are, hon. Really fast.'

'I thought I was going to die. Like Nona.'

'No.' Pip wound her fingers tightly over Alice's. 'You're going to be fine. And the operation you've had means that you probably won't ever get those sore tummies again.'

'Is Nona still going to die?'

'Not for a while, I hope. She's feeling quite a lot better at the moment. We'll look after her.'

'Where is she?'

'Asleep. In the chair over there by the window.'

'Where's Toni?'

'He's here somewhere. There was a sick little girl he had to go and see.'

'I'm a sick little girl.'

'This one's a lot sicker than you are now. She needed him. I expect he'll come and see you again before he goes home. He's been taking very good care of you.'

'I don't really hate him, you know.'

'I know.'

'You didn't have to stop going out with him.'

'I was trying to make things better for you.'

'Will you go out with him again?'

'I don't know.'

'Don't you *want* to go out with him again?'

Pip was silent for a moment. Alice was still a child in many ways. And for the first time, thanks to the trauma of the last few weeks, Alice felt completely *her* child. Somehow, during this period, Shona had relinquished her role of being Alice's mother and, miraculously, Pip seemed to have stepped into the breach without failing as much as she'd thought she had.

There was still the extra dimension to their relationship, however. The friendly 'sister' component. And Pip could see that as a positive thing now. It would give them a closeness not many mothers would have with their daughters. Even so, how much should she tell her?

What was it Toni had said that time? That you have to do what feels right as a parent and that you can only do your best.

'I don't want to go out with Toni at the moment if it means that I'm going to fight with you, Alice,' she said finally. 'I want home to be the best place. For all of us.'

'But do you *want* to? Are you in love with him?'

'Yes. I do love Toni, hon. Not the same way I love you. It's completely different but very, very special.'

'I'm sorry I was so awful about it. I didn't really mean it, you know, about the babies and stuff. I think it would be cool. I'd be like another mother, wouldn't I?'

'You sure would. You'd be almost the age I was when I had you.'

'So you will marry him, then? And have babies?'

'I don't know, hon. He might not want to go out with me any more.'

'Why *not*?' Even in her increasingly drowsy state, Alice's tone held an indignation that made Pip smile. How could she have doubted the strength of love Alice had for her?

'I think I hurt his feelings when I agreed that it would be a good idea if we didn't see each other at the moment.'

'You mean it was his idea?'

'Yes.' Pip tried to banish the conviction that it would have come eventually, anyway. That Toni didn't feel the same way. She didn't want Alice to know how sad that made her. 'He understands that I've got other things in my life that are very important.'

'Like me?' Was it Pip's imagination or was there a satisfied note in Alice's voice? The knowledge that she was important enough to have been put first.

'Like you,' Pip agreed. 'But there *are* some other things

we need to talk about.' Like those babies Alice might be a second mother to.

A quiet sound from near the window made Pip realise her mother was awake and had been listening.

'You should do that, then,' Shona said. 'Go and talk to him.'

'I will,' Pip responded. 'He's busy at the moment and it's getting late. I'll do it as soon as I get the chance.'

'And you'll tell him that you're in love with him?' Alice said.

'Yes.'

Shona hadn't been the only person to hear Pip's conversation with Alice. Toni had to swallow hard to clear the lump in his throat when he'd paused to listen to Pippa singing to her daughter at this quiet end of the ward.

And then he'd waited, not wanting to interrupt that first proper conversation she'd been able to have with her daughter since she'd become so ill.

But he couldn't wait any longer. Not after hearing that admission that she intended to tell him she loved him. She *loved* him. His heart singing, he moved to step into Alice's room.

His smile was a little embarrassed. 'I couldn't help overhearing,' he lied. Then his gaze fastened on Pip. 'Would now be a good time for that talk, do you think?'

Alice's grin was weak but much more like her old self. 'You are so busted,' she told her mother.

'I guess I am.' But Pip didn't care. In the pale gleam of the nightlight in Alice's room, she could still clearly see the way Toni was looking at her.

'Go,' Shona ordered. 'I'll be here with Alice.'

Toni wasn't looking at Pip any longer. 'Is that all right with you, Alice?'

'Sure. But you'll come back, won't you, Mum?'

'Of course I will.'

Shona waved her hand at the couple as Pip slowly walked towards the door and took Toni's outstretched hand.

'Play nicely, children,' she said.

And Alice giggled.

'She's sounding so much better.'

'Isn't she? It's like the clock's been turned back. To before she started having those attacks. Before Mum got sick.'

'To before we started seeing each other?'

'Except that I think she sees you as part of the picture now.'

'Is that what you want, Pippa?' Toni's hand pulled her to a stop near the lifts where their aimless wandering had taken them. 'Do you want me as part of *your* picture?'

The lift doors were open and, by tacit consent, they both stepped inside. Toni pushed the button to close the doors. He looked at Pip.

'Yes.' Pip felt shy because she knew Toni had overheard her telling Alice that she was in love with him but she didn't know if he felt the same way. Then, having made herself vulnerable to that extent, she knew she may as well go the whole distance. 'You're so much part of the picture I want, Toni. You make it bigger. Clearer. The colours brighter. It even has a frame that makes it perfect.'

'Not a solid frame, I hope?'

Pip could have basked for ever in the look she was receiving. It was so warm. So full of…love.

'Why not?'

'Because we might want to make that picture bigger.'

Pip's heart skipped a beat. 'You mean…with our own children?'

'No.' Toni shook his head quickly. 'I would never ask you to do something that frightened you too much, Pippa. Or something that you really didn't want to do. It's enough for me to be with you. Knowing that we have our whole lives to add to that picture. Places to go. Things to share.'

'Do you mean you don't *want* children?'

'I mean I want *you* more, *cara*. There's no one else I would want to be the mother of my children so if I don't have you, I will have nothing. You must know how much I love you.'

'You…*love* me?' The words caused a peculiar tingle that coursed through Pip. She had never felt anything like this. Like liquid hope. Or joy.

Toni was looking perplexed. 'Of course I love you. I've told you many times. Ever since that first night we spent together when you made me burn my spaghetti sauce.'

'Oh…' Maybe the meaning of those sexy, foreign phrases hadn't been as clear as Pip had believed. 'You told me that in Italian?'

'Did I? I don't remember. Maybe. I was speaking from my heart, not my head. I thought you understood.'

'Maybe I did,' Pip confessed, 'but what's said in bed can sometimes be…not the real thing.'

'I never say anything in bed I don't mean.'

Toni's touch as he pulled her close to him was as convincing as his words. The strength of the love Pip felt for Toni was enough to render her speechless for a moment, but it didn't matter because he was still talking. Pip could feel as well as hear the low rumble of his words as she revelled in the closeness of their embrace.

'I love all of you, Pippa. Not just your beautiful body or your clever mind. I love the way you love your mother and your daughter. And if Alice will allow me to be a father to her, I will be honoured, but it's *you* I love, Pippa Murdoch—with all my heart and soul. It's you I want to marry and spend the rest of my life with.' He bent his head and kissed Pip's lips. 'I've missed you so much, my love. These last few days have felt like months.' He kissed her again.

The lift doors chose that moment to open. A startled-looking cleaner had to stop the forward movement of his polishing machine.

'Sorry,' Toni said firmly. 'This lift is occupied.' He pushed the button to close the doors again and then hit a random floor number so the lift started moving upwards.

'Now, where we were?' he murmured. 'Ah, yes. I think I was asking you to marry me, Pippa.'

'Were you?' Pip couldn't help trying to spin this delicious moment out just a little longer.

'Most definitely.'

Pip had to wait for another kiss to finish before hearing the words that thrilled her even more than she could have expected.

'Will you marry me, Pippa? Will you be my love? My wife? And let me love you for the rest of my life?'

'Yes.' Pip didn't bother trying to blink away the tears of joy that sprang to her eyes. 'I love you, too, Toni. And I love that you think I'm enough for you without having to be a mother again.'

'You are.'

'But I *want* to be the mother of your children.' Pip would have had to brush away tears that were now rolling down the side of her nose except that Toni was doing it for her. Cradling her face with both hands and using his thumbs to dry her tears. 'I want to have your babies, Toni. I want you to be a father. *Us* to be a whole family.'

The smile lit up his face. 'You really *want* that? After all you went through with Alice?'

'I love you enough to make me brave,' Pip said softly. 'If I have you with me, I can do anything.'

Toni kissed her yet again. Slowly. Tenderly. 'You have your mother's incredible strength, Pippa,' he said eventually. 'She told me that love has the power to conquer fear. She said she wasn't afraid to die because of the love she shared with your father.'

'She told me something, too.'

The lift was moving downwards again but Toni didn't seem to notice. 'What was that?'

'That it would be nice if she could plan for a wedding instead of a funeral.'

'She will,' Toni avowed. 'And maybe she'll still be with us for long enough to welcome a new grandchild.'

'It's possible.' Pip would remember this moment of hope and hang onto it for as long as she could. 'But, just to be on the safe side, do you think we should get married soon?'

'The sooner, the better.'

The lift doors opened and the cleaner was still standing with his machine on the floor they'd left, his foot tapping impatiently.

Not that Toni or Pip noticed. Wrapped in each other's arms, their kiss advertised the promise of future dreams and it firmly excluded the rest of the world.

The cleaner sighed wearily and hauled his heavy machine backwards so he could change direction and head for a different lift.

Clearly, his preferred choice was not going to be available for quite some time.

LATIN LOVERS COLLECTION

Intense romances with gorgeous
Mediterranean heroes

Greek Tycoons
1st July 2011

**Hot-Blooded
Sicilians**
5th August 2011

Italian Playboys
2nd September
2011

**Passionate
Spaniards**
7th October
2011

**Seductive
Frenchmen**
4th November
2011

**Italian
Husbands**
2nd December
2011

Collect all six!

www.millsandboon.co.uk

Have Your Say

You've just finished your book.
So what did you think?

We'd love to hear your thoughts on our
'Have your say' online panel
www.millsandboon.co.uk/haveyoursay

- ❧ Easy to use
- ❧ Short questionnaire
- ❧ Chance to win Mills & Boon® goodies

The World of Mills & Boon®

There's a Mills & Boon® series that's perfect for you. We publish ten series and with new titles every month, you never have to wait long for your favourite to come along.

Blaze.
Scorching hot, sexy reads

By Request
Relive the romance with the best of the best

Cherish™
Romance to melt the heart every time

Desire™
Passionate and dramatic love stories

Visit us Online

Browse our books before you buy online at
www.millsandboon.co.uk

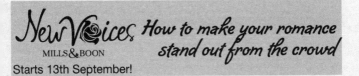
Avoiding the dreaded cliché

Open your story book with a bang—hook your reader in on the first page and show them instantly that this story is unique.

A successful writer can use a conventional theme and twist it to deliver something with real wow factor!

Once you've established the direction of your story, bring in fresh takes and new twists to these traditional storylines.

Here are four things to remember:

- 🌹 Stretch your imagination
- 🌹 Stay true to the genre
- 🌹 It's all about the characters—start with them, not the plot!
- 🌹 M&B is about creating fantasy out of reality. Surprise us with your characters, stories and ideas!

So whether it's a marriage of convenience story, a secret baby theme, a traumatic past or a blackmail story, make sure you add your own unique sparkle which will make your readers come back for more!

Good luck with your writing!

We look forward to meeting your fabulous heroines and drop-dead gorgeous heroes!

For more writing tips, check out:
www.romanceisnotdead.com

Visit us Online

NEWVOICESTIPS/B